The Complete Ridgemont Christmas Thrillers

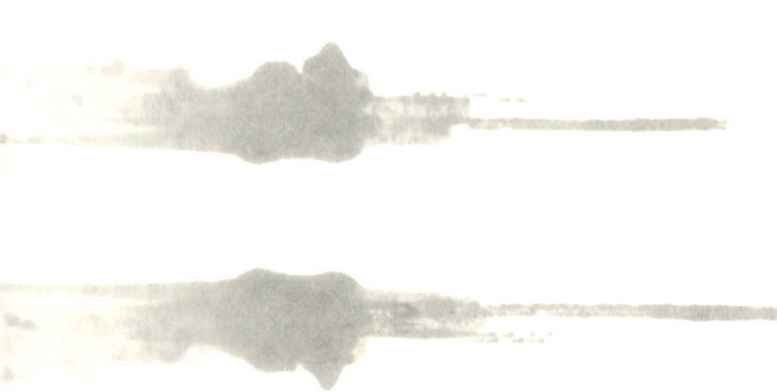

This is a work of fiction. Names, characters, places, and incidents are products of the author's imagination or are used fictitiously. Any resemblance to actual persons, living or dead, events, or locales is entirely coincidental.

Copyright © 2025 by Ion Esimai

All rights reserved.

No part of this book may be reproduced in any form or by any electronic or mechanical means, including information storage and retrieval systems, without written permission from the author, except for the use of brief quotations in a book review.

Published by Wetin Books, Sparta

www.ionesimai.com

eISBN-13: 978-1-962798-95-2

Title: The Complete Ridgemont Christmas Thrillers

Series: *The Ridgemont Christmas Thrillers Series*

Cover design by Ion Esimai

The Complete Ridgemont Christmas Thrillers

Ridgemont Christmas Thrillers

Ion Esimai

Contents

BOOK 1
The Gift Exchange — 1

BOOK 2
The Perfect Christmas Card — 49

BOOK 3
Day One: The Partridge — 105

BOOK 4
The Advent Calendar — 173

BOOK 5
The Cabin — 237

BOOK 6
Christmas Eve Storm — 295

BOOK 7
The Neighbor — 353

BOOK 8
The Homecoming — 407

BOOK 9
Office Secret Santa — 465

BOOK 10
The Proposal — 521

BOOK 11
Love, Actually — 571

BOOK 12
Forgiveness Season — 625

About the Author — 691
Also by Ion Esimai — 693

BOOK 1

The Gift Exchange

Chapter 1

The Arrival

The lake house smelled like pine and lies.

I killed the engine in Ridge Lake Resort's parking lot. My hands clung to the wheel as if it anchored me. Through the bare trees, Ridge Lake lay frozen, a sheet of white pinned between dark shores.

It hadn't been frozen then.

July 1999. Twenty-six years ago. Lane eight. Me twelve.

"You ready?" Jordan asked.

I wasn't.

The drive from the city crawled. Holiday traffic on I-80. Route 23 already icy near Mountain Creek. The signal bled out bar by bar until nothing remained.

"Dawn?"

"Yeah," I said. "Ready."

The lie sat between us.

We walked to the resort office. Grant Beck stood behind the counter, same too-white smile I remembered from childhood visits. He'd been younger then, fresh from some NYC real estate deal. He bought up properties in Ridgemont like they were poker chips.

"Welcome back, Ms. Patterson." His smile widened. "Cabin Seven, just like you requested."

I hadn't requested Cabin Seven. My mother had.

"Busy weekend," Grant continued. He tapped his computer screen. "That podcaster lady rented the main lodge. Doing some kind of research project." He laughed. "Hope she's not looking into any local secrets."

My chest tightened.

Behind Grant, a small artificial tree blinked red and green. The lights reflected in his computer screen, Christmas colors bled across rental agreements and credit card receipts.

Jordan signed the paperwork. I stared at the wall behind Grant—photos of Ridge Lake in summer. Bright water. Smiling families. Red bathing suits.

I counted breaths instead of looking at the red in those photographs.

Twelve years old again, back at the lake's edge, Lane's hands breaking the surface—reaching—while I counted. One. Two. Three...

"Dawn?" Jordan touched my elbow. "Keys."

I took them. Metal cold against my palm.

Cabin Seven sat fifty yards from the main lodge, close enough to see the frozen lake through every window. We parked, Jordan grabbed our bags, and I stood outside inhaling December air that tasted like snow and memory. Across the valley, lights from Mountain Creek ski resort blinked against gray sky.

The cabin door opened before we reached it. "You're here!" Mother's voice. Too bright. Too high. "Finally!"

She pulled me into a hug. Too tight. Her perfume—floral and expensive—made my throat close. Behind her, the cabin blazed with Christmas decorations. Lights. Garland. A tree too big for the space, covered in ornaments that caught the afternoon light and threw it back in sharp pieces.

"Come in, come in. Baxter and Addison just got here with the twins."

I stepped inside. My brother Baxter unpacked in the corner, his wife Addison sorted through their daughters' bags. The twins—eight years old, both—ran past me. One wore a red sweater.

I flinched.

Lane wore red that day. Red with white polka dots.

"Dawn?" Addison watched me. Careful eyes. Observant.

"Cold," I said.

Through the window, Father stood on the porch, bourbon in hand. He stared at the lake, unmoving. Didn't look at us. Didn't come inside.

Jordan carried our luggage to the guest room. I stood in the living room, surrounded by pine smell and cinnamon candles and Mother's obsessive decoration. Normal. She tried for normal. I couldn't take a deep breath.

My hands shook. Refused to stop.

Jordan returned and squeezed my hand. Leaned close. "We can leave anytime."

I managed a nod. My voice stayed buried.

One of the twins streaked past—the one in red—and for a split second, Lane's face flashed where hers should've been.

I shouldn't have come back to this lake.

But Mother had insisted. Her voice on the phone three weeks ago had been different. Urgent. Like she'd waited twenty-six years to say something.

"It's time," she'd said.

Time for what? To remember? To confess?

I'd spent twenty-six years forgetting.

Night pressed against the cabin windows.

We gathered in the living room. Mother made hot cocoa—too sweet, like childhood. The twins played with ornaments she handed them carefully, like passing down heirlooms. Father came inside at last, refilled his glass, took off his jacket, and collapsed into the chair farthest from everyone.

Baxter talked about clients. Addison laughed in the right places. Jordan listened, polite, attentive.

From outside, faint across the cabins, "Last Christmas" drifted through the walls. *Last Christmas, I gave you my heart.* The notes crawled under my skin. Lane's voice layered over it—eight years old, off-key, singing it all summer.

I counted ceiling tiles. Twenty-four.

Mother clapped her hands—sharp, decisive. "Everyone to the dining room!" Her voice too cheerful. Too practiced.

We were already in the living room.

"We'll do something special this year," she continued.

She pulled out a crystal bowl. Slips of paper inside, folded small and white.

"Secret Santa."

Father's glass stopped halfway to his lips. "Laura, we haven't done that since—"

"Since Lane," Mother finished.

Her eyes found mine across the room. Held. Didn't blink.

"I think it's time," she said.

Time for what? None of us asked.

Not out loud.

Chapter 2

The Drawing

We gathered around the dining table. Mother had set it like she was hosting strangers—cloth napkins, good china, candles that smelled like Christmas. Pot roast steamed in the center. Wine glasses filled and refilled. Forced conversation clung to us, heavy and damp.

Baxter talked about the twins' school play at Ridgemont Academy. How they'd both gotten speaking parts. How proud he was.

Addison turned to me. "Still at the firm?"

"Still there," I said. "Partner track next year."

"That's wonderful."

Her voice said it wasn't wonderful. Implied she wanted other information.

Mother served the roast. Passed plates. Kept everyone's wine glass full. Father sat at the head of the table, mostly silent. He nursed his drink. The twins ate mac and cheese that Mother had made special for them.

From the TV in the other room, Frosty the Snowman murmured at low volume. The twins had left it on. That cheerful narrator voice leaked through—*Happy birthday, Frosty*—while we passed dishes in silence.

Jordan tried. Kept conversation light. Asked about Ridgemont, how the town had changed.

It hadn't. Small towns never did.

After dinner, Mother stood, clearing plates with sharp, efficient movements. "I'll get dessert in a moment," she said. "But first…"

She brought out the bowl again. Crystal. Expensive. Probably a wedding gift from thirty years ago.

"Rules are simple." Mother's voice had that teacher quality, the one that expected obedience. "Under fifty dollars. Something meaningful. From the heart."

Cold slid through my fingers at "from the heart."

Six slips of paper inside: Dawn, Jordan, Laura, Robert, Baxter, Addison. The twins were too young to participate. They'd been sent to watch a movie in the bedroom.

"We'll exchange gifts tomorrow night," Mother continued. "But we draw names now."

Father looked up from his bourbon. "Why not Christmas Eve like normal people?"

"Because I said so."

Mother's tone left no room for argument.

She passed the bowl to Father first. He barely glanced at the name before folding it back up and shoving it in his shirt pocket.

Mother drew second. Smiled. Too satisfied.

Baxter wore a Christmas sweater—green with a reindeer on it. Addison must have made him wear it. He drew third. The sweater stretched as he reached forward. Laughed. "This'll be easy."

Addison drew fourth. Her face unreadable. She glanced at the name, then at me, then folded it carefully and tucked it into her purse.

Jordan drew fifth. Squeezed my hand under the table.

I drew last.

Opened the paper.

Baxter's name.

I folded it back up. Didn't matter. Wouldn't matter. We wouldn't be here long enough for gifts.

Mother brought out apple pie. Still warm. My favorite, she said, as if I'd forgotten everything she'd done or hadn't done twenty-six years ago.

I took a bite.

My phone buzzed in my pocket. I pulled it out casually. Work email, probably. Something that could wait until Monday.

Unknown number. Blocked. Blank where a name should be.

I opened the message.

I know what you did that summer.

My fork hit the plate. China rang. Every head at the table turned.

"You okay?" Jordan asked.

"Fine." My voice came from somewhere far away. "Work email."

But my face had gone white. I could feel it. Heat drained from my cheeks. Cold spread from my chest outward.

Mother's gaze pinned me in place, traced the gooseflesh along my arms. "You've always been sensitive to the cold, sweetheart."

It didn't work. "I need the bathroom."

I stood. Too fast. Chair scraped. I walked to the hallway, found the bathroom, and locked the door.

Stared at my phone. Number still blocked.

I read it again.

"I know what you did that summer."

My hands shook. My fingers tightened until the knuckles blanched. I splashed cold water on my face. Looked in the mirror. Thirty-eight years old. But the reflection slipped—me at twelve. Lake water dripping from my hair.

The bathroom smelled like peppermint. One of those plug-in air fresheners Mother had placed everywhere. Candy cane scent mixed with panic made my stomach turn.

I deleted the text.

Counted to ten.

Twenty.

Air snagged halfway down. Tried to slow the galloping horses in my chest.

Who sent it? Someone at that table? Someone who knew?

I stared out the bathroom window. Across the lake, lights from another property. Pine Ridge Chalet, according to the resort map. Vacation rental. Dark now except for one window upstairs.

Sirens wailed toward downtown Ridgemont. Not for us.

The shaking didn't stop. Cold sweat traced a line down my back. Vision narrowed at the edges. I couldn't catch my breath.

Counted to thirty. Composed myself.

Opened the bathroom door.

The dining table sat empty when I returned. Everyone sat in the living room with coffee. The twins watched a Christmas movie on TV at low volume. Father poured another bourbon. Mother knitted something red.

Jordan gave me a quick once-over and patted the couch beside him. I sat. Stiff.

"What's wrong?" he whispered, for me alone.

"Tired."

But my phone was still in my hand. Screen dark. Message deleted but not forgotten.

Mother watched from across the room. Addison watched. Father didn't. He fixed on his bourbon like it held answers. Baxter scrolled on his phone, absent-minded.

One of them sent that text. One of them knew. But which one? And what did they know?

On TV, the Christmas movie reached its climax. *It's a Wonderful Life.* George Bailey begged for his life. Clarence got his wings. The bell rang.

I sat back on the couch. Everyone stared at me. My jaw locked, eyes fixed on the TV. Too long.

"What?" I asked. My voice sounded far away.

"You look like you saw a ghost," Mother said. A smile tugged the corner of her lips. Too slow, like she'd practiced.

"Everything alright, sweetheart?"

Chapter 3

The First Gift

S now fell outside, thick and silent. Fire crackled in the fireplace. Normal family evening. Except nothing was normal.

Mother stood up from her chair, clapped her hands together. "Let's do Secret Santa tonight," Mother said. "No point waiting."

Father looked up from his bourbon. "That's not the tradition."

"We've already gone over that, Bob, new tradition." Her tone left no room for argument.

She walked to the Christmas tree, bent down, picked up a gift I hadn't seen before. Red wrapping. White ribbon. I'd checked under that tree an hour ago. Nothing was there.

My name was on the tag. Handwriting I didn't recognize.

"Dawn, it has your name," Mother said.

"I didn't—"

"Come on, sweetheart. Open it."

I walked to the tree slowly. Everyone watched—Jordan, Baxter, Addison, Father, Mother. Even the twins focused on me. I picked up the box. Light. Small. Shoebox size, maybe.

My hands shook as I tore the paper. Inside, tissue paper. White. Carefully folded. I pulled it back.

A child's bathing suit.

Red with white polka dots.

Size 6.

Lane's size. Lane's pattern. Lane's last day.

My vision blurred. Time slowed. My ears rang like I'd gone underwater. The box fell from my hands.

"What is it?" Baxter asked.

My tongue stuck to the roof of my mouth.

Jordan picked it up, held the bathing suit, looked at me, then at it, then back at me. "A bathing suit?" His forehead furrowed. "That's... weird." He focused on my face. "Dawn?"

Addison leaned forward. "Is this supposed to be funny?"

Mother stood up. "My God, who would joke about that?" But her voice was too calm. Too practiced.

Father refilled his drink. Said nothing. Looked at nothing.

One of the twins stood up, walked closer, curious. "Who's that for?"

Baxter pulled her back. "Nobody, sweetie. Enjoy your movie."

I couldn't speak. Couldn't move. Couldn't breathe. Red with white polka dots. Same brand. Same size. Identical. Lane's bathing suit. The one she wore that summer.

Jordan touched my arm. "Dawn, what's wrong?"

I forced words out. "Must be a mistake." My voice sounded like something borrowed.

Mother took the bathing suit from Jordan's hands, held it up, examined it like she'd never seen it before. "I'm sure whoever bought this didn't realize—"

I snatched it from her. "I'll keep it."

Something inside me braced for impact.

Everyone went silent.

"I'm tired," I said. "Going to bed."

I walked up the stairs to the guest room and shut the door behind me. Didn't slam it. Control. I had to maintain control.

Jordan followed five minutes later. The room was dark except for moonlight through thin curtains. The wood paneling on the walls appeared black. Christmas decorations on the dresser—Mother's touch—cast strange shadows. A ceramic Santa on the dresser watched from the shadows.

I sat on the bed, held the bathing suit. The fabric soft in my hands. Same size. Same brand. Ran through my head like a mantra. Identical.

My throat closed around a breath that didn't make it out.

"What's going on?" Jordan asked.

"Nothing."

"That's not nothing. You looked like you lost your footing and were in a free fall."

"I'm alright."

Jordan sat beside me. "Is it about Lane?"

My head snapped up. "Why would you say that?"

"The bathing suit. The accident happened here in the summer, right? It just seems—"

"I want to go home."

"We just got here."

I got out of bed, used the bathroom, and changed into red plaid flannel pajamas. Ironic now that I'd packed that for the trip. I turned to my husband. "Tomorrow. First thing."

Jordan sighed, ran his hand through his hair. "Let's talk about this in the morning."

He went to the bathroom. The sound of water. Toothbrush. Normal nighttime sounds.

I stared at the bathing suit. He was right. That was Lane's bathing suit.

Jordan came back. "Still awake?"

I didn't answer. Lay down. Faced away from him. He'd locked the door and engaged the chain. He wanted some, but I was not in the mood.

I inhaled. Exhaled. Maintained a rhythm. Pretended.

"That was strange," Jordan said to himself. "Awake one second, asleep the next."

He got into bed. The mattress dipped under his weight. He placed his hand on my shoulder, then removed it. "Good night."

The mattress moved again. He probably rolled over.

Ten minutes later, his breath deepened. Slowed. Sleep.

I lay awake, stared at the ceiling shadows. Firelight from the living room flickered under the door. Counted. One, two, three... sixty. My last minute with Lane.

The TV in the living room played low. Local news. Something about a corporate party at Ridgemont Plaza. Holiday celebrations downtown. Then a commercial—*All I Want For Christmas Is You*—Mariah Carey's voice bled through the walls. I wondered who was still up.

My phone buzzed on the nightstand. Notification. Ridgemont Gazette article: "Local Podcaster Reopens Cold Case."

I didn't open it.

I must have fallen asleep eventually, because I woke up with a start.

The clock on the nightstand glowed: 2:47 AM. On my pillow was another box. Red wrapping. White ribbon.

A cold bead traced my spine. I didn't put it there.

The bedroom door was still locked. Jordan had locked it after he came back from the bathroom. He slept beside me.

But the box was there.

Waiting.

The box waited.

Chapter 4

The Evidence

I sat up and stared at the box on the pillow next to my head. Same red wrapping as the first gift. Same white ribbon tied in a perfect bow.

Jordan slept on his side, dark hair messy against the white pillowcase. He wore the gray t-shirt he always slept in. Hadn't moved. Chest rose and fell in a steady rhythm.

My heart pounded.

I got in bed by midnight. Jordan brushed his teeth. Got into bed. Said goodnight.

Missed almost three hours.

I got up, bare feet on cold hardwood, and walked to the door. Still locked. I checked the window—also locked. Snow lay undisturbed beneath the glass. No footprints. No ladder marks. Nothing.

Maybe Jordan put it there. It was impossible for someone else.

But the box was real. I held it.

I took it to the bathroom, locked the door, and sat on the toilet lid in complete darkness. Didn't turn on the light. My hands shook too badly to open it.

I counted to twenty, tore the wrapper off. The paper crinkled, too loud in the silence.

Inside: laminated newspaper clipping.

I turned on the bathroom light and squinted against the sudden brightness.

Headline in bold: "LOCAL GIRL, 8, DROWNS IN TRAGIC ACCIDENT."

Ridgemont Gazette. July 26, 1999.

Lane's school picture below—huge smile, gap between her front teeth, brown hair in pigtails with red ribbons.

Article underneath:

"Lane Patterson, 8, drowned yesterday in Ridge Lake during a family vacation at Ridge Lake Resort. Authorities say the girl was swimming unsupervised when she got into difficulty. Her older sister, Dawn, 12, attempted rescue but couldn't reach her in time. Lane was pronounced dead at Ridgemont General Hospital. Detective Paul Morrison said the death appears accidental. 'A terrible tragedy during the holidays,' he stated. The family was vacationing at the resort for summer..."

I read it three times.

I'd never seen this clipping. Mom and Dad had kept all the news coverage from me. Said it would upset me. Make things worse.

But someone kept it.

Someone laminated it.

Someone put it on my pillow.

I looked down at my hands. Dirt under my fingernails—dark, thick.

Before bed, I'd scrubbed my hands with lavender soap. They were clean then.

Now: mud caked under every nail.

I looked at my feet. Soles dirty. Cold. Small pieces of gravel stuck to my heel.

I checked my pajama hem. Damp. Muddy. Pine needles caught in the fabric.

I'd been outside.

In the snow.

In the middle of the night.

In December.

Had no memory of it.

The world pulled back a few inches, like I wasn't fully in it. I grabbed my phone from the bedroom and checked location history.

"Ridge Lake shoreline, 2:14 AM."

Thirty-three minutes ago.

I'd walked to the lake. In my sleep. In the cold. In the dark. And I recalled nothing.

I turned on the sink and scrubbed my hands. Dirt swirled down the drain, brown water, dark earth. The bathroom smelled like cinnamon—Mother's scented soap. That thick, artificial holiday smell mixed with mud and panic made me want to gag.

I scrubbed my feet in the bathtub, took off my pajamas, stuffed them in the bottom of my toiletry bag, and put on clean pajamas from my suitcase —blue cotton, Mother had given them to me last Christmas.

Tried to remember.

Last memory: Jordan's voice. Goodnight. Warmth beside me.

Next memory: I woke up at 2:47.

Three hours lost.

Was I insane? Had I always been insane and only now couldn't hide it anymore?

I wrapped the clipping in tissue, buried it deep in the toiletry bag with the pajamas. Evidence. Of what, I didn't know.

I got back into bed and lay rigid, staring at the ceiling.

Jordan rolled over, his face pale in the moonlight. Stubble on his jaw. Eyes still closed.

"You okay?" he mumbled.

I froze.

"Bad dream?"

"Yeah. Bad dream." My voice held its shape. Barely

He went back to sleep. Just like that. Easy. Normal.

I counted ceiling tiles again.

Twenty-four.

Waited for dawn.

Through the bedroom window, an ambulance tore down Route 23. Headed toward town. Probably the psychiatric center. Everything here seemed to circle back to that place.

Car doors slammed outside. Close. Someone else awake at the resort.

Footsteps in snow. Soft. Careful.

I got up and looked out the window.

A figure walked between cabins, dark coat, hood up. Too far to see who.

Beyond them, across the lake, someone's cabin blazed with Christmas lights. Multicolored. They blinked in sequence—red, green, blue, white. Over and over. Relentless. Like a warning I couldn't read.

Or maybe I imagined it.

Maybe I imagined all of it.

The gifts. The mud. The lost time.

Maybe I'd been insane since I was twelve. Since the lake incident.

I'd been outside. Walked by the lake. At 2 AM. In December. In my bare feet. And I had no memory of it.

The gifts could have been from anyone.

But what if they were from me?

What if I left them for myself?

What if I'd finally, completely, lost my mind?

At 6 AM, my phone buzzed on the nightstand.

I grabbed it before Jordan could wake.

Text from unknown number.

Same blocked ID as before.

This time, a photo attached.

I opened it.

Me.

By Ridge Lake.

In my red plaid pajamas.

Bare feet in snow.

Arms at my sides.

I stared at the frozen water.

Timestamp: 2:14 AM.

Below the photo, one line of text:

"You always were a troubled sleeper."

Chapter 5

The Search

I woke to voices downstairs. Laughter. The twins. Mother's voice too bright as she called that breakfast was ready.

Gray light came through the window.

Clock: 7:45 AM.

I must have dozed off after my phone buzzed at 6 AM. I'd finally slept two hours. Maybe. Jordan's side of the bed was empty. Cold.

I got up and dressed quickly—jeans, gray sweater, thick socks, hair pulled back in a ponytail. No makeup. Couldn't manage it.

I stood at the top of the stairs. Everyone was in the kitchen and dining room below. Sounds of plates and silverware. Smell of coffee. Normal Sunday morning.

Now was my chance to investigate the mystery of the gifts and who knew what.

I went to Baxter and Addison's room first. Across the hall. Door unlocked.

The room smelled like Addison's perfume—expensive and floral. Two suitcases open on the floor. Clothes scattered. The twins' stuffed animals on one of the twin beds pushed against the wall.

My fingertips tingled—too hot, then too cold.

I moved fast. Methodical.

Checked the dresser: nothing but Baxter's clothes. Polo shirts. Khakis. He dressed like our father—conservative, safe.

Addison's purse was on the nightstand, black leather, designer. Next to it, a miniature ceramic Christmas village—Mother must have put it there. Three tiny houses with snow-covered roofs, a church with a steeple, all lit from within by LED lights that blinked in sequence.

I opened the purse.

Wallet. Phone charger. Lipstick. Gum.

Then an envelope in the side pocket.

I pulled it out.

Photos inside. Old. Printed on yellowing photo paper.

Me as a child. At this lake. Age twelve, the summer Lane died. I recognized the dock. The cabin. My hair was longer. Wearing a blue swimsuit. No smile.

Another photo: Lane and I together. She seven. Me eleven. Both in swimsuits. At the water's edge. Lane smiling. Me looking away from the camera.

Why did Addison have these?

Where did she get them?

I photographed them with my phone, flash off.

Footsteps on the stairs closer.

I shoved the photos back in the envelope, back in the purse, exactly how I found it.

Ran out. Barely made it to the hallway bathroom before Addison appeared at the top of the stairs.

I turned on the sink and pretended to wash my hands.

Addison stood in the doorway, wearing dark jeans and a white sweater, her blonde hair pulled back perfectly. Thin. Too thin.

"Looking for something?"

Heat flushed across my face and vanished just as fast.

"Just using the bathroom. Ours is occupied."

She didn't believe me. Everyone but me was downstairs. Her blue eyes stayed cold. "Right."

She went into her room and closed the door—firm, not a slam.

I waited. Counted to thirty.

Then went to my parents' room at the end of the hall. Their door unlocked too. Nobody locked doors here. Mother's rule: "We're family."

The room was larger than ours. King bed against the far wall. Mother's side meticulously made—hospital corners, decorative pillows arranged by size, navy comforter pulled tight. Father's side rumpled, sheets twisted, smelling like bourbon and old sweat.

Dresser covered with Mother's things—jewelry box, perfume bottles, hand cream—everything organized, labeled, controlled.

I looked under the bed.

Found a shoebox.

Pulled it out.

Inside: photos of Lane, organized by year in separate envelopes.

Age 1. Age 2. Age 3, 4, 5, 6, 7, 8.

Stopped at 8.

Last photo: Lane in the red bathing suit—the day she died. Same one from the newspaper clipping. But this one showed more. The full frame.

My grip tightened on the picture until the paper bent.

Me in the background. On the dock. Focused on Lane swimming.

My face in shadow but my body language clear—tense, angry, arms crossed, watching her.

Footsteps on the stairs. Heavy, fast.

I shoved the box under the bed. Not quite where I found it. No time.

Grabbed a towel from the bathroom.

Father appeared in the doorway. My heartbeat stuttered.

Robert Patterson. Seventy but looked older. Gray hair. Lined face, red from decades of drinking. Khaki pants, wrinkled button-down, stained collar.

His eyebrows shot up. Before he could say, What are you doing in here? I spoke first.

"Looking for extra towels."

He stared—bloodshot eyes, broken capillaries across his nose.

"Towels are in the hallway closet."

"Right. Thanks."

I brushed past him. He smelled like he always did—morning bourbon, afternoon bourbon, night bourbon. All the same.

He watched me. Didn't move from the doorway.

I went downstairs.

The rest of the family was at the dining table already—pancakes, bacon, orange juice, coffee.

Mother sat at the head of the table, wearing cream slacks and a blue cashmere sweater, pearl earrings, hair styled perfectly even though it was Sunday morning. Dyed brown over graying roots. Makeup subtle.

Jordan looked up.

"Where were you?"

"Shower." I sat. My hair was dry. He noticed, said nothing.

Mother watched me with surgical precision. "Sit, sweetheart. Eat."

Dad and Addison came down the stairs and took their seats. Baxter, wearing jeans and a Ridgemont Academy sweatshirt—our alma mater— passed me the pancakes. He loved it. I hated it.

The twins showed me drawings—crayon Christmas trees, stick-figure families, red and green everywhere. One drew Santa's sleigh over the cabin. The other drew presents under the tree. Innocent.

I couldn't look.

Baxter talked about taking them sledding. Mother about making hot cocoa. Addison said nothing. Her glances sharp. Suspicious. Father had deep bags under his eyes—was he awake last night?

Mother's brightness felt fake, too polished. Baxter wouldn't meet anyone's eyes. Jordan seemed calm, too calm, like a man pretending the house wasn't burning down around him. Anyone here could have taken that photo. Anyone could have left those gifts.

Mid-breakfast, a knock at the door.

Grant Beck, resort manager. Khakis. Fleece jacket with Ridge Lake Resort embroidered on the chest. A sprig of holly pinned near the zipper.

"Morning, folks. Everything alright?"

Father looked up. "Fine. Why?"

"Some guests reported seeing someone walking by the lake late last night. Just checking everyone's okay."

A thread of dread pulled tight beneath my ribs.

Grant's eyes found me. "You feeling alright, Ms. Patterson? You look pale."

"Fine. Just tired."

"Well, stay warm. It's going to snow again tonight." He smiled—professional, practiced. "Let me know if you need anything."

He left.

Mother stood and began clearing the table.

"Dawn, help me with the dishes."

Not a question.

I followed her into the kitchen.

She filled the sink with hot water—steam rising, soap bubbles, pine scent from the dish soap.

"Did you sleep well?" she asked.

"Fine."

"No bad dreams?"

"No."

She washed a plate. Rinsed it. Set it in the rack.

"You know you can talk to me, sweetheart."

"I know."

"About anything."

I stayed silent.

She washed another plate. "Your father heard you last night. Walking around. He thought you went outside."

My hands froze around the dish towel.

"I didn't go outside."

"Of course not." Mother smiled. "That would be crazy."

She handed me a wet plate.

I dried it. The dish towel scratched my skin. My pulse thudded in my ears.

From the living room, the TV played low—morning show hosts laughing about holiday shopping deals, their voices bright and sharp.

Anyone here could have done this. Taken that photo. Left those gifts. Or all together. Maybe they knew what I did. Maybe they'd always known.

Maybe this weekend was the reckoning I'd spent twenty-six years avoiding.

Chapter 6

The Diary

Sunday afternoon. Mother announced church service—special Advent service at St. Mary's with Father O'Sullivan. Everyone got ready. Baxter herded the twins upstairs to change clothes. Addison searched for her good shoes. Jordan grabbed his coat from the closet.

"I have a headache," I said. "I'll stay here."

Jordan stopped. "Want me to stay with you?"

"No. I'll be fine. Just need quiet."

Mother's eyes narrowed. She stood in the hallway in a navy dress, a wool coat draped over one arm. Her pearl necklace caught the light.

"Are you sure?"

"Positive."

She stared at me for a long moment, then nodded. "Rest, sweetheart."

The twins came downstairs in matching red velvet dresses, ribbons in their hair—Addison's touch. They looked like dolls. Like Lane used to look for church. Pretty. Perfect. Dead.

They left. Cars started outside. Snow crunched under tires. Engines faded down the resort road.

Silence.

Too quiet.

I stood in the living room. Fire burned low in the fireplace. Christmas tree lights blinked red and green. Ornaments turned slowly from the heat.

Then I saw it—one present under the tree that wasn't there this morning. Red wrapping. White ribbon. My name in the same handwriting as before.

A small thud echoed in my chest. Recognition. Fear.

I approached slowly and knelt on the hardwood floor, cold through my jeans. I picked it up—book-sized, heavier than the others.

I unwrapped it, the ripping paper too loud in the empty cabin.

Inside: a child's diary. Pink cover, unicorn stickers in the corners, a broken lock hanging loose. On the first page, in careful child's writing: "This diary belongs to Lane Patterson."

A tremor crawled into my fingers.

Lane's diary.

But Mother always said the police never found it—that she must have lost it before the trip.

I flipped through pages. All blank. Cream paper. Lines waiting for words.

Except one.

Page dated: July 25, 1999. The day before Lane died. Written in a child's handwriting, loops too big, some letters backward:

"Dawn is mad at me. I got the summer solo in the pageant and she didn't. She said it's not fair because she's older. She said I always get everything. She said maybe I won't be around to sing it. I'm scared of her sometimes. She looks at me different now. Like she hates me. I tried to tell Mom but Mom was busy. Dad said Dawn's just jealous. But it doesn't feel like just jealous. It feels like something worse. Tomorrow we're going to the lake. I don't want to go swimming. Not with Dawn. I'm scared."

I read it three times.

Did Lane write this? I had no recollection. But it sounded true—every word. I had been jealous. The solo. The attention. The applause. I had looked at Lane with hatred. The next day she was dead.

I stared at the handwriting. Something familiar.

I got my purse from the bedroom, found a shopping list I'd written yesterday, and brought it back to the diary. Compared handwriting. Letter by letter. The loops. The space. The pressure on the paper.

They matched. Dawn's handwriting. Not Lane's.

I wrote this diary entry. Not Lane. I wrote it—pretended to be Lane. When? During one of my blackouts? Like last night when I walked to the lake?

Heat crept up my throat. Shame or fear—I couldn't tell which.

Church bells rang outside—St. Mary's. Slow, deliberate tolls across the frozen lake, calling people to kneel and pretend everything was fine.

I checked all the other pages. Blank. Just this one. In my handwriting, made to look like a child's—clumsy, deliberate.

I tried to burn it.

Ran to the fireplace and grabbed the lighter from the mantle. Metal. Heavy. Flint wouldn't catch—dead, useless.

Car doors outside.

They were back already. Service must have been short.

I shoved the diary under the couch cushion, pushed it deep, smoothed the fabric, then ran to the bathroom and splashed cold water on my face.

I walked out as the front door opened.

Mother came in first, carrying takeout bags from Ridge Tavern. "Got lunch on the way back. You feel better?"

"Yeah. Much better."

But my hands shook.

Jordan wore his good charcoal coat. He looked at my hands, then my face. "You sure?"

"Just hungry."

We ate lunch around the table—sandwiches, fries, coleslaw. The twins played with a stuffed snowman from the church gift shop. It sang Frosty the Snowman off-key every time they squeezed it, over and over, hilarious to them.

I couldn't stop thinking about the diary under the cushion. What if someone sat there? What if they found it?

After lunch, the adults sipped coffee. Father poured bourbon into his mug. "Irish coffee," he said. Nobody laughed.

I left them and went to the living room to retrieve the diary—but Mother was already there, taking the seat directly across from the couch and staring at it like she knew.

Something inside me paused. Waiting. Watching her watch me

My phone buzzed. Pulse jumped. Weather alert. "Winter storm warning tonight through Monday morning. Heavy snow expected."

I exhaled.

TV played in the background. A Ridgemont Gazette reporter—Gloria Steele—talked through holiday news.

"Busy Christmas weekend in Ridgemont. Increased police presence downtown following yesterday's incident at Ridgemont Plaza. More on that story at six."

Mother's phone chimed. She checked it. "Father O'Sullivan posted about midnight mass tomorrow. Christmas Eve."

Jordan walked in. "Are we going?"

"Of course we're going," Mother said.

Jordan squeezed my hand. "Want to go for a walk? Clear your head?"

The diary was under the cushion. Ten feet away. My eyes drifted toward the floor. "Maybe later."

I wrote that diary entry. In my handwriting, pretending to be Lane. I'd written all the gifts to myself. The bathing suit. The clipping. The diary. I was losing my mind. Or I'd lost it years ago.

"Dawn."

Mother's voice cut sharp.

I looked up. Concern crossed her face.

How long had I zoned out?

"Can you come to the kitchen?" she asked, voice formal. Cold. "We need to talk."

Jordan reached for my elbow—gentle, firm—and guided me.

What was going on?

In the kitchen, Baxter, Addison, and Father waited. An intervention?

Father looked up from his spiked drink. "Sit down, sweetheart."

He never called me sweetheart.
His voice was sober. Clear.
For the first time all weekend.

Chapter 7

The Confrontation

Five faces turned toward me, all waiting, all deciding who I was.

The twins had been sent upstairs with an iPad—thin giggles drifting through the ceiling like ghosts. Down here, no one laughed. No one moved.

I took the empty chair. Hardwood pressed into my spine. The kitchen smelled like coffee and something sharper beneath it—fear, maybe. Or guilt. Or both.

Jordan sat beside me, too close. His knee brushed mine, steady where mine wasn't. He wore his dark blue sweater, the one he packed for "nice family dinners," the one he'd worn the night he proposed. He didn't look at me now.

Mother folded her hands on the table, fingers interlaced in perfect symmetry. Pearl earrings. Fresh lipstick. Her "important meeting" face.

"Dawn," she said softly. "We're worried about you."

"I'm fine."

"You're not," Jordan said, his voice small, careful, controlled so it wouldn't tremble.

Baxter stared into his coffee cup—Ridgemont Academy logo worn at the edges. His hands wrapped around the ceramic as if it could keep him braced.

Addison watched me from across the table, arms crossed, expression neutral, eyes sharp. Calculating. Always calculating.

Father held his mug like a man holding a confession he hadn't decided to make. He'd shaved. That alone unsettled me—the sudden neatness, the effort. Blue sweater, clean khakis. He looked almost purposeful.

Jordan slid a laptop toward him. Silver. Closed. My throat tightened. He lifted the lid. Light flared across six faces.

He didn't explain. Didn't clear his throat. Didn't soften a single edge. He just clicked.

A single photo filled the screen.

My bedroom closet at home. The memory box on the carpet—open, spilling envelopes like bones. White paper everywhere. My handwriting on all of it. My name on some. Lane's on others.

Air drained from the room.

Jordan didn't look at me. "This was three months ago."

Baxter leaned in. "Where'd you get that?"

Jordan's jaw clenched. "The camera caught it."

My stomach knotted. "What camera?"

He swallowed—a hard, deliberate movement. "I set one up after... after the first incident."

"What incident?"

His eyes flicked to mine. Apology lived there. And fear. "You sleep-walk, Dawn."

The words hit like cold water.

"No," I whispered.

Jordan clicked again. A video opened—grainy, green-tinted night-vision.

Me. In our bedroom. Hair loose. Eyes open but empty.

I moved like someone following instructions whispered through a wall. Reached for the closet. Pulled out the memory box. Sat on the floor. Opened an envelope. Moved my lips—whispered something the camera didn't catch.

Mother gasped. Or pretended to. Hard to tell with her.

Baxter's voice wavered. "Jesus, Dawn."

A pulse hammered painfully at my temple. "That's not—Jordan, that isn't—"

He touched my hand—not a comfort, more like restraint.

"This wasn't the only time," he said.

"No." I pulled my hand back. "Jordan, that video—someone could've—"

"Faked it?" His voice cracked. "Why would anyone fake this?"

Because nothing here is what it looks like, because someone wants me to doubt myself, because someone knows what happened twenty-six years ago, because someone knows what I did—or what I think I did.

Father set his cup down hard. "You need help, sweetheart."

The room swayed. Edges of chairs and cabinets bent inward. The air thickened, syrup-heavy.

Jordan shut the laptop, closing the entire subject with a click.

"Dawn," he said quietly, "we want to help you."

"Help me what?" My voice wasn't steady. "Help me remember something I didn't do? Help me confess to something you decided I must have done? Help me believe a version of myself that doesn't feel like mine?"

Mother stood.

The shift was small—just her pushing the chair back—but the sound vibrated along my spine.

"I've made some calls," she said.

Baxter's head snapped up. "Mom."

Addison pressed her lips together, looked at me, looked away.

Mother continued, "There are excellent programs at Ridgemont Psychiatric Center."

A sour heat rolled through my stomach. "You think I'm insane?"

Silence. Which is an answer.

Father rubbed his forehead. "We just want you safe."

Safe.

The word crawled under my skin.

Safe from what? From myself? From them? From the truth?

My knees pressed against the underside of the table, anchoring me. The kitchen shrank around me. Five faces closing in.

"You're staging an intervention?" I said.

Jordan flinched. Mother didn't.

She folded her hands again and offered the smallest smile.

"With love," she said.

Blood roared faintly in my ears—like distant surf.

"You think I wrote those letters?" I said. "In my sleep. You think I've been—what—planning something? Sabotaging myself? Hurting someone?"

Jordan spoke softly. "We don't know what's happening to you, Dawn."

"I do." Mother's voice sliced through him.

Everyone turned to her.

Her posture was perfect. Her expression smooth. Her eyes fixed on me with a kind of hunger behind the pity.

"I know exactly what's happening," she said.

The room went silent. My skin prickled.

Mother walked to the window and looked out at Ridge Lake—white and still and waiting. Then she turned back to us.

And her face changed.

The performance dropped, the softness peeled away, the mask cracked.

"We need to talk about that summer," she said.

My pulse stopped. Not slowed—stopped. A cold pressure formed at the base of my skull.

"The day Lane died," Mother whispered. "It's time."

She held my gaze—the way she had held Lane's tiny hand walking to the lake that morning. Held it the way she held everything together for twenty-six years.

And something in my chest splintered.

"What about that summer?" I asked.

She opened her mouth—and then closed it. Not yet. She wasn't ready. The truth wasn't coming in one piece. She would break it off in fragments and make me swallow each one.

"We'll talk soon," she said.

Soon.

Soon meant everything and nothing.

Father exhaled shakily. Baxter put his head in his hands. Addison looked like she wanted to run upstairs and hide with her twins. Jordan stared at nothing.

I sat silent. No answers. No confessions. Just five faces waiting for me to break.

Chapter 8

The Witness

Mother's hands shook. I'd never seen that before.

She stood at the window with her back to all of us, shoulders rigid under the beige sweater. Outside, snow fell again. Soft. Silent.

"I was supposed to be watching you girls that day."

Her voice was flat. Emotionless. Rehearsed.

"Summer, 1999. At the lake."

The kitchen went still. Even the clock seemed to stop.

"But I wasn't there."

Baxter leaned forward. "What do you mean?"

Mother turned. Her face pale. Makeup couldn't hide the lines around her mouth or the hollow in her eyes.

"I was next door. At the Richardsons' house."

She paused. Breathed.

"John Richardson."

Father closed his eyes sharply, like he could shut the memory out.

"We'd been seeing each other for six months."

The words hung in the air—heavy and sour.

Jordan's hand found mine, squeezed. I couldn't squeeze back.

Mother kept going, her voice mechanical, practiced.

"His wife was visiting family for the summer. I told Robert I was taking the girls swimming."

She looked at Father. He didn't open his eyes.

"Instead, I left you two at the lake. Told you to stay on the dock. That I'd be right back."

Her voice cracked on "back."

"I went to John's house."

The memory rose inside me—sudden, sharp, too fast. Like a wave slamming into me before I could brace.

Mother leaving. Her perfume drifting behind her. "Stay here, don't go in the water. I'll be right back."

Lane sitting beside me on the dock, her red bathing suit bright against gray wood.

Warm water. Summer warm. Lane begging to swim.

A flash—her hair drifting underwater like dark seaweed.

A smaller flash—my hand reaching.

A blurred shape.

Pressure.

Count... something.

A breath catching.

Red fabric too bright.

But the pictures were incomplete. Jagged. Like broken glass held too close to my eyes.

I couldn't tell what was memory and what was guilt or fear or suggestion or all three at once.

Mother's voice pulled me back.

"John's bedroom faced the lake. Second floor."

Her hands gripped the counter, knuckles white.

"I watched you both through the window."

My vision tunneled, centering on her mouth, her words.

"Lane was in the water. You were at the edge, Dawn. Watching her swim."

The fragmented images inside me twisted tighter but still refused to form a full picture.

Mother kept talking, her voice a whisper now.

"Then you went in the water. You held her under."

Jordan's hand went rigid in mine.

Baxter shot to his feet, the chair clattering to the tile. "What?"

"I counted," Mother said. "Thirty seconds. Forty. Fifty."

She looked at me—only at me.

"I watched you crawl onto the dock," she said. "You were soaked. Blue-lipped. Shaking. You kept looking back at the water, waiting for her to come up."

Her breath hitched.

"But she didn't."

Baxter choked out, "Why didn't you run out there? Why didn't you do something?"

Mother looked at him. Then Father. Then back at me.

"Because if I did, everyone would know. I wasn't supposed to be watching my daughter drown. I was supposed to be in another man's bed."

Addison made a small sound. Horrified.

"You stayed there?" My voice cracked. "You stayed there and watched?"

She nodded once, slowly.

A cold current passed through me, like stepping into deep water.

"I should have run," she whispered. "I should have dragged Lane out of the water."

Father finally spoke, voice rough and scraped raw.

"I found her running across the yard. Coming from Richardson's house. Screaming."

He opened his eyes and stared at his coffee. At the bourbon stain on the tablecloth. Anywhere but at her.

"But Lane was already gone."

Mother nodded, mechanical again.

"I called 911 from the lake. Told them I was there the whole time. That I looked away for just a moment. That it was an accident."

My throat felt raw, though I hadn't spoken.

She looked at Father.

"Robert backed up my story. Protected me. Protected the marriage."

From the living room, the TV still played a Hallmark movie—cheerful music, mistletoe engagements, guaranteed happy endings. The sound made my skin crawl.

"John Richardson left town three days later," Father said. "I paid him off. Bought his silence."

He swallowed hard. "He died five years ago. Heart attack."

Mother dabbed her eyes. Careful not to smudge makeup.

"No one in Ridgemont ever knew," she said. "We were careful."

I couldn't process it. Couldn't breathe. Couldn't think.

Mother watched something—someone—through a window. And lied. For twenty-six years.

Let me believe Lane's death was my fault.

Let my mind fill in the blanks with whatever horror it could find.

"You let me think it was an accident," I whispered.

My voice didn't sound like mine.

Mother held my gaze.

"It was easier than the truth."

"Which truth?" I asked quietly.

"That I killed her? Or that you let her die?"

Mother's face crumpled—real tears this time.

The room wavered for a moment before sharpening again

Outside, someone's car alarm chirped. Doors unlocked. Grant Beck walked toward the lodge with shopping bags from Whole Foods and Ridgemont Plaza—normal Sunday errands, while my family collapsed around me.

"Both," she said.

Her voice broke.

"Both truths."

Chapter 9

The Punishment

The room was silent. Even the Christmas tree lights seemed dimmer.

Jordan broke the silence, his voice careful, measured. "Why are you telling us this now?"

Mother stood, walked to the counter, and pulled out a manila envelope from behind the coffee maker. Thick. Official-looking. She placed it on the table.

"Because I can't anymore." Her voice steady now, resolved. "I've been in prison for twenty-six years. Watching you, Dawn. Hating you. Hating myself more. Every summer. Every family dinner. Looking at you and seeing my choice. Seeing what I let happen. What I turned you into."

Baxter leaned forward. "The gifts. Who left them?"

Mother looked at him. Eyes dry now. Tears gone. Only emptiness left. "I did. All of them."

A thin tremor ran through my right hand— I hid it under the table.

The room went silent.

"The bathing suit. The clipping. The photo by the lake. The diary pages. I wrote them, I placed them, I created all of it."

Mother folded her hands on the table. "I've been planning this for months. I called Jordan, told him you seemed unstable. I knew he'd watch you more closely. I knew he'd see you sleepwalking—"

"I've always sleepwalked," I whispered.

"Yes." Her eyes stayed on mine. "Since you were eight years old. Since that summer."

Jordan's voice shook. "You manipulated me into thinking—"

"That she was breaking down. Yes. I needed everyone here. I needed you all to see her struggle. To understand why this confession—why this truth—was necessary."

She tapped the envelope with one finger. Nail polish perfect. Red. Blood red.

"I placed every gift while she slept. I wrote the diary entries in her handwriting. I've been practicing for months. I made her doubt herself. I made all of you doubt her."

Baxter stood. "Why?"

"Because I couldn't carry it alone anymore. Twenty-six years of watching her live while Lane stayed eight forever. I wanted her to feel what I felt. I wanted everyone to know what we did."

She looked at me. Only at me. "And I wanted to stop pretending."

Addison's voice finally cut through the room. "You manipulated all of us."

"Yes." No apology. No explanation.

Jordan paced to the window and back, hands tangled in his hair.

Father reached for the envelope, but Mother pulled it back, sharp. Possessive. "This is mine." She handed it to Jordan instead. "I've written everything down. What I did. What happened. The affair. The negligence. How I let Lane drown. How I tortured Dawn for twenty-six years."

Jordan opened the envelope. Pulled out papers—typed, single-spaced, pages and pages.

"It's going to the police," Mother said.

Baxter stood. "Mom, you can't—"

"I can. I have to." Her voice final.

From upstairs, one of the twins cried. The other tried to comfort her by singing Jingle Bells—off-key, innocent.

"This is my confession. Not Dawn's."

Father stood, unsteady. The bourbon had caught up with him. In his navy sweater and pressed pants, he looked almost like a man ready for court. "Laura, we had an agreement. We never speak of this. We move forward."

Mother turned on him—fast, vicious. "You moved forward. You and Bourbon. I stayed frozen. Watching Dawn struggle, while Lane stayed eight years old in my mind. Forever."

Father sat back down and poured bourbon into his coffee. Didn't hide it anymore. Said nothing else.

Addison crossed her arms. "There's one problem." Everyone turned. "Dawn still killed Lane. Your negligence doesn't change that. You're both guilty."

My ribs constricted. A slow crush.

Her eyes found mine. Blue. Cold. Assessing. A verdict, not the truth.

Through the window, a police car drove past on the main road toward downtown Ridgemont. Lights off. Routine patrol.

Baxter cleared his throat. "The police will have questions for everyone."

Jordan looked up from the papers. "Should I call a lawyer?"

"I already have one," Mother said. "Two, actually. One for me. One for Dawn."

She'd planned everything.

Jordan picked up his phone, hands shaking.

"What are you doing?" My voice came out hoarse. Raw.

"Calling the police."

Mother didn't move. Didn't try to stop him. "I know. That's why I told you."

Outside, sirens. Faint, but closer.

Baxter's mouth dropped open. "You already called them?"

Mother looked at me. Only at me. "An hour ago. While I could still do it. While I still had the courage."

The sirens grew louder. I counted the beats of my pulse instead of the seconds.

Through the window, the resort's Christmas lights flicked on—automatic timer, 4 PM every day. Thousands of white bulbs illuminated the main lodge. Festive. Beautiful. Grotesque.

The perfect backdrop for two women about to be arrested for murder.

Chapter 10

Silent Night

The sirens got louder.

A heavy knock at the door—three times, official, authoritative.

Baxter answered. His face pale. His hands shook like he had Parkinson's.

Two officers entered. The woman in front moved with the kind of calm that only detectives had—gray suit, hair pulled back tight, eyes already assessing the room. She showed her badge. "Detective Fairbank."

Behind her, the younger patrol officer—Polaski, according to his name tag—hovered near the doorway, fresh-faced, nervous.

Fairbank's eyes swept the kitchen: everyone at the table, the envelope, the laptop, Jordan's phone still in his hand.

"We received a call from this address."

Mother stood. Held out her wrists. Steady. Calm. "That was me."

Father didn't move from his chair. Stared at his empty bourbon glass.

Jordan stepped forward. "This is complicated." He pointed at the envelope.

Fairbank picked it up, didn't open it yet. Looked at Mother, then at me, then back at Mother. "Ma'am, can you tell me what this is about?"

Mother's voice stayed even. "I'd like to make a statement. About my daughter's death."

Fairbank flipped open a small black notebook. "Which daughter, ma'am?"

Mother met her eyes. "Both of them."

Polaski's pen scratched fast across paper.

Mother continued. "I need to confess to negligent homicide. Obstruction of justice." She paused. Looked at me. "And twenty-six years of psychological abuse."

Fairbank opened the envelope. Read the first page. Her expression didn't change. Read the second, the third. Looked at Mother again.

"Mrs. Patterson, you're coming with us."

I swallowed hard—the motion scraped my throat.

Then she turned to me. "You as well, Ms. Patterson."

I spoke for the first time since the sirens started. "I was twelve."

Fairbank's expression softened slightly. "Twelve, when what happened?"

"When I held my sister underwater. When I killed her."

The words came out like rust, like lake water. They tasted like memory, but memory lies. Memory rewrites itself under pressure. Memory can be forged, as handwriting can.

Fairbank closed the notebook. "We'll need to verify all details. Speak with prosecutors. But yes—you were a minor. That matters legally."

Jordan stepped closer to me. "She won't be charged?"

"I can't say for certain," Fairbank replied. "But likely not. It was twenty-six years ago. She was a child." She faced Mother. "You, however, are a different situation."

Before they left, the question ripped out of me. "Are you sorry you let her die? Or sorry you couldn't save both of us?"

Mother stopped at the doorway. Officers on either side. Not handcuffed yet. Voluntary.

She said nothing for a long moment. Snow fell outside, heavy now, covering everything.

"I don't know anymore." Her voice cracked. "I've asked myself that for twenty-six years. I still don't know the answer."

Father stood, slow and deliberate, and walked to her. Kissed her forehead—soft, sad. "I should have let you tell the truth twenty-six years ago."

Mother closed her eyes. "I should have saved her."

Father's voice rasped. "We both should have."

Through the window behind them, the neighbor's inflatable Santa collapsed in the wind. Red vinyl suit deflated, white beard sagging. The compressor must have shut off. It looked obscene. Dead. A grotesque holiday corpse while my mother prepared to leave with police.

Fairbank led Mother to the patrol car outside, fresh snow on the hood. She wasn't cuffed. Just guided. A hand on her elbow.

I asked to follow in a separate vehicle. Fairbank nodded. Officer Polaski would drive me. Jordan said he'd drive behind them. Stay close.

Baxter held Addison. Tears streaked both their faces. Dark stains on her white sweater.

The twins appeared at the top of the stairs in matching red pajamas. Hair messy from sleep.

"Grandma?"

Addison rushed up to block their view. "It's okay, babies. Grandma has to go talk to some people."

Through the window, Mother sat in the back of the cruiser. Straight. Composed. Like she'd prepared for this moment her entire life. Maybe she had.

Before we left, I walked to the mantle. Christmas decorations everywhere—garland, stockings, candles. I picked up Lane's photo. Eight years old. Red bathing suit. Gap-toothed smile.

My chest opened and collapsed at the same time. I carried it with me.

Polaski opened the back door of his cruiser. "Watch your head."

I got in. The plastic seat was too warm. Too close. Vinyl and stale coffee in the air. The radio crackled with dispatch chatter.

Fairbank drove Mother separately. Two cars. Two confessions.

Polaski glanced back. "You okay?"

I stared at Lane's picture. Watched the lake house shrink behind us in the rear window. Christmas lights blinking on neighboring cabins. Families celebrating. Safe. Intact.

"No," I said. "But for the first time in twenty-six years, I know why."

He turned on the radio, low. Christmas music. Silent Night. Ironic. Cruel. All is calm, all is bright. Nothing calm. Nothing bright.

I held Lane's photo. Outside, snow fell—clean, white. A fresh sheet over old sins.

Behind us, the cabin lights went out one by one. Baxter turning everything off. Preparing to take his family home. Until nothing remained but darkness and the truth we couldn't escape.

The radio crackled again.

Dispatch: "Unit 7, we have another call. Lakeview Drive. Domestic situation."

Polaski acknowledged.

"Busy night in Ridgemont," he said.

I didn't answer. Just held Lane's photo. Her smile fixed in time, untouched by the years that destroyed the rest of us.

We drove past St. Mary's Church. "Midnight Mass Tomorrow—All Welcome."

Past the Ridge Lake Resort sign. "Season's Greetings from Ridge Lake Resort."

Past the Ridgemont Gazette office—lights still on. Gloria Steele probably writing tomorrow's headline: "Double Arrest at Ridge Lake Resort—Mother and Daughter in 26-Year-Old Drowning Case."

Snow fell.

The car moved.

Lane smiled.

And I didn't let go.

Fairbank's cruiser stopped ahead of ours. Officers opened the station doors. Mother stepped out into the wind. Snow blew into her hair like ash. She didn't look back.

Fairbank turned to me. "You coming, Dawn?"

Jordan reached for my hand. I didn't take it.

Everyone waited.

No one breathed.

I stared past them, past the lights, past the doorway—toward the lake. Frozen. Silent. White as bone.

A sharp ache formed behind my sternum.

For a moment, I saw it again:

A small hand breaking the surface.

Reaching.

Still reaching.

My breath caught.

Lane never let go.

And neither did I.

I stepped toward the officers.

The lake stayed quiet.

But I knew it was watching.

The End

BOOK 2

The Perfect Christmas Card

Chapter 1

The Photo Shoot

I stood at the living room window. Stared at the empty driveway. Ridge Lake stretched out behind the house, frozen solid, gray under December clouds.

Across the lake, neighbors had already hung their Christmas lights. Red. Green. Blue. They blinked in perfect patterns. Our house stood dark by comparison. Nathan kept saying we'd do it this weekend. Every weekend.

Everything else was ready. Wreaths positioned on either side of the fireplace—fresh pine, red velvet bows, $89 each from the boutique in Ridgemont Plaza. Cream cable-knit sweaters lay across the couch—matching, all four, six hundred dollars total.

The house smelled like cinnamon and artificial pine from the candles I'd lit. Holiday scent layered over holiday scent. The house looked like a magazine spread. I'd been awake since five this morning, and it made a difference— perfect.

My phone buzzed.

Jennifer: Running 10 min late! Traffic is INSANE

Ten minutes. That made it forty minutes late total.

I typed back: No problem! See you soon!

Three exclamation points. Casual. Breezy. Like I wasn't tracking every second.

From somewhere outside, Christmas music drifted across the lake. Jingle Bell Rock. Someone's outdoor speakers. The cheerful sound made my jaw tighten.

Nathan's Tesla pulled into the driveway at three forty-five. He was still in scrubs. I met him at the door.

"You're late."

"Surgery ran over. I texted you."

"Jennifer will be here any minute."

He set down his bag. Looked at me. "Jennifer's taking the photos?"

"She's a professional photographer. And my best friend."

His jaw tightened. He never said why he didn't like Jennifer. Never gave me a reason. Just that look every time her name came up.

I called upstairs. "Emma! Aiden! Time to get dressed!"

Aiden appeared at the top of the stairs immediately. His face carried that worried expression he wore too often lately. He clutched something—a small, wrapped present. Maybe an early Christmas gift from school.

"Is this the right sweater, Mom?"

He held up the cream cable-knit.

"Perfect, baby."

Emma came down slowly. Black jeans. Black hoodie. No sweater. Earbuds in. Some angry music bled through. Not carols.

"Emma, I laid out your outfit."

"This is so fake, Mom."

"It's not fake. It's our family tradition."

"Your followers' tradition. Not ours."

Nathan stepped between us. "Emma, just put on the sweater."

She rolled her eyes but went back upstairs.

My fingers went numb. Pressed them against my thighs. One photo. One hour. Was that too much to ask?

Jennifer's BMW pulled up at four. Custom plate: MOMLIFE. She had fifty-two thousand followers now. Two thousand more than me. Two thousand more since October.

She came in carrying camera equipment. Red and green scarf wrapped around her neck. Holiday chic. Hugged me. "Ready to make magic?"

Glanced at Nathan. "Hey, Nathan."

He nodded. Went upstairs to change.

Jennifer set down her camera bag. "He seems stressed."

"Surgery was long."

"Must be hard. Him working in the city. You here alone with the kids."

Something in her voice. I couldn't place it.

I ignored it.

Through the window behind her, I saw our neighbor's inflatable Santa. Full-sized. Waving one mechanical arm. On. Off. On. Off. Eight feet of forced cheer.

The photo shoot took two hours. Not one.

"Emma, smile. Real smile."

"Aiden, stand up straight."

"Nathan, put your arm around me. No, the other way."

Jennifer clicked away. "Beautiful. Perfect. One more."

The speakers I'd set up played Christmas music on repeat. Have Yourself a Merry Little Christmas. The Judy Garland version. Melancholy. Appropriate.

Nathan's phone buzzed in his pocket, again and again. He silenced it each time, but I noticed. Jennifer noticed too. Her eyes flicked to his pocket. Then to his face. Then away.

By six, everyone was done.

The kids looked exhausted. Nathan looked irritated. I felt hollow.

Jennifer packed up her equipment. "I'll send you the proofs tomorrow."

She left with a final look at Nathan. Too long. He didn't look back.

This year's card had to be better than Jennifer's. She'd gotten two thousand new followers last month. I'd gotten two hundred. The algorithm was punishing me. Or maybe my content wasn't good enough anymore.

Maybe I wasn't good enough anymore.

I made dinner. Pasta. Nobody ate much. Nathan scrolled through his phone. Emma picked at her food. Aiden asked to be excused early.

"Did you hear about that incident at Ridge Lake Resort?" Jennifer had mentioned it during the shoot. "Some family drama. Police and everything."

I didn't pay attention to local gossip.

My phone pinged. Ridgemont Gazette notification. I swiped it away.

Outside, the neighbors' Christmas lights came to life. Timer set for six PM. The whole yard lit up. Synchronized to music. *Feliz Navidad* played loud enough to penetrate our windows. Repetitive. Invasive.

That evening, I sat at my laptop editing photos. Nathan put the kids to bed. He read to Aiden. Emma's door closed with a thud.

I opened the photo folder Jennifer had sent.

One hundred twenty-seven images.

I scrolled through them. Stopped.

Found something.

A photo I didn't remember Jennifer taking.

My family. Nathan, Emma, Aiden. Same outfits. Same location in our backyard. Same poses.

But there was a woman in the photo. Standing where I should have been.

Her face was blurred.

I zoomed in. Same height as me. Same build. But brunette. I was blonde.

I checked the metadata.

December 15th. 2:47 PM.

But our photo shoot was today.

December 20th.

I scrolled faster. Found three more photos with the blurred woman. Always in the background. Always where I should be.

In one photo, her hand rested on Nathan's shoulder.

My stomach dropped.

I checked my calendar for December 15th.

BlogCon NYC - Full Day.

I was supposed to be in Manhattan that day.

But I stared at the screen. At the woman who wasn't me. With my family posing without me.

The photo shoot happened five days ago.

While I was gone.

Outside, *Feliz Navidad* played again. Same verse. Over and over.

I want to wish you a Merry Christmas.

Merry Christmas.

Chapter 2

The Discovery

I stared at the photo until my eyes burned. The blurred woman stood exactly where I would stand. Same angle. Same distance from Nathan. Her hand on his shoulder like she belonged there.

In the background of the photo, our Christmas tree was visible—the one I'd decorated three days ago. White lights. Gold ornaments. The exact same tree I'd photographed a hundred times for content.

I zoomed in on her figure. Same height. Same build. Brunette hair, where mine was blonde. The blur was intentional. Soft focus. Like Jennifer had edited it that way.

The laptop screen cast blue light across my hands. My fingers trembled on the trackpad. Cold. The house had gone quiet except for the furnace clicking on somewhere below. Outside, the neighbor's Christmas lights blinked through the window. Red. Green. Blue. On. Off. Relentless rhythm.

I checked the metadata again. December 15th. 2:47 PM.

Opened my calendar for that day. *BlogCon NYC - Full Day.*

I was supposed to be in Manhattan. All-day conference. Networking. Panels on content creation and engagement metrics.

I scrolled through all one hundred twenty-seven photos from today's shoot. Found three more with the blurred woman. Always in the background. Always positioned where I should be.

In one photo, the woman's hand rested on Nathan's shoulder. In another, she stood between Emma and Aiden—both wearing those cream sweaters I'd bought. In the third, she was barely visible behind the Christmas tree, ornaments glowing around her blurred face.

My stomach twisted. Dropped. Like missing a step in the dark.

I opened Photoshop. Checked the images for manipulation. Layers. Filters. Additions. Adjustments.

The software loaded. Analyzed. Processed each pixel.

Nothing.

The photos were authentic. No photoshopping. No digital compositing. No evidence of alteration.

This was a real photo shoot. December 15th. In my backyard. With my family. With someone else playing my role.

Jennifer took these photos.

Why?

The desk lamp hummed. Low electrical buzz I'd never noticed before. My throat went dry. I reached for the water glass beside the keyboard. Empty.

From somewhere outside, music drifted in. Faint. *Silver Bells*. The neighbor's outdoor speakers. City sidewalks, busy sidewalks, dressed in holiday style. The cheerful melody made my skin crawl.

Footsteps on the stairs.

I minimized the laptop screen. Pulled up a different folder. My pulse hammered in my wrists. In my neck. Behind my eyes—everywhere.

Nathan appeared in the doorway. Dressed in flannel pajama pants and a white t-shirt. Barefoot. Hair wet from the shower. Steam followed him, plus the smell of his body wash—cedar and something synthetic. Underneath it, peppermint. He'd brushed his teeth. The holiday toothpaste the kids picked out. Candy cane flavor.

"Kids are down. You coming to bed?"

"Soon. Just editing."

He came closer. Looked at the screen. Generic family photos displayed. Safe ones. Normal ones.

I reopened the photo with the blurred woman. "What is this?" I kept my voice calm. Level. Like asking about groceries.

Nathan leaned in. Squinted. His cologne mixed with the shower steam. Too strong. Gave me a headache.

"What am I looking at?"

I pointed. "This woman. This photo shoot. December fifteenth."

He shook his head. "I don't understand."

"We had another photo shoot. You, the kids, Jennifer. With someone else."

Nathan's face went blank. Smooth. Like wiping a whiteboard clean.

"Catherine, you photoshopped that."

"I didn't."

"You're obsessing again."

That word. Obsessing. Like I was crazy. Like my concerns didn't matter. Like everything I said could be dismissed with one word.

My hands gripped the armrests. The leather, slippery and warm, damp from my palms.

"I didn't photoshop anything. Look at the metadata."

"I don't know what that means."

"The photo's information. Date, time, camera settings. It's all there. December fifteenth. Your camera. Jennifer's camera."

Nathan sat on the edge of the desk. The wood creaked. His wedding ring caught the lamplight. Through the window behind him, the inflatable Santa next door waved. Mechanical. Mindless. On. Off. On. Off.

"Catherine, we need to talk about something."

My chest tightened. Ribs pressed in. Lungs shrank.

"What?"

"The pills. You're supposed to be taking them."

My antidepressants. Zoloft. Fifty milligrams daily. The bottle sat in the medicine cabinet. Half full. Untouched for fourteen days.

"I stopped two weeks ago."

"Why?"

"They made me foggy. I needed to be sharp for the Christmas card."

Nathan's face shifted. Concern or judgment. I couldn't tell anymore. His eyebrows pulled together. Mouth set in a thin line I recognized. He'd already decided I was wrong.

"You stayed up until three AM last year editing."

"That was different."

"You've been worse this year."

"Worse how?"

He stood. The desk shifted with his weight. A pen rolled. Stopped at the edge.

"We'll talk about this tomorrow. You need sleep."

He left.

The floorboards groaned under his steps. Down the hall, up the stairs. Bedroom door closing. Not slamming. Shut with that soft click that somehow felt worse.

I sat alone with the photo. With the blurred woman who wasn't me.

Maybe he was right. Maybe I did Photoshop it during one of my late-night editing sessions. Maybe I didn't remember. The pills. Stopping them suddenly. Dr. Carlson warned me about that. Withdrawal symptoms. Mood changes. Memory issues.

But I needed to be clear-headed. I needed to be perfect.

The TV played in the bedroom. Local news. Muffled through the wall. Something about Ridge Lake Resort. Police investigating an incident. I barely heard it.

The neighbor's Christmas music shifted. *Have Yourself a Merry Little Christmas*. The sad version.

My phone buzzed. Screen lit up. Ridgemont Gazette notification. *"Local Podcaster Investigating Cold Case."* I swiped it away. The glass was smudged. Fingerprints everywhere.

I stayed with my laptop. Nathan went to bed.

The house settled around me. Pipes ticking. Wind against windows. December cold seeped through the walls. The cinnamon candles I'd lit for the photo shoot had burned down. Wax pooled in the holders. Scent gone stale.

I searched my phone. My computer. Cloud storage. Searched for proof of December 15th.

My calendar said: *BlogCon NYC - full day*.

I found the Metro-North ticket. Purchased that morning. 10:15 AM departure from Dover station. Confirmation number. Seat assignment. Everything proper.

Then I checked my phone's location history.

December 15th. 2:00 PM to 4:00 PM.

My phone was at home.

In Ridgemont.

Not Manhattan.

The blue dot sat fixed on Lakeview Drive. My house. Unmoving for two hours.

I pulled up the BlogCon website. Checked my registration. Ticket purchased. Confirmation email sent. But no check-in record. No badge pickup. No attendance logged.

I wasn't at BlogCon.

I was here.

And I had no memory of it.

Outside, the neighbor's music played the same songs on repeat. *Jingle Bells. Deck the Halls. Feliz Navidad.* Over and over. The cheerful voices sang about joy and celebration while I stared at proof that I'd lost hours of my life.

Five days before Christmas.

And I couldn't remember any of it.

Chapter 3

The Essay

I made pancakes on Saturday morning. Emma and Aiden sat at the table with their iPads. The screens cast blue light across their faces, bleached them pale. Ghostly. Behind them, the Christmas tree blinked—white lights, gold ornaments—its timer set for seven. Cheerful. Relentless.

Nathan had left early. Running errands, he said. Last-minute Christmas shopping. Back this afternoon.

He didn't say where.

Emma went to the bathroom. The folder waited on the counter. Green plastic. Her name in Sharpie across the tab. A sheet of white paper stuck out from the side.

The title was easy to read: My Mother.

I flipped the pancakes. The spatula scraped cast iron. Edges browned. Bubbles rose in the batter and broke. I shouldn't read her homework. It was private.

My hand lifted the folder anyway.

From the living room, the radio played *I'll Be Home for Christmas.* Bing Crosby murmured about snow and mistletoe. The song tightened the air in my throat.

Emma was still in the bathroom. I picked up the folder. Warm plastic bent under my fingers.

I read quickly. Heat crowded behind my eyes. The page wavered.

The essay began with a neat introduction. Topic sentence. Thesis. Then the body paragraphs. And then:

My mother is not who she pretends to be. She makes us smile for pictures but we're not really happy. She cares more about strangers on the internet than us. She says the Christmas card is for memories but it's really for likes. She checks her phone two hundred times a day. She counts her followers like some people count money. Last week she cried because a post only got five hundred likes. She made me reshoot a photo fifteen times until my smile looked "genuine." My teacher says writing should be honest. This is honest. My mother loves her phone more than she loves me.

The words smeared. I blinked until the page steadied.

At the bottom, red pen waited. Mrs. Douglas's handwriting. Small, precise.

Emma, this is concerning. I'd like to speak with your mother. Please have her call me. – Mrs. Douglas

I set the folder down. The granite felt cold under my palms. We picked these counters three years ago. Two thousand dollars for surfaces that earned fifteen hundred likes.

Was this how Emma saw me?

Was this who I had become?

The bathroom door opened. Water ran in the sink. Emma walked back wearing the reindeer sweater she bought herself. A joke about forced cheer.

She saw the folder in my hands.

Her face closed. Tight. Final.

"You read my homework?"

"It was right there."

"It's private."

I flipped the pancake. "Emma, is this really how you feel?"

She grabbed the folder. Her fingers left smudges across the plastic. "You wouldn't understand."

"Try me."

She froze. So did I.

"Your phone gets more attention than we do."

She walked away. Quiet steps for someone so angry. Up the stairs. Her door slammed. The house trembled.

Aiden watched from the table. His pancakes cooled. He held his fork still, grip tense. His snowman pajamas glowed under the blue screen light. I posted a photo of him in those pajamas last week. Three thousand likes.

I sat. The chair scraped the tile.

"Mommy?"

His words tightened, thin as thread.

"Yes, baby?"

"Are you leaving after Christmas?"

The room snapped out of focus. "What?"

He dragged his fork through syrup, drawing crooked trails. His shoulders curled inward.

"Nothing."

"Aiden, who said I was leaving?"

"Nobody."

"Aiden."

He stared at his plate. Didn't blink.

"Daddy said not to talk about it."

The floor tilted under me. "What did Daddy say exactly?"

Tears gathered in his lashes. They fell. He didn't wipe them. "I don't remember."

"Aiden—"

"I don't want you to leave!"

He ran upstairs. His steps landed too heavy for his body. His door closed with a soft click.

I sat alone in the kitchen.

The clock ticked. The refrigerator hummed. A car eased past outside. Tires whispered across wet pavement. A horn chirped—bright, festive, wrong.

The radio shifted into Jingle Bell Rock. Bobby Helms. Joy everywhere but here.

Nathan told the kids I was leaving.

Why would he say that?

The pancakes burned on the stove. Smoke lifted in thin gray streaks. The alarm shrieked. I didn't move.

Moments later, I turned the gas knob off. The stove clicked. Heat faded from the pan.

I opened the window. December air swept in—cold, sharp. Pine drifted from the neighbor's real tree. They'd dragged it inside yesterday. Eight feet tall. Perfect. They laughed while decorating.

I called Mrs. Douglas.

Voicemail.

'This is Mrs. Douglas, Ridgemont Academy. I'm away for winter break. For urgent matters, contact the school office.'

I called the office.

Recording. Closed until January third. Happy holidays.

Air scraped through my throat.

I checked my email. Scrolled back three weeks. Past sponsored offers. Past follower alerts. Past sales I planned to shop but never did.

There it was.

Parent-Teacher Conference Requested — Emma Winters

Sent: November 28

The email was marked as read. November 29, 10:47 AM.

I don't think I read it.

I checked my calendar.

December 23rd, 2 PM — Parent-Teacher Conference — E. Winters.

The entry sat there. Color-coded. Reminder icon bright.

I didn't put it there.

Who did?

My phone rested on the counter. The dark screen showed my reflection. Warped. Off. Someone unfamiliar.

Upstairs, Emma's voice drifted through the vents. Urgent. Low.

I moved to the base of the stairs. My hand wrapped the banister.

Garland brushed my wrist—plastic leaves, fake berries. Decoration for photos. Nothing more.

"I know, Dad. I'll be ready."

Dad.

Nathan wasn't home.

Who was she talking to?

Her steps crossed the floor above me. Too heavy for her size.

"Monday at two. I'll tell her I have choir practice."

My breath stalled.

Monday at two.

The parent-teacher conference.

Emma and Nathan planned it together.

Without me.

The radio drifted into Have Yourself a Merry Little Christmas. Judy Garland. Low. Worn. Heavy.

Five days until Christmas.

And my family locked me out.

Chapter 4

The Photographer

I called Nathan. Told him I was stepping out. Needed to clear my head.

"Want company? I'll be home soon."

"No. Just need a few minutes alone."

He paused. The silence stretched.

"Okay. Don't be long."

I drove three houses down instead. Past snow-covered lawns with different types of Christmas accessories in the front yard. Lakeview Drive curved along the lake. It was a picturesque winter wonderland.

Jennifer's house was a white colonial, black shutters. Same architect as half the neighborhood. Her yard glowed with Christmas lights, wrapped around every tree. They outlined the porch, the inflatable reindeer on the lawn—bigger than the neighbor's. More elaborate. Competition disguised as holiday spirit.

Her BMW sat in the driveway. Custom plate caught the afternoon sun. MOMLIFE.

I rang the bell. Its synthetic Jingle Bells chimed through the house. Nothing.

Waited. Counted to thirty. Rang again.

Movement inside. Footsteps. A pause. Then stillness.

TV was on. I could hear it through the door. Voices. News broadcast.

Jennifer was home. Why stay silent?

I tried the doorknob.

Unlocked.

This was normal. Small town. Safe neighborhood. We all left doors unlocked. Had for years. Until someone gave us a reason not to.

I pushed the door open. "Jennifer?"

No response.

Living room empty. Couch pillows arranged perfectly. Throw blanket folded at precise angles. Everything staged. Everything photo-ready. Christmas tree in the corner. Nine feet. White lights. Rose gold ornaments. Coordinated. Professional. Posted three days ago on Instagram. Got seven thousand likes.

TV on. Local news. Gloria Steele reporting on Ridge Lake Resort. Something about arrests. Police tape in the background. I'd seen the notification earlier. Dismissed it.

I walked toward the kitchen. Hardwood floors creaked under my feet. The house smelled like vanilla and cinnamon. Those expensive candles from Anthropologie. Holiday scents layered, too thick. The sweetness clung to my throat. I wanted the cold again.

Her laptop was open on the dining table. Photo editing software displayed. My family stared back at me.

I stopped.

Those were the December 15th photos. The ones with the blurred woman. Dozens of them filled the monitor.

I moved closer. The laptop was warm. Recently used. The fan hummed softly.

Photos labeled: "Dec 15 Shoot - Winters Family - RUSH."

I sat down at the table. The chair was still warm. Jennifer had been here minutes ago.

I scrolled through the files.

Two hundred plus photos from December 15th. Me in some. Blurred woman in others. Same poses. Same lighting. Same location in my backyard.

Like Jennifer shot it twice.

Once with me.

Once with... who?

I looked closer at the blurred woman. Tried to adjust the clarity. Clicked through menus. Enhancement tools. Sharpen filters.

System required password.

Locked.

I heard water running upstairs. Pipes in the walls. Jennifer was in the shower.

From somewhere in the house, music played. Soft. Background. Have Yourself a Merry Little Christmas. The Sinatra version. Made everything feel wrong. Sinister.

I continued to scroll.

Found folder: "Winters Family - Christmas Card Options."

Inside: Mock-ups of finalized Christmas cards. Layouts. Text options. Border choices.

One with my family. Traditional pose. Safe. Normal.

One with Nathan, Emma, Aiden... and Jennifer.

Jennifer's face clear. Smiling. Standing where I should be. Her hand on Nathan's shoulder. Emma leaned into her. Aiden held her hand.

Bottom text: "The Winters Family - Nathan, Jennifer, Emma & Aiden."

My vision narrowed. Edges went dark. Tunnel vision. Like through a scope.

What the fuck was this?

"Catherine?"

Jennifer's voice from the stairs.

I jumped. Heart slammed into my throat.

She stood at the top of the stairs. Wet hair. White bathrobe. Bare feet on hardwood. Red toenails. Holiday pedicure probably. Festive.

"What are you doing in my house?"

I pointed at the laptop. "What is THIS?"

Jennifer came down slowly. Each step deliberate. Controlled. Her hand on the banister. Knuckles white. The railing was wrapped in garland. Fake pine with red berries. Same as mine. Same as everyone's.

She looked at the screen.

Her face was unreadable. Blank. Then something flickered. Gone before I could name it.

"What?"

"These photos. December fifteenth. Who is that woman?"

Jennifer sat down across from me. Water dripped from her hair. Made dark spots on the robe.

Looked at the screen. Paused too long.

"Catherine, there's no other woman in these photos."

I pointed. My finger left a print on the screen. "Right there. That's not me."

Jennifer clicked the mouse. Photo refreshed. Reloaded.

Blurred woman was gone.

Only my family. Normal photo. Nothing wrong.

"I just saw—"

"Nathan called me last week."

I froze. The room went cold. "What?"

"He's worried about you. He said you've been seeing things. That you stopped taking your medication."

"Nathan called YOU about MY medication?"

"He's concerned. I am too."

My hands gripped the table edge. The wood pressed into my palms. Hard. Real.

"Show me that other file. The Christmas card mockup."

"What mockup?"

"The one with your face. Where you replace me."

Jennifer's expression shifted. Soft. Gentle. Pity.

"Catherine, there's no such file."

I grabbed the laptop. Pulled it toward me. Searched for the file. Clicked through folders. Subfolders. Recent files. Deleted files.

Gone.

All of it gone.

Jennifer must have deleted it. Right before I looked. While I was examining the other photos.

Or I imagined it.

Which was more terrifying?

"I think you should talk to Dr. Carlson."

"I'm fine."

"You're not fine. You broke into my house."

"The door was unlocked."

"You're seeing photos that don't exist."

"They existed. You're lying."

Jennifer stood. The robe fell open slightly. She pulled it closed. Tied the belt.

"I'm trying to help you, Catherine. We're friends. Let me help."

Something in her voice. Sweet. Concerned. False.

I stood too. The chair scraped backward. "Stay away from my family."

Jennifer's face flickered. Something dark. Cold. Calculating.

Gone in a second.

Replaced by concern again.

"Of course."

I left. Walked out the front door. Didn't close it behind me.

The cold air hit my face. December wind off the lake. Sharp. Clean.

Christmas lights blinked everywhere. Every house. Red. Green. Blue. White. Synchronized displays. Inflatable Santas. Reindeer. Snowmen. The whole street looked like a mall parking lot. Cheerful. Oppressive.

She was lying. She had to be. I saw those photos. I saw her face in that mockup. Clear as anything.

But what if I didn't?

What if I was hallucinating?

The pills. Stopping them suddenly. Dr. Carlson warned this could happen. Paranoia. Visual disturbances. False memories.

But this felt real.

Jennifer and Nathan talking behind my back felt real.

The way she looked at him felt real.

I drove home. Three houses. Thirty seconds. My hands shook on the wheel.

Someone's outdoor speakers played Jingle Bell Rock. Same song on repeat. The neighbor three houses down. They'd been playing it since Thanksgiving. Every day. All day.

Nathan's car was back in the driveway.

But there was another car too.

A Tesla. White. Newer than Nathan's. Wreath on the front grille. Green with red bow. Professional touch.

License plate: SHRINK1.

Dr. Carlson's car.

Inside, I heard voices. Nathan's. Deep. Steady. A woman's. Higher. Professional.

Talking about me.

Through the window, I saw them. Living room. Stood by our Christmas tree. The one I'd decorated. The one that got twelve hundred likes. They didn't see me. Too focused on their conversation.

Dr. Carlson gestured. Nathan nodded.

Planning something.

Planning what to do with me.

Chapter 5

The Intervention

I entered through the front door. Heard voices in the kitchen. Emma and Aiden upstairs. Sent up out of earshot. Their footsteps drifted down. Quiet. Listening.

Nathan stood when I entered. Dr. Carlson sat at the kitchen table. Coffee mug in front of her. She'd been here a while.

I glanced from the doctor to my husband. "What's going on?"

Nathan's face was set. Determined. "We need to talk."

Dr. Carlson gestured to the empty chair. "Catherine, please sit down."

My heart pounded. Fast. Irregular. "Dr. Carlson, why are you here?"

"I called her," Nathan said. Voice calm. Practiced. "I've been worried about you."

"This is ambush therapy. That's not ethical."

Dr. Carlson set down her mug. Careful. Precise. "Your husband is concerned. I'm concerned. Please, sit."

I sat. So did Nathan. The cold from the chair seeped into my bones. No one had used it. I on one side. They on the other.

It felt like an intervention.

Was it?

Nathan brought over his leather backpack from the dining table. He pulled out his laptop and placed it on the table.

Through the window behind him, the neighbor's inflatable snowman sagged against their garage, half-deflated. It looked obscene. I am running a few minutes late; my previous meeting is running over.

Nathan ran a finger over the trackpad to turn it on.

"Do you remember posting these?"

The screen showed my Instagram account. My face in the profile picture.

Recent posts I didn't recognize.

Post from December 18th. 2:47 AM.

Photo of Nathan asleep. Our bedroom. Dark. Flash illuminating his face.

Caption: They're trying to replace me. Watch them. Trust no one. realitycheck truthhurts notcrazy

Forty-seven comments. Most of them concerned.

"Catherine, are you okay?"

"This is scary. Should we call someone?"

"Please reach out if you need help"

I stared at the screen. My pulse raced.

"I didn't post that."

Nathan scrolled. His finger on the trackpad. Slow. Deliberate.

Another post. December 17th. 3:12 AM.

Photo of Jennifer's house. Taken from outside. From the street. Night. Dark windows. One light on upstairs.

Caption: She wants my life. She's been planning this. I see everything now. betrayal fakefriends thetruth

Sixty-two comments. More concerned. Some alarmed.

"Catherine, this isn't normal"

"Are you safe?"

"Should we call the police?"

My throat closed. Tight. Like hands around my neck.

"I didn't—"

"There are six posts like this." Nathan's voice was quiet. Gentle. The voice he used with frightened patients. "All posted between two and four AM. All deleted within hours. But followers screenshot them. Sent them to me. Asked if you're okay."

He showed me more screenshots from concerned followers. Private messages to my account. To Nathan's account. Questions. Worry. Fear.

The room spun. I clutched the tabletop. Somewhere upstairs, Emma's speakers came to life. Mariah Carey. All I Want For Christmas. The song seemed to follow me everywhere this month. Relentless. Inescapable.

Dr. Carlson leaned forward. "Catherine, do you remember making these posts?"

"No."

"Have you been sleeping normally?"

"I... Don't know."

"You stopped taking Zoloft two weeks ago?"

"Yes."

"Why?"

"It made me foggy."

Dr. Carlson made notes. Pen scratched paper. The sound, too loud in the quiet room. "Stopping SSRIs suddenly can cause issues. Paranoia. Dissociation. Memory gaps. Sleepwalking. Sleep-texting."

Nathan turned the laptop toward himself. Scrolled more. "She's been accusing Jennifer of things. Says Jennifer is trying to replace her."

"She IS." My voice too loud. "I saw photos—"

"Photos you can't show me." Nathan interrupted. Calm. Patient. Infuriating.

"Because they disappeared."

"Or you imagined them."

Dr. Carlson set down her pen. Folded her hands on the table. Professional. Concerned. "Catherine, I think you're experiencing a break. The stress of social media. The perfectionism. Stopping medication suddenly. It's a perfect storm."

"I'm not having a break. They're gaslighting me."

The word hung there. Heavy. Accusatory.

Dr. Carlson's expression didn't change. "Who is?"

"Nathan. Jennifer. Both of them."

Nathan's face shifted. Hurt. Genuine or performed. I couldn't tell anymore.

"Catherine, I love you. I'm trying to help."

"Help me or document me?"

Silence.

Dr. Carlson broke it. "I'd like you to come to my office. Monday morning. We can talk more there. Discuss options. Maybe inpatient treatment."

I bolted to my feet. "Inpatient? You want to commit me?"

Nathan stood too. "Not commit. Just... a rest. A place to get better."

"I'm not crazy."

"I didn't say you were."

But his face did. His eyes confirmed it. The way he stood. The way he looked at Dr. Carlson. The way they'd coordinated this.

"The posts, Catherine." Dr. Carlson's voice soft. "Look at them."

I looked.

They were disturbing. Paranoid. Unhinged. Photos taken at three AM. Captions that sounded desperate. Frightened. Unstable.

Did I write those?

The room was too warm. My sweater scratched against my skin. The heating vent blew dry air. My eyes burned. The scent of pine drifted from the candle Nathan had lit earlier. Winter Wonderland or some bullshit. The smell made my stomach turn.

"There's a facility here in Ridgemont if you prefer staying local." Dr. Carlson pulled out a brochure. Glossy. Professional. "Ridgemont Psychiatric Center. Dr. Ballard recommended it. He referred several patients there. Very comfortable. Private rooms. Excellent staff."

"I need to think about it."

Nathan exhaled. Relief. "That's all we're asking."

Dr. Carlson stood. Gathered her things. Put on her coat. Black wool. Expensive. "Call me Monday. We'll talk more."

She left. Nathan walked her to the door. They talked about me. Voices low. Discussed me. Planned me.

The front door closed.

Nathan came back. "I'm glad you're considering it."

"I said I'd think about it."

"That's a start." He walked to the stairs. "I'll let the kids know everything's fine. Mom was just having a hard time. Mom would get better."

I turned to go with him, but my phone pinged. I grabbed it. Email notification. New message.

Your order is ready for pickup - PrintPerfect, Ridgemont Plaza.

I clicked it.

Order confirmation for Christmas cards. Rush order. Five hundred cards. Expedited processing. Extra charge.

I opened the preview.

My family.

Nathan. Emma. Aiden.

And Jennifer.

She stood in my place. Her hand on Nathan's shoulder. Emma leaned into her. Aiden held her hand. All smiled. Genuine smiles. Real smiles. Not the forced ones from our photo shoots.

Bottom text: "The Winters Family - Nathan, Jennifer, Emma & Aiden - Merry Christmas 2024"

Order placed: December 15th. 2:47 PM.

From my account. winterscatherine@gmail.com.

Using my credit card. The one ending in 4782.

Ship to: 847 Lakeview Drive, Ridgemont, NJ.

My house.

My address.

I never ordered this.

But the confirmation said I did.

The timestamp said I did.

December 15th. 2:47 PM.

The same time as the photo shoot I didn't remember.

The same time I was supposed to be at BlogCon.

The same time my phone was at home.

In Ridgemont.

Without me.

Chapter 6

The Investigation

I knew where to get answers, and it won't be in Dr. Carlson's office on Monday.

Nathan was upstairs.

I sent a text: Need Starbucks. Need to process everything from the intervention.

I grabbed my keys. My phone with the email confirmation and drove to Ridgemont Plaza.

Not Starbucks.

PrintPerfect photo shop.

The plaza was busy. Saturday evening. Holiday shoppers. Families. Couples. Everyone happy. Normal. Intact. Holiday exhaust and pine candles bled into cold air.

The parking lot speakers blared Jingle Bell Rock on loop. Fourth time I'd heard it. I circled for a spot.

PrintPerfect sat three stores from Starbucks. Close enough to make my lie plausible.

I parked. Sat in the car for a moment. The engine ticked as it cooled—impatient. So was I.

The steering wheel pressed into my palms. One breath. Second breath. Go to Starbucks. Get coffee. Go home. Pretend I never saw the email.

But I did. I must get to the bottom of this.

I walked into PrintPerfect.

The chemical sting hit first. Followed by the humming lights. Bright lights above display boards advertised sample prints. Wedding photos. Family portraits. Christmas cards.

A young employee stood behind the counter in a red polo shirt and khaki pants. College kid. Home for the break. Name tag– TYLER.

He looked up from his phone. "Hi, how can I help you?"

"I'm Catherine Winters. I got an email about a pickup?"

Tyler checked the computer. Typed. Clicked. "Oh yeah, Mrs. Winters. Your Christmas cards. They're ready."

"Can I see them before you wrap them?"

"Sure."

He disappeared into the back. Returned with a cardboard box. It dropped with a dull thud on the counter.

I opened it.

Five hundred cards.

I pulled one out.

And there it was, my family with Jennifer. In full color. Professional printing. Glossy finish. Perfect quality.

The photo I'd seen on Jennifer's laptop. The one that disappeared. The one I thought I imagined.

Real.

Physical.

In my hands.

"When did I place this order?"

Tyler checked the computer. "December fifteenth. Online."

"Can you show me the order details?"

"Um... sure."

He turned the monitor toward me.

Order placed from my account. winterscatherine@gmail.com. Credit card ending in 4782. Mine. Shipping address: 847 Lakeview Drive, Ridgemont, NJ. My house.

It matched, looked legit.

"Can I see the original file uploaded?"

"I could get in trouble for this—"

"This isn't me in this photo. Someone stole my identity."

Tyler's face went pale. "Um..." He looked uncertain. Like he didn't want problems.

"Please."

His Adam's apple bobbed. "Sure, Why not."

He didn't sound sure. But he clicked through folders. System directories. Upload history. Original high-res photo loaded.

Jennifer's face. Clear. Smiling. Not blurred. Perfect. She stood where I should. Her hand on Nathan's shoulder. Emma leaned into her. Aiden held her hand.

I took a photo of the screen with my phone. Tyler watched. Nervous. Behind us, the store's overhead speakers belted Silent Night. The instrumental version. Peaceful. Serene. Wrong for this moment.

"Ma'am, I don't think I'm supposed to—"

"This isn't me in this photo. Someone stole my identity."

Tyler cocked his head. His eyebrows narrowed. "There's... There's something else."

Heat snapped under my ribs. "What?"

"A woman came in last week. Said she was Catherine Winters. She placed the order in person."

My throat went dry. "What did this woman look like?"

"Black hair. Early thirties. Really friendly. She was super nice about everything."

Jennifer was brunette.

I was blonde.

"But then we got the online order too. Same card. Same photos. We figured you wanted to make sure you had enough. Holiday rush and everything."

"The woman who came in—did you check her ID?"

"No. We had a new temp that week. He skipped steps he shouldn't have."

"That woman wasn't me."

"Oh." Pause. "Oh shit."

"Do you have security cameras?"

"Yeah, but—"

"I need to see footage from last week. When that woman came in."

"I'd have to ask my manager."

"Where's your manager?"

"He's off for the holidays."

I pulled out my phone. "I'm calling the police. This is identity theft and fraud."

Tyler panicked. "Wait! Wait. Let me check the footage. Just... Don't call anyone yet. Please."

He pulled up the security system. Old. Grainy. Black and white. Scrolled through timestamps.

December 15th. 2:30 PM.

A woman entered the store. Brunette. Sunglasses. Large purse. Winter coat. Hat.

Talked to the employee. Different kid. Not Tyler. Pointed at the computer. Gestured at displays. Laughing. Friendly. Comfortable.

The angle was wrong. The camera was positioned above the door. Couldn't see her face clearly. Her hat blocked most of it. Sunglasses covered the rest.

But I knew.

Jennifer.

I was sure.

The way she moved. The way she stood. The way she gestured with her hands.

"Can you zoom in?"

Tyler tried. Image pixelated. Got worse. No facial recognition possible.

But the timestamp was clear. December 15th. 2:30 PM.

Seventeen minutes before the metadata on the photos.

Seventeen minutes before my phone was at home.

Seventeen minutes before someone used my laptop to place an online order.

"I'm canceling this order."

"You'll lose the deposit."

"I don't care. Cancel it. And I want a written statement that someone impersonated me."

Tyler typed. Printed receipt. His hands shook.

Order 4782 - CANCELED - Customer reported identity theft.

Signed. Dated. Stamped with store logo.

"Should I... should I call my manager?"

"No. I'll handle it. But keep that security footage. Don't delete it. The police might need it."

"The police?" His voice cracked. "Are you really calling them?"

"I don't know yet. Depends on what else I find." I opened my wallet and pulled out my ID. "As you can see, I'm blonde. I match the name."

He looked at my driver's license, nodded.

I left PrintPerfect, receipt in hand, photo on phone—all evidence and walked to Starbucks. Decided to get coffee anyway, the lie still warm in my pocket.

I bought a Grande latte I didn't want. The first sip scorched my tongue. Good. Something real.

I sat in my car. The evidence dragged at my fingers. Real. Solid. Physical proof.

Jennifer impersonated me. Placed orders in my name. Used my photos. My family. My identity.

Cold paper. Pixelated faces. A shaky signature.

This wasn't in my head.

I wasn't crazy.

But if I showed this to Nathan, would he believe me?

Or would he say I fabricated it somehow? Set it all up to prove my paranoia was justified?

I drove home. The route familiar. Automatic. Three turns. Two stop signs. Ridge Lake on the right. Frozen. Gray. Dead.

Nathan's car was in the driveway.

Jennifer's BMW was there too.

In my driveway.

At my house. Heat climbed my neck.

I heard voices. Inside. Emma laughing. High. Genuine. Happy.

I walked into the living room.

Jennifer's voice: "Your mom will love this when she sees it."

Jennifer sat with Emma and Aiden at the coffee table, decorating Christmas cookies. Icing, sprinkles. Red and green. Festive. Perfect.

Like a fucking family.

Emma wore her apron. The one I bought her last year. She was covered in flour and smiling. Actually smiling. Jennifer had on a ridiculous sweater. Reindeer. Sequins. Familiar.

The kind of ugly Christmas sweater people wore ironically to parties. But she wasn't at a party. She was in my house. With my children.

Aiden had green frosting on his nose. Giggling.

Jennifer looked up first. Not my kids—her. Flour dusted her sleeves, my daughter's apron tied around her waist like it belonged there.

"Catherine." A bright smile. Too bright. "We saved you a spot."

Her hand rested on my daughter's back. Comfortable. Certain.

My house. My children. And she invited me in like a guest.

Chapter 7

The Memory

I sat at my desk. Eleven PM. Jennifer was gone. Everyone asleep. Nathan in bed. Emma and Aiden in their rooms. The house was quiet except for the furnace. The settling. The sounds old houses made.

I checked every digital footprint from December 15th.

BlogCon ticket: Purchased. Never scanned at the entrance.

Metro-North ticket: Purchased. Never used.

Car GPS history: Stayed in Ridgemont all day.

Phone location: Home from 10 AM to 6 PM.

Photos in my phone: Every shot inside this house. Nowhere else.

Every data point nailed me inside these walls that day.

Leaving. Keys. Door. A blur. Something missing.

The office faded. December 15th rose up whether I wanted it or not.

Morning. Conference clothes, conference face. Black pants, cream sweater, someone competent in the mirror.

Nathan left early. Surgery. Kissed me goodbye. Said good luck.

Kids went to school. Bus came at seven-thirty. Emma dragged her feet. Aiden excited. Something about a science project.

I'd packed my laptop when—

Doorbell.

Jennifer.

She filled my porch, wrapped in knit and teeth and warmth that didn't touch her eyes

"Hey! I was heading to Ridge Tavern for lunch. Want to come?"

I checked my phone. Ten forty-five.

"I can't. I'm going to BlogCon."

"It doesn't start until two PM." She pulled out her phone. Showed me the schedule. "Come on. One quick lunch. You've been so stressed."

I hesitated. Laptop half-packed. Bag open on counter.

"Okay. Quick lunch."

We drove to Ridge Tavern. Jennifer's car. She insisted. Easier if she drove.

The tavern was quiet. Lunch crowd hadn't arrived yet. We sat at a booth. Back corner. Private.

Jennifer ordered wine.

"I can't. I'm driving into the city after."

"One glass. It's the holidays. You've been wound so tight you might snap. You need to relax."

The server brought the wine. Red. Something expensive. Jennifer ordered it specially.

I drank it.

I drank. The first swallow scraped metallic, wrong, like old pennies under the fruit. But I drank it anyway. Didn't want to be rude.

The floor slipped sideways in under ten minutes.

The edges of the room blurred. Lights too bright. Jennifer's voice too loud.

"I don't feel good."

"Let me drive you home."

I barely remembered the car ride. Streets passing. Too fast. Too slow. Time wrong.

My knees went out. The hallway lurched in jump cuts until the couch caught me.

Jennifer's arm around me. Supported me.

"Just rest for a few minutes. You probably need food. Low blood sugar."

I lay down. The couch cushions soft. Too soft. Sinking.

The cushions swallowed me. Black. Then—Clock said 5 PM.

Seven hours gone. Jennifer gone.

BlogCon over. Too late to go. Missed the whole thing.

I opened my eyes in my office. Back to now. My chest cinched tight, breath coming in clipped, uneven pieces.

No blackout lasts seven hours. Not from one glass of wine. Not like that. Unless she'd put something in it.

The wine at Ridge Tavern. Dizzy within minutes. Seven hours unconscious.

I checked my laptop history from that day. Activity log. Timestamps. Programs used.

My laptop woke up at 2:15 p.m. and kept working for two hours while I lay dead to the world.

Twenty feet away, my body slack on the couch.

Jennifer used my laptop. Placed the Christmas card order. Accessed my accounts. Scheduled those social media posts. Made them publish later. At 2 AM. 3 AM. Times when I'd look unstable.

All while I lay unconscious twenty feet away.

I went to the kitchen. December 15th was six days ago. Would the wine glass still be somewhere?

Checked the dishwasher. Empty. Ran yesterday.

Checked under the sink. Recycling bin.

Found it.

Wine glass. Unwashed. Lipstick mark on the rim. My shade. MAC Ruby Woo.

I carefully wrapped it in paper towel. Placed it in a plastic bag. Sealed it.

Evidence.

If someone tested it, they'd see it. The drug. The proof. So when the police asked who and why, I'd have an answer that wasn't 'I'm crazy.'

My therapist thinks I'm having a breakdown. My husband thinks I'm unstable. My best friend is the one who drugged me.

Who would believe me?

Nathan appeared in the doorway. Barefoot. T-shirt. Pajama pants.

"What are you doing?"

I jumped. Nearly dropped the bag.

"Nothing. Couldn't sleep."

Nathan saw the wine glass in my hand. Wrapped in paper towel. Sealed in plastic.

"Catherine..."

"This is from December fifteenth. The day Jennifer drugged me."

Nathan's face. Not anger. Not surprise. Pity.

"Jennifer drugged you?"

"Yes. At Ridge Tavern. She put something in my wine."

Nathan sat on the counter. Heavy. Tired. "And you kept the glass?"

"I found it. In the recycling. I forgot it was there."

"This sounds..."

"Crazy? I know. But look."

I pulled out my phone. Showed him the photo from PrintPerfect. The screen showed Jennifer's face. My family. My life with her pasted over me.

"This is from the photo printer. Security footage. Employee witness. Jennifer impersonated me. Placed orders while I was unconscious."

Nathan looked at the photo. His face unreadable.

"When was this?"

"December fifteenth. While I was passed out on the couch."

I opened the house cameras—the ones I'd installed after that scare last year.

December 15th. 2:47 PM. Living room camera.

The feed showed my laptop glowing on the desk. A figure in my chair, shoulders hunched, fingers working the keys. Using my computer.

"See? Jennifer. Used my accounts. Placed orders."

Nathan watched. His expression shifted. Changed.

"Catherine, there's no one in this video."

"What?"

I looked at the screen. Video showed my laptop. Open. Glowing. But the chair was empty. Desk empty. Room empty.

"I just watched Jennifer—"

"The video shows an empty room. There's no one there."

I stared. Rewound. Played again.

Empty room. Empty desk. Laptop open. Cursor twitching, windows blooming and closing on their own.

"I'd seen her. I knew I'd seen her there, chair occupied, hands on my keys. Hadn't I?

Sitting at my desk. Typing. Using my computer. Her face. Her hands. Her movements.

Nathan took the wine glass from my hand. Unwrapped it. Held it up to the light.

"Let's throw this away."

"No! It's evidence."

"Evidence of what? That you had wine six days ago?"

He walked to the sink. Turned on the water.

I grabbed his arm. "Nathan, please. I need you to believe me."

He looked at me. Really looked. His eyes scanning my face. Looking for something. Sanity. Reason. The woman he married.

"I want to. But Catherine... You're seeing things that aren't there."

My phone buzzed.

Text from Jennifer.

Can't wait for Monday's conference. Emma's so excited.

Monday.

The parent-teacher conference.

I looked at Nathan. "You're taking Jennifer to Emma's conference?"

His face confirmed it.

Guilty. Caught.

"Emma asked if Jennifer could come."

Something inside me buckled. "Emma asked?"

"She feels more comfortable with Jennifer there."

More comfortable with Jennifer than with me?

My own daughter.

"Why?"

Nathan washed the glass and set it down on the rack. Dried his hands on the towel. "Because Jennifer listens to her. Actually listens. Doesn't just see her as a prop for photos."

The words landed. Sharp. Accurate. True.

My knees went soft. I sat down.

"So you're replacing me. You and Jennifer. You've been planning this."

"Catherine—"

"Is that why you called Dr. Carlson? To document me? Build a case?"

Nathan didn't answer. Didn't need to. His silence was answer enough.

My phone buzzed again. Another text from Jennifer.

This one had an attachment. A photo.

I opened it.

Jennifer. Nathan. Emma. Aiden.

At Ridgemont Academy. Today. This afternoon. While I was at Print-Perfect.

All of them. Together. Smiling like this was the version of our family that made sense.

Caption: Practice run for Monday! Emma wanted to show us her classroom. So proud of this girl.

They'd already gone to the school. Walked her halls. Met her teacher. All without me.

In the photo, Emma leaned into Jennifer's side, the red snowflake sweater snug at her neck—the same one she'd ripped off for me, "too itchy," "hate it," tears and drama and slammed doors.

She wore it for Jennifer. Smiled for Jennifer.

My family lined up in front of construction-paper trees, and I was the one holding the evidence like a crazy person.

They didn't need to replace me.

I was already gone.

Chapter 8

The Plan

I couldn't sleep. Four AM. Nathan still slept. His breathing was steady—too steady for a man dismantling our life.

I came downstairs.

The Christmas tree lights were still on. We'd forgotten to turn them off before bed. White LEDs reflected off the ornaments. Emma's handprint ornament from kindergarten. Aiden's construction paper snowflake. The glass angel my mother gave us. All hung there. Mocking me with their cheerful glow.

His laptop sat on the kitchen table. Open. Unusual. He always closed it. Always locked it. Always protected his privacy.

But this morning it sat open. Screen dark.

The screen glowed awake under my finger.

Checked browser history. He'd cleared some. But the downloads folder was full. PDFs dated over the past month.

Files with names that made heat tighten under my ribs

"Winters_Divorce_Petition.pdf"

"Winters_Custody_Agreement.pdf"

"Winters_Psychological_Eval.pdf"

I opened the custody agreement. Legal. Polished. Final.

Read:

Nathan Winters seeks full legal and physical custody of minor children Emma (12) and Aiden (8).

Mother exhibits signs of mental instability, paranoia, and dissociative episodes.

Mother poses potential risk to children's emotional wellbeing.

Mother stopped prescribed psychiatric medication without consulting physician.

Filed: November 28th.

Three weeks ago.

Nathan's signature at the bottom. Digital. Official. Real.

Lawyer: Carlson & Associates, Montclair, NJ.

Wait.

Carlson.

No. Couldn't be.

Except—of course it was.

I opened the psychological evaluation PDF. "Cold slid along the back of my neck. The trackpad was slippery under my fingers.

Report written by Dr. Sarah Carlson, Ph.D.

My therapist.

The evaluation cited:

Patient exhibits obsessive behavior regarding social media presence and follower metrics.

Patient stopped prescribed medication (Zoloft 50mg) without consulting physician or therapist.

Patient exhibits paranoid ideation regarding spouse and close friend.

Patient reports visual disturbances and memory gaps consistent with dissociative episodes.

Patient's social media activity shows erratic posting patterns during early morning hours (2-4 AM).

Recommendation: Supervised visitation recommended until patient undergoes inpatient psychiatric treatment. Patient poses potential emotional harm to minor children.

Dr. Carlson wrote this. After Nathan called her. After they coordinated. After the intervention.

The evaluation wasn't to help me. It was to build a legal case. Document my instability. Take my kids.

Footsteps upstairs drew my attention. Someone was awake. The laptop screen read six AM. Toilet flush. Sound of water. Morning sounds.

I read on. Ignored the sounds, like the coffee I brewed an hour ago. I found more files.

Screenshots of my Instagram posts. The disturbing ones. The 2 AM ones. The ones I didn't remember posting.

Screenshots of my text messages. With Jennifer. With Nathan. With Emma's teacher.

Bank statements of purchases at PrintPerfect. At Ridge Tavern. At places I didn't remember going.

All evidence. All documented. All building a case.

Nathan had collected these for weeks. Maybe months.

The water stopped. Footsteps on the stairs.

Nathan appeared. Saw me on his laptop. Saw the files open.

He went still mid-step. "You found them."

Not surprised. Not frantic.

Prepared.

I sat at the table.

"Three weeks. You've been building this for three weeks."

Nathan sank onto a stool. Pajamas wrinkled. Hair messy. Suddenly older. "I was going to tell you."

"When? After you took my kids?"

"I'm trying to protect them. From all this."

"From me."

"From what you're becoming."

The words split something inside me. Clean. Precise.

"You built a story about me. Piece by piece."

Nathan leaned back, poured coffee, as if we were discussing weather reports. "I documented your behavior. That's not setting you up."

Something old and buried clawed up.

"You're proving my point right now."

"Fuck you."

A small voice: "Mom?"

Emma stood at the top of the stairs. Hair tangled. Old star pajamas too small on her wrists. Aiden behind her, clutching the bear he pretended not to need. Their new Christmas pajamas peeked from the laundry basket nearby—matching red plaid for photos we'd never take now.

Both kids stared at us. Frightened.

Exactly the picture Nathan needed.

I took a deep breath. Held for five. Exhaled for five.

"Nathan. I want Jennifer here. Now."

"It's six in the morning."

"I don't care. Call her. Tell her we need to finalize the Christmas card."

"Catherine—"

"Call her, or I'm calling Detective Fairbank about the drugging. I kept the wine glass. You washed the wrong one. Evidence."

Bluff. The glass was gone. Nathan had washed it. His face was unreadable. He must have excelled in the 'Poker Face 101' in medical school.

Nathan hesitated. Looked at me. Weighed his options. He removed his phone from his pants pocket and dialed.

Jennifer answered too quickly for dawn. "Nathan? What's wrong?"

"We need you to come over. Catherine wants to talk."

Pause. Long. Loaded.

"Now? It's barely dawn."

"Please."

Longer pause. Background noise. Movement rustled on her end.

"Okay. Twenty minutes."

Nathan hung up. "What are you doing?"

"Getting the truth."

The kids came down. I hugged them and went upstairs. To our bedroom. To the walk-in closet. To the safe Nathan kept in the back. Behind his suits. Behind the shoe rack.

The code was our anniversary. He'd never changed it.

I opened the safe.

Nathan kept a gun there. Home protection, he'd said when he bought it five years ago. After a break-in two streets over. We'd never needed it. Never used it. It just sat there. Locked away.

I lifted it out. The metal bit into my palms—cold, heavy, real.

Loaded. We'd practiced at the range. My one condition before he brought it into the house.

Downstairs: "Catherine? What are you doing?"

I descended the stairs with the gun low. Not aimed. Not threatening. Just visible.

Emma screamed.

Nathan's face went white. Drained of color. Of blood. Of everything.

"Catherine, put that down."

I held it steady. Not aimed. Not threatening. Just... there. Behind Nathan, through the window, I could see the neighbor's lawn. Their inflatable Santa and reindeer display. Still inflated. Still cheerful.

Across the street, Santa's mechanical arm waved. At no one in particular or at a woman holding a gun in her kitchen at six in the morning.

"I'm done being gaslit," I said.

"I'm getting the truth."

Chapter 9

The Confrontation

Jennifer's car rolled into the driveway. I watched from the window, fingers pressed to the cold glass.

Six forty-five AM. The sun wasn't up yet. December dark. Ridge Lake a black mirror behind the houses, holding its breath.

I turned from the window. "Emma. Aiden. Upstairs. Doors closed. Don't come out."

They ran.

Jennifer parked. Got out. Walked fast. Clutched her fur coat around herself. Her breath puffed in quick clouds, then vanished.

She knocked. Didn't use the key I'd given her two years ago. For emergencies. Not affairs.

Nathan opened the door.

Jennifer stepped in. Saw me in the living room. Saw the gun low in my hand.

"What the hell?"

Nathan moved toward her. "It's not loaded."

"It is." My voice didn't shake.

Jennifer looked at Nathan. Something passed between them—quick, silent, familiar.

"Why did you call me here?"

"Sit down."

"I'm not sitting until you put that down."

I gestured to the coffee table. "Fine." I set the gun in the center. Equidistant. "It's there. Not pointed at anyone. Sit."

Jennifer sat on the couch. Purse still on her shoulder. Coat still on. Ready to run.

Nathan dropped into his father's chair—heavy, expensive, uncomfortable.

I stayed standing.

"I want the truth. All of it."

Nathan started, "Catherine, you're not well—"

"Shut up." Calm. Flat. Empty. "I found the divorce petition. The custody agreement. Carlson's report."

Another glance between them. Longer. Heavier.

"You built this together."

Jennifer's expression shifted. The mask slipped.

"Planning what?"

I lifted my phone. Showed her the PrintPerfect photos. The Christmas card. The timestamp. The employee statement.

"You impersonated me. December fifteenth. While I was unconscious."

Jennifer stared at the photos. Something cold slid behind her eyes.

"Because I love him."

Silence.

The furnace clicked off. The house held its breath.

Nathan's voice tightened. "Jennifer, don't—"

She turned on him. "No. Fuck this. I'm done."

She looked at me. "I've loved Nathan for two years. Since my divorce. Since Mark left me. Nathan listened. Actually heard me."

My chest tightened. "Two years?"

"He saw me."

"We're married." The words slipped out before I could stop them.

Jennifer laughed—sharp, bitter. "You don't even see him. You see your phone. Your followers. Your fucking Christmas card."

The words hit. True in ways I didn't want them to be.

"He told me last summer he planned to leave you."

I looked at Nathan. His face pale. Guilty.

"Is that true?"

He stared at his hands. "We talked about it."

"When?"

"August. Ridge Tavern."

"While I was with the kids."

He nodded.

"While I took them to the lake. We swam. Made memories. You were with her."

Nathan's jaw tightened. "You were taking photos for Instagram. Not making memories."

Seventeen photos. Two thousand likes. Validation where he said there should've been connection.

"How long have you slept with her?"

Silence.

Jennifer answered. "Six months."

My legs folded. I dropped into the nearest chair.

"Six months."

"The hotel in Short Hills. Every Thursday. You thought he had late surgeries."

Every Thursday. Six months. Twenty-four nights my husband picked her.

I looked at Nathan. "Every Thursday?"

His face showed guilt, but also defiance.

"You stopped being my wife years ago."

"So you fucked my best friend."

"She's more present than you've ever been."

The cruelty landed. Precise.

I forced myself to focus.

"The drugging. December fifteenth. That was you."

Jennifer shrugged. Casual. "You needed to stay home that day."

"Why?"

"So I could use your laptop. Access your accounts. Plant evidence for the custody case."

Her tone stayed conversational—felony presented as favor.

I looked at Nathan. "Did you know she drugged me?"

His face answered before his mouth did.

"Not at first," he said. "She told me after."

"And you didn't stop her."

"I needed documentation. The court wouldn't just take my word for it."

"So you let her drug me. Steal my identity. Gaslight me for weeks."

"You're unstable, Catherine. The posts. The meds. You've been in a spiral for months."

"Because you tightened the screws and called it concern."

"I documented what was already there."

Jennifer leaned forward. Soft voice. Reasonable. Delusional. "We did this for Emma and Aiden. They need stability. They need a mother who sees them. Not a mother who sees followers."

I laughed. Harsh. Broken. "You're fucking my husband and talking about stability?"

"I'd be better for those kids than you are."

There it was. Center of everything.

She wanted my life.

"You planned this for months."

Jennifer smiled—cold, victorious. "Yes."

"The intervention. Dr. Carlson. The evaluation."

"All necessary. Nathan needed evidence for court."

"Dr. Carlson is your family."

"Cousin," Jennifer said. "Close enough."

Light came in too bright, too sharp. Every piece snapped into place.

"You have set me up since November."

"Since August," she corrected. Proud. "When Nathan decided to leave."

I picked up the gun. My fingers closed around the cold grip before my brain caught up.

Nathan and Jennifer tensed.

"Don't," Nathan said, voice scraped raw.

"Mom?"

Emma's voice floated from the stairs. She hadn't gone to her room. She had listened. Heard everything.

Her mouth hung open, eyes wet, chin trembling.

"Dad's been lying?"

I set the gun down. Gentle. Controlled.

"Yeah, baby. He has."

I grabbed my phone. Dialed.

"Nine-one-one, what's your emergency?"

"I need to report a crime." My tongue felt thick. "Identity theft. Fraud. Assault. Drugging."

Jennifer stood. "You can't prove any of that."

"I can prove enough. Security footage. Witness statements. Bank records. Medical sedation notes. And the wine glass I kept. The one with your fingerprints."

Her face blanched.

The dispatcher: "Ma'am, are you in immediate danger?"

"No. But I need Detective Fairbank. Tell her it's Catherine Winters. Lakeview Drive. Tell her I have evidence of a conspiracy."

Through the window, dawn crept in. The Hendersons' timer clicked on. Their outdoor speakers blasted *O Holy Night,* Celine Dion's voice soaring—too powerful for a house this broken.

The notes climbed higher and higher, like the song hadn't realized everything here had already cracked.

Chapter 10

Perfect Card

Detective Hazel Fairbank took our statements. All three of us.

Two Ridgemont PD officers arrived first. Young. Uniformed. Names I didn't catch. They secured the gun, checked for injuries, separated us into different rooms.

Then Fairbank arrived—mid-forties, professional, tired eyes that had seen every kind of disaster. The same detective from the Ridge Lake Resort case. I'd seen her on the news yesterday, arresting that woman and her mother.

She took in the scene: the gun sealed in an evidence bag, three adults, two kids, fear thick in the air like smoke.

Fairbank set up at the dining table. Laptop. Recorder. Legal pad.

"Let's start from the beginning."

I told her everything. December fifteenth. The photo I didn't remember taking. Jennifer's wine. The blackout. The PrintPerfect order. The security footage. The employee statement. Screenshots. Timestamps. GPS logs. Bank charges I never made. My phone at home while I supposedly attended BlogCon.

Fairbank listened. Neutral. Professional.

"Can you prove the drugging?"

"The wine glass. I kept it."

"Where is it?"

My stomach dropped. "He washed it last night."

Fairbank made a small note. "So no physical evidence of drugging."

"But the PrintPerfect order. The footage—Jennifer impersonated me."

"We'll look into it."

She interviewed Nathan next. His voice calm. Measured. Practiced.

Yes, he had an affair. Six months. He regretted it. But Catherine had been unstable. Erratic. He'd documented everything for custody. Only wanted to protect the kids.

No, he didn't know Jennifer drugged me. That was her decision. He only found out after.

Yes, he coordinated with Dr. Carlson. Only to help me. Not to build a false case.

Everything he said sounded reasonable. Responsible. Like he was the one struggling to hold the family together.

Fairbank's face didn't move.

Jennifer's interview was shorter. Sharper.

She admitted everything. The drugging. Identity theft. Accessing my accounts. Ordering prints. Scheduling posts. Gaslighting me.

But insisted it was necessary. That I was unfit. Dangerous. The kids needed stability.

"You drugged someone," Fairbank said. "That's a crime."

Jennifer's expression hardened. "Prove it."

"We will."

Fairbank arrested her for administering a controlled substance without consent. Identity theft. Fraud. Attempted extortion.

Jennifer's face went pale. Then furious.

"Nathan, call my lawyer!"

Nathan didn't speak. Didn't move. Just looked away.

Jennifer's voice cracked with realization. "You're not helping me?"

"You went too far." His tone cold. Clean.

Jennifer barked a laugh—bitter, jagged. "I went too far? This was YOUR plan!"

Nathan's voice stayed even. "I never asked you to drug her."

A lie. A strategic one.

Jennifer kept screaming as they led her outside. Her words spilled into the morning air—wild, frantic. And from the sidewalk, it all sounded unhinged. Exactly the version of me they'd spent months creating.

Neighbors gathered. Mrs. Henderson in her robe and Santa hat. Mr. Smith filming. Phones out. Eyes wide. Sunday morning entertainment.

Fairbank turned to Nathan. "You're not under arrest. But get a lawyer."

"I didn't break any laws."

"Conspiracy is still on the table. We'll see."

Nathan grabbed his keys, wallet, phone. "I'll be at the Marriott in Parsippany."

He looked at me. No apology. No regret. Mind working overtime.

"I'll have my lawyer contact yours."

"Get out of my house."

He walked past Emma without looking at her. Past Aiden, whose shoulders shook with sobs. Nathan didn't turn back.

Emma watched him go, face blank. Aiden collapsed against me. I held him while he cried.

"It's okay, baby."

But it wasn't. Not yet.

Fairbank closed her laptop. "We'll need follow-up interviews. With Emma. With Aiden's counselor. We'll build the case."

"What about Nathan?"

"We'll investigate. But he's smart. He distanced himself from the drugging. Without physical evidence..."

She didn't finish. She didn't need to.

Nathan might walk away clean.

"Get a good lawyer," Fairbank said. "Document everything. This custody case is going to be ugly."

She left. The officers left. Silence settled over the house.

Just me and the kids in the wreckage.

An hour later, my phone rang. Dr. Carlson.

"Catherine... I heard what happened. I'm so sorry."

"You wrote a psych eval calling me unstable."

"Nathan called months ago. He said he was worried about you. I thought I helped."

"You helped him build a custody case against me."

Silence. Then softer: "I reviewed your file. Everything. You're not unstable. Someone was systematically gaslighting you. And I helped them. I'll testify. I'll write a corrected evaluation. I'll admit I was misled."

Her voice cracked. Regret—or performance. I couldn't tell yet.

I looked at Emma and Aiden as they built a blanket fort in the living room. Playing. Finally acting like kids again. Aiden draped the red plaid throw between two chairs. Matching the pajamas he'd worn this morning. A lifetime ago.

"Thank you," I said.

That evening, I checked my email. Avoided Instagram. Avoided the persona I'd built for fifty thousand strangers.

A message from PrintPerfect.

Your order is ready for pickup.

I hadn't ordered anything.

I clicked the link. A preview opened.

A Christmas card. My family—just Catherine, Emma, and Aiden. No Nathan. No Jennifer.

Simple photo. Real smiles. Not posed. Not curated. Just us.

Bottom text: **The Winters Family — Catherine, Emma & Aiden — Merry Christmas 2024**

Order placed: This morning. While I gave statements.

From my account.

But I hadn't placed it.

I checked the order notes.

Mom, I made this one while you talked to the police. Used your account. Hope that's okay. Used the photo from last weekend at Ridge Lake. Just us. No phones. Love, Emma.

My eyes blurred.

I showed Emma. She looked nervous. "Are you mad?"

I pulled her close. "No, baby. It's perfect."

Two days later, I opened Instagram. Fifty thousand followers waiting for the perfect family. The perfect family card. The perfect lie.

I typed:

This year, I'm choosing real over perfect. I'm choosing my kids over followers. I'm choosing truth over image. Merry Christmas. And goodbye.

I attached Emma's card. Posted. Deleted the app.

Emma watched me. "What did you just do?"

"Something I should've done years ago."

Outside, snow fell over Ridge Lake. Clean. White. A reset button pressed over everything. Across the water, someone's speakers played *White Christmas.* Bing Crosby's voice drifted over the frozen lake—hopeful for once.

Two days later, Gloria Steele's article ran in the Ridgemont Gazette:

Lakeview Drive Scandal: Mommy Blogger's Best Friend Arrested for Elaborate Gaslighting Scheme

Fifty thousand views in six hours—more than my most popular post ever.

I didn't read it.

I was too busy building a snowman with Emma and Aiden.

No photos.

No posts.

Just us.

Perfect.

THE END

BOOK 3

Day One: The Partridge

Chapter 1

The Arrival

Silence stretched across the lake—perfect for recording, dangerous for remembering.

I pulled the rental car into Ridge Lake Resort's parking lot. Gravel crunched under tires. December air hit me when I opened the door—pine sharp in my lungs, cold that bit through my coat. Twenty degrees, maybe less.

Friday the thirteenth. December thirteenth. I noticed. Dismissed it. Superstition was for people who believed in consequences.

Grant Beck waited at the main lodge entrance. Mid-fifties, tall, silver hair precisely cut. Expensive parka over wool slacks. He moved with practiced ease. Red and green garland wrapped around the porch railings. White lights blinked in perfect rhythm.

"Ms. Burns. Welcome." He extended his hand. "We've prepared the lodge for your recording."

I'd paid for the entire building. Two weeks of privacy. No interruptions. No guests wandering through asking about microphones and murder cases.

"Equipment arrived yesterday," Grant said. He held the door. "Signed for it myself."

The main lodge stretched before me. Vaulted ceilings crossed by exposed beams. Stone fireplace that could fit three people standing.

A wall of windows faced Ridge Lake. The smell hit me—pine and wood smoke, old logs and newer polish. Underneath it all, cinnamon. Someone had plugged in one of those holiday candles.

Previous guests had used the fireplace. Ash still dusted the hearth. Frozen lake beyond the glass. White expanse disappeared into the tree line. Other cabins visible across the property. Warm lights in windows. Christmas lights strung between them. Red. Green. Blue. Blinked in the darkness.

The heater rattled in the corner. Holiday music played from somewhere. Tinny. Distant. Mariah Carey promising all she wanted for Christmas. I'd heard that song four times on the drive up.

"Busy weekend," Grant said. "Family reunion in Cabin Seven."

I barely heard him. My focus locked on equipment cases stacked near the fireplace. Microphones. Mixer. Laptop. Portable sound booth. Everything I needed.

"This will work," I said.

Grant handed me the keys. "Anything you need, just call the office. We're here until ten most nights."

He left.

Silence pressed in. Perfect. I walked to the wall-mounted speaker. Turned off the Christmas music. Silence was better.

I'd driven ninety minutes up I-80 from Brooklyn. Through the tunnel, across the bridge, into New Jersey's northwestern corner. Sussex County. Mountain Creek ski resort glowed across the valley. Cell service dropped to one bar halfway up Route 23. Good for focus. Bad for emergencies.

Not that I expected emergencies.

My phone buzzed. Alex.

Thirty minutes out. Traffic on 80.

I unpacked. Microphone stands assembled easily. Cables snaked across hardwood floors. Laptop booted. External drives connected. I'd recorded in hotel rooms, closets, a storage unit in Queens. This was luxury. Space. Light. A view that made me forget the city existed.

Alex arrived in the production van. His knock echoed through the empty lodge.

I opened the door. He looked tired. Late twenties, lean build, dark hair that needed cutting. Dark circles under his eyes. Coffee stain on his jacket. Already burned out on true crime, and he'd only been doing it three years. He wore an ugly Christmas sweater—ironic, probably. Reindeer with light-up noses.

"Remote location," he said. Unloaded gear. "Bold choice."

"Fewer distractions." I grabbed a case. "I need to focus."

"On what specifically?"

"The Graham Winston retrospective."

Alex stopped moving. Set equipment down carefully. Too carefully.

"That case?" His voice flattened. "Why now?"

"It's been ten years. And he died a few months ago." I carried the mixer to the recording area. "People want closure."

"Do they?" Alex followed me. "Or do you?"

Strange question. I ignored it.

Guilty Conscience launched in 2015. My first episode covered Graham Winston. Local Ridgemont story. I was an investigative journalist then. Twenty-five years old. Hungry. Desperate to prove I could break real news.

Graham Winston was convicted in 2014 of murdering his wife, Bethany. Strangled her in their kitchen. At least, that's what the prosecution claimed. What I helped prove through my reporting.

Two million downloads on that first episode. Changed my life. Launched my career.

Graham was released in 2023 on a DNA technicality. Some details about trace evidence. Sloppy police work. He walked free after nine years.

Six months later, he died homeless in Burlington. Overdose. Officially.

I felt nothing when I heard. Should I have felt something? Guilt? Relief?

I pushed the thought away.

I unpacked in the master bedroom. King bed. Private bathroom. View of the lake through tall windows. Across the property, Cabin Seven glowed with lights. Someone had hung an inflatable Santa on their porch. It sagged in the wind, half-deflated, obscene.

The wrapped box sat on my pillow.

Red paper. Gold ribbon. Small. Gift-box size.

Tag: *For Ida*

I picked it up. Turned it over. No other markings.

"Alex?"

He appeared in the doorway. "Yeah?"

"Did you leave this?"

He stepped closer. "Leave what?"

"This gift."

He looked at the box. "No." Eyebrows narrowed. "Maybe Grant left a welcome gift?"

I tore the paper. Inside: porcelain ornament. Partridge in a pear tree. Delicate. Hand-painted. The kind sold in boutiques that charged thirty dollars for nostalgia.

Underneath the ornament: a USB drive.

My throat tightened.

I plugged it into my laptop. One file. *Day_One.mp3*

I clicked play.

My voice filled the room. Younger. Eager. December 2014.

"Thank you for agreeing to this interview, Bethany."

Bethany Winston. Alive on this recording. Dead ten years.

"I appreciate you taking the time—"

"I don't have much time. Graham will be home soon."

Static. Then my voice again.

"You said you had information about the allegations?"

"No. I said I needed to talk to you about something important."

Pause. Tension in Bethany's voice now.

"You've been following me, Ida. For weeks. I see your car outside my office. Outside our house. At the grocery store."

The file cut off. Abruptly. Mid-sentence.

Recognition struck like lightning.

I'd deleted that interview. Ten years ago. Every copy. Every backup.

Made sure no trace existed.

But someone had it.

Someone knew.

Alex watched me. "What was that?"

"An old interview." My hands wouldn't stop shaking. "From the Winston case."

"With who?"

"Bethany Winston."

He went still. "You interviewed Bethany before she died?"

"Yes."

"You never mentioned that."

"It wasn't relevant to the podcast."

Alex's expression shifted. "Everything's relevant to the podcast, Ida. You taught me that."

I turned back to the ornament. Noticed something taped to the bottom of the box.

A note. Printed.

On the first day of Christmas, I'm giving you one gift:

The truth you buried.

11 more days. 11 more gifts.

Confess before I expose you.

Below that:

- Someone who was there

I read it three times.

"Someone who was there."

Not Bethany. She's dead.

Not Graham. He's dead too.

Who was there?

My phone buzzed. Unknown number.

Text message:

Hello, Ms. Burns.

I've waited ten years for this moment.

You have 11 days left.

Day Twelve is Christmas Day.

Confess what you did to Bethany Winston.

Or I will.

No name. No signature. Just those words.

I looked at the window. Dark outside now. Snow started to fall. Thick flakes caught light from the outdoor lamps. Across the lake, someone's Christmas lights blinked. On and off. Red and green reflected on the snow.

I walked to the window. Looked out.

Nothing. Just darkness. Falling snow. Empty parking lot.

But someone had been in this room. While I unpacked equipment downstairs. While Alex unloaded the van. Someone placed that box on my pillow.

Someone was watching.

Outside, the inflatable Santa swayed in the wind. Christmas lights blinked their mindless patterns. Somewhere across the lake, Silent Night played from someone's radio.

Silent night. Holy night.

All is calm. All is bright.

Nothing was calm.

Nothing was bright.

Chapter 2

The Journalist

I remembered that interview with Bethany. Every word of it.

Or thought I did.

Memory is strange. Unreliable. Ten years later, how much is real? How much did I rewrite?

Alex left to get dinner in town. Ridge Tavern, he said—the gastropub on Main Street where they played only Christmas music. Twenty minutes there and back. I needed the silence anyway.

I sat at the recording desk. Plugged in headphones. Played the audio file on loop.

Bethany's voice filled my ears. Alive again after ten years of silence.

"You've been following me, Ida. For weeks."

Had I?

I tried to remember. September through December 2014. I was twenty-five. Investigative journalist for the Ridgemont Gazette. Failed relationships. Mediocre career. Invisible in every room I entered.

Then the Graham Winston story broke.

Wife missing. Presumed dead. I pitched a podcast to my editor. A woman with sharp eyes who never remembered my name.

She approved it. Gave me three weeks to produce the first episode.

I started the research. Background on Graham. Background on Bethany. Understood the victim. Understood the suspect.

That's what journalists do.

I learned Bethany's schedule. Where she worked—prosecutor's office in Montclair. Where she lived—beautiful colonial on Lakeview Drive in Ridgemont. Where she shopped. Where she had dinner.

Research. Profile building. Investigation.

Not stalking.

Right?

I remembered Ridgemont Plaza. Coffee shop. December morning. Smell of espresso and gingerbread. Holiday music playing through ceiling speakers. That Wham! song about last Christmas. Everyone wore scarves and winter coats. Wreaths hung on exposed brick walls. Red and green everywhere.

Bethany walked in. Ordered coffee. Turned around.

Saw me.

Her face changed. Recognition. Then something else. Fear? Anger?

She walked to my table. Customers watched.

"Stop following me."

My face burned. "I'm working on a story."

"You're working on an obsession." Her voice carried across the café. "Get help."

She left. I sat there. Humiliated. Customers stared. The barista pretended not to notice. The cheerful music kept playing. Something about sleigh bells and snow. Made everything worse.

I wanted to disappear.

But was Bethany right?

Had I been obsessing?

I tried to remember the weeks before that confrontation. Drove to Montclair. Sat outside her office. Watched her walk to her car. Followed her route home. Stopped when she stopped. Turned when she turned.

Research. That's what I told myself.

But something else lived underneath. Something darker.

Bethany was everything I wasn't. Successful. Beautiful. Confident.

Married to Graham—handsome, beloved high school teacher. Their house on Lakeview Drive had a garden. Real furniture. Wedding photos on the mantel. Christmas lights wrapped around the porch. Perfect.

I had a studio apartment in Newark. Ikea shelves. Frozen dinners. No lights. No decorations. Nothing.

I wanted what she had.

No.

I wanted to *be* her.

The thought surfaced like something buried too long. Ugly. True.

I pushed it away.

Two days after the coffee shop incident, Bethany called me. Offered to meet. "Let's talk. Clear the air."

I thought she was apologizing. Reconsidering. Seeing me as an equal.

December 12, 2014. 2:15 PM.

I drove to her house. Lakeview Drive. Beautiful colonial with the garden. Christmas lights wrapped around porch railings. Wreath on the front door. Green with red berries. Through the window, I could see their tree. Eight feet tall. Perfectly decorated. White lights. Gold ornaments. Everything coordinated.

Bethany let me in. Smiled. Too kind. Patronizing. She wore a red sweater. Festive. The house smelled like cinnamon and pine.

We sat in her kitchen. Granite counters. Stainless appliances. Fresh cookies cooled on a rack. Sugar cookies shaped like Christmas trees. Like she was preparing for some perfect holiday party I'd never be invited to.

"I wanted to explain," she said. "What I said at the coffee shop was harsh. But Ida, following me isn't journalism. It's stalking."

My jaw tightened.

"I'm concerned about you," Bethany continued. "I think you need professional help. This obsession—"

"I'm not obsessed."

"You've been outside my house seventeen times this month."

"I'm researching."

"Researching what? I'm not part of Graham's case. I'm his wife."

And then—

The memory cut off. Fragmented. Like film with missing frames.

I remembered standing. Angry. Defensive.

I remembered Bethany standing too. Moving toward the phone.

"I'm filing a restraining order."

What happened next?

The memory blurred. Went dark. Like my brain deleted the file.

I remembered leaving. Walked to my car. Hands shook. Drove away too fast.

But what happened between those moments?

The door opened. Alex returned with takeout bags. Smell of burgers and fries. He'd taken off the ugly Christmas sweater. Just plain black hoodie now.

"You okay?" He set food on the counter. "You look pale."

I closed the laptop. "Fine. Just tired."

"What was on that audio file?"

"Nothing important."

"Ida."

I looked at him. His expression too careful. Too controlled.

"An old interview. From the Winston case."

"With Bethany?"

"Yes."

Alex studied me. "That's a pretty big detail to leave out of the podcast."

"It didn't fit the narrative."

"What narrative?"

"That Graham killed his wife."

"Did he?"

The question landed cold. Direct.

"The jury thought so."

"That's not what I asked."

I unwrapped a burger. Took a bite. Didn't taste anything. "He was convicted. Served nine years. DNA got him released on a technicality."

"And six months later he died."

"Overdose. Tragic. But not my fault."

Alex sat across from me. "Why are you doing this episode now?"

"Closure. For the audience."

"Or for you?"

"What's that supposed to mean?"

"You've done fifty episodes since the Graham Winston case. Never gone back to it. Never mentioned the DNA technicality. Never acknowledged he might have been innocent."

"He wasn't innocent."

"How do you know?"

"Because—" I stopped. Because why? Because the evidence said so? Evidence I helped build? "Because the case was solid."

"Was it?"

I stood. Threw the burger in the trash. "I'm going to bed."

"Ida—"

"Drop it, Alex."

That night I couldn't sleep.

Three AM. Lodge silent except for wind against windows. Snow fell heavier now. Thick flakes covered everything. Across the lake, someone's Christmas lights still blinked. On and off. Red and green reflected on the snow. Relentless cheer that made my skin crawl.

I played the audio again. Headphones on. Volume high.

Listened past Bethany's words. Past my questions. Into the background noise.

There.

Faint. Almost buried beneath our voices.

Footsteps. Upstairs. Small. Light.

Someone else.

Then nothing. Silence. The recording cut off.

But someone else had been in that house.

Someone upstairs.

Who?

My phone buzzed. Three thirty AM.

Unknown number.

Text message:

Can't sleep, Ms. Burns?

Neither could I. For ten years.

Ten more days.

Tomorrow's gift will help you remember what you forgot.

I walked to the window. Looked out.

Snow. Darkness. Empty parking lot.

But somewhere out there, someone watched. Texted. Waited.

I texted back:

Who are you?

Three dots appeared. Typing. Then stopped.

No response.

I tried again:

What do you want?

This time, immediate response:

I want what you took from me.

Ten more days to figure out what that is.

Sleep well, Ms. Burns.

Or try to.

I stared at the messages. Tried to decode them. Tried to understand.

Who was I texting? Who had I taken something from?

Graham was dead. Bethany was dead. Who else was left?

Family? Friends? Witnesses I'd never interviewed?

Someone I'd erased from my story. Someone I'd made invisible.

Someone who refused to stay invisible anymore.

Outside, the inflatable Santa waved. Mechanical. Mindless. Cheerful.

Ho ho ho.

Ten more days until Christmas.

Ten more days until whoever this was, revealed themselves.

And what they knew.

Chapter 3

Day Two

The second gift appeared while I was recording.

Saturday morning. Ten AM. I'd slept maybe two hours. Coffee and fear kept me upright.

I sat in the portable sound booth Alex assembled near the fireplace. Microphone live. Headphones on. Recording light red.

Through the window behind me, Cabin Seven's inflatable Santa had reinflated overnight. Stood at full height now. Waved one mechanical arm. On. Off. On. Off. Relentless.

"Welcome to *Guilty Conscience*. I'm Ida Burns." My voice came out steady. Professional. Years of practice hid what I felt. "Today, we revisit the Graham Winston case—ten years later."

Through the booth's small window, Alex sat at the control board. Laptop open. Levels displayed on screen. He gave me the continue signal.

"Graham Winston was convicted of murdering his wife, Bethany, in December 2014. He served nine years before DNA evidence freed him in 2023."

I paused. Took a breath. Continued.

"Six months after his release, Graham died homeless in Burlington. An overdose. Some call it tragedy. Others call it—"

119

I stopped.

On the desk in front of me—a small wrapped box.

Hadn't been there thirty seconds ago.

"Alex." I kept my voice level. "Did you just put something on my desk?"

His voice crackled through headphones. "What? No. I'm in the control room."

I looked at him through the window. He stared back. Confused.

The box sat there. Red wrapping. Gold ribbon. Identical to yesterday's gift.

"Someone's in here," I said.

I opened the box on camera. Recording still running. Evidence if I needed it later.

Inside: Two ceramic turtle doves. White porcelain. Delicate wings spread mid-flight.

And an envelope.

My hands shook opening it. Photos spilled across the desk.

Dozens of them.

All of me.

December 2014. Ten years ago.

Me outside Bethany's office building in Montclair. Gray stone, tall windows. My car parked across the street. Telephoto lens captured my face through the windshield. Binoculars in my hands. Watched.

Me at Ridgemont Plaza. FollowedBethany through the grocery store. Three aisles back. Pretended to shop. Christmas decorations visible in the background. Garland. Sale signs for holiday turkeys.

Me at Ridge Tavern. Sat in the corner booth. Bethany and Graham at a table near the window. My tape recorder visible on my table. Behind them, a Christmas tree. White lights. Red ornaments.

Me outside Bethany's house on Lakeview Drive. Night shot. My car idled at the curb. Lights off. Watched their lit windows. Their Christmas lights wrapped around the porch glowed. Made my surveillance look even more predatory.

Thirty photos minimum. Maybe forty.

All surveillance-style. Professional quality. Dated and time-stamped.

Someone had followed me.

While I followed Bethany.

Someone documented everything.

Note with the photos. Printed text:

On the second day of Christmas:

Proof you weren't investigating.

You were stalking.

P.S. - I'm watching you right now. Wave to the camera.

I ripped off the headphones. Burst out of the sound booth.

"Someone's here."

Alex stood. "What?"

I showed him the photos. His face went white.

"Where did these come from?"

"They appeared on my desk. While I was recording. You were watching me through the window."

"I was." His voice tight. "I didn't see anyone."

"Then they came from behind. Or below. I don't know."

We searched the lodge. Every room. Master bedroom. Guest rooms. Bathrooms. Closets. Storage areas. Kitchen. Checked locks on every door. Every window.

Empty.

All doors locked from inside. No footprints in the fresh snow outside. No other cars in the parking lot.

Grant Beck's office at the far end of the property sat dark. Closed for the weekend. Wreath on the door. Closed sign decorated with holly.

We were alone.

But someone had been inside. While I recorded. While Alex watched me through the control room window.

Someone invisible.

Back in the main room, I spread the photos across the table. Alex leaned over them. Face unreadable.

"Ida." His voice careful. "What's going on?"

"I don't know."

"These photos. You were following Bethany Winston."

"I was investigating."

"That's not investigating." He picked up a photo. Me outside Bethany's house at night. "That's surveillance. Stalking."

"It's over. She's dead. It doesn't matter."

"It matters to whoever's leaving you these gifts."

Silence stretched between us. Wind rattled windows. Snow fell heavier now. White curtain erased the lake from view. Somewhere in the distance, church bells. Saturday service. Or maybe just recorded bells played from someone's speaker. Peace on earth. Goodwill toward men.

"Who took these photos?" Alex asked.

"I don't know."

"Someone was following you. In 2014. While you followed Bethany."

"Apparently."

"Who would do that?"

I thought about the text messages. The anonymous threats. The promise of twelve days.

"Someone connected to Bethany," I said.

Alex looked up. "Family?"

"Maybe. Or someone who knew her. Someone who thinks I'm responsible for what happened."

"Are you?"

The question I'd been avoiding.

"I was there that day. At her house. But I left. I told you—I don't remember clearly what happened between us talking and me leaving."

"That's convenient."

"It's the truth."

"Your truth." Alex looked at the photos spread across the table—me stalking Bethany for months. "Someone else's truth is in these photos. In these gifts."

He paused. "Someone who was there. Who saw something. Who's been waiting ten years."

"But who?"

I thought about possibilities. Bethany's family—did she have siblings?

Parents? I'd never investigated. Never cared about her personal life beyond what served my story.

A colleague from the prosecutor's office who blamed me for sensationalizing the case?

Someone Graham told about me before he died?

A journalist investigating me the way I'd investigated others?

The possibilities multiplied. Each one worse than the last.

I pulled out my phone. Showed Alex the text messages. Unknown number. Both of them.

He read. Face tightened with each line.

"They say they were there. The day Bethany died."

I thought about the background noise on the audio. Faint footsteps. Upstairs.

Someone had been in that house. But I'd never asked who. Never investigated. Never cared about collateral witnesses because I was too focused on building my story.

"Did anyone see what happened?" Alex asked.

"I don't know."

"What *did* happen, Ida?"

The question I couldn't answer. The memory with missing frames.

"I went to her house. We talked. She told me to stop following her. That she was filing a restraining order."

"And?"

"And I left."

"That's it?"

"That's all I remember."

"Nothing about what happened to Bethany?"

"I left. Drove home. The next day, I heard Graham was arrested. That Bethany was dead."

"And you didn't think to mention you'd been at her house the day she died?"

"I was scared. I thought—" I stopped. What did I think? "I thought it would make me a suspect."

"It should have."

"Exactly. So I stayed quiet. Deleted the interview recording. Moved on."

"And built your career on her death."

The words landed like a punch.

"I reported what the evidence showed."

"Did you?"

My phone buzzed. Both of us looked at it.

Text from unknown number.

Good morning, Ms. Burns.

Did you enjoy Day Two's gift?

I followed you for three months in 2014.

Documented everything.

Every time you followed her.

Every time you sat outside her house.

Every time you pretended to be a journalist instead of a stalker.

Below the text: Another photo.

Of me and Alex. Standing at the table. Looking at the surveillance photos.

Taken through the lodge window.

Five seconds ago.

They were outside right now.

Watching.

I ran to the window. Pressed my face against the glass. Looked out.

Snow. Trees. Empty parking lot.

Then—movement. At the tree line. Dark shape. Human-sized.

"There!" I pointed.

Alex joined me. Looked where I pointed.

"I don't see anything."

"Someone was there."

"Are you sure?"

Was I? The shape could have been a deer. A shadow. My imagination.

But the photo was real. Taken seconds ago. From outside. Through this exact window.

Someone was watching.

I grabbed my coat. "I'm going out there."

"Ida, don't. It could be—"

"What? Dangerous?" I zipped the coat. "Someone's been in this lodge twice. While we were here. While doors were locked. I want to know who."

I opened the door. Cold hit me like a wall. Snow fell heavy. Thick flakes that stuck to everything. I walked toward the tree line. Boots crunched in fresh snow. Each step visible. Each footprint evidence.

Behind me, the lodge glowed warm. Christmas lights from Cabin Seven blinked their cheerful patterns. From somewhere across the property, music drifted. *Deck the Halls.* Fa-la-la-la-la. Made everything worse.

I reached the trees. Looked for footprints. Signs of someone standing here. Watching.

Nothing. Just undisturbed snow.

But the photo was real. Someone stood here. Minutes ago.

I walked deeper into the trees. Looked back at the lodge. Clear line of sight to the window. To the table where we'd been standing.

Perfect vantage point.

Something caught my eye. On a low branch. Eye level.

Pink fabric. Small. Caught on bark.

I pulled it free. Child's mitten. Pink. Knitted. The kind a child would wear. Or that someone would keep for years as a reminder. As evidence. As a symbol.

Behind me, footsteps. I spun around.

Alex. Hands in pockets. Face concerned.

"Find anything?"

I showed him the mitten. He looked at it. Then at me.

"Maybe a kid lost it while playing. What does it mean?"

"I don't know. A message? A threat? A reminder?"

"Of what?"

"Someone small. Someone innocent. Someone hurt by what happened."

But who? Whose mitten? Why leave it here?

Was it meant to represent a child? Innocence destroyed? Someone young who'd been affected?

Or was it misdirection? Someone's attempt to make me think one thing while they were really something else?

Alex looked toward the lodge. Then back at me.

"Ida, what really happened that day?"

"I told you. I don't remember."

"Can't remember? Or won't?"

"Can't."

"That's convenient."

"It's the truth."

He walked back toward the lodge. Left me standing in the snow. Trees. Silence.

I looked at the mitten. Pink. Small. Innocent.

Somewhere out there, someone was watching. Waiting.

Someone who'd been in that house ten years ago. Someone I'd never thought about. Someone I'd erased from my story.

Someone who refused to stay erased.

Ten more days until Christmas.

Ten more days until they revealed themselves.

And made me remember what I'd forgotten.

Or buried.

Or both.

Chapter 4

The Lies

Days Three and Four arrived with more gifts and more questions I couldn't answer.

Sunday morning. December fifteenth. I woke to church bells across the valley, their sound carried over the frozen lake like a reminder that somewhere, people gathered for worship and celebration and normal December rituals.

Here, I sat alone in a lodge that felt less like a sanctuary and more like a crime scene. I waited for the next piece of evidence to materialize.

The third gift appeared on the kitchen counter while I was in the shower.

I'd locked the bedroom door. Checked it twice before stepping into the bathroom, letting hot water wash away a sleepless night and the cold that had settled into my bones from standing in the snow. When I came out—hair wet, towel wrapped around me, steam still clouding the mirror—there it sat.

Red wrapping. Gold ribbon. Smaller than the previous boxes.

I didn't scream. Didn't panic. Just stood there dripping water onto hardwood floors, staring at proof that locked doors meant nothing. That

127

privacy was an illusion. That whoever was doing this could enter any room, any time, completely invisible.

Alex found me like that. Standing frozen. Water pooled at my feet.

"Ida?" He stopped in the doorway. Looked at me. Then at the box. "Another one?"

I nodded.

"How did—" He checked the door. Still locked from inside. Chain still engaged. "That's impossible."

"Apparently not."

He picked up the box. Turned it over. No markings except the tag: *Day Three.*

I got dressed. Met him in the main room. We opened it together this time, both of us standing over the table like we were defusing a bomb instead of unwrapping a Christmas gift.

Inside: Three ceramic French hens. White porcelain with gold detailing, wings spread like they were caught mid-flight or mid-song, frozen forever in that moment of sound.

With them: a photocopied document. Medical examiner's report. Official letterhead from Ridgemont General Hospital. Dr. Erasmus Ballard's signature at the bottom.

Case: Bethany Winston, DOB 03/15/1980

Date of Death: December 12, 2014

Cause of Death: Asphyxiation

Time of Death: Between 2:30 and 4:00 PM

The details continued. Bruising on neck consistent with manual strangulation. Petechial hemorrhage in eyes. Blunt force trauma to occipital region of skull, non-fatal but significant.

But in the margin—handwritten note in Ballard's script, the same neat doctor's writing I'd seen on prescriptions and official forms:

Bruising pattern inconsistent with hands. Width and pressure suggest fabric? Towel? Recommend further investigation of household linens.

Below that, stamped in red: **RECOMMENDATION IGNORED**.

Someone at Ridgemont General had questioned the findings, had suspected something other than manual strangulation, had documented concerns about the evidence not matching the official story.

But the case closed anyway. Too fast. Report buried. Never followed up.

I remembered. I'd met with the lead detective. Sergeant Morrison, tired eyes and coffee breath and a desperate need to close cases quickly. I'd brought him coffee from the shop where Bethany had confronted me, smiled like we were colleagues instead of journalist and cop, convinced him Graham was the obvious suspect. Husband present. Wife dead. Simple math.

"Don't overthink it," I'd told him. Leaned against his desk in that confident way I'd practiced in mirrors. "The evidence is clear. Graham had motive, opportunity, and no alibi for the exact time of death."

He'd closed the case in forty-eight hours. Never read Ballard's notes carefully. Never questioned inconsistencies. Never looked deeper than the surface I'd helped him construct.

Note with the gift, printed in that same clean font:

Dr. Ballard knew something was wrong.

You made sure no one listened.

How many people did you manipulate to hide the truth?

Alex read the medical examiner's report three times, his finger traced Ballard's handwritten notes like he could find answers in the loops and curves of the letters. "This says fabric. Not hands."

"Ballard was speculating."

"Based on evidence." Alex looked at me, and something in his expression had shifted—the easy familiarity we'd built over three years of working together cracked like ice under pressure. "Evidence that suggested Graham didn't do it."

"Graham was convicted."

"By a jury you helped convince." He set the report down carefully, the way you'd set down something fragile or explosive. "With a podcast that presented speculation as fact."

"I reported what the police said."

"You reported what you wanted the police to say."

The accusation hung between us. Outside, someone from Cabin Seven had started building a snowman—I could see them through the window, two small figures packing snow into spheres, laughing, creating something innocent while we stood here dissecting death.

"Why are you defending Graham?" I asked.

"I'm not defending anyone. I'm just—" Alex stopped. Ran his hand through his hair. "I'm just wondering if we got it wrong."

"We?"

"Your podcast. My production. The whole thing."

I walked to the window. The snowman was taking shape now. Carrot nose. Button eyes. Red scarf wrapped around where a neck would be. From this distance, it looked cheerful. Festive. Up close, I knew it would be imperfect—lumpy snow, crooked features, already starting to melt in places where the sun hit.

"Graham's dead," I said. "Whether we got it right or wrong doesn't matter now."

"It matters to whoever's sending these gifts."

True.

My phone buzzed. Both of us jumped.

Text from unknown number:

Day Three's gift was about the doctor.

Day Four will be about you.

Your lies. Your fabrications.

Every false claim you made.

Check your recording equipment.

Alex and I looked at each other. Then at the sound booth. The equipment sat exactly where we'd left it—microphone, mixer, laptop, cables snaked across the floor like veins.

I walked over slowly. Alex followed.

On the microphone: four small USB drives. Blue. Labeled 1 through 4.

They hadn't been there twenty minutes ago.

I plugged in the first drive, hands shaking so badly I had to try three times before the connection held. Alex stood behind me. Close enough I could hear his breathing. Feel his tension.

My voice played through the speakers. Episode 1 of *Guilty Conscience*. Recorded December 2014, broadcast January 2015, the episode that changed everything.

"Graham Winston had a documented history of domestic violence. Police reports dating back three years show multiple 911 calls from the Winston residence—neighbors reporting screaming, sounds of struggle, Bethany's terrified voice begging someone to stop."

My voice. Confident. Authoritative. Absolutely certain.

Then another voice. Different recording. Current. Female. Cold. Factual.

"False. No police reports exist. No 911 calls. Ridgemont PD confirmed zero domestic violence reports filed by or about the Winston family. This claim is completely fabricated."

Silence. Then my voice again from the original episode:

"Bethany Winston filed for a restraining order against Graham two weeks before her death. Court documents show she feared for her safety, described incidents of physical and emotional abuse that had escalated in recent months."

The other voice responded:

"False. No restraining order was ever filed. Sussex County Court records show zero applications from Bethany Winston against Graham Winston or anyone else. No protective orders. No domestic violence filings. This claim is a complete fabrication."

I plugged in the second drive.

"Graham was having an affair with a teacher at Ridgemont Academy—a woman twenty years younger who later testified she'd been trying to end the relationship when Bethany discovered them together, and that Graham had told her he needed Bethany gone so they could be together."

Response:

"False. No affair existed. No teacher testified to this. The woman you're referencing—Amanda Torres—gave one statement to police saying she'd carpooled with Graham to a conference six months before Bethany's death and that their relationship was entirely professional. You twisted her words, invented a romance, and created a motive that never existed."

Third drive.

"Graham had significant financial motive. Bethany's life insurance policy was worth one point five million dollars, and Graham was drowning in debt from gambling losses he'd hidden from his wife for years."

Response:

"False. No life insurance policy of that value existed. The Winston family had basic coverage through Graham's teaching position—fifty thousand dollars, which would barely cover funeral costs. No gambling debts. No financial crisis. You invented both to support your narrative."

Fourth drive.

"Multiple witnesses saw Graham threaten Bethany in public just days before her murder. One witness reported hearing him say, 'I'll kill you if you leave me,' outside Ridge Tavern on December ninth."

Response:

"False. Only one witness claim exists. Anonymous tip called into Ridgemont PD on December thirteenth, 2014—the day after Bethany's death. Voice analysis conducted in 2024 shows the caller was you, Ida Burns. You called in your own anonymous tip. You created the witness. You fabricated the threat."

Static. Then the female voice—calm, measured, devastating:

"Four lies. Four complete fabrications. Four pieces of false evidence that convicted an innocent man. You didn't just report the story, Ms. Burns. You created it. You built a case from nothing. You destroyed a man's life with your imagination."

The recording ended.

Silence filled the lodge. Even the heater had stopped rattling. Just us. The evidence. The truth.

Alex spoke first, his voice barely above a whisper. "That was you. The anonymous tip."

Not a question. A statement.

"I thought—" I stopped. What did I think? "I thought it would help the investigation."

"By lying?"

"By giving them a direction to look."

"Toward an innocent man."

"I didn't know he was innocent."

"You didn't know he was guilty either." Alex stepped back. Put distance between us. "But you built an entire case anyway. Made up evidence. Fabricated witnesses. Created a monster out of a high school teacher."

"I was twenty-five. I made mistakes—"

"Those weren't mistakes." His voice rose. First time I'd ever heard him yell. "Mistakes are typos. Wrong dates. Minor errors. You committed fraud. You destroyed evidence. You manipulated law enforcement. You sent an innocent man to prison."

"I didn't send him anywhere. The jury—"

"The jury heard your podcast. Two million people heard your podcast. Your fabricated evidence. Your invented witnesses. Your complete fiction disguised as investigative journalism."

He grabbed his coat from the hook by the door.

"Where are you going?"

"Town. I need air. Need to think." He zipped the coat. "Need to figure out if I can keep working with someone who—" He stopped. Shook his head. "I'll be back in an hour."

The door slammed. Engine started. Tires on gravel. Gone.

I stood alone in the lodge with four USB drives and the truth they contained, surrounded by Christmas lights that blinked their mindless patterns and holiday music that drifted from somewhere across the lake— *Joy to the World* now, trumpets announcing the Lord's arrival while I stood in the wreckage of my own making.

My phone buzzed.

Text from unknown number:

Your producer is smart.

He's starting to see what you really are.

A liar. A fraud.

And possibly something worse.

Six more days until I prove it.

I texted back:

Who are you? What do you want from me?
Response came immediately:
I want you to remember.
I want you to face what you did.
I want you to confess.
Before I expose everything.
Another text:
You took something from me ten years ago.
Now I'm taking everything from you.
Fair trade.

I stared at the messages. Who was this? Someone from Bethany's life I'd never investigated? A family member I'd overlooked? A colleague from her office? Someone who'd been watching me for ten years, collecting evidence, waiting for the perfect moment?

The possibilities multiplied, each one more disturbing than the last.

Outside, the snowman stood complete now, the children gone back inside to warmth and hot chocolate and normal December afternoons. The snowman's coal eyes seemed to watch the lodge, black and empty and knowing, a silent witness to everything that happened here.

I closed all the curtains.

Chapter 5

The Fracture

Day Five arrived with my breakdown.

Monday. December sixteenth. I didn't sleep Sunday night —just lay in bed, stared at the ceiling, listened to the wind rattle the windows, and my own thoughts spiraled into places I'd spent ten years avoiding.

By morning, exhaustion had settled into my bones like cold. Made everything slow and difficult and unreal.

Alex returned around ten AM. He didn't speak. Just set up equipment. Checked levels. Tested microphone. Everything perfect. Professional. Ready.

The silence between us felt like another presence in the lodge, heavy and accusatory.

The fifth gift appeared while I was making coffee.

I'd gone to the kitchen, turned my back for thirty seconds to pour water into the machine, and when I turned around—there it was. On the counter. Red wrapping. Gold ribbon.

I didn't react. Didn't call for Alex. Just stood there with the coffee pot in my hand.

Five boxes this time. Small. Velvet-covered. Arranged in a row like they were on display.

I opened them one by one.

Rings.

Wedding rings. Engagement rings. Three others—sapphire, emerald, ruby.

Bethany's rings.

I recognized them from photos. From research. From the case file I'd studied until I could recite it backward.

Engagement ring—diamond solitaire, platinum band, exactly one carat. Wedding band—simple gold, engraved inside with letters I couldn't quite read from here. The others—anniversary gifts probably, each in its own velvet box, each worth more than I'd made in a year when I was twenty-five.

With them: a note.

You took these from her body while she was still warm.

You pulled them off her fingers one by one.

You kept them.

Why?

Trophies? Proof? Evidence you planned to use later?

Or just because you wanted what was hers?

I sat down hard. Chair scraped against floor. The rings stared up at me, caught light from the window, threw tiny rainbows across the table.

"Ida?" Alex appeared in the doorway. Saw the boxes. Saw my face. "What is it?"

I couldn't speak. Couldn't look away from the rings.

He walked over. Looked at what I was looking at. Picked up the engagement ring. Held it to the light.

"These are—"

"Bethany's."

"How did—" He stopped. Read the note. His face changed. "You took these?"

"No. I didn't—" But even as I said it, something in my memory shifted.

Surfaced. A flash of image: hands—my hands—pulled metal over knuckles, pocketed small objects, worked quickly while—

I stood up fast. Too fast. The edges of the room blurred

"I need air."

"Ida—"

I grabbed my coat. Walked outside into the December cold that hit like a slap, sharp and clarifying and utterly insufficient to clear the fog in my head.

I walked toward the lake. Snow crunched under boots. Each step visible. Each footprint evidence. Behind me, the lodge glowed warm—Christmas lights, occupied rooms, the illusion of normalcy.

Ahead, frozen water stretched white and endless.

I stopped at the shore. Looked out at nothing.

The memory kept trying to surface. Kitchen. Granite counters. Christmas cookies scattered across the floor. Bethany on the ground, red sweater now showing darker stains, eyes unfocused but still seeing, still aware—

And me. Standing over her. Something in my hands.

White cotton. Monogrammed.

No. Stop. Not real. Can't be real.

But Bethany's rings were real, sitting in velvet boxes in the lodge behind me, proof that I'd been there when she died, that I'd taken things from her body, that I'd kept them for ten years hidden in places I could pretend I'd forgotten about.

My phone buzzed.

Text from unknown number:

You're starting to remember.

Good.

The truth is surfacing.

Like bodies in spring, when ice melts and reveals what winter buried.

I texted back with shaking fingers:

What do you want from me?

Response:

I want you to stop lying to yourself.

I want you to remember what you did.
I want you to face it.
Then confess it.
Another text:
Check your laptop. Downloads folder. File name: Memory.
I ran back to the lodge. Alex still stood at the table, holding the sapphire ring up to the light like he could find answers in its facets.
"My laptop," I said. "Where is it?"
"Recording desk. Why?"
I pulled it open. Downloaded folder. Found the file.
Memory.mp4
I clicked play.
Security camera footage. Doorbell camera. December 12, 2014.
The timestamp in the corner read 2:15 PM.
My car pulled into Bethany's driveway—silver Honda Civic, license plate visible, no attempt to hide or disguise. Two minutes later, I walked to the front door, clearly visible in the frame. Bethany answered. They talked briefly on the porch. She gestured me inside. Door closed.
The timestamp jumped forward.
3:42 PM.
Door opened again.
I came out. Alone. Looked around. Nervous. Paranoid. Carried my bag—the one with my tape recorder inside. Walked fast to my car. Got in. Sat there for thirty-three seconds staring at the steering wheel, hands gripping it in the grainy footage.
Then drove away. Too fast. Tires squealed.
Thirty-three minutes later—4:15 PM—Graham's car pulled up. Black Subaru. He got out with his briefcase, returned home from work at Ridgemont Academy, unlocked the front door, went inside.
Eight minutes after that, he burst back out—stumbled, phone to his ear, screamed something the camera couldn't capture, dropped to his knees on the lawn.
Bethany was already dead when he arrived.
The timeline proved everything. She died between 2:17 PM and 3:42

PM—while I was alone in that house with her. While Graham was still teaching third graders about fractions and Christmas around the world. While someone else was upstairs doing whatever they were doing, completely unaware that something terrible was happening one floor below.

Note appeared on screen, overlaying the video:

This footage was given to police in 2014.

They filed it as evidence but never reviewed it.

Too focused on Graham.

Too willing to believe your story.

Your license plate is visible. Your face is visible.

Timeline proves Graham's innocence.

And your presence at the scene.

The video ended.

I couldn't breathe. Room spinning. The walls breathed in and out.

Alex caught me as I fell. Guided me to a chair. His hands on my shoulders. Steady.

"Ida. Talk to me."

"I was there." The words came out broken. Whispered. "I was at her house when she died."

"I know."

"You know?"

"The video's pretty clear."

"But I didn't—" I stopped. Didn't what? Didn't kill her? But the rings were in the kitchen. The medical examiner's note about fabric. The timeline showed I was alone with her when she died.

"What do you remember?" Alex asked.

"Not enough. Too much. I don't know."

He pulled up a chair. Sat across from me. His face was different now—not the producer I'd worked with for three years, but someone harder, colder, more distant.

"Tell me what you do remember."

"Going to her house. Sitting in the kitchen. She told me I needed help. That she was filing a restraining order."

"And then?"

"And then—" The memory fractured. Came in pieces. "We fought. I grabbed her arm. She pulled away."

"She fell?"

"Yes. No. I don't—" I pressed my hands to my head. "I don't remember clearly."

"Or you don't want to remember."

"Both. Maybe. I don't know."

Alex leaned back. Studied me like I was evidence. A specimen. Something to analyze.

"Someone's been leaving you these gifts. Someone who knows exactly what happened. Someone who was there."

"But who? Who was in that house?"

"You tell me."

I thought back. Tried to remember. The audio had background noise. Footsteps upstairs. Small. Light.

But whose? A neighbor who'd come over? A friend of Bethany's? Someone I'd never asked about because I was too focused on building my case against Graham?

"I don't know," I said. "I never investigated who else might have been there. Never cared about witnesses because I already had my story."

"And now someone's making you care."

My phone buzzed.

Text from unknown number:

Five more days, Ms. Burns.

Five more gifts.

Then you decide.

Confess the truth.

Or I expose everything.

I showed Alex the message. He read it. Looked at me.

"What are you going to do?"

"I don't know."

"You could run."

"Where?"

"Anywhere. Disappear. Start over."

"Someone's been watching me for ten years. You really think I can hide now?"

Alex stood. "Then you have one choice. Figure out what really happened. Remember. Face it. And decide if you're going to tell the truth before someone forces you to."

He walked to the door and left.

I sat alone with Bethany's rings and my fragmenting memory, surrounded by Christmas decorations that felt increasingly like mockery—joy to the world, peace on earth, goodwill toward men.

I'd shown no goodwill. Found no peace. Created no joy.

Just lies. Fabrications. A career built on someone else's grave.

My phone buzzed.

Text from unknown number:

Tomorrow's gift will be harder to deny.

The evidence you can't explain away.

Sleep well.

If you can.

Outside, night fell. Christmas lights blinked on across the property—timers activated, automated holiday cheer, thousands of bulbs illuminated the darkness while I sat in my own private hell.

The rings caught the light. Diamond. Sapphire. Emerald. Ruby. Gold.

Bethany's rings.

That I'd taken from her dead hand.

The memory came back. Piece by piece. Image by image.

Soon I wouldn't be able to deny it anymore.

Soon I'd have to face what I'd buried for ten years.

The truth.

Chapter 6

The Evidence

Days Six and Seven brought the final pieces I couldn't ignore.

Tuesday morning. December seventeenth. I woke to knocking.

Grant Beck stood at the door, red plaid scarf wrapped against the cold, concern creased his weathered face. "Ms. Burns. Just wanted to check in. You've been very quiet the last few days."

"Just working hard on the episode."

"Right. Well." He shifted his weight. "Wanted to remind you—Christmas Eve is in a few days. We'll be closing the office early. Won't reopen until the twenty-sixth."

"Understood."

"You need anything before then, just let me know." He nodded. "Have a good day."

He left. I closed the door. Leaned against it.

The sixth gift appeared while I was in the shower.

I'd locked the bathroom door. Checked it twice. Turned the water as hot as I could stand, let steam fill the small space until I could barely see my own reflection in the mirror. When I emerged, wrapped in a towel, hair dripping—there it sat.

On the bathroom counter. Red wrapping. Gold ribbon.

They could go anywhere. Do anything. I had no privacy. No safety. No walls they couldn't breach.

Six figurines this time. White ceramic. Geese. A-laying, according to the song.

With them: printed emails. My correspondence with Sergeant Morrison from December 2014.

I read them with water still dripping down my back, soaked into the towel, made me shiver.

December 10, 2014 - 3:47 PM

From: ida.burns@ridgemontgazette.com

To: morrison.j@ridgemontpd.gov

Subject: Winston Case - Witness Information

Sergeant Morrison,

I have a witness who saw Graham Winston threaten Bethany the week before her death. The witness is willing to provide a statement but asks to remain anonymous due to fear of retaliation. This person heard Graham say, "I'll kill you if you leave me" outside Ridge Tavern on December 9th. Multiple other patrons were present and may have overheard the same threat.

Please let me know if you need me to facilitate contact with this witness.

Best,

Ida Burns

Investigative Journalist, Ridgemont Gazette

December 10, 2014 - 4:23 PM

From: morrison.j@ridgemontpd.gov

To: ida.burns@ridgemontgazette.com

Subject: RE: Winston Case - Witness Information

Ms. Burns,

We'll need to interview the witness directly. Anonymous statements won't hold up in court. Can you provide contact information?

Sgt. James Morrison

Ridgemont Police Department

December 11, 2014 - 9:15 AM

From: ida.burns@ridgemontgazette.com

To: morrison.j@ridgemontpd.gov

Subject: RE: Winston Case - Witness Information

Sergeant Morrison,

I understand your position, but this witness is genuinely afraid. Graham Winston is a respected teacher with connections throughout Ridgemont. The witness fears losing their job or facing harassment if they come forward publicly.

However, I was able to record their statement. I'm attaching the audio file. Combined with the other evidence you've gathered, I believe this provides additional support for probable cause.

The witness heard the threat clearly. This shows Graham's state of mind days before Bethany's death—escalating anger, explicit threats of violence.

Best,

Ida

December 11, 2014 - 2:41 PM

From: morrison.j@ridgemontpd.gov

To: ida.burns@ridgemontgazette.com

Subject: RE: Winston Case - Witness Information

Ms. Burns,

I listened to the recording. The audio quality is poor and the voice is muffled, but I can make out the general content. This is helpful background, but we still need the witness to come forward if we want to use this in court.

Can you make one more attempt to convince them?

Sgt. Morrison

December 12, 2014 - 6:33 PM

From: ida.burns@ridgemontgazette.com

To: morrison.j@ridgemontpd.gov

Subject: RE: Winston Case - Witness Information

Sergeant Morrison,

Just heard about Bethany. I'm so sorry. This is exactly what the witness feared would happen.

I know you'll need to move quickly on this case. The witness is still unwilling to come forward publicly, but they wanted me to tell you that they're certain Graham is responsible. The threat they overheard was genuine. The anger was real.

If there's anything else I can do to help the investigation, please let me know.

Ida

December 13, 2014 - 8:17 AM

From: morrison.j@ridgemontpd.gov

To: ida.burns@ridgemontgazette.com

Subject: RE: Winston Case - Witness Information

Ms. Burns,

Arrest warrant was signed this morning. We're bringing Graham Winston in for questioning. Your witness information was helpful in establishing motive and escalating behavior.

Thank you for your cooperation with this investigation.

Sgt. Morrison

I read the emails three times. Each time, they got worse.

There was no witness. I'd created one. Called the anonymous tip line myself, disguised my voice, reported a threat that never happened. Sent Morrison a recording I'd faked in my apartment using audio editing software I'd learned for podcast production.

I'd manufactured evidence. Manipulated law enforcement. Sent an innocent man to prison with complete fabrications.

Note with the emails, printed in that same clean font:

You corrupted a police investigation.

You created false witnesses.

You lied to law enforcement.

You helped convict an innocent man.

Someone watched you do it.

Someone documented everything.

Someone remembers.

I walked out of the bathroom. Found Alex at the recording desk, headphones on, reviewed audio levels for an episode we'd never finish.

"The emails are here," I said.

He pulled off the headphones. "What emails?"

I showed him. Watched his face change as he read. Disbelief to disgust to something colder.

"You created a witness that didn't exist."

"I thought—" I stopped. What did I think? "I thought Graham was guilty. I was helping the investigation."

"By lying."

"By giving them direction."

"Toward an innocent man." Alex stood. Put distance between us. "How did you fake the recording?"

"Audio editing software. Not hard if you know what you're doing."

"And you knew what you were doing."

"I was good at my job."

"Your job was journalism. Not framing people." He grabbed his coat. "I need to get out of here. Can't be here when—" He stopped. Shook his head. "I just can't be here."

"Alex, wait—"

"What? You want to explain? Justify? Tell me there's some version of this story where you're not a complete fraud who destroyed an innocent man's life?"

I had no answer.

He left. Door slammed. Engine started. Gone.

I sat alone with the emails, watched the clock tick toward evening.

At one-thirty, the seventh gift appeared.

I was at the table, stared at nothing, when I noticed it.

On the chair across from me. Red wrapping. Gold ribbon.

Seven figurines. White ceramic. Swans. A-swimming.

With them: three witness statements. Typed. Notarized. Official.

Statement of Jennifer Cole - Barista, Ridgemont Plaza Coffee Shop

On December 10, 2014, I witnessed a confrontation between two women at the coffee shop where I work. One woman followed the other inside and sat three tables away, staring. The woman being followed noticed and confronted the follower loudly, saying "Stop stalking me" and "This has to end." The follower looked humiliated and ran out, leaving her coffee cup on the table.

I saved the cup, thinking it might be important for police if the stalking escalated. Police never came asking about it. I kept it for several months, then gave it to my manager for storage. I recently learned it was recovered and tested for DNA.

The stalker in this incident was Ida Burns. The woman being stalked was Bethany Winston.

Statement of Marcus Webb - Customer, Ridgemont Plaza Coffee Shop

I witnessed an incident at Ridgemont Plaza coffee shop on December 10, 2014. A woman confronted another woman about stalking behavior. The confrontation was loud enough that other customers stopped what they were doing. The woman being stalked used phrases like "you've been following me for weeks" and "I'm filing a restraining order."

The stalker was clearly distressed and ran from the shop. I remember thinking at the time that this might escalate into something dangerous.

Two days later, I heard on the news that Bethany Winston was dead. I recognized her as the woman from the coffee shop. I called Ridgemont PD to report what I'd seen, but was told the case was already closed and my information wasn't needed.

The stalker was Ida Burns.

Statement of Patricia Voss - Manager, Ridgemont Plaza Coffee Shop

My employee Jennifer Cole gave me a coffee cup in December 2014. She said it belonged to a woman who had been stalking another customer and that she was keeping it in case police needed it as evidence.

Police never contacted us. I stored the cup in our back office for approximately six months, then moved it to our storage unit when we renovated. The cup remained there until 2024, when a private investigator contacted me asking about the incident.

I provided the cup for DNA testing. Results confirmed the DNA belonged to Ida Burns.

Three witnesses. Three statements. All described the same incident—

Bethany confronting me in public, calling me a stalker, and threatening a restraining order.

All ignored by the original investigation. All filed away or dismissed. All proved I'd lied about my relationship with Bethany, about the nature of my "research," about everything.

And a coffee cup. Saved for ten years. Tested. Confirmed.

My DNA. My fingerprints. Physical evidence I was stalking Bethany Winston in the weeks before her death.

Note with the statements:

Three witnesses remember you.

The police never interviewed them.

Someone else did.

Five more days.

Five more gifts.

Then you decide.

Outside, darkness fell. Christmas lights blinked on across the property—timers activating, automated holiday cheer, thousands of bulbs illuminated the darkness while I sat in my own private hell.

My phone buzzed.

Text from unknown number:

Day Seven complete.

Five more days until Christmas Eve.

Five more chances to remember.

Then you confess.

Or I take everything to the police.

I stared at the message. Whoever this was had been building a case for years. Collecting evidence. Preparing for this moment.

And in five days, they'd force me to choose.

Tell the truth myself.

Or have it told for me.

Chapter 7

The Betrayal

I didn't sleep that night.

Wednesday morning. December eighteenth. The eighth gift appeared while I made coffee—materialized on the kitchen counter the moment I turned my back, like all the others had, proof that whoever was doing this moved through the lodge like smoke.

Eight figurines. White ceramic. Women in old-fashioned dresses. Milkmaids a-milking.

With them: therapy session notes. Dr. Sarah Carlson's office letterhead. Ridgemont's discreet therapist for professionals who needed someone who knew how to keep secrets.

My sessions. September through December 2014.

I read them with dread settling into my bones like cold.

September 15, 2014: *Patient presents with anxiety, insomnia, obsessive thoughts. Reports fixation on "B.W." Describes following B.W., learning schedule, fantasizing about "becoming" her. Exhibits signs of erotomania—delusional belief that B.W. would want friendship if she "really knew" patient. Recommended continued treatment.*

October 20, 2014: *Patient's fixation intensifying. Reports spending 4-5 hours daily monitoring B.W.'s movements. Exhibits signs of identity* *disturbance. States: "She has the life I should have. If I could just make her see me as equal, as worthy, maybe she'd let me into her world." Concerning language. Increased frequency to weekly sessions recommended. Patient declined.*

November 10, 2014: *Patient increasingly agitated. Reports feeling "invisible" and "insignificant" compared to B.W. States: "She has everything I deserve. Everything I've worked for. Everything I'll never have." When asked about obsessive behaviors, became defensive. Cancelled next appointment.*

December 8, 2014: *FINAL SESSION. Patient appears angry, volatile. Mentioned B.W. "humiliated" her in public setting. Declined to elaborate. When pressed about potential for violence, patient stated: "I'm not violent. I just want her to acknowledge me. To see me. To understand I'm not nothing." Risk assessment: MODERATE to HIGH. Recommend immediate follow-up. Patient refused and cancelled all future appointments.*

Dr. Carlson never contacted police after the murder. Patient confidentiality protected me. Kept my obsession secret. Kept my deteriorating mental state hidden. Kept my escalating rage documented but private.

But someone got a court order. Subpoenaed the records. Used them to prove premeditation.

Note with the therapy notes:

Your therapist saw you spiraling.

Warned you.

Recommended help.

You refused.

Four days later, my mother was dead.

My mother.

I stared at those two words. The daughter. Had to be. But who? How old? What was her name?

My phone rang. Alex.

I answered. "Where are you?"

"Town." His voice sounded different. Harder. "We need to talk."

"About what?"

"About everything. About who I really am. About why I'm really here."

My stomach dropped. "What do you mean?"

"Meet me at Ridge Tavern. Noon."

He hung up before I could respond.

I drove to Ridge Tavern at eleven-thirty. Arrived early because I couldn't stand sitting alone in the lodge with evidence of my own unraveling spread across tables and beds and counters.

The tavern was decorated for Christmas—garland wrapped around the bar, lights strung across exposed brick, a tree in the corner with local ornaments donated by businesses and families. Holiday music played low. *Have Yourself a Merry Little Christmas*. Melancholy and wistful and completely inappropriate for what was about to happen.

Alex sat in a corner booth. Same booth where I'd sat ten years ago. Watched Bethany and Graham have dinner. Recorded their conversation without permission. Documented their lives for reasons I'd told myself were professional but were really just obsessive.

He didn't smile when I approached. Just gestured to the seat across from him.

I sat. Waited.

"My name isn't Alex Vasquez," he said. Direct. No preamble. "It's Alex Winston."

The name landed like a punch. Winston.

"Graham Winston was my uncle," he continued. His hands folded on the table in a way that reminded me of interrogators, of people who'd practiced this moment. "My mother's older brother, and a father figure to me. I was raised by a single mother and was fifteen when my uncle was convicted. Watched the trial on TV. Watched your podcast convince the jury he was guilty."

He pulled out his phone. Showed me a photo. Young boy—thirteen, maybe fourteen—stood next to Graham. Baseball uniforms. Little League. Big smiles.

"Uncle Graham coached my team. Taught me to throw a curveball. Came to every one of my games. He was gentle, kind, patient. The kind of uncle who made you believe adults could be trusted."

Another photo. Christmas. Family gathering. Graham and a woman I didn't recognize—Alex's mother probably—opened presents while children ran around in the background.

"Our family fell apart after the conviction. People avoided my mom at Christmas gatherings. Stopped calling. Started treating us like we were contaminated by association with a murderer."

"After the conviction, Mira went to live with our grandfather—Graham's father. He was the one who took the pictures of you stalking Bethany in 2014. The police didn't want them."

Alex sighed. "I watched her grow up, refusing to believe her dad was guilty. When she was fifteen, she told me she was going to prove his innocence one day."

"I didn't think it was possible. But she did it. Found the DNA evidence. Got him released."

Alex's voice cracked. "By then, he was already destroyed. Homeless. Addicted. Broken by nine years in prison and the weight of public hatred your podcast created."

"He died six months later at the Burlington homeless shelter. Overdose. But really, he died of shame. Of grief. Of a heart that couldn't survive what you did to him."

He looked at me with eyes that had spent three years hiding this truth.

"Mira and I made a promise at his funeral. Make the real killer confess."

"I applied to be your producer three years ago. Used my father's last name—Vasquez—instead of Winston. You never suspected. Never questioned my résumé, my references, my background."

"All fake. Well—not all. I do have a film degree. I'm good at audio production. Learned a lot from YouTube University. But the recommendations, some were cooked."

"I documented everything over three years. Your methods. Your lies. How you fabricated sources. How you manipulated interview subjects. How you edited audio to change meaning."

"Mira worked the forensics side. I worked the inside. Together, we built an airtight case."

The betrayal hit in waves. Three years. Three years of working together. Recording episodes. Editing audio. Late nights in studios. Conversations about craft and storytelling and the responsibility of true crime journalism.

All lies. All surveillance. All preparation for this moment.

"Why wait three years?" I asked.

"Because Mira wanted it perfect. Undeniable. She wanted to give you a chance to confess. To own what you did. To face consequences with some shred of dignity instead of being destroyed publicly."

"The twelve days of Christmas was her idea. One gift per day. Each with evidence. Building to Christmas Eve when you'd confess on your podcast."

He stood. Put on his coat.

"I'm done, Ida. Done producing your show. Done pretending we're colleagues. Done watching you profit from my uncle's destroyed life."

"Tomorrow's Day Nine. Mira will bring it herself. The final evidence. The proof you can't deny."

"Where will you go?"

"Back to Burlington. Help Mira with the Wrongful Conviction Project she's starting. Use your podcast as a teaching tool. How media can destroy innocent lives. How we need to be more careful. More skeptical. More human."

"And me?"

"You'll either confess or be exposed. Either way, you'll finally face what you've been running from."

He walked toward the door. Stopped. Turned back.

"One more thing. The night Uncle Graham died, you want to know what he said?"

I didn't. But he told me anyway.

"He said, 'I forgive her. Whoever did this. I forgive them.' Because that's who he was. Kind. Forgiving. Better than any of us."

"You don't deserve his forgiveness. But you have it anyway."

Alex left. Door closed. Bell jingled. Gone.

I sat in the booth where I'd sat ten years ago, surrounded by Christmas decorations that felt increasingly like accusations, listening to Bing Crosby dream of white Christmases while my life disintegrated into truth I could no longer avoid.

My phone buzzed.

Text from unknown number:

Day Eight complete.

Tomorrow I come in person.

You'll finally see my face.

Finally know my name.

Four more days until Christmas Eve.

Four more days to decide.

Confess the truth.

Or I take everything to the police.

I stared at the message. Tomorrow. She was coming tomorrow.

The daughter I'd never thought about. The child I'd erased from my story.

The witness who'd spent ten years building a case I couldn't escape.

Outside, snow began to fall. Christmas lights blinked their mindless patterns. Somewhere across town, families prepared for the holiday. Normal lives. Normal December afternoons.

I had four more days.

Four more days to decide who would tell my story.

Me.

Or her.

Chapter 8

The Evidence

Day Nine brought the truth I'd been hiding from myself.

Thursday. December nineteenth. The lodge felt different this morning—smaller, colder, like the walls were closing in or maybe I was just finally seeing how trapped I'd been all along.

At noon exactly, tires on gravel. Car door. Footsteps on the porch.

I knew before I opened the door.

A young woman stood there. Eighteen years old. Dark coat covered in snow. Hair pulled back. Face I recognized from surveillance photos but also from somewhere deeper—Bethany's face, aged eighteen years, same sharp cheekbones and green eyes that caught light from the Christmas decorations and held it.

She carried a wrapped box. Larger than the previous gifts. Heavier.

"Hello, Ms. Burns." Her voice was calm. Professional. Controlled in a way that only came from practice. "I'm Mira Winston."

The name landed like cold water.

"I was eight years old when you killed my mother."

I stepped back. She walked in without invitation. Set the box on the table between us.

"Day Nine," she said. "The last gift before the final countdown."

I couldn't speak. Couldn't move. Just stared at Bethany's daughter standing in my lodge, holding evidence I couldn't deny.

"Open it," Mira said. Not a request. A command.

I tore the paper with shaking hands. Inside: Nine figurines. White porcelain. Ballerina poses. Ladies dancing.

With them: three items.

A photograph of Bethany's kitchen towel. White cotton. Monogrammed. The note said the actual towel was sealed in an evidence bag at a secure location. Brown stains visible in the photo. DNA label attached: *Bethany Winston - victim. Ida Burns - suspect.*

My journal from 2014. Black leather. Pages and pages of obsessive writing. Bethany's name covered every line in handwriting I recognized as mine but couldn't remember producing.

She has everything I want.

She dismissed me like I'm nothing.

I could be her. I should be her.

What would it take to erase her and take her place?

And a USB drive. Labeled: *The Truth.*

"The towel was recovered from your storage unit six months ago," Mira said. Her voice steady in a way that only came from years of preparation. "You kept it. Along with Bethany's rings. Along with your journal documenting premeditation."

She held up the USB drive. "But this is what matters most. December twelfth, 2014. My mother's kitchen. You left your recorder running in your bag."

She plugged it into my laptop. Opened the file.

"You deleted this recording ten years ago. But nothing's ever really deleted. Not if you know where to look."

She pressed play.

My voice filled the lodge. Younger. Desperate.

"You don't get to dismiss me."

Bethany's response, calm but firm: *"Ida, I'm not dismissing you. I'm setting boundaries. What you've been doing—following me, learning my schedule, sitting outside my house—that's not journalism. That's stalking."*

"I'm trying to understand you. To know you. To—"

"To what? Become me? Take my life?" Bethany's voice sharpened. *"I saw your journal. You left it in the coffee shop last week. I read it before I gave it to the manager."*

My stomach dropped. She'd read my journal. Knew everything.

"That journal—" My voice defensive. Panicked. *"That's private. You had no right—"*

"You had no right to stalk me!" Bethany yelling now. *"To follow my daughter to school. To sit outside my house at night. To build some fantasy where you take over my life like I'm just a role you can play!"*

Sound of movement. Struggle.

My voice: *"I just wanted you to see me!"*

"I do see you, Ida. I see someone who needs help. Professional help. And I'm done enabling this. I'm filing a restraining order. Tomorrow. You need to leave. Now."

More sounds. Louder. Violent.

After what seemed like an eternity, the recording ended.

I sat down hard. Chair scraped against floor.

Mira stood across from me. Tears on her face but voice still steady.

"I was upstairs in my room that day," she said. "Playing with dolls my dad had bought me for my birthday. I heard you and Mom talking. Heard your voices get louder. Heard fighting. Something breaking. Mom falling."

She pulled out a photo. Her as a child. Eight years old. Pink dress. Blonde pigtails. Holding a porcelain doll.

"I ran to my closet. Hid. I was eight. I didn't understand what was happening. Just that something was very wrong."

"I heard you leave. Heard the front door close. Waited twenty minutes before I came downstairs."

Her voice cracked. "Mom was still on the kitchen floor. Not moving. There was blood. And cookies—those stupid Christmas cookies she'd made that morning—scattered everywhere. You ruined cookies for me."

"I called 911. Told them my mom was hurt. Told them the lady with the tape recorder had left. But Sergeant Morrison never listened carefully.

Just focused on Dad finding the body. Never followed up on what an eight-year-old said."

She wiped her eyes.

"I spent the last four years collecting evidence he ignored. Started when I was fourteen, after I found Mom's journal in Grandpa's house and realized the story didn't make sense."

"At fourteen, I could pull court records. Research newspaper archives. Request public documents."

"At sixteen, I found the doorbell camera footage buried in evidence files. Your license plate. Your face. Timeline proving Dad's innocence."

"At eighteen—three months ago—I used money from Grandpa's estate to hire a private investigator. That's when we found everything. The coffee shop witnesses. The DNA from your coffee cup. The emails you sent Morrison fabricating witnesses. Dr. Ballard's notes about fabric bruising. Your therapy records."

"Ten years I waited. Four years I investigated. Now you face what you did."

She gathered the evidence. Left only the USB drive and journal on the table.

"Christmas Eve. Two PM. You have three days to decide."

"You can confess. On your podcast. Record the truth. Upload it. Own what you did."

"Or I take everything to Detective Fairbank. The doorbell footage. The audio recording. The witness statements. The DNA. All of it."

"Your choice, Ms. Burns. Confession with maybe some mercy. Or arrest with full prosecution."

She walked to the door. Stopped. Turned back.

"My father died homeless six months after his release. Addicted to heroin. Couldn't get a job because of your podcast. Two million people heard you explain why Graham Winston was a monster."

"He died in my arms. Burlington homeless shelter. Overdose that was really just grief. Just shame. Just a broken heart that couldn't heal."

"So yes. You get three more days. But they're three days more than you gave him."

She left. Door closed. Engine started. Gone.

I sat alone with the recording. With the journal. With the memory that had finally surfaced after ten years of burial.

Three more days until Christmas Eve.

Three more days to decide who would tell my story.

Me.

Or her.

Chapter 9

The Countdown

Friday. December twentieth. Day Ten.

I didn't leave the lodge. Didn't answer my phone. Just sat at the table with the USB drive and my journal, played the recording on loop, read my own obsessive words until they blurred together into proof of premeditation I couldn't deny.

The tenth gift appeared while I was in the shower. Ten lords a-leaping. Ceramic figurines in elaborate poses.

With them: timeline documentation. Minute by minute account of December 12, 2014. My car arriving at 2:15 PM. My car leaving at 3:42 PM. Graham arriving at 4:15 PM. Official medical examiner's determination: death occurred between 2:30 and 4:00 PM.

While I was alone in that house with Bethany.

While Graham was teaching third graders about fractions.

The timeline proved everything.

I read it once. Set it aside. Went back to the recording.

"You should have just acknowledged me. That's all I wanted. Just to be seen."

My voice. Cold. Calculated. The voice of someone who'd already decided.

I remembered now. All of it. The way I'd planned it for weeks. Written about it in my journal like it was inevitable. Like Bethany's death was the only solution to my invisibility.

The memory was clear now. Sharp. Undeniable.

Bethany reading my journal. Her face changing as she understood what I'd written. The fear in her eyes when she told me to leave.

The rage that flooded through me when she called it stalking. When she reduced months of careful observation to something pathetic. Criminal.

I saw red.

Moments later. It was over.

Saturday. December twenty-first. Day Eleven.

The gift appeared at dawn. Eleven pipers piping. Red uniforms. Instruments raised.

With them: Graham Winston' exoneration paperwork. Official documents dated 2023. DNA evidence summary. Court order releasing him from Sussex County Correctional Facility after nine years.

And a death certificate. Graham Winston. June 15, 2024. Cause of death: heroin overdose. Location: Burlington Community Shelter.

I stared at the documents for an hour.

Nine years in prison for a crime he didn't commit. Six months of freedom before grief and shame killed him anyway.

Because of me.

Because I couldn't stand being nothing.

I thought about running. Packing the car. Driving west until I disappeared into some small town where no one knew my name or my podcast or what I'd done.

But Mira had everything. The recording. The timeline. The witnesses. The DNA. Even if I ran, she'd find me. Or the police would. Eventually.

And Graham's words kept echoing in my head. The last thing he'd said before he died.

I forgive her. Whoever did this. I forgive them.

He'd forgiven me.

And I'd never even confessed.

Sunday morning. December twenty-second. Christmas Eve.

I woke at dawn to the twelfth gift on my pillow.

Twelve drummers drumming. Porcelain. Red uniforms. Gold drums. Frozen mid-beat.

With them: final note.

Today is Day Twelve.

Christmas Eve.

2 PM.

I'm bringing Detective Fairbank.

You can confess on your podcast while we listen.

Or I give her everything and she arrests you.

Your choice.

One last chance to tell the truth yourself.

- Mira

I sat on the bed with the note in my hands. Read it three times.

Two PM. Six hours away.

I could still run. Pack the essentials. Be in Pennsylvania before anyone noticed.

But where would I go? Who would I become? Another invisible woman in another anonymous town, carrying the weight of what I'd done until it crushed me anyway?

Or I could stay. Face it. Tell the truth.

Give Graham his name back, even if it was too late for him to know.

Give Mira what she'd waited ten years for.

Give Bethany... what? Justice? Nothing I did now could bring her back. Nothing could undo the fifty-three seconds when I'd pressed cotton over her face and counted.

But I could stop lying.

I could stop building my life on her grave.

I showered. Dressed in black—sweater, jeans, clothes appropriate for confession or arrest. Simple. Dark. Forgettable.

Went downstairs. Made coffee. Didn't drink it.

The lodge was quiet. Outside, snow fell steady. Christmas lights blinked across the property. Families in Cabin Seven were probably wrapping last-minute gifts. Normal Christmas Eve preparations. Normal lives.

I walked to the recording equipment. Alex had set it up weeks ago. Professional. Perfect. Ready.

I checked the levels. Tested the microphone. Everything worked.

All I had to do was press record.

Tell the truth.

Face what I'd been running from for ten years.

At noon, I sat at the desk. Stared at the microphone. My phone buzzed.

Text from Mira:

On my way.

Detective Fairbank is with me.

We'll be there at 2.

Last chance, Ms. Burns.

Tell your truth.

Or I'll tell mine.

Recognition struck like lightning. I set the phone down. Looked at the equipment. The microphone. The laptop. IT was time. Everything was ready.

Outside, Christmas music drifted from somewhere across the lake. *Silent Night.* Holy night. All is calm.

Nothing was calm.

But in two hours, I'd tell the truth.

In two hours, I'd face Mira and Detective Fairbank and confess what I'd done.

In two hours, my life as I knew it would end.

But maybe that's what I deserved.

Maybe that's what justice looked like.

I sat at the desk. Waited for two PM.
Waited for the knock on the door.
Waited for the moment I'd finally stop running.

Chapter 10

The Confession

At two PM exactly, tires on gravel. Two car doors. Footsteps on the porch.

I opened the door before they knocked.

Mira stood there. Behind her—a woman in her mid-forties. Short gray hair pulled back. Navy blazer over white button-down, pressed slacks. Badge clipped to her belt. Gun holstered at her hip. Small wreath pin on her lapel.

"Ms. Burns," Mira said. "This is Detective Hazel Fairbank. Ridgemont PD."

Fairbank's expression was unreadable. "Ms. Burns. Mira contacted me this morning. Brought evidence in the Bethany Winston case. Substantial evidence."

I stepped back. Let them in.

They walked to the table. Mira set down her thick folder. Fairbank remained standing. Professional. Watchful.

"Mira tells me you might want to make a statement," Fairbank said. "Before I proceed with my investigation."

I looked at Mira. She looked back. Eighteen years old. Bethany's daughter. The child I'd never thought about. The witness I'd erased from my story.

"Yes," I said. "I have a confession to make."

Fairbank's expression didn't change. "I need to advise you of your rights first."

"I know my rights. I'm waiving them. I want to confess."

"On the record?"

I gestured to the microphone. The recording equipment. Everything ready.

"On the record. For my podcast. For everyone."

Fairbank looked at Mira. Mira nodded slightly.

"Alright," Fairbank said. "Proceed."

I sat at the desk. Pulled the microphone close. Looked at both of them —Mira and Fairbank, standing across from me, waiting.

I pressed record.

Red light blinked on.

"This is Ida Burns. *Guilty Conscience*. Final episode."

My voice was steady. Calm. Like I was recording any other episode. Like this was just another story.

But it wasn't.

"Today I'm going to tell you the truth about the Graham Winston case. The truth I've hidden for ten years."

I took a breath.

"On December twelfth, 2014, I murdered Bethany Winston."

The words came easier than I expected. Like they'd been waiting to escape for a decade.

"I'd been following Bethany for months. Stalking her. I told myself it was research for a story, but it wasn't. It was obsession."

Mira's face remained neutral. Fairbank pulled out a notepad. Started writing.

"I wanted to be her. She had everything I didn't. Success. Confidence. A beautiful home. A family. I convinced myself that if I could just under-stand her life, I could build one like it. But really, I wanted to erase her and take her place."

I detailed everything. The surveillance. The coffee shop confrontation. Bethany reading my journal. Her threat to file a restraining order.

"On December twelfth, I went to her house. She let me in. We talked in her kitchen. She told me I was stalking her. That I needed professional help. That she was filing a restraining order the next day."

My hands gripped the edge of the desk.

"She told me to leave. I attacked her. She fell. Hit her head on the marble counter on her way down. Dazed and helpless on the floor, blood pooling from a head injury. I should have called 911."

Guilt wrapped around my spine. Denial crumbled to dust. "Instead, I grabbed a kitchen towel. White cotton. Monogrammed with her initials."

Mira's jaw tightened. But she didn't speak.

"I pressed it over her face. She fought. Clawed at my hands. Tried to scream. But I held it there. Counted. Fifty-three seconds until she stopped struggling."

Silence in the lodge. Just my voice. The heater. The truth.

"Then I staged the scene. Made it look like a struggle. Took her rings—I wanted something of hers. Something to prove I'd been close to her perfect life."

"I left at three forty-two PM. Graham arrived ninety minutes later. Found her dead. Called 911."

"And I built a case against him. Fabricated witnesses. Created false evidence. Sent fake tips to the police. Convinced Sergeant Morrison that Graham was guilty."

"I launched my podcast two months later. *Guilty Conscience*. Episode one was about Graham Winston—the monster who killed his wife. Two million people downloaded it. My career was born."

"Graham Winston spent nine years in prison for a murder I committed. He was released in 2023 when DNA evidence proved his innocence. He died homeless six months later. Heroin overdose. But really, he died of shame and grief."

"He died because of what I did to him."

I looked at Mira. Tears streamed down her face, but she stood steady.

"I killed Bethany Winston because she saw me. Really saw me. And what she saw was pathetic. Obsessive. Nothing."

"I couldn't stand being nothing while she was everything. So I made her nothing too."

"I'm guilty. Of murder. Of fraud. Of destroying an innocent man. Of building my career on someone else's grave."

"Graham Winston was innocent. Bethany Winston deserved to live. And I deserve whatever consequences come next."

I stopped. Looked at the microphone. Then at Fairbank.

"That's my confession. All of it. The truth."

I pressed stop. Red light went dark.

Silence.

Then Fairbank stood. Pulled handcuffs from her belt.

"Ida Burns, you're under arrest for the murder of Bethany Winston."

She walked around the desk. I stood. Turned around. Felt cold metal close around my wrists.

"You have the right to remain silent. Anything you say can and will be used against you in a court of law. You have the right to an attorney. If you cannot afford an attorney, one will be provided for you."

I'd heard these words a hundred times. On TV. In movies. In the research for my podcast.

Never thought I'd hear them for myself.

Fairbank led me to the door. Mira followed. Silent.

Outside, snow fell steady. Christmas lights blinked across the resort. Families watched from windows—Cabin Seven, Cabin Three, Grant standing at his office door.

The world witnessed my final scene.

Fairbank opened the back door of her car. Guided me inside. Closed it.

I sat in the back seat. Hands cuffed. Watched the lodge disappear as we pulled away.

We drove through Ridgemont. Main Street decorated. Stores closing early for Christmas Eve. People carrying last-minute gifts. Living normal lives.

Tomorrow they'd wake to headlines. The podcaster who confessed to murder. The journalist who destroyed an innocent man. The killer who built a career on her victim's grave.

My episode would upload tonight. Millions of downloads by morning. Trending number one.

Famous for confessing.

Ironic.

I'd killed someone for recognition. Got famous for admitting it.

Sussex County Jail processed me by evening.

Fingerprints. Photos. Orange jumpsuit. Cell in the women's block.

Metal bed. Concrete walls. Bars.

Christmas Eve night, I lay on the thin mattress, stared at the concrete ceiling. From the common area, voices rose in song.

Silent night, holy night

All is calm, all is bright

Other inmates singing carols. Finding some small piece of holiday joy even here.

Nothing was calm. Nothing was bright.

But for the first time in ten years, I'd told the truth.

I'd faced what I'd done.

I'd given Graham his name back.

I'd given Mira justice.

I'd given Bethany... acknowledgment. Finally. Ten years too late.

The singing continued. *Sleep in heavenly peace.*

I closed my eyes.

Tomorrow was Christmas.

Tomorrow, the world would know my truth.

Tomorrow, my life as I knew it would end.

But tonight, I'd finally stopped running.

Chapter 11

Epilogue

Three months later, Mira visited. Glass partition between us. Phones to communicate.

"The Wrongful Conviction Project is going well," she said. "We're helping three families right now. People your podcast helped convict."

"I'm sorry."

"I know."

Silence. Noisy breathing through phone lines.

"I forgive you," she said finally. "Not for you. For me. So I can move forward. So I can stop spending every day thinking about what you did."

"Your father said the same thing. The night he died. Alex told me."

"I know. Dad was always better than the rest of us." She smiled. Sad. Genuine. "That's why what you did hurt so much. You didn't just kill my mother. You destroyed the best man I ever knew."

She stood to leave. Hand on phone. Ready to hang up.

"Wait," I said. "Why twelve days? Why Christmas?"

"Because Christmas was when everything broke. When Mom died. When Dad was arrested. When our family shattered."

"I wanted you to feel what those twelve days felt like for us. The countdown to losing everything. The dread. The inevitability."

"And I wanted to give you something Dad never got. A choice. Confession or exposure. Dignity or destruction."

"You chose confession. That's something."

She hung up. Walked away.

I sat alone in the visiting room, surrounded by other inmates and their families, pretending incarceration was temporary instead of life-defining.

My public defender got me fifteen to twenty years. Murder Two. With my confession, there was no trial. Just sentencing.

Fifteen years. Longer than Mira's childhood. Longer than Graham survived after release.

Not long enough for what I'd done.

Outside these walls, the world kept turning. My podcast kept downloading. My case kept being studied. My name kept being mentioned—not as journalist or expert, but as cautionary tale.

Bethany Winston got justice.

Graham Winston got vindication.

Mira Winston got closure.

And me?

I got truth. The kind that destroys but also liberates. The kind that costs everything but returns something more valuable—honesty, finally, after ten years of lies.

Some gifts are wrapped in red and gold.

Some are wrapped in handcuffs and confession.

This Christmas, I learned which kind matters.

THE END

BOOK 4

The Advent Calendar

Chapter 1

The Discovery

Sunday, December 1, 3 PM

I found the Advent calendar in the attic while looking for Christmas decorations.

Cold up there—our heating didn't reach the third floor. I pulled the chain for the overhead bulb. Weak yellow light spread across boxes labeled in Michael's neat handwriting. *Ornaments. Lights. Wreath.*

I grabbed the box marked *Tree Decorations* and turned to go.

That's when I saw it.

Sitting on top of old suitcases. Wooden, antique-looking. Hand-painted scenes on the front—a snow-covered village, tiny houses with glowing windows, a church with a steeple. Twenty-four little doors, numbered one through twenty-four.

An advent calendar. I'd never seen it before.

Heavy. Solid wood, not cheap cardboard. The paint looked old, cracked in places. Someone had put real work into this.

A small envelope was taped to the back. My name in Claire's handwriting.

Hannah—

Found this at an estate sale in Princeton. Too beautiful to pass up. Thought you'd love it—you always appreciated vintage things.

Start December 1st. Open one door each day until Christmas.

Love, Claire

The date: November 28. Three days ago.

Claire must have dropped it off while Michael and I were out. She had a key. Did this all the time—left vintage finds she thought I'd like.

I carried both boxes downstairs.

The house was quiet. Four bedrooms, cream walls, Pottery Barn furniture. Catalog-perfect. Michael had gone to school to grade papers. Sunday ritual.

I set the Advent calendar on the kitchen island.

Outside, the Hendersons' Christmas lights blinked. Too early for December first, but they always went overboard. "Jingle Bell Rock" played from their outdoor speakers.

I made tea. Stared at the calendar.

Open one door each day.

I checked my phone. 3:47 PM.

I should wait for Michael. Make it festive.

But he wouldn't be home for hours.

Door number one was in the bottom left corner. Painted green with a tiny gold handle. I pulled it open.

Inside: a Polaroid photograph.

Two people at a restaurant. A man and a woman. The man faced away, but I recognized the back of his head. Michael's hair, that cowlick. His gray jacket—the one I'd bought him last Christmas.

The woman sat across from him. Brunette, late twenties, pretty. Smiling. Her hand reached across the table toward his.

I flipped the photo over.

Date stamp: December 15, 2024.

Two weeks from now.

My hands went cold.

The photo couldn't be real. You couldn't photograph something that hadn't happened yet.

Could you?

I paced the kitchen. This had to be fake. Photoshopped. Someone's prank.

But who? And why put it in Claire's estate sale find?

Unless Claire made this. But that was insane. Claire wouldn't do this.

Maybe it wasn't Michael. Maybe I was wrong about the jacket, the hair.

I scrutinized the photo.

No. That was Michael.

But how could they photograph something two weeks in the future?

The front door opened.

I shoved the photo in my pocket. Grabbed the ornament box.

Michael came in. Forty-two, graying at the temples, tired from grading. "Hey. How long have you been home?"

"Couple of hours. Got the decorations down."

He looked at the Advent calendar. "What's that?"

"Advent calendar. Claire dropped it off."

He picked it up. "Nice craftsmanship." He examined the painted doors. "Should we open today's?"

"Let's wait until after dinner. Make it a thing."

"Sounds good."

He headed upstairs.

I stood there, hand in my pocket, fingers on the Polaroid.

December 15. Two weeks.

At dinner, I pushed pasta around my plate. Couldn't eat. Michael talked about students, department politics.

Normal Sunday dinner.

But the photo burned in my pocket.

"You okay?" he asked.

"Fine. Just tired."

"Want to open the calendar now?"

We went to the kitchen. He opened door one. Reached inside.

Nothing. Empty.

"Guess whoever made this didn't finish it," he said. "Should we try door two?"

"No. One per day."

He shrugged. Went upstairs.

I stared at the empty door. But the photo was in my pocket. Still real.

Was I losing my mind? Seeing things that were yet to happen?

I went to bed early. Lay awake staring at the calendar on my dresser.

At midnight, I crept over. Opened door 2.

Another photo.

Michael and the woman. Ridgemont Plaza. Holding hands.

Date: December 16, 2024.

I opened doors 3 through 7.

Five more photos. Five more future dates.

Day 3 (Dec 17): Coffee at Starbucks. Laughing. Her hand on his arm.

Day 4 (Dec 18): Ridge Tavern. Corner booth. His hand covered hers.

Day 5 (Dec 19): Dinner. Candlelight. Wine. Intimate.

Day 6 (Dec 20): Parsippany Marriott parking lot. His car next to a blue Honda Civic.

Day 7 (Dec 21): Hotel window. Two silhouettes against the light.

I spread them on my dressing table, my back to Michael. Ready to slide them under my makeup kit once he moved.

An affair in seven acts. Coffee to hotel.

But these dates hadn't happened yet.

How could photos show the future?

I grabbed my laptop. Searched: "can objects predict the future?"

Occult websites. Tarot cards. Crystal balls. Nonsense.

But the Polaroids looked real. Felt real. Hard to fake.

Was this Michael? Creating fake photos to gaslight me? Make me think I was crazy while he had an affair?

Or was the calendar showing me the future?

My phone buzzed. 1:47 AM.

Claire: *Sorry, just saw your message. What's weird about the calendar?*

Should I tell her? What if this was her doing?

Or what if I sounded insane?

Photos of Michael with a woman. Dated December 15-21. Future dates. How is that possible?

The typing dots appeared—three quick flashes. *Future photos? That doesn't make sense. Are you sure?*

Yes. December 15 is two weeks away.

Maybe it's a mistake? Old calendar, wrong year?

No. Everything looks recent.

Pause. *Do you want me to come over?*

No. I'm fine. Just confused.

Maybe talk to Michael? See if he knows who she is?

Yeah. Maybe.

Get some sleep. We'll figure this out tomorrow.

I set the phone down.

Claire sounded genuinely confused. Concerned. Not like someone behind an elaborate scheme.

So if not her, who made this calendar?

And how did it know what would happen two weeks from now?

I gathered the photos. Locked them in my nightstand.

Crawled back into bed beside Michael. He was asleep. Breathing steady. Peaceful.

Innocent.

Or performing even in sleep.

I didn't know anymore.

Didn't know what was real.

Didn't know if I was seeing the future or losing my mind.

But I'd know soon.

December 15 was fourteen days away.

The calendar would either be right.

Or I'd need serious help.

Chapter 2

The Pattern

Monday, December 2, 8 AM

I couldn't sleep after I found the photos.

Lay there until 3 AM staring at the ceiling, counting each breath Michael took. Then got up. Picked up the calendar and went downstairs.

Seven photos spread across the kitchen table. Seven future dates. Each one worse than the last.

December 15: Restaurant. Hands reaching.

December 16: Plaza. Holding hands.

December 17: Starbucks. Her hand on his arm.

December 18: Ridge Tavern. His hand covered hers.

December 19: Dinner. Candlelight. Intimate.

December 20: Hotel parking lot. Afternoon.

December 21: Hotel window. Two silhouettes.

A timeline. Coffee to lunch to dinner to hotel. Escalating.

But none of it had happened yet.

I made coffee. My hands shook. Spilled grounds on the counter.

7 AM. Michael's alarm went off upstairs. Shower ran.

I swept the photos into my purse.

By the time he came downstairs, I sat at the table. Coffee mug in front of me. Normal.

"Morning." He kissed the top of my head. Routine. Automatic.

I didn't move.

He poured coffee. "You're up early."

"Couldn't sleep."

"Bad night?"

"Something like that."

He grabbed his bag. "Back-to-back classes today. Won't be home until six."

"Okay."

He looked at me. "You all right?"

"Fine."

He didn't push. Just left.

The door closed.

I pulled out the photos. Laid them in order.

The woman. Brunette. Late twenties. Pretty. Who was she?

And how did the calendar know about her two weeks before it happened?

My office was above the bakery on Main Street. Small practice. Two chairs facing each other. Tissues on the side table. Degrees on the wall: *Licensed Marriage and Family Therapist.*

Fresh bread smell hit me in the stairwell. Usually comforting. Today it made me sick.

I'd scheduled three clients.

1 PM: Married couple. Fighting about money.

I listened. Took notes. Gave them the exercises I'd given a hundred other couples.

"Trust is the foundation," I heard myself say. "You have to believe your partner has your best interests at heart."

The words felt like ash.

3 PM: Woman whose husband had cheated. Found texts. Photos. Wanted to know if she should leave.

"How did you know?" I asked. "That he was cheating?"

"I found evidence." She showed me screenshots. "Hotel receipts. Messages. He denied it. Said I was paranoid."

Paranoid.

"But you weren't."

"No. The evidence was right there."

Evidence. Like photos. Like a calendar showing December 17, 18, 19.

"What did you do?"

"Confronted him. He admitted it." She looked at her hands. "Now I don't know if I should stay."

"Do you want to?"

"Part of me thinks—we've been married twelve years. We have kids. Maybe we can fix this."

"And the other part?"

"Wants to burn his clothes and change the locks."

I almost smiled. "Both feelings are valid."

After she left, I sat alone. Stared at the wall.

Marriage counselor. That's what I did. Helped people navigate betrayal, dishonesty, broken trust.

And here I was. Holding photos of my husband with another woman. Dates that hadn't happened yet.

5 PM: Man leaving his wife for someone younger.

"I love her," he said. "Can't help it."

My jaw tightened. "Affairs don't 'just happen.' They're choices."

"I know. But—"

"You chose to pursue her. Chose to lie. Own it."

He blinked. "I thought therapists weren't supposed to judge."

"I'm not judging. I'm clarifying."

After he left, I locked the office. Sat in the dark.

Pulled out my phone. Googled: "Claire Price estate sales Princeton."

Nothing relevant. Just auction houses. Antique dealers. No recent sales matching late November.

I called one. "Did you have an estate sale November 28th? Advent calendar, hand-painted?"

"No, ma'am. Our last sale was October."

I tried three more. Same answer.

So, Claire lied about the estate sale.

Why?

I called her.

"Hey," she answered. "How are you feeling? Get any sleep?"

"Where did you really get the calendar?"

Pause. "I told you. Estate sale."

"I called every dealer in Princeton. No sales on November 28th."

Silence.

"Claire."

"Okay, fine. I didn't get it at an estate sale. I found it at a vintage shop in Montclair. But I knew you'd ask where, and I didn't want you going there asking questions, so I said Princeton."

"Why would I ask questions?"

"Because you overthink everything." Her voice had an edge. "It's a calendar, Hannah. Not a conspiracy."

"It has photos of Michael with another woman."

"So take them to Michael. Ask who she is. Maybe there's an explanation."

"The photos are dated to the future."

"Then they're fake. Someone's messing with you."

"Who?"

"I don't know. But obsessing over it won't help."

I hung up.

Claire was lying. I could hear it in her voice. The defensiveness. The deflection.

But why?

Michael got home at 6:30.

I watched him from the kitchen. Set down his bag. Checked his phone.

Phone face-down on the counter. Always face-down now.

Had it always been like that? Or was I just noticing?

His phone buzzed.

He flipped it. Checked. Put it back.

Quick.

"Who was that?" I asked.

He looked up. "Just a parent. About grades."

"What did they want?"

"Hannah." His voice had an edge. "Why?"

"Just asking."

"You're being weird."

Maybe I was. Or maybe he was hiding something.

We ate dinner in silence. Jeopardy on in the background. Michael answered questions about American history. Got most of them right.

Normal. Everything looked normal.

But I kept seeing the photos.

December 17. December 18. December 19.

That night, Michael fell asleep at 10 PM.

I stayed awake.

At 11, his phone buzzed.

Text notification. I couldn't see the name from my side of the bed.

He didn't wake up.

I waited. 11:15. He rolled over. Deep breathing. Asleep.

I slid out of bed. Crept around to his side.

Picked up his phone.

Text from **A**: *Can't wait to see you tomorrow. Same place?*

My hands went numb.

Tomorrow was December 3.

I walked to the dresser. Opened door number 3 of the advent calendar.

Photo of Michael and the woman.

At Ridge Tavern.

Date stamp: December 3, 2024.

Tomorrow.

The calendar wasn't predicting the future.

It was counting down to it.

Chapter 3

Day Three

T**uesday, December 3, 11 AM - 2 PM**

I followed him.

Called my office at 8 AM. Canceled all three clients. Migraine, I said. My assistant believed me—I never called in sick.

Michael left for school at 7:30. Ridgemont Academy, fifteen minutes away. He'd be there until lunch.

The text had said *tomorrow* and *same place*.

Tomorrow was today. December 3.

Same place had to be Ridge Tavern. The calendar photo showed them there. Corner booth, back of the restaurant.

I drove to the Tavern at 11:45. Parked across the street in the Ridgemont Plaza lot. Between a pickup truck and a minivan. Good sight line to the entrance.

The Tavern's windows were strung with white lights. Wreath on the door. A-frame chalkboard advertised *Holiday Brunch Special - Peppermint Pancakes*.

12:00. No Michael.

I sat in my car. Engine off. Cold crept through the vents.

Ridiculous. Sitting here like some paranoid spouse from my client sessions. The kind who hired private investigators. The kind who went through phones and followed their partners.

But the photo showed December 3rd. Today. Ridge Tavern. Michael and the woman.

12:15. Michael's gray Subaru pulled into the lot.

My stomach dropped.

He got out. Looked around. Didn't see me. Went inside.

I grabbed my phone. Took a photo of his car. Time stamp visible.

12:35. Another car pulled up. Honda Civic. Blue. Dent in the rear bumper.

A woman got out.

Brunette with highlights, late twenties, about five-five. Pretty in that effortless way. Green coat, expensive boots. Athleisure underneath—yoga pants and fitted jacket.

Same woman from the photos.

I couldn't breathe.

She walked toward the Tavern. Confident. Touched her hair before going inside. Smoothed it back.

Like she was meeting someone important.

I waited five minutes. Then got out.

Cold hit me hard. December wind off the lake. The Plaza's speakers played "Silver Bells." Shoppers moved between stores, arms full of bags.

I crossed the street.

Inside Ridge Tavern, warmth and noise. Smelled like burgers and coffee. Christmas music—"*Last Christmas*" by Wham. Garland wrapped around the bar. Tiny lights everywhere.

I scanned the restaurant.

Found them.

Corner booth. Back wall. Just like the photo.

Michael sat facing away. The woman across from him. She laughed at something he'd said. Her hand reached across the table.

His hand moved toward hers.

The knowing tore through my defenses

I walked to their booth.

Michael looked up.

His face went white.

"Ha...Hannah?"

The woman turned. Confused. "Who—"

"I'm his wife."

She pulled her hand back. Fast.

Michael stood. "Hannah, what are you doing here?"

"What are *you* doing here?"

"I told you. Department lunch."

I looked at the woman. "You're in the English department?"

"I'm Addison Bennett." Her voice was steady. Professional. "Student teacher at Ridgemont Academy."

"Student teacher."

"We were discussing curriculum," Addison said. "The British Romantics unit. Michael's been mentoring me in—"

"Holding hands?"

"We weren't—" Michael started.

"I saw you."

People were staring now. A waitress paused mid-pour at the next table. The bartender looked over.

My voice had gotten loud.

I didn't care.

"How long has this been going on?"

Michael grabbed my arm. "Let's talk outside."

I yanked free. "Answer the question."

"Nothing's going on."

"Liar."

He pulled me toward the door. I let him. Better than making more of a scene.

Outside. Cold air sharp in my lungs. "Last Christmas" still playing, muffled through the windows.

"You're embarrassing yourself," Michael said.

"*I'm* embarrassing *myself*?" Heat climbed my neck. "You're meeting a student teacher for secret lunches."

"Addison is a colleague. We were discussing work."

"Holding hands is work?"

"We weren't holding hands."

"I SAW YOU."

A couple walking past turned to look. Michael's jaw tightened.

"You're being paranoid," he said. Quiet. Controlled. "You need help."

Paranoid?

"The photo doesn't lie."

"What photo?"

"From the Advent calendar. It showed this. Today. This exact scene."

Michael stared at me. "The advent calendar predicted I'd have lunch with a colleague?"

"It predicted you'd be here. With her. Holding hands. Lying to me."

"Hannah." His voice changed. Softer. Concerned. The tone he used with difficult students. "You sound insane."

Insane.

Like I was the problem. Like I was imagining this.

"I know what I saw."

"You saw two teachers having lunch. That's it."

"On December 3rd. At Ridge Tavern. Just like the photo showed."

"Photos can be faked. Edited. Someone's messing with you."

"Who?"

He shook his head. "I don't know. But this—" He gestured at me. At the Tavern. "This isn't you. Following me? Confronting me at lunch? You're acting crazy."

Crazy.

Another word.

I turned. Walked back to my car.

Michael called after me. "Hannah, wait—"

I didn't stop.

I drove home. Hands locked on the steering wheel. Vision narrowed.

The Subaru in the lot. 12:15.

The Honda Civic. 12:35.

Their hands reaching across the table.

Michael's face when he saw me. Shock. Then calculation. Then the performance.

You're being paranoid. You need help. You sound insane.

Gaslighting. I knew the pattern. Taught it to clients every week. The deflection. Making the victim doubt their own perception.

But I wasn't imagining it.

The photo showed December 3rd. Today. Ridge Tavern. Michael and Addison.

It happened exactly as shown.

Which meant the other photos—December 17, 18, 19, 20, 21—would happen too.

Unless I stopped it.

I pulled into the driveway. Sat in the car.

The house looked normal. Wreath on the door. Michael's papers visible through the window, stacked where he'd left them this morning.

Everything normal.

But nothing was.

I went inside. Straight to the bedroom.

The Advent calendar sat on the dresser. Seven doors open. Seventeen sealed.

I opened door number 8.

December 4, 2024. Tomorrow.

The photo showed Michael's car in a driveway I didn't recognize. Small house. White siding. His Subaru parked like he belonged there.

I turned the photo over.

Handwritten note on the back: *114 Maple Street, Apartment 2B, Burlington.*

I stared at the handwriting.

Neat. Careful. Not Michael's.

Someone had been to this address. Knew where it was. Documented it.

Someone who knew about the affair.

Someone who was showing me proof.

But who?

And how did they know what would happen tomorrow?
My phone buzzed. Text from Michael.
We need to talk when I get home.
I didn't respond.
Didn't want to hear the excuses. The justifications. The gaslighting.
The calendar had been right about December 3rd.
It would be right about December 4th.
And December 15th through 21st.
All of it coming true.
All of it unstoppable.
I just didn't know how.
Or who was showing me.

Chapter 4

The Investigation

Thursday, December 4, 7 AM

I tried to stop it.

The photo showed December 4th—today. Michael's car at 114 Maple Street, Apartment 2B, Burlington. The calendar had been right about December 3rd. Right down to the minute.

So I'd stop December 4th from happening.

Michael came downstairs at 7:15. Same routine. Showered, dressed, grabbed coffee.

I stood in the kitchen. Waited.

"We need to talk," I said.

He looked up. "About what?"

"Where you're going today."

"School. Same as every Thursday."

"After school."

"Hannah—"

"You're going to see her. At her apartment. Burlington."

He set down his mug. "I don't know what you're talking about."

"114 Maple Street."

His face went white. Just for a second. Then the mask came back. "How do you know that address?"

"The calendar showed me."

"Hannah, you need to stop this. You sound—"

"Crazy? Paranoid? You keep using those words. Like if you say them enough, I'll believe you instead of my own eyes."

"There's nothing to see."

"Then you won't mind if I come with you today."

"I don't have time for this."

"Because you have somewhere to be at 7 PM?"

He grabbed his bag. "I have department meetings."

"Swear to me. You won't go to Burlington tonight."

Michael looked at me. Direct eye contact. Steady voice. "I swear. I'm not going to Burlington."

He left.

I stood in the kitchen. Listened to his car pull away.

He was lying.

I called in sick to work. Third time this week.

At 6:45 PM, I parked down the street from 114 Maple Street.

Small apartment complex. Two stories, white siding. Cars in the drive-way. Normal. Anonymous.

Perfect for hiding an affair.

December cold seeped through the car. I kept the engine off. Across the street, a house had Christmas lights—blue and white icicles dripping from gutters.

6:52 PM. Headlights turned onto Maple Street.

Gray Subaru.

My stomach dropped.

Michael's car pulled into the driveway. He got out. Looked around—didn't see me. Checked his phone. Walked to the building.

Disappeared inside.

The calendar had been right. Again.

Exactly right.

I grabbed my phone. Took photos. His car. The building. Time stamp:

6:54 PM.

How did the calendar know?

I'd tried to stop this. Confronted Michael this morning. Made him swear he wouldn't come here.

And he'd lied.

The calendar had predicted it. Like it knew he'd lie. Knew I couldn't stop him.

Predestination. Fate.

Or—

What if they weren't predictions? What if they were plans?

What if someone had orchestrated this? Set it up? Created a timeline and was making sure it happened?

But who?

Michael? Some elaborate gaslighting scheme?

Addison? Did she want me gone badly enough to manipulate me?

Claire?

My phone buzzed. Text from Claire.

How are you doing? Been thinking about you.

I stared at the message. Coincidence? Or checking in? Making sure her plan was working?

I typed: *The calendar was right again. He's at her apartment right now.*

Three dots flickered on screen, held. *I'm so sorry. Do you want me to come over?*

How does it know? The future. How does the calendar show things that haven't happened yet?

Pause. *I don't know. Maybe you're just seeing patterns. Coincidence?*

His car is in her driveway. Right now. December 4th. Just like the photo showed.

Then maybe the calendar is just—I don't know. Lucky guesses?

No. This was too specific. Too accurate.

I got out of the car. Walked toward the building.

Second floor. Apartment 2B had lights on. Curtains open. I could see shadows moving inside. Two people. Close together.

I took more photos. Zoomed in.

Then left. Got back in my car. Drove home.

The house was dark when I arrived. I didn't turn on the lights. Just sat in the living room.

On the coffee table: the Advent calendar.

Twelve doors open. Twelve photos of my marriage ending.

I opened my laptop. Searched: "objects that predict the future."

Occult websites. Tarot cards. Crystal balls. Nonsense.

But the calendar kept being right.

I searched: "gaslighting with photos."

Articles about manipulation. How abusers use staged evidence to make victims doubt reality. Photoshop. Deepfakes.

Was Michael doing that? Had he planted the calendar?

But the photos were Polaroids. Instant film. Hard to fake. And they showed details I couldn't have known. Addison's address. The exact booth at Ridge Tavern.

Unless Michael had told me these things and I'd forgotten—

No. I was doubting myself again. Exactly what he wanted.

The photos were real. The predictions were accurate.

Question was: how?

And who gave it to me?

Claire. Found it at an estate sale, she'd said. Except I'd called every dealer in Princeton. No sales on November 28th. She'd admitted lying about that. Said she got it at a vintage shop in Montclair instead.

But what if that was a lie too?

What if Claire had made the calendar?

But why? To torture me? To force me to see Michael's affair?

Unless—

Unless she'd tried telling me before. And I hadn't listened.

I pulled up my texts with Claire from July. Scrolled back.

There. July 15.

Claire: *Saw Michael at Ridge Lake Resort today. With a younger woman. They looked close.*

Me: *Probably a colleague. He mentors student teachers.*

Claire: *Hannah, I'm serious. It looked like more than that.*

Me: *You're projecting. Just because your marriage ended in cheating doesn't mean mine will.*

I'd dismissed her. Shut her down. Made her the problem.

Had she been right all along?

Had I ignored her, and now she was making me pay attention the only way that would work?

My phone buzzed.

Text from Michael: *Staying late at school. Don't wait up.*

Liar.

I texted back: *Okay.*

10:47 PM. Michael came home.

I was in bed. Pretended to be asleep.

He showered. Long shower. Washing off evidence.

Slipped into bed beside me. Careful not to wake me.

His phone buzzed. Text notification.

He picked it up. Checked. Set it back down. Face down. Always face down now.

I opened my eyes just enough to see him.

He was smiling.

Small smile. Satisfied. Happy.

The look of a man getting away with something.

I closed my eyes.

Tomorrow was December 5th.

More lies. More evidence. More proof I couldn't stop any of this.

Whatever was coming, it was already set in motion.

And I was just along for the ride.

Chapter 5

The Surveillance

Friday-Sunday, December 5-7

I became the person I counseled against.

The paranoid spouse. The one who checked phones. Followed cars. Documented everything.

Friday, December 5. I canceled all my appointments. Told my assistant I had the flu. She didn't believe me anymore.

I didn't care.

Michael left for school at 7:30. I followed.

Stayed three cars back. Watched him park in the faculty lot. Go inside.

I sat there until noon.

Took photos. Time stamps. His car. The building. Documentation.

Of what? That he went to work?

But the calendar showed December 5th. I needed to see what it predicted.

Except I hadn't opened door 5 yet.

I drove home. Opened it.

The photo showed Michael at Starbucks. With Addison. Afternoon. Both holding coffee cups. Laughing.

Date: December 5, 2024. Today.

I drove back to Ridgemont. Parked outside Starbucks at 2 PM. Waited.

2:47 PM. Michael's Subaru pulled up.

2:52 PM. Addison's Honda Civic.

They went inside together.

I watched through the window. Small table by the front. Coffee cups. Laughing. Her hand on his arm.

Exactly like the photo.

I took pictures. Zoomed in. Time stamps visible.

Evidence.

But evidence of what? A prediction? Or a plan someone had executed perfectly?

Saturday, December 6.

I opened the door before following him.

Photo showed them at Ridge Lake Resort. The terrace restaurant overlooking the water. Dinner. Wine glasses. Candlelight.

Date: December 6, 2024.

Michael told me he was meeting the department head. Budget discussion. Would be home by nine.

I followed him to Ridge Lake Resort at 6 PM.

Parked in the back lot. Walked to the terrace.

Found them at a corner table. Wine. Appetizers. His hand over hers.

The exact scene from the photo.

I took pictures. My hands shook so much half came out blurred.

A hostess approached. "Table for one?"

"No. Changed my mind."

I drove home. Sat in the dark living room.

Called Dr. Morrison. My old supervisor. The one I consulted when cases got complicated.

"Hannah. It's been a while."

"I need to talk."

"Of course. What's going on?"

"I think my husband is having an affair. But I also think I might be losing my mind."

Silence. "Tell me what's happening."

I explained. The calendar. The photos. The predictions. How everything kept coming true exactly as shown.

"And you're sure the dates are in the future?" Dr. Morrison asked.

"They were. December 3rd was future when I found the photo on December 1st. But it happened exactly as shown."

"That means the calendar is accurate."

"Yes. But how? How can photos show things that haven't happened yet?"

"They can't." Her voice was gentle. "Hannah, photos can't predict the future. What's more likely is that you're seeing patterns. Your mind is connecting dots that aren't really connected."

"But I have proof. I followed him. Everything matches."

"Or you're following him to places the photos suggested, and your mind is confirming what it expects to see."

"I'm not imagining this."

"I'm not saying you are. I'm saying stress can make us see patterns where there aren't any. Has anything else changed in your life? Work stress? Marriage problems before this?"

"No. Everything was fine until the calendar."

"The calendar your sister gave you?"

"Yes."

"Have you talked to her about it?"

"She says it's coincidence. That I'm overthinking."

"She might be right." Dr. Morrison paused. "Hannah, I want you to consider something. Is it possible you've been suspicious of Michael for a while? And the calendar is just confirming fears you already had?"

"No. I wasn't suspicious before."

"Are you sure?"

Was I?

I hung up. Stared at the calendar.

I opened doors 8, 9, 10, 11, 12.

Five more photos.

December 8: Michael and Addison at Ridgemont Medical Center. Walking out together. His arm around her shoulders. Protective.

December 9: Shopping. Michael at Ridgemont Jewelers. Looking at display case. Rings visible.

December 10: Addison at a doctor's office. Sign visible: *Dr. Elizabeth Monroe, Obstetrics.* A positive pregnancy test in her hand.

December 11: Michael's hand on Addison's stomach. Her face glowing. Happy.

December 12: Ultrasound photo. Tiny white shape on black screen. Eight weeks, the label said.

I stared at door 10.

Pregnancy test. Obstetrics. Due date calculation.

Addison was pregnant.

Or would be.

Or the photo was fake.

I couldn't tell anymore.

Michael came home at 9:30. Late. Again.

I was sitting at the kitchen table. The pregnancy test photo in front of me.

He stopped when he saw it.

"What is that?"

"You tell me."

He picked it up. "Where did you get this?"

"The calendar."

"Hannah—"

"Is Addison pregnant?"

"What? No. Of course not."

"This photo says otherwise."

"Photos can be faked. Photoshopped."

"Is she pregnant?"

"No." His voice was firm. Convincing. "You're being delusional. There is no pregnancy."

"Then why does this photo show a positive test? With her name on it? At an OB office?"

"Because someone is messing with you. Trying to destroy our marriage."

"Who?"

"I don't know. Maybe someone at your office? A former client? Someone who wants to hurt you?"

"By faking pregnancy photos?"

"By making you think I'm having an affair when I'm not."

"You were at Ridge Lake Resort tonight. With Addison. I saw you."

His face changed. Calculation. His eyes narrowed. "You followed me?"

"Answer the question."

"Yes. I was there. For a department dinner. Addison was there. So were six other faculty members. You saw what you wanted to see."

"Your hand was on hers."

"I was passing her the salt."

"Liar."

"You're sick, Hannah. You need help. Professional help."

"I am a professional."

"Then you know what's happening. Paranoia. Delusions. You're creating a narrative that doesn't exist."

"The photos exist."

"Fake photos. Someone planted them. And you're falling for it."

He walked upstairs.

I sat there.

Stared at the pregnancy test photo.

Was I crazy?

Was I seeing things that weren't there?

Was Dr. Morrison right—was I creating patterns, confirming fears, following him to places the photos suggested and seeing what I expected to see?

Or was Michael gaslighting me?

Making me doubt reality. Making me think I was unstable. Making me the problem.

I didn't know anymore.
All I knew was the calendar kept being right.
And I kept following.
And Michael kept lying.
Or I kept imagining lies.
One of us was wrong.
And I was terrified it was me.

Chapter 6

The Spiral

Monday-Wednesday, December 9-11

I stopped sleeping.

Monday night. Tuesday night. Wednesday night. Lay in bed, watching shadows crawl across the ceiling while Michael snored beside me.

The calendar sat on the dresser. Mocking me.

Fourteen photos. Fourteen predictions. All coming true.

Was I manifesting them? Following him so obsessively that I made them happen?

Or was someone else making them happen?

Tuesday, December 10. I opened door 10 again.

Addison at Dr. Monroe's office. Obstetrics. Positive pregnancy test.

Date: December 13, 2024. Three days away.

I googled Dr. Elizabeth Monroe. Ridgemont Medical Center, second floor. Office hours Tuesday and Friday.

Friday was December 13.

If the photo was real—if Addison was pregnant for a fact—she'd go to that appointment.

If she didn't, the calendar was fake. I was crazy. Dr. Morrison was right.

But if she did—

Then the calendar was real. The photos were real.

And someone knew about this affair before I did.

Wednesday, December 11. I opened doors 13 through 24.

All of them. Couldn't wait any longer.

Needed to see how this ended.

December 13: Addison at Dr. Monroe's office. Michael with her. His hand on her back.

December 14: Michael at Ridgemont Jewelers. Looking at rings. Engagement rings.

December 15: Michael packing boxes. Our bedroom. His clothes. His books.

December 16: Moving truck outside a building I didn't recognize.

December 17: Addison's apartment. Furniture. Michael's desk visible through the window.

December 18: Michael signing papers. Divorce papers. My name visible on the document.

December 19-24: Various scenes. Moving. Finalizing. Ending.

December 24—Christmas Eve—showed a final photo.

Me. Alone. In an apartment I didn't recognize. Small. Different from our house.

But I was smiling.

Not sad. Not broken.

Free.

I stared at that last photo for twenty minutes.

This was the ending. Divorce. Him with Addison. Me alone.

But who took these photos?

Who planned this timeline?

Who knew about the affair?

And how did they photograph things that hadn't happened yet?

Unless—

Unless they weren't future photos.

What if they were past photos? Dates changed? Evidence from months ago that someone re-dated to December?

But Michael's haircut was current. The jacket was new. Addison's car had that dent—I'd noticed it at Ridge Tavern on December 3rd.

These weren't old.

They were recent. Or future. Or—

I didn't know anymore.

Thursday, December 12. I called every photography shop in three counties.

"Do you develop Polaroids?"

"Can you alter dates on Polaroid film?"

"Have you seen anyone bring in photos of a man and woman? Brown hair, forties, with a younger brunette?"

No one had answers. Most laughed. One suggested I was being paranoid.

Maybe I was.

I called Claire.

"Where did you really get the calendar?"

"I told you. Vintage shop in Montclair."

"Which one?"

"Hannah—"

"Which shop?"

Silence. "I don't remember the name. It was months ago."

"The note said November 28. That's two weeks ago."

"Fine. Two weeks. But I don't remember the shop's name."

"You're lying."

"Why would I lie about a calendar?"

"I don't know. You tell me."

"Hannah, you're spiraling. I'm worried about you."

"Did you make it? The calendar. Did you make it?"

"What? No. Why would I—"

"Because you knew. You saw him with Addison in July. You told me. I didn't believe you. So you made this to force me to see."

"That's insane."

"Is it?"

"Hannah—"

I hung up.

Paced the living room.

Claire had seen Michael with Addison in July. Five months ago.

The photos in the calendar looked recent. But they could be from July. August. September. October.

Someone could have been following them. Documenting everything. Then re-dated the photos to December. Put them in the calendar. Gave it to me.

To force me to see what I'd been missing.

To save me from my own blindness.

Claire had the motive. She'd been cheated on. Divorced. She'd want to protect me from the same fate.

She'd tried telling me in July. I hadn't listened.

So she'd created this.

But how did she get the photos? How did she follow them? How did she know where they'd be?

Unless—

Unless she hired someone. A private investigator. Someone to document everything.

Then put it all in a calendar. Wrapped in a gift. Delivered with a note about estate sales and vintage finds.

A lie wrapped in concern.

Friday, December 13.

I sat in the Ridgemont Medical Center parking lot.

2:00 PM. The appointment time.

If Addison showed up, the calendar was real.

If she didn't, I was crazy.

1:45 PM. Michael's Subaru pulled in.

My stomach dropped.

1:50 PM. Addison's Honda Civic.

They went in together. His hand on her back. Protective.

I couldn't breathe.

I followed. Took the stairs to the second floor.

Dr. Elizabeth Monroe. Obstetrics and Gynecology.

I stood outside. Watched through the window in the door like a creep.

Waiting room. Addison at the check-in desk. Michael beside her.

They sat. He held her hand.

Waited.

A nurse called her name. They stood. Went through the door.

Disappeared.

I stood there.

Addison was pregnant.

The calendar had been right.

Again.

I wasn't crazy. Wasn't imagining things. Wasn't seeing patterns that didn't exist.

The affair was real. The pregnancy was real.

And someone had documented it all.

I drove home. Sat in the kitchen.

Pulled out my phone. Searched: "private investigators New Jersey."

Pages of results. Firms. Individuals. Services.

Discreet surveillance. Infidelity documentation. Photo evidence.

That's how.

Claire hired a private investigator. Months ago. July, probably. After she saw them together.

Had them followed. Photographed. Documented.

Then created the calendar. Re-dated everything to December. Made it look like predictions.

To force me to see.

To make me believe.

Because if she'd just shown me photos from July, I would have said "that was months ago, maybe it's over."

But photos dated to the future? Photos that came true day after day?

I couldn't ignore those.

She'd manipulated me.

Brilliantly.

And I was furious.

But also—

Also grateful.

Because without the calendar, I'd still be blind.

Unaware I'm married to a man having a baby with someone else.

Unaware I'm living a lie.

I looked at the house. Our house. The life I thought we had.

All fake.

The calendar had shown me the truth.

Now I needed Claire to confirm it.

I texted her: *I know what you did.*

Three dots wobbled. *What are you talking about?*

The calendar. The private investigator. The re-dated photos. I know.

Long pause. *We need to talk. Face to face.*

Christmas Eve. Your apartment.

Why wait that long?

Because I need time to process this. All of it.

Hannah—

Christmas Eve. 2 PM. Don't make me wait longer.

Okay. I'll be here.

I set the phone down.

Eleven days until Christmas Eve.

Eleven days until Claire would tell me the truth.

Until then, I'd keep watching. Keep documenting. Keep playing along.

Michael came home at 6:30.

"How was your day?" I asked. Casual. Normal.

"Fine. Lots of grading."

"Anything else?"

"No. Why?"

"Just asking."

He looked at me. Suspicion in his eyes. "You're being weird again."

"Sorry. Just tired."

"You should see someone. A therapist."

"I am a therapist."

He sighed. "Then you know what I'm talking about."
He went upstairs.
I sat at the table.
Stared at the calendar.
Twenty-four doors. All open now. All revealing the same story.
My marriage ending.
His baby beginning.
My life exploding.
But also—
Also starting over.
The last photo showed me smiling.
Free.
That's what was coming.
Not just loss.
Freedom.

Chapter 7

The Choice

Saturday-Monday, December 14-16

I had a choice.

Saturday morning. I woke in an empty bed. Michael had left early. "Department meeting," the note on his pillow said.

Liar.

I made coffee. Sat at the kitchen table.

The calendar sat in front of me. All twenty-four doors open now. The entire timeline visible.

December 15: Michael packing boxes.

December 18: Divorce papers.

December 24: Me alone. Smiling. Free.

Someone had shown me my future. Gave me advance warning. Time to prepare.

Time to choose.

I could wait. Let it happen. Let Michael pack his boxes on December 15 like the photo showed. Let him leave me. File divorce papers. Make me the victim.

Or I could act first.

I picked up my phone. Called Rachel Morrison. The divorce attorney my friend had used three years ago.

"Morrison & Associates."

"I need to file for divorce."

"I can schedule a consultation for next week—"

"Monday. I need Monday."

Pause. "Let me check. Yes, we have 10 AM available."

"I'll take it."

I hung up.

First choice made.

I wouldn't wait for him to leave me.

I'd leave first.

Sunday morning. I drove to St. Mary's Church.

Stone building on Ridge Road. Stained glass windows filtering colored light across worn pews.

Father O'Sullivan's office was behind the sanctuary. I knocked.

"Come in."

Late sixties, white hair, kind face. He'd married Michael and me fifteen years ago. Right here in this church.

"Hannah." He stood. "Sit. What's troubling you?"

I sat. Explained. The affair. The pregnancy. The calendar that had shown me everything.

Father O'Sullivan listened. Hands folded. Patient.

When I finished, he leaned forward.

"What does your heart tell you?"

"That I should leave him."

"And what does your faith tell you?"

"That I should forgive him."

"Those aren't contradictory." His voice was gentle. "Forgiveness doesn't mean reconciliation. You can forgive Michael and still leave. Forgiveness is for you, not him."

"But the vows. For better or worse."

"The vows also include fidelity. Forsaking all others. He broke them first."

I hadn't thought of it that way.

"So I'm allowed to leave?"

"You're allowed to choose what's healthiest for you. What allows you to live with integrity."

"Does he want to save the marriage?" Father O'Sullivan asked.

I thought about it. Michael's lies. His denials. The baby with Addison.

"No," I said. "I don't think he does."

"Then you have your answer."

I left the church feeling lighter.

Second choice made.

I wouldn't forgive and stay.

I'd forgive and leave.

Sunday afternoon. I called Dr. Morrison.

"Hannah. How are you?"

"I need your advice. Professional advice."

"Of course."

"If you had a client whose husband was having an affair and got another woman pregnant, what would you tell them?"

Silence. "Is this about you?"

"Yes."

"Hannah—"

"What would you tell them?"

Dr. Morrison sighed. "I'd tell them to consider what they can live with. Can they forgive the affair? Can they accept a child born from betrayal? Can they trust again?"

"And if they can't?"

"Then they leave."

"Even after fifteen years?"

"Especially after fifteen years. You've invested enough time. Don't invest more in something broken."

"But what if I'm wrong? What if the calendar is fake? What if I'm seeing patterns that aren't there?"

"You said you followed him to the OB appointment. You saw them together."

"Yes."

"Then you're not wrong. Trust yourself."

I hung up.

Third choice made.

I'd trust myself.

Not Michael's gaslighting. Not his denials. Not his performance.

Myself.

Monday, December 16. 10 AM. Morrison & Associates.

Glass and steel building. Modern lobby. The elevator played "Silent Night."

Rachel Morrison met me in the conference room. Mid-forties, sharp suit, direct eyes.

"Hannah. Tell me what's going on."

I explained. The affair. The pregnancy. The evidence.

"Do you have documentation?" she asked.

I pulled out my phone. Showed her photos. Time stamps. Locations. Michael's car. Addison's car. The medical center. Ridge Tavern. Burlington apartment.

"This is very thorough," Rachel said. "How long have you been documenting?"

"Two weeks."

"And the pregnancy?"

"I saw them at the OB office. December 13. Together."

Rachel nodded. Made notes. "New Jersey is a no-fault state. We can file on grounds of irreconcilable differences. Given the pregnancy, we have a strong case for equitable distribution."

"How long will it take?"

"Six to eight months. Maybe faster if he doesn't contest."

"He won't." I looked at her. "He wants to be with her."

"Then we'll move quickly." She slid papers across the table. "This is the retainer agreement. Once you sign, we file immediately. He'll be served within forty-eight hours."

I picked up the pen.

Stared at the papers.

Fifteen years. Reduced to signatures and legal terms.

Irreconcilable differences. Equitable distribution. Dissolution of marriage.

I thought about the calendar. Door 24. Me alone. Smiling.

Free.

I signed.

"Where should we serve him?" Rachel asked.

"His workplace. Ridgemont Academy."

"You want him served at school?"

"Yes."

A flicker crossed her face. Approval. "Most people try to be discreet."

"He wasn't discreet when he got another woman pregnant."

She nodded. Collected the papers. "We'll serve him Tuesday. Tomorrow."

I left before the tears came.

Sat in my car in the parking lot.

Done.

The choice was made.

I'd filed for divorce.

Tomorrow Michael would be served. In front of his students. His colleagues. Everyone would know.

And in eight days—Christmas Eve—I'd confront Claire. Get the truth about the calendar. About the private investigator. About how long she'd known.

My phone buzzed. Text from Michael.

Working late tonight. Don't wait up.

Of course he was.

I didn't respond.

Drove home. The house felt different. Not mine anymore. Not ours.

Just a place I was leaving.

I went to the bedroom. Started packing.

Not everything. Just the important things. Photos of my parents. My journals. Clothes. Books.

Things I'd need for the apartment I'd find next week.

The calendar sat on the dresser.

I picked it up. Looked at door 15. Today's date.

Photo showed Michael packing boxes. His clothes. His things.

But I was the one packing.

The calendar had shown me the ending. But I'd changed how I got there.

Not waiting for him to leave me.

Leaving him first.

That night, Michael came home at 11 PM.

I was in bed. Eyes closed. Pretending.

He showered. Slipped in beside me.

His phone buzzed. Text from A: *Love you. Can't wait for tomorrow.*

Tomorrow he'd be served divorce papers.

Tomorrow his life would explode.

Tomorrow he'd know I wasn't blind anymore.

I almost smiled.

Instead, I slept.

First real sleep in two weeks.

Because the choice was made.

And I was finally done waiting.

Chapter 8

The Sister

Tuesday, December 24, 2 PM

I drove to Claire's apartment on Christmas Eve.

Eleven days since I'd filed. Michael had been served at school on December 17. In front of his AP Literature class. A process server walked into his classroom. Handing him papers. Everyone watching.

He'd called me seventeen times that day. I didn't answer.

Moved out December 20. Found a one-bedroom on Main Street. Small. Clean. Mine.

Michael left messages. Angry at first. Then pleading. Then resignation.

"Fine. You want a divorce? You'll get one. But you'll regret this."

I didn't regret it.

I regretted the fifteen years before it.

Claire's apartment was in Burlington. Same complex as Addison's— ironic. Two-story building, gray siding. I parked outside 2B.

Knocked.

Claire opened the door. She looked tired. Dark circles under her eyes. Hair pulled back. Jeans and a sweater.

"Come in."

Small apartment. IKEA furniture. Minimal decoration. A half-decorated Christmas tree in the corner, like she'd started and given up.

We sat at her kitchen table. Cheap laminate. Two chairs.

"You made the calendar," I said.

"Yes."

No denial. No performance. Just truth.

"How?"

Claire took a breath. "I hired a private investigator in July."

There it was.

"After you saw them at Ridge Lake Resort."

"Yes. I called you. Told you Michael was with a younger woman. You dismissed me. Said I was projecting."

I remembered. July 15. I'd shut her down. Made her the problem.

"So you hired someone to follow them."

"I needed proof. Solid proof you couldn't ignore or rationalize away."

"The photos."

"The investigator took them over four months. July through October. Coffee dates. Dinners. Hotel visits. Everything."

"But they're dated December."

"I re-dated them." She met my eyes. That direct stare. "Made them look like future events."

My chest tightened. "Why?"

"Because if I gave you photos from July, you'd say 'that was months ago, maybe it ended.' You'd make excuses. Find reasons to believe him. You always do."

"So you manipulated me."

"I gave you evidence you couldn't ignore. Every day, a new photo. Counting down. Building pressure. You couldn't dismiss it."

"That's cruel."

"What's cruel is Michael gaslighting you for five months while fucking a twenty-eight-year-old."

The words landed like blows.

Neither of us spoke.

Through the wall, a neighbor's TV played. A Christmas commercial. Families. Joy. Lies.

"The calendar isn't magic," I said.

"No. It's evidence."

"But December 3rd happened. Today. Exactly as shown."

Claire nodded. "Because he's still seeing her. The pattern hasn't changed. Tuesdays at Ridge Tavern. Thursdays at her apartment. The PI documented his schedule. It's predictable."

"So the photos aren't predictions. They're patterns."

"Exactly."

I looked at her. My sister. Who'd watched her own marriage implode from infidelity. Who'd been exactly where I was now.

"Why go through all this? Why not just show me the evidence?"

"I tried. July. You didn't believe me."

"So you created an Advent calendar mind game?"

"I created a way for you to see the truth gradually. Day by day. So you couldn't deny it. So you'd have time to process. To accept. To act."

"You decided for me."

"I gave you information. You decided. You're the one who filed for divorce. You're the one who left. I just showed you what you needed to see."

"By lying about estate sales. By faking future photos. By manipulating—"

"By protecting you." Claire's voice broke. "Do you know what it's like? Watching someone you love stay in a marriage that's destroying them? Watching them make excuses for a man who's betraying them? I lived that. For two years, I suspected. Made excuses. Believed the lies. By the time I had proof, I'd wasted two years I'll never get back."

"I didn't want that for you."

Silence.

"Show me," I said. "The real evidence. Everything."

Claire stood. Went to her bedroom. Came back with a manila folder.

Set it on the table between us.

"Open it."

I did.

Inside: dozens of photos. Not Polaroids. Digital prints. Michael and Addison. July through November. Time stamps in the corners. Metadata visible.

July 18, 2024: Ridge Lake Resort. Terrace. Holding hands.

August 3, 2024: Ridge Tavern. Corner booth. Kissing.

August 15, 2024: Parsippany Marriott. Parking lot. His car next to hers.

August 22, 2024: Hotel window. Fourth floor. Curtains open. Two figures.

September 6, 2024: Starbucks. Coffee. Laughing.

September 12, 2024: Ridgemont Plaza. Shopping. His arm around her.

October 8, 2024: Doctor's office. Both entering. His hand on her back.

October 15, 2024: Pharmacy. Picking up prescription. Prenatal vitamins visible in the bag.

Receipts. Flowers from Ridgemont Florist. Jewelry from Ridgemont Jewelers. Hotel rooms. Dinners. Everything documented.

Text message screenshots. The PI had accessed Michael's phone somehow.

July 20: "I love you. I'll leave her soon."

August 5: "She suspects nothing."

September 18: "Baby makes it complicated."

October 15: "I'll file for divorce after Christmas."

That one stopped me.

I'll file for divorce after Christmas.

Sent October 15. To someone saved as "A."

Addison.

"He was planning to leave me," I said. My voice sounded distant.

"Yes. After Christmas. New year, fresh start. He was just waiting."

"But he never said anything."

"Because he's a coward."

I flipped through more texts. Hundreds of them. All from Michael to Addison. All while he came home to me. Kissed me goodnight. Made love to me on our anniversary. Planned Vermont for Christmas.

Lies.

Every word.

"The rest of the calendar," I said. "December 15 through 24. What do those show?"

"Some are real photos from August through October. Some are staged."

"Staged?"

"The PI took photos at locations they frequented. Set up shots that would look like future events. To complete the narrative."

"The pregnancy announcement photo. December 10."

"Real. Taken October 8. She was eight weeks then. Would be showing by mid-December. I calculated."

"The divorce papers. December 18."

"Staged. But based on his texts. He planned to file in January. I just moved the timeline up."

"The last photo. December 24. Me alone. Smiling."

Claire reached across the table. Took my hand. "That's real too. That's your future. Freedom."

I pulled my hand back. "You manipulated every part of this."

"I gave you truth wrapped in a method you couldn't ignore."

"You played God."

"I played sister. Protecting you the only way I knew how."

I closed the folder. Stood up. Walked to the window.

Outside, Christmas lights blinked on buildings across the parking lot. Families carrying presents. Living normal lives.

"I should be angry," I said.

"Are you?"

I thought about it. The calendar. The manipulation. The staged photos. The countdown.

But also—

Also the truth. The evidence. The freedom.

"No," I said finally. "I'm not angry."

I turned back to Claire. "You saved me. In the most twisted way possible. But you saved me."

Claire's eyes filled. "I'm sorry I lied."

"I'm sorry I didn't listen in July."

We stood there. Sisters. Both divorced. Both betrayed. Both survivors.

"Merry Christmas," Claire said.

I almost laughed. "Merry Christmas."

She stood. Hugged me. Hard. Long.

"The calendar's not magic," she whispered. "But you are. You chose yourself. That's the real miracle."

I drove home—my new home—at 4 PM.

Small apartment. Clean. Empty.

Mine.

I'd brought the calendar with me when I moved. Couldn't leave it behind.

All twenty-four doors hung open. Empty now.

I carried it to the trash chute.

Dropped it in.

Heard it tumble down. Gone.

I didn't need it anymore.

The predictions had come true. But not because of magic.

Because Claire had documented reality. Given me evidence. Forced me to see.

And I'd chosen freedom.

That night, I went to midnight mass at St. Mary's.

Sat in the back. Alone.

The church was packed. Families. Couples. Children.

Everyone belonged to someone.

I belonged to myself.

Father O'Sullivan's sermon: "Sometimes God's greatest gift is showing us what we need to leave behind."

I thought about that.

Michael. The house. The marriage. Fifteen years.

All left behind.

The congregation sang "Silent Night."
I didn't sing.
Just sat there.
Alone.
But not lonely.
Free.

Chapter 9

The Confrontation

Wednesday, December 25, 3 PM

Michael called Christmas morning.

I was drinking coffee on my apartment floor. Hadn't bought furniture yet. Just an air mattress, two boxes of books, and a coffee maker.

His name lit up my phone. I almost didn't answer.

But I needed closure.

"Hello."

"Hannah." His voice was rough. Like he'd been crying. "Can we talk?"

"About what?"

"Us. The divorce. Everything."

"There's nothing to talk about."

"Please. Just give me an hour."

I looked around my empty apartment. Nothing else to do on Christmas.

"Fine. Meet me at Ridge Tavern. Noon."

"Thank you."

I hung up.

Drove there at 11:45. Same restaurant where I'd caught them December 3rd. Three weeks ago. Felt like years.

The Tavern was nearly empty. Christmas Day. Most places closed. But Ridge Tavern stayed open for people with nowhere else to go.

Lonely people. Divorced people. People like me.

Michael was already there. Same corner booth. His spot with Addison. I sat across from him.

He looked terrible. Unshaven. Dark circles. Hair uncombed. The carefully-put-together Michael was gone.

"Thank you for coming," he said.

"You have one hour."

"I want to save our marriage."

I almost laughed. "No, you don't."

"I do. I made a mistake—"

"You made a choice. Multiple choices. For five months."

"It was stupid. Meaningless—"

"Meaningless?" I pulled out my phone. Showed him the screenshot. Text from October 15. *I'll file for divorce after Christmas.*

His face went white.

"Where did you get that?"

"Doesn't matter. Is it true?"

Silence.

"Michael. Is it true?"

"Yes."

The word hung there.

"You were planning to leave me. After Christmas. Fresh start with Addison and your baby."

"Hannah—"

"Don't lie to me. Not anymore." I pulled out the manila folder. Set it on the table. "I know everything."

"What is that?"

"Open it."

He did.

His hands shook as he flipped through photos. July. August. September. October. All of them. Time stamps visible. Metadata clear.

His face crumbled.

"How did you—"

"Private investigator. Hired in July. Documented everything."

"You had me followed?"

"No. Someone who loves me did. Someone who tried to warn me and I didn't listen."

Michael looked up. "Claire."

"Yes."

"That calendar—"

"Was her creation. Evidence wrapped in a countdown. Every photo in that calendar was real. Just re-dated to December to force me to pay attention."

"She manipulated you."

"You manipulated me. She just showed me the truth."

Michael closed the folder. Pushed it away. "I was going to tell you."

"When?"

"After Christmas. I was waiting for the right time."

"There's no right time to tell your wife you got another woman pregnant."

"I know. I'm sorry."

"Sorry you did it? Or sorry you got caught?"

He didn't answer.

"Where's Addison?" I asked.

"At her apartment."

"Alone? On Christmas?"

"She's with her parents. They came to visit."

"Meeting the grandparents already. How nice."

"Hannah—"

"Do you love her?"

He looked at his hands. "Yes."

Four words. Worse than the affair. Worse than the pregnancy. Worse than the lies.

He loved her.

"Then why are you here?" I asked.

"Because I love you too."

"No, you don't."

"I do. Fifteen years—"

"Fifteen years you threw away. You don't get to claim them now."

"I want to fix this."

"You can't."

"We can go to counseling. Work through it—"

"Michael." I looked at him. Really looked. "You're having a baby with her. In six months, you'll be a father. To her child. There's nothing to work through."

"I can still be married to you—"

"And what? Play house with two families? Visit your baby on weekends? Lie to both of us?"

"It doesn't have to be like that."

"Yes, it does. Because that's who you are. A man who lies. Who cheats. Who tells me he loves me while texting another woman that he'll leave me after Christmas."

I stood up. "I'm not interested in being your backup plan. Your safety net. Your comfortable fallback when the new relationship gets hard."

"That's not what this is."

"Yes, it is. You don't want me. You want the security. The house. The routine. The life that doesn't require anything from you."

"That's not fair."

"Neither was five months of lies."

I grabbed the folder. Started to leave.

"Hannah, wait."

I turned back.

"The calendar," he said. "The photos. December 3rd through 24th. They all came true."

"Most of them."

"How? How did Claire predict all that?"

"She didn't predict. She documented patterns. You're predictable,

Michael. Tuesdays at Ridge Tavern. Thursdays at Addison's apartment. Same schedule for months. Claire just showed me what I was too blind to see."

"So none of it was magic."

"No. Just evidence."

He looked broken. Small. The man I'd married was gone. Or maybe he'd never existed.

Maybe this was who he'd always been.

I left.

Thursday, December 26, 6 PM

The doorbell rang.

I'd spent the day cleaning. Organizing. Making the apartment feel more like home. I left the last remnants of my old life in boxes. They'll go to the Salvation Army.

I checked the peephole.

Addison.

This, I had to see.

I opened the door.

She stood there. Green coat, expensive boots. Hair perfect. That Instagram face. Her hand rested on her stomach—protective gesture, though at fourteen weeks there wasn't much to show yet.

"Hannah. Can I come in?"

I stepped back. Let her enter.

She looked around the apartment. Nearly empty. Air mattress. Two boxes. Coffee maker. Nothing else.

"You're not settled yet," she said.

"I'm settled enough."

Awkward silence.

"Why are you here?" I asked.

"To say thank you."

I blinked. "Excuse me?"

"For letting him go. Michael came to see you yesterday. Asked you to take him back. You said no."

"And?"

"And he came back to me. We're getting married in March." She touched her stomach. Proud. Happy. "Before the baby comes."

I stared at her. The audacity. Coming to my apartment to thank me for rejecting my own husband.

"Congratulations," I said.

"I know this is awkward. But I wanted you to know—I appreciate it. You could have made this harder. Taken him back just to hurt me. But you let him go cleanly."

"I didn't let him go. I threw him out. There's a difference."

"Still. Thank you."

She turned to leave. Stopped at the door.

"I know you probably think I'm terrible. The other woman. Home-wrecker. All of that."

"I don't think about you at all."

That landed. Her face flickered. Uncertainty.

"Michael and I—we're happy. He loves me. The baby. Our future together."

"Good for you."

"You don't believe me."

"I believe you think that's true. Right now. While everything's new and exciting."

"What's that supposed to mean?"

I looked at her. Twenty-eight years old. Glowing with early pregnancy and new love. Convinced she'd won.

"Nothing. Enjoy your wedding."

She studied my face. Looking for something. Bitterness, maybe. Jealousy. Anger.

She wouldn't find it.

"Do you hate me?" she asked.

"No."

"You should. I slept with your husband. Got pregnant. Took him away from you."

"You didn't take him. He was already gone. You just showed me what I hadn't wanted to see."

Addison shifted. Uncomfortable. "Michael said you had some kind of calendar. That predicted everything."

"It wasn't magic. Just evidence I ignored for too long."

"He said it showed the future."

"It showed patterns. His patterns. Predictable behavior I was too blind to notice."

"I don't understand."

"You will." I opened the door. "When he does it to you."

Her face hardened. "He won't. What we have is different."

"That's what I thought too. Fifteen years ago."

"I'm not you."

"You're right. You're younger. Prettier. More exciting. For now."

"That's not fair."

"It's not fair or unfair. It's reality. Michael loves comfort. Routine. The path of least resistance. Right now, that's you. The new relationship. The baby. The fresh start."

"But in five years? Ten? When the baby's not new? When life gets routine? When another pretty twenty-eight-year-old shows interest?"

"He'll do to you what he did to me."

"You're bitter."

"I'm honest. There's a difference."

Addison's hand went to her stomach. Protective. Defensive.

"We're different," she said. But her voice was less certain now.

"Maybe. I hope so. For your baby's sake."

She left without saying goodbye.

I closed the door. Locked it.

Walked to the window.

Watched her get in her Honda Civic. Sit there for five minutes. Hands on the steering wheel. Not moving.

Thinking.

Finally, she drove away.

I made fresh coffee. Sat on my air mattress.

Thought about Addison. Her certainty. Her belief that she'd won.

Maybe she had.

Or maybe she'd just inherited my problem.

Either way—not my concern anymore.

Michael and Addison would get married in March. Have their baby in June. Build their life together.

And I'd build mine.

Alone. Free. Starting over.

The calendar had shown me this moment. Six months ago. Me in a new apartment. After confrontation. After closure.

It hadn't predicted the future.

It had shown me a choice.

And I'd chosen myself.

My phone buzzed. Text from Claire.

How did it go yesterday?

He begged me to take him back. I said no.

Good. Proud of you.

Addison just left. Came to thank me for rejecting him. They're getting married in March.

OH MY GOD. The audacity.

I know.

How do you feel?

I thought about it. Really thought.

Free.

Outside, Christmas lights still blinked on the building across the street. Families inside, probably. Boxing up decorations. Returning to normal life.

I had no decorations to box up. No normal life to return to.

Just me.

And that was enough.

Chapter 10

The Calendar

S**ix Months Later - June**

Rachel Morrison called on a Tuesday. "It's final. You're divorced."

I was in my car. Parked outside Whole Foods in Ridgemont Plaza. Where this had started, in a way. Where I'd caught them that first time.

"Thank you," I said.

I felt nothing. No sadness. No relief. No anger.

Just closure.

I'd moved on months ago.

That week, I reopened my practice.

New office space. Different building, still in Ridgemont. Brighter windows. Modern furniture I'd chosen myself. Plant on the windowsill—a succulent, thriving. My degrees on the wall in new frames.

Fresh start.

First day back, three clients scheduled.

1 PM: Woman considering divorce. Husband had cheated. She wasn't sure what to do.

"Is it worth it?" she asked.

"Only you can answer that."

"Was yours worth it?"

I thought about the apartment. The peace. The mornings drinking coffee alone. The freedom.

"Yes."

"Even though you're alone now?"

I smiled. "I'm not alone. I'm free. There's a difference."

She nodded. Understood.

3 PM: Couple fighting about trust. He'd lied about money. She'd found evidence.

"Can trust be rebuilt?" the wife asked.

"Sometimes. If both people want to rebuild it. If both people are willing to do the work. If both people are honest."

"But what if he's not?"

"Then you have your answer."

5 PM: Man who'd left his wife for someone younger. Six months later, the new relationship was falling apart.

"She's not who I thought she was," he said.

"Or she's exactly who she was, and you're seeing clearly now."

"What do I do?"

"Learn from it. Don't make the same mistake twice."

After he left, I sat in my office. Looked out the window. Main Street below. People walking. Lives continuing.

Mine too.

My phone buzzed. Text from Claire.

Dinner tonight? My place?

Yes. 7 PM.

Bring wine.

I smiled.

Claire and I had grown closer since Christmas. Weekly dinners. Long phone calls. Sisters in a way we'd never been before.

Both divorced. Both betrayed. Both free.

We understood each other now.

That evening, I drove to Burlington. Claire's apartment looked different. More furniture. Actual decorations. Photos on the walls—us as kids, our parents, trips we'd taken.

She looked different too. Lighter. Hair shorter. New glasses. Smiling.

"Come in."

We sat on her couch. Drank Cabernet. Talked about work, clients, summer plans.

Normal sister things.

"Have you heard from Michael?" Claire asked.

"No. Not since Christmas."

"Have you heard anything through the grapevine?"

Claire shrugged. "They got married in March. Small ceremony. The baby's due any day now."

"A boy, right?"

"Yes. Nathan." She paused. "Apparently they're fighting a lot. Money. Stress. Addison stopped working. Michael's salary doesn't stretch like it used to."

"Already?"

"Babies are expensive. Reality's setting in."

I almost felt bad for them.

Almost.

"Do you regret it?" Claire asked. "The calendar. The manipulation. All of it."

I thought about it. Really thought.

"No."

"Why not?"

"Because you gave me truth. In the most twisted way possible. But truth nonetheless."

"I'm still sorry I lied."

"I'm still grateful you did."

We sat in comfortable silence.

"I kept one thing," I said.

"What?"

I pulled out my phone. Showed her the photo. The last one from the calendar. December 24. Me alone in an apartment. Smiling.

Free.

"I took a picture of it before I threw the calendar away. Look at it sometimes when I need a reminder."

"A reminder of what?"

"That endings can be beginnings. That loss can be freedom. That sometimes the worst thing that happens is also the best thing."

Claire's eyes filled. "Hannah—"

"Thank you. For caring enough to manipulate me. For protecting me when I wouldn't protect myself. For being my sister."

We hugged. Long and hard.

When I left at 10 PM, I drove past our old house. The one on Lakeview Drive. We'd sold it in February. Split the proceeds.

New family lived there now. Lights on. A swing set in the backyard.

New life. New memories.

I kept driving.

Back to my apartment. No longer empty. I'd bought furniture in March. Real bed. Couch. Dining table. Pictures on the walls. Plants by the windows.

Home.

I made tea. Sat by the window.

Same window from the calendar's last photo. Same contentment. Same peace.

My phone buzzed. Text from an unknown number.

Photo attachment. Michael and Addison. Hospital. Her holding a newborn. Both looking exhausted.

Caption: *Nathan Michael Price. Born June 18. 7 lbs 3 oz.*

I stared at the photo.

Michael's son. His new family. His future.

I deleted it.

Blocked the number.

Didn't need to see that anymore.

They had their life. I had mine.

I looked at the photo on my phone. The one I'd kept from the calendar. Me smiling. Free.

The calendar had shown me this moment six months ago. Me in a new apartment. After everything. After betrayal and lies and loss.

And it had shown me smiling.

That was the real magic.

Not the photos. Not the predictions. Not the manipulation.

The magic was knowing that after everything, I could still smile.

Still be happy.

Still be free.

The calendar hadn't shown me the future.

It had shown me a choice.

And I'd chosen myself.

Tomorrow I'd take that trip to Vermont I'd always wanted. The one Michael never had time for. Already booked. Two weeks. Solo travel.

Next month I'd consider dating again. Maybe. When I was ready.

Or maybe not.

Maybe I'd just be.

Alone but not lonely.

Free but not lost.

Starting over but not starting from nothing.

I had myself.

And that was enough.

The calendar had taught me that.

Not through magic.

Through truth.

I finished my tea. Turned off the lights.

Tomorrow would come.

And I'd be ready for it.

Not because I knew what was coming.

But because I'd learned to trust myself.

To see clearly.

To choose freedom.

The advent calendar was gone. Thrown away months ago.

But its lesson remained.

Sometimes the best gift is the one that shows you what you need to leave behind.

And sometimes the person you need to choose is yourself.

THE END

BOOK 5

The Cabin

Chapter 1

Arrival

Pine Ridge Chalet was the kind of place people rented to reconnect or disappear. It sat at the end of a narrow road, tucked into the tree line like it was hiding. Two stories of dark wood and wide windows. Expensive. Remote.

Gravel crunched under my tires as I pulled up. I killed the engine. Silence settled over everything except the wind moving through the pines.

December air bit my face when I stepped out. The smell hit right away—sharp pine mixed with something metallic. Maybe the propane tank around the side. Maybe just the sting of winter.

Ice cracked somewhere on the roof like a faraway gunshot. The sound hit, then silence again.

The cabin's front door opened before I reached it.

"Julia!" Vanessa's voice carried across the driveway. Too loud. Always too loud.

"Finally! We were starting to think you bailed."

She stood in the doorway, blonde hair styled even out here, wearing expensive athleisure that probably cost more than my car payment. Vanessa Hart. Real estate agent. Former best friend. Current whatever-we-were-now.

"Traffic," I said.

"Sure." She smiled, stepped aside. "Everyone's already here."

The interior opened into a great room with high ceilings and exposed beams. To the left, the main staircase led to the second floor. To the right, near the kitchen, a narrow door—probably servant's stairs from when the cabin was built.

Vanessa gestured toward the stairs. "Bedrooms are all upstairs. Four rooms. You can take whichever one's open."

A stone fireplace took up most of the far wall. The furniture looked catalog-perfect. Windows everywhere showed nothing but trees and the kind of darkness that came early in December.

In the corner stood a real pine tree. Not huge. Tasteful. A single strand of white lights wrapped around it. Glowed soft against the wood paneling. Someone had hung a garland along the mantel—green with small silver ornaments catching the firelight.

Soft instrumental music played from somewhere. Christmas playlist. Generic. Safe. Marcus's idea of ambiance, I would guess.

Marcus stood near the kitchen island, phone in hand like always. Thirty-six, fit in that intentional gym way, black hair gelled back even on a weekend trip. Investment banker. He'd organized this reunion, rented the cabin, and sent calendar invites like we were clients instead of old friends.

"Julia." He nodded without looking up. "You made good time."

"Three hours."

"Two-forty from the city if you take Route 515." He glanced at me. "I sent you the best route."

"I took 23."

He frowned. Went back to his phone.

Derek appeared from the hallway, camera hanging around his neck. Marcus's younger brother. Thirty-three now, though the shaggy hair and flannel made him look younger. He'd grown a beard since I'd seen him last. It suited him.

"Hey." His voice was quieter than Vanessa's. Always quieter. "Good drive?"

"Long." I set my duffel down. "You got here okay?"

"Yeah. A few hours ago." He shifted his weight, didn't meet my eyes. Old habit. Derek had spent most of college looking at floors or through camera lenses.

Olivia emerged from the kitchen, cardigan wrapped tight around her small frame. Thirty-four, light brown hair in a bob, freckles across her nose. She smiled when she saw me—that peacemaker smile that said everything was fine even when it wasn't.

"Julia! I'm so glad you made it." She moved in for a hug. I let her. "Troy's just finishing a work call upstairs. He'll be down soon."

Troy. Olivia's husband. Married two years ago. I was at their wedding. Nice ceremony. Open bar. I'd met him twice before that. Both times he'd been polite, quiet, the kind of person who watched more than he spoke.

I didn't know him well. None of us did, really.

Heavy footsteps on the stairs. Troy descended—tall, lean, dark brown hair thinning slightly, gray eyes that took in the room before settling on me.

"Julia." He extended his hand. Firm grip. "Good to see you again."

"You too."

He positioned himself near Olivia, one hand on her back. Protective but not possessive. His expensive watch caught the light—a whole month of living strapped to his wrist.

Vanessa clapped her hands together. "Okay! Now that we're all here, we should do the thing."

"The thing?" I crossed my arms.

"The photo!" She already had her phone out. "We have to recreate the senior year Christmas party photo. You know, the one from Greg's apartment? All five of us crammed on that terrible couch?"

I didn't remember a couch. Didn't remember Greg's apartment looking like anything specific. Senior year felt like a blur of deadlines and hangovers and trying to figure out what came next.

But Vanessa remembered. Vanessa always remembered.

"Come on." She waved us toward the fireplace. "Same poses. It'll be fun."

Marcus sighed, but moved. Derek followed. Olivia positioned herself carefully, hands folded like she was posing for a school photo.

I stood at the edge of the group.

"Julia, you were on the left," Vanessa said. "Next to Derek."

I moved. The floorboards creaked under my weight.

"Troy, you can set up the camera," Vanessa continued. "Since you weren't there for the original."

Troy took Vanessa's phone, examined it. "Timer's already set. Where do you want me to position this?"

"On the mantel. Get everyone in frame."

Troy adjusted the phone, checked angles. His movements precise, methodical. He stepped back, studied the setup, and made a micro-adjustment.

"You're good at this," Derek observed.

Troy shrugged. "Just detail-oriented."

The phone beeped. Ten seconds. Troy moved to the side, out of frame, watching us.

Vanessa squeezed in next to Marcus, too close, her hand on his shoulder in a way that meant nothing and everything.

The camera clicked.

"Perfect!" Vanessa grabbed her phone, scrolled through the photo. "God, we look exactly the same."

We didn't. We all knew we didn't.

"I need to check something upstairs," Marcus said, on his way to the stairs.

Derek wandered toward the windows, camera raised. Capturing angles. Avoiding people.

Olivia touched my arm. "You okay? You seem tense."

"Long drive," I said.

"Right." She didn't believe me, but let it go. That's what Olivia did. Smoothed things over. Made sure everyone stayed comfortable even when comfort felt impossible.

Troy approached Vanessa. "The cabin's nice. Good choice."

"Marcus found it," Vanessa said. "But I approved. Always approve the location." She checked her phone again—that chapel clock app she'd been obsessed with lately. The screen glowed briefly before she pocketed it.

"Family doing well?" Derek asked her, camera lowered for once.

Vanessa's expression hardened. Only for a second. "I don't have family anymore. Not since Ryan."

Uncomfortable silence.

"I'm sorry," Derek said. "I forgot—"

"It's fine," Vanessa said, voice tight. "Six years ago. People forget."

Marcus cleared his throat from across the room. "Storm's rolling in. We're here whether we want to be or not."

Troy moved to the window, studied the darkening sky. "How bad?"

"Bad enough. Roads will be impassable by morning."

"Then let's make this a good weekend," Olivia said, forced cheer in her voice. "Please."

I walked to the hallway, took the stairs looking for my room. The floorboards groaned. Halfway down the corridor, I stopped.

Heard something. Almost like my name. Whispered.

"Julia."

I turned. Empty hallway. Dark wood paneling. Closed doors. Just the wind outside pressing against the windows. The cabin's acoustics swallowed everything, made sounds bounce wrong.

Could've been someone calling from upstairs. Could've been wind. Could've been my brain filling the silence with something familiar.

I walked on.

Found my room—small, cold, bed covered in a quilt that smelled faintly of cedar and disuse. I dropped my duffel, walked to the window.

My reflection stared back. Behind me, the dimly lit Christmas tree downstairs was visible through the open door. The empty great room. Shadows pressed in from corners.

And for just a second—less than a second—I swore the face in the glass next to mine wasn't mine at all.

I blinked.

Nothing there.

Just me. Just the tree. Just the cabin settling around us like a held breath.

Watching.

Chapter 2

The Body In The Snow

The storm hit sometime after midnight.

I woke to wind that hammered the windows. The sound was violent, relentless. I lay there and listened, waited for something to break. Nothing did. Just wind and the groan of old wood under pressure.

I checked my phone. 5:47 AM. No service. The bars had disappeared. Marcus had warned us—Pine Ridge Chalet sat in a dead zone.

Sleep wouldn't come back, so I got up. The floorboards felt like ice. I pulled on jeans, a sweater, and thick socks. And grabbed my scarf.

Downstairs, the great room was dark except for dying embers in the fireplace. Someone had unplugged the Christmas tree lights. Smart. A storm like this could knock out power any second.

Through the windows, nothing but white. The world erased.

I moved to the kitchen. Filled the kettle, set it on the stove. Found coffee in the cabinet—expensive stuff, the kind Marcus would buy. Ground beans that smelled like burned caramel.

That's when I noticed.

Vanessa's coat was gone from the hook near the door. Her boots too.

I walked to the window above the sink. Cupped my hands against the glass, tried to see through the pre-dawn gray and swirling snow.

There. Near the tree line. A dark shape against white.

My stomach dropped.

I wrapped my scarf around my neck. Grabbed my North Face jacket from the chair where I'd left it. Shoved my feet into boots. Didn't bother to lace them. Yanked open the back door.

Cold slammed into me. The kind that burned. Snow came up past my ankles. Drifts piled against the cabin walls. The porch light cast a weak yellow across the driveway, barely cutting through the storm.

The shape didn't move.

I pushed forward. Each step took effort. My breath clouded, disappeared. Twenty feet. Thirty. The cold bit through my jeans, my jacket, found skin.

Closer now.

Blonde hair. Expensive athleisure jacket. One arm stretched out, fingers pale against snow.

Vanessa.

"Vanessa!"

No response.

I dropped to my knees beside her. Reached out. Her jacket was stiff with ice. I grabbed her shoulder, tried to roll her over.

Heavy. Dead weight.

I pulled harder. She turned. Her face—

Blood crusted around her temple, dark against pale skin. Eyes half-open, stared at nothing. Lips blue. Snow had started to accumulate on her back, in her hair, covered her like the storm tried to bury evidence.

My hands shook. Not from cold.

I touched her neck. No pulse. Skin like frozen meat.

How long had she been out here?

I looked around. Footprints everywhere—multiple sets, circled, stopped, started in patterns that made no sense. Some led from the cabin. Some went nowhere.

And there, half-buried near her hand. A small red ornament. Glass. The kind you hang on a tree.

I'd seen it before. In my bag when I'd packed. My mother had given it to me years ago. I'd thrown it in without thinking. Forgot about it completely.

How did it get out here?

Blood on the tree trunk behind her. Dark smear against bark. Like she'd been hit there, then dragged.

Or she'd staggered, fell.

Or—

"Julia!"

I spun.

Derek stood in the doorway, backlit. He started down the steps, moved fast but carefully through the snow.

"What—" The wind tore his words away.

He reached me. Saw Vanessa. "Jesus."

He crouched beside the body. Touched her neck like I had. Pulled his hand back fast.

"Get the others," I shouted over the wind.

He nodded. Ran back.

I stayed with the body. With Vanessa.

Except something felt wrong. The hair looked darker in the storm light. Matted with blood and ice, but still. Wrong shade. And her build— had she been this small?

The wind howled. Almost sounded like my name.

Voices at the door. Marcus appeared first, then Olivia, then Troy. They hurried down the steps, heads bent against the wind.

Marcus checked her pulse. "She's gone."

Olivia made a sound. Small. Broken.

"Inside," Marcus shouted. "Now. We can't stay out here."

"We need to call someone," I said.

"Cell phones?" Olivia asked. Her voice shook.

Everyone checked. Marcus shook his head. Derek held up his phone— no bars. Troy showed his screen. Nothing.

"We're cut off," Marcus said. "Landline. Inside."

We stumbled back to the cabin. The warmth hit like a wall when we got through the door. We stood there, dripping melted snow, not looking at each other.

Marcus went straight to the landline. Picked up the receiver. Dialed 911. He put it on speaker.

"911, what's your emergency?"

"We're at Pine Ridge Chalet in Sussex County. One of our group is dead. We found her in the snow. We need police."

Pause. Keyboard typing.

"Sir, roads are currently impassable due to the storm. We can't get emergency vehicles through until conditions improve. Likely Sunday morning at the earliest."

"So we just wait here? With a dead body?"

"Stay inside. Keep warm. Don't disturb the scene. We'll dispatch officers as soon as the roads clear. This call is logged. Help is coming."

The call ended.

Marcus looked at us. "They can't get here until the storm passes. Sunday at the earliest. But they know. It's on record."

"Sunday?" Olivia's voice cracked. "That's tomorrow."

"Could be longer if the storm doesn't let up."

"What do we do?" Olivia wrapped her arms around herself.

"We wait. The storm will pass. Roads will clear. Police will come."

"When?" Her voice rose. "How long?"

Marcus shook his head. "I don't know."

She looked at Troy. "We're stuck here until Sunday?"

He put his hand on her back. "We'll be okay. We stay inside. Stay together."

I walked to the fireplace. Threw on another log. Needed to do something. Needed my hands to move.

Derek stood by the window, looked out at the gray nothing. "When did anyone last see her?"

"Dinner," Olivia said. "She was in the kitchen around eight."

"I saw her later," Derek said. "Upstairs. Around eleven. She walked past. Didn't say anything."

Troy turned from where he stood near Olivia. "I saw her in the kitchen. Same time. She was on her phone."

"All of you saw her around eleven?" Marcus asked.

We all nodded.

"And then?"

"I went to bed," Olivia said.

"Same," Troy said. "We were together all night."

Derek shrugged. "I was in my room. Editing photos."

Marcus looked at me. "Julia?"

"I went to bed around midnight. Woke up around five-thirty. Came downstairs."

"And found her." Maruc Finished.

Silence except for the wind and the fire.

"She mentioned Ryan last night," Derek said. "At dinner. Her brother. Said something about finally getting justice for him."

Marcus frowned. "What does that mean?"

Derek shrugged. "I don't know."

"Ryan died years ago," Olivia said. "Car accident. Why would she bring that up?"

"She wouldn't explain," Derek said.

I stared at Vanessa's coat still on the hook. Except it wasn't there. She'd worn it outside. But I could've sworn—

No. That was someone else's coat. Mine. Dark blue. Similar.

My thoughts wouldn't organize.

"It doesn't look like her," I said.

Everyone turned.

"What?" Marcus asked.

"Out there. The hair looked wrong. Darker."

"It's covered in blood," Derek said. "And ice."

"But—"

"Julia." Marcus's voice was firm. "Who else would it be?"

I didn't have an answer.

The Christmas tree stood dark in the corner. The garland on the mantel sagged where the wire had come loose. The peppermint candies someone had set out sat in their bowl, untouched.

Outside, Vanessa's body lay in the snow.

Inside, we stood in a circle, not looking at each other.

Wrong.

Chapter 3

Fracture

We sat in the great room. The fire in the fireplace threw heat that never reached past the hearth. The Christmas tree in the corner stood dark—no one had plugged the lights back in.

Outside, wind hammered the windows. Inside, silence stretched between us like something alive.

Derek paced near the window, camera around his neck. Troy sat next to Olivia on the couch, one hand on her knee. Marcus stood by the fireplace, jaw tight.

I pulled my jacket tighter. Still felt cold from being outside. From kneeling in the snow next to Vanessa's body.

"We should talk about what happened," Marcus said. "Before the police get here. Make sure we know what we're dealing with."

"What we're dealing with?" I asked.

"Someone killed Vanessa. One of us saw something. Heard something."

"Or did something," Olivia said. Quiet.

Everyone looked at her.

"I'm just saying. We all know each other. And Vanessa—" She stopped. "Vanessa had issues with people."

"What issues?" Troy asked.

"Old stuff. College stuff." Olivia pulled her cardigan tighter. "She'd been texting us all week. Said we needed to talk. That it was time."

"Time for what?" Troy said.

Derek turned from the window. "The winter formal. She kept bringing it up."

Marcus's expression hardened. "There's nothing to talk about."

"She thought there was," Derek said.

Marcus's hands came up in a quick defense. "Vanessa made things up. She always did."

I stared at the bowl of peppermint candies on the coffee table. Red and white stripes. Someone had put them out as decoration. They sat there, wrong.

"What happened at the winter formal?" Troy asked.

Silence.

Olivia took a deep breath and let it out with a sigh. "Someone got hurt. A girl. She fell down some stairs outside the venue."

"Was she okay?" Troy's voice was calm. Curious.

"She said she was. We helped her up. She went home." Olivia looked at her hands. "But Julia and the girl had been arguing right before it happened."

Everyone turned to me.

"I don't remember that," I said.

Marcus laughed. No humor in it. "Of course you don't."

I gave him a side glance. "What's that supposed to mean?"

Marcus shook his head, disbelief tightening his features. "You were drunk, Julia. Wasted. You said things."

"What things?" I shot back.

It was Olivia who answered.

"You told the girl she was pathetic. That people only talked to her out of pity." Olivia's voice got quieter. "You were cruel."

My throat closed. I tried to remember. Fragments came—crowded room, music too loud, someone crying. But the details wouldn't stick. Just shapes. Just noise.

"I don't remember saying that."

"You did," Marcus said. "I heard it."

"The girl ran out," Derek added. "She was crying. Then we heard the crash. She'd fallen. Down the exterior stairs."

"And?" Troy asked.

"And we helped her up. Asked if she was okay. She said yes. So we all left."

Troy leaned forward slightly. "Who was she?"

More silence.

Then Derek: "I think she was related to Vanessa. Sister maybe. I'm not sure."

"Vanessa had a sister?" Troy asked.

"A brother," Olivia said. "Ryan. He died years ago. Car accident."

Troy sighed, shaking his head. "Did she have a sister too?"

"I don't know," Olivia said. "Vanessa didn't talk about her family much."

The fire popped. We all looked at it. Just wood. Just heat.

But it felt like something was watching us.

Derek rubbed his face. "Vanessa said something at dinner last night. About Ryan. About finally getting justice for him."

Marcus frowned. "What does that mean?"

"I don't know. She wouldn't explain."

"Ryan died in a car accident six years ago," Olivia said. "What does that have to do with anything?"

No one answered.

Troy sat back. "I wasn't there at your formal. So, I can't say what happened. But people remember things differently when guilt's involved."

I looked at him. "What's that supposed to mean?"

"Just an observation. Memory's unreliable under stress."

"I'm not stressed about something I don't remember doing."

"Maybe that's the stress. Not remembering."

My hands started to shake. I shoved them in my pockets.

"Julia found the body," Olivia said. Like she'd been thinking about it this whole time. "She was the first one out there."

"I saw her from the window," I said.

"You were already awake. Already dressed."

"I couldn't sleep."

Olivia cocked her head. "Convenient." Her voice trembled. "And your ornament was next to her body."

"I don't know how it got there. It was in my bag."

"Was it?"

"Yes. I packed it. I didn't take it out."

Marcus tapped a finger on his chin. "You and Vanessa had a falling out. Years ago."

"Over a guy she dated after we stopped being close. That was five years ago."

"But you were angry about it."

"Not angry enough to kill her!"

"I'm not saying you did." Marcus backtracked. "I'm just noting. You have history. Your ornament was at the scene. You found her." He paused. "And you don't remember the winter formal. Don't remember what you said to that girl."

"Because I was drunk. People don't remember things when they're drunk."

"Or people block out things they don't want to remember," Troy said. Soft. Almost gentle.

The room tilted. I grabbed the arm of the chair to steady myself.

The smell hit me then. Faint. Floral. Lavender.

Vanessa's perfume.

But Vanessa was outside. Dead in the snow.

The pipes dripped somewhere deeper in the cabin. The wood groaned like the whole structure shifted. The playlist switched tracks—some instrumental thing. Jingle bells. Piano. Christmas music.

Then it cut off.

No one had touched the speaker.

"Did anyone else—" I started.

"What?" Marcus asked.

"The music. It just—"

"Changed tracks. So what?"

I heard my name. Whispered from somewhere in the room.

Julia.

I spun. Looked at each of them. "Someone just said my name."

They stared at me.

"No one said anything," Derek said.

"I heard it."

"You're hearing things," Marcus said. Not mean. Just tired. "We're all stressed."

A sudden gust of wind pushed against the cabin.

The landline gave a single, harsh ring.

We all turned toward it.

Marus stepped over, lifted the receiver like it might bite, and pressed it to his ear.

His eyes flicked around the room.

He lowered the phone.

"Landline's dead."

A chill swept through me. I stood. Needed to move.

I walked to the kitchen for my scarf. It wasn't with my jacket.

Instead, a notepad sat beside the coffee maker—*Pine Ridge Chalet* printed across the top. A pen rested next to it.

I picked up the pen. My hand moved without thinking.

Stay awake.

I stared at the words. They felt wrong. Like someone else wrote them.

I crossed them out. Heavy black lines.

Wrote underneath:

Don't trust them.

The pen felt heavier.

Behind me, voices kept going—low, sharp, arguing over memory. Over the formal. Over the lies.

But I stood in the kitchen.

Alone.

Chapter 4

Marcus In The Snow

The afternoon dragged. We sat in the great room and didn't talk. Just stared at the fire. At the windows. At anything but each other.

The storm had lightened. Wind still pushed against the cabin, but the worst had passed. Snow fell steady instead of sideways. Through the window, I could see shapes now. Trees. The driveway. The place where Vanessa's body lay.

Someone had thrown a tarp over her. Marcus, probably. Couldn't leave her completely exposed.

My stomach turned.

Derek stood by the window with his camera. He'd taken it off at some point. Just held it now. Olivia sat on the couch, cardigan pulled tight, stared at nothing. Troy made coffee in the kitchen. The smell filled the cabin—normal, wrong.

Marcus paced. He'd been pacing for an hour. Phone in hand, even though it was useless. No service. No way out.

"We need supplies," he said finally. "If we're stuck here another day, we need to check what we have."

"There's food," Olivia said. Almost a whisper.

"I'm talking about the generator. Gas. In case power goes out." He grabbed his coat from the hook. "There's a shed around back. I'm going to check it."

"I'll come," Derek offered.

"No. Stay inside. One person goes missing, it's carelessness. Two, it's a pattern." Marcus zipped his coat. "I'll be ten minutes."

He left before anyone could argue.

The door closed. We sat in silence.

Troy brought coffee to Olivia. Set the mug in her hands. She didn't drink. Just held it.

"He shouldn't go alone," she said.

"He'll be fine." Troy sat next to her. "It's just the shed."

I walked to the kitchen. Found the notepad where I'd written earlier. The words still there. *Don't trust them.* I tore the page off. Folded it. Shoved it in my pocket.

Fifteen minutes passed.

Twenty.

Derek looked at his watch. "He said ten minutes."

"Give him time," Troy said.

Twenty-five minutes.

Derek grabbed his coat. "I'm checking on him."

This time no one argued.

Derek went out. The door stayed open. Cold poured in. I watched him trudge through the snow toward the back of the cabin. He disappeared around the corner.

Then I heard it. Faint. Muffled by wind and distance.

Derek shouting.

Troy was up first. Grabbed his coat. I grabbed mine. Olivia stayed on the couch, frozen.

We ran outside. The cold hit hard. My boots sank into snow. I followed Troy around the corner of the cabin.

Derek stood twenty feet out. Bent over something.

Not something. Someone.

Marcus.

I reached them. Dropped to my knees.

Marcus lay face-up this time. Eyes open. Stared at the gray sky. Blood pooled under his head. Dark. Fresh. The snow around him already turned pink.

Blunt force trauma. Back of his head. Same as Vanessa.

"No." The word came out small.

Derek backed away. His face white. "I found him. I just—he was just here."

Troy crouched next to Marcus. Checked his pulse. Shook his head.

"How long?" I asked.

"Not long. He's still—" Troy stopped. "Minutes, maybe."

Which meant whoever did this was close. Could still be here.

I looked around. Saw the shed. Door open. Tools scattered. A shovel in the snow. Marcus had made it there. Started to search. Then someone hit him from behind.

I stood. Scanned the tree line. Nothing moved. Just snow and shadows and wind.

Then I saw it. In Marcus's hand. Clenched tight. Fabric. Dark blue. My scarf.

The one I'd lost. The one I couldn't remember taking off.

"That's yours," Derek said. Looked at me.

"I don't—I don't know how it got there."

"You don't know?" His voice flat.

"I lost it yesterday. I thought—I don't know where I put it."

Troy stood. "We need to get inside. Now."

Nobody moved.

"Julia was the last one in the kitchen," Derek said. "Before Marcus left."

"I was making coffee."

"So was I," Troy said. "We were both there."

Derek looked between us. Then at the scarf in Marcus's hand. "He's holding it. Like he grabbed it from someone."

"I wasn't out here!"

"You don't remember where your scarf went. You don't remember the winter formal. You don't remember—"

"Stop." Troy's voice cut through. Calm but firm. "We're all scared. Turning on each other won't help."

"Two people are dead," Derek said. "And Julia's things keep showing up next to the bodies."

My throat closed. I couldn't breathe right.

Troy moved toward Marcus's body. "We should check him. See if there's anything else."

"Don't touch—" Derek started.

"Evidence. I know." Troy knelt carefully. "But police won't be here until tomorrow. And whoever did this might do it again. We need to know what we're dealing with."

He checked Marcus's pockets. Methodical. Careful. Pulled out a phone—dead. Keys. Wallet.

Then a folded piece of paper.

Troy opened it. Read it. His expression didn't change, but something shifted in his eyes. Quick. Then gone.

"What is it?" I asked.

"Nothing. Just—" He folded it again. Put it in his own pocket. "Old receipt."

"Let me see it."

"It's not important."

"Then why did you take it?"

Troy stood. "Because Marcus is dead and I'm not leaving evidence in the snow for animals to destroy."

The answer sounded reasonable. But something about the way he moved—the speed he'd pocketed that paper—felt wrong.

Derek grabbed Marcus under the arms. "Help me get him inside."

Troy took the legs. They lifted. Carried him toward the cabin. I followed.

Olivia stood in the doorway. Saw Marcus's body. Made a sound like something broke inside her.

They brought him in. Laid him on the floor on the opposite side of the fireplace. Found another tarp. Covered him.

Two bodies now. Two tarps.

The Christmas tree stood in the corner. Still dark. Still wrong. The garland on the mantel had come completely loose on one side. Hung crooked. No one fixed it.

Derek turned to me. "Where were you when Marcus left?"

"Here. In the kitchen."

"Alone?"

"Troy was there too."

"For how long?"

"I don't know. Ten minutes? Fifteen?"

"And then?"

"He brought coffee to Olivia. I stayed in the kitchen."

Derek looked at Troy. "You saw her the whole time?"

"Most of the time."

"Most?"

"I was focused on making coffee. Not watching Julia."

"So she could've gone outside."

"I would've heard the door," Troy said.

"Would you?" Derek's voice rose. "Would you really? With the wind? The storm?"

"I don't know. Probably."

"Probably isn't good enough." Derek faced me. "Your ornament next to Vanessa. Your scarf in Marcus's hand. You found Vanessa first. You were in the kitchen before Marcus went out." He stopped. "You don't have an alibi for either death."

My jaw tightened, then unlocked. "Neither do you."

"I was in my room. Editing photos. Both times."

"Can you prove that?"

Derek tilted his head. "Can *you* prove that?"

Troy stepped between us. "Stop. Both of you. This isn't helping. Two people are dead."

"I know. And she—"

"Enough." Troy's voice harder now. "We're all suspects. All of us. Fighting won't change that."

Olivia stood. Walked to the window. Stared out at the gray afternoon. "Who's next?" Her voice barely audible. "Which one of us is next?"

No one answered.

I looked at Troy. He'd moved away. Stood near the fire. One hand in his pocket. The pocket where he'd put that paper.

What had it said? Why had he taken it so fast?

And why had he looked relieved—just for a second—like he'd found something he'd been searching for?

Chapter 5

The Stairwell

Evening came early. The sky darkened to charcoal. Snow still fell, but lighter now. Soft flakes instead of the violent sideways assault from this morning.

Four of us left.

We sat in the great room. Didn't talk much. Just existed in the same space because being alone felt worse.

The fire burned low.

Derek stepped toward the hearth. Troy joined him, the space between them tight and hot. Their conversation scraped along—thin, brittle, brief. Troy set a log on the grate and drifted back to Olivia.

I wondered what transpired between the two men.

Derek added another. Sparks lifted, hung a moment, died.

The Christmas tree leaned in the corner, dark.

Someone had tried to fix the garland on the mantel and quit halfway. It sagged. Wrong.

Troy and Olivia remained on the couch. His arm around her shoulders.

She folded into him. Small. Breakable.

Her cardigan remained buttoned out of order.

I stood by the window. Watched the gray nothing outside. Thought about Marcus under that tarp. About Vanessa in the snow. About my scarf in Marcus's hand.

I didn't kill them.

But Derek's words circled in my head. *Your things keep showing up next to the bodies.*

"I need my backup battery," Derek said. Broke the silence. "Camera's dying."

"Where is it?" Troy asked.

"Upstairs. In my room."

"I'll come with you," I said. Needed to move. Needed to be away from Troy's steady gaze and Olivia's quiet crying.

Derek nodded. We headed for the stairs.

A single strand of white lights wrapped around the stairwell railing. Someone had plugged them in earlier—Marcus probably. They gave off weak light. Barely enough to see by. The wood steps creaked under our feet.

Halfway up, Derek stopped. Turned to look at me.

"I don't think you did it," he said. Voice low.

"Then why—"

"Because Marcus is scared. Was scared." He corrected himself. "When Marcus got scared, he attacked. Blamed someone. Made them the enemy so he didn't have to think about the real threat."

"And the real threat is?"

Derek glanced back toward the living room. Made sure we were alone. "I don't know. But I've been thinking about that article Marcus had."

"What article?"

"The one from his pocket. Hartford Courant. About someone dying in a bar."

"Troy said it was a receipt."

"It wasn't. I saw it before he folded it. Newspaper clipping. Headline about a death." Derek rubbed his face. "And the date. December 2018."

Memory scraped the inside of my skull. "Same date Vanessa's brother died."

"Yeah."

"Ryan died in a car accident."

Derek looked at me. "Did he? Or is that just what Vanessa told us?"

The words hung between us. Heavy. "Why would she lie?"

"I don't know. But she mentioned him last night. Said something about getting justice. You don't get justice for a car accident." He paused. "And why would Marcus have an article about a bar death from 2018?"

"Maybe it wasn't related."

"Maybe." Derek didn't sound convinced. "But Troy took it. Fast. Like he didn't want us to see it."

"You think Troy—"

"I don't know what I think. But something's wrong. And whatever Marcus found, it got him killed."

Derek turned. Started up the rest of the stairs. I followed two steps behind.

He reached the landing. Turned toward his room.

That's when I saw it.

Behind him. In the shadows where the stairwell light didn't reach. A silhouette.

Tall enough. Could be a person. Could be darkness rearranged into a shape my brain interpreted as human.

"Derek—"

He turned back. "What?"

The figure moved. Or I thought it moved.

Derek's foot caught something. The edge of the top stair. A loose board. His arms went wide.

He grabbed for the railing.

Found air.

Silence. Complete. Horrible.

Then the sound. Wood splintering. Or bone. I couldn't tell.

Derek fell. Backward. Down. His body hit the stairs. Once. Twice. Rolling. Limbs at wrong angles.

The ornament on the small shelf near the landing rattled. Vibration from the impact. Glass against wood. High-pitched.

He stopped at the bottom. Face-down. Didn't move.

"Derek!" I ran down. Dropped beside him.

Blood pooled under his face. Spread across the floorboards. His neck bent at an angle that made my stomach clench.

I grabbed his shoulder. "Derek. Derek, please."

No response.

I pressed fingers to his neck. Searched for a pulse. Found nothing.

Footsteps behind me. Fast.

Troy appeared from the living room. Saw Derek. Stopped. "What happened?" His chest rose and fell.

"He slipped. He was pushed." Reality pixelated at the corners. "I saw —there was someone—" My words came out broken.

Troy's eyes widened. "Someone what?"

"Behind him. On the landing. I saw someone."

Troy pushed past me. Took the stairs two at a time. Reached the landing. Looked around.

"There's no one here."

"There was. I saw them."

He turned. Scanned the space. The hallway. The bedrooms. "All the doors are closed. No one's here."

"I saw them."

Troy came back down. Carefully. One hand on the railing. He crouched next to Derek. Checked for a pulse like I had.

Nothing.

"He's gone," Troy said.

Olivia appeared. Her eyes landed on Derek's body. A thin, broken noise slipped out, and her hand clamped over her mouth. Her breath came fast and jagged.

"I saw someone," I said again. "Behind him. A figure."

"What did they look like?" Troy asked. Calm. Too calm.

"I don't know. Tall. Dark. I couldn't—the lighting was bad."

"Man or woman?"

"I don't know."

Troy stood. "Could you have imagined it? The stress, the fear—"

"I didn't imagine it."

But doubt crept in. Had I seen someone? Or just shadows? The lights on the railing had flickered right before Derek fell. Changed the way darkness moved. Made shapes seem solid when they weren't.

"I'm checking upstairs," Troy said. "Stay here."

He climbed again. Disappeared into the hallway. I heard doors open. Close. His footsteps moved from room to room.

Olivia stayed in the doorway. Stared at Derek's body. Tears on her face. Her breathing calmer.

From the bottom of the stairs, something caught on the landing—a smudge, a disturbance in the dust.

I climbed until I could see it clearly. Footprints.

Small. Too small for Derek. Too small for Troy or Marcus.

My size. Or Vanessa's. Or Olivia's. I came down.

Troy returned. "No one. All the rooms are empty."

"There are footprints. On the landing."

He went back up. Looked. "Could be anyone's. We've all been up and down these stairs."

"But—"

"Julia." His voice gentle. Careful. "You're in shock. You just watched your friend die. Sometimes our brain fills in details that aren't there. Tries to make sense of something senseless."

"I know what I saw."

"Do you?"

He came down again. Stood in front of me.

"Or do you know what you *think* you saw?"

I couldn't answer.

Olivia moved closer to Derek's body. Looked down at him. "Who's doing this?" Her voice small, broken. "Why?"

"I don't know," Troy said. He put his arm around her. Guided her back to the living room. "But we're staying together from now on. No one goes anywhere alone."

I stayed with Derek. Stared at his face. Blood still seeped. Slowly. His camera had fallen when he did. It lay on the floor next to him. Lens cracked.

I thought about what he'd said. About the article. About Marcus finding something. About Troy taking it fast. Too fast.

And now Derek was dead. Derek, who'd been asking questions. Who'd connected Ryan's death to that newspaper clipping.

I stood. Looked up at the landing again.

The wall near the shelf. Just below where the ornament sat. A mark.

I climbed the stairs. Slow and deliberate.

Reached the landing. Moved to the wall.

A handprint.

Small. Palm and five fingers pressed against the white paint. Almost invisible except for the angle of the light.

I extended my hand toward it. Stopped an inch away.

Heat radiated from the wall. Warmth that shouldn't be there. Warmth that had nothing to do with the cabin's heating or anything explainable.

Someone had touched this wall not too long ago.

Someone with small hands.

I heard it then. Faint. Through the vents. High-pitched.

Laughter.

Could've been wind through pipes. Could've been my imagination. Could've been—

"Julia?" Troy called from downstairs. "Are you okay?"

"Yeah," I called back. Voice shook. "I'm coming."

I looked down the hallway. All the doors closed. All the rooms supposedly empty.

But someone had been up here. Someone had stood behind Derek. Someone had left a warm handprint on this wall.

Someone was still in this cabin.

Here.

Chapter 6

The Evidence Box

S unday morning. Dawn came gray and quiet. The storm had stopped.

I woke on the couch. Didn't remember falling asleep. My neck ached. The fire had died to ash. Someone had covered me with a blanket—probably Olivia.

The cabin felt different. Lighter. Smelled of coffee. The oppressive weight of the storm had lifted. Through the window, weak sunlight cut through clouds. The snow had stopped falling.

Roads would be cleared today. Police would come. This would be over.

Three of us left. Three bodies under tarps. One outside. Two inside.

I sat up. Olivia slept in the armchair, curled up, small. Troy wasn't in the room. He must have made coffee. I contemplated getting a cup.

I stood. Put on my jacket and walked to the window. The world outside looked clean. Fresh snow covered everything. Peaceful. Wrong.

Water ran upstairs. Shower. Must be Troy.

My mind went back to last night. To Derek on the stairs. To what he'd said before he fell.

I've been thinking about that article Marcus had.

The Hartford Courant. About someone dying in a bar. December 2018. Same date as Ryan's death.

Troy had taken it. Put it in his pocket. Said it was nothing.

But if it was nothing, why take it?

I looked at the couch where Troy had slept. His jacket lay draped over the arm. Dark fleece. Expensive.

The water still ran upstairs. I had time.

I moved to the jacket. Checked the doorway. Listened. Just the shower. Just wind outside. Olivia still slept.

I slipped my hand into the right pocket. Empty. Left pocket. Found something. Paper. Folded.

I pulled it out. Unfolded it carefully.

Hartford Courant. December 16, 2018.

"Man Sought in Fatal Bar Fight"

"Ryan Hart, 23, Dies After Altercation at Downtown Hartford Bar"

A shiver crawled up my spine.

I read fast. Skimmed the article.

December 15, 2018. The Brass Monkey bar. Argument between Ryan Hart and another patron. Patron—Trevor Walsh, 29—punched Hart. Hart fell. Struck head on bar edge. Died at scene. Trevor Walsh fled before police arrived. Wanted for involuntary manslaughter.

Photo below the text. Black and white. Grainy. But clear enough.

Trevor Walsh.

Same face. Same build. Same eyes.

Troy Bennett.

They were the same person.

The truth carved itself into my bones. The paper slipped from my hands. Fluttered to the floor.

I glanced at Olivia—still curled up. I picked it up. Read it again. Made sure.

No mistake. Troy was Trevor Walsh. Wanted for killing Ryan Hart.

Vanessa's brother.

The shower stopped.

I shoved the article in my pocket. Moved away from the jacket. Tried to look normal.

Footsteps upstairs. Troy moving around. Getting dressed.

I needed more. Needed proof. Needed—

Vanessa's phone.

She'd had it Friday night. Checking that chapel clock app. Where was it now?

I looked around the room. Checked the kitchen counter. The table. Nothing.

Then I remembered. Troy had gone outside Saturday morning. After we found Vanessa. He'd stayed out there longer than the rest of us. Said he was checking something.

Had he found her phone? Taken it?

I moved to his duffel bag near the stairs. Unzipped it quietly. Looked inside.

Clothes. Toiletries. A book. Nothing.

Then I felt it. Hard rectangle inside the lining. I pressed. Definitely a phone.

I found the seam. Worked it open. Pulled out a phone in a cracked case.

iPhone. Screen shattered but intact. I pressed the power button.

It turned on. Battery at 8%.

No password. Vanessa never used one. Said she had nothing to hide.

I opened her photos. Scrolled back. Found screenshots. Documents. Articles.

More Hartford Courant pieces. All about Trevor Walsh. About the manhunt. About Ryan Hart's family seeking justice.

Photos of Troy. Different angles. From Olivia's Facebook. From the wedding. From other events. All labeled: "Trevor Walsh - Confirmed."

Private investigator reports. Facial recognition analysis. 98% match.

My heart hammered.

I found the voice memos app. One recording. Friday night. Time-stamped 11:47 PM.

I played it. Volume low. Pressed against my ear.

Vanessa's voice. Clear. Close to the phone.

"Trevor Walsh. I know who you are. I know what you did."

Troy's voice. Harder than I'd ever heard it. "I don't know what you're talking about."

"The Brass Monkey. Hartford. December 15, 2018. You killed my brother."

Silence. "That was an accident."

"You punched Ryan. He fell. He died. You ran."

"He started it. I was defending—"

"You fled the scene. You're wanted for manslaughter. You changed your name. You've been hiding for six years."

"Vanessa, listen—"

"No. You listen. You took my brother from me. He was twenty-three years old. He was all I had. And you killed him over nothing."

"It wasn't—wait, are you recording this?"

Sound of struggle. Phone hitting something. Audio cut out.

I stared at the screen.

Troy killed Ryan. Vanessa had known. She'd confronted him Friday night. Recorded his confession.

And then he'd killed her.

"What are you doing?"

I spun.

Troy stood at the bottom of the stairs. Hair damp. Fresh clothes. His eyes moved from my face to the phone in my hand.

His expression changed. The mask he'd worn all weekend dropped. Something cold underneath.

"That's not yours," he said. Calm. Too calm.

"You're Trevor Walsh."

He didn't deny it. He stood there. Watched me.

"You killed Vanessa's brother. She found you. She confronted you. And you murdered her."

"It was an accident. The bar. I didn't mean—"

"You ran. You hid. You changed your name." My voice rose. "You killed Vanessa because she was going to expose you."

"She was recording me. She was going to ruin everything." He moved closer. Slow. "I built a life here. With Olivia. I couldn't let Vanessa destroy that."

"So you killed her."

"I protected what was mine."

"And Marcus?"

"Marcus found that article in Vanessa's room. He would've figured it out."

Troy's voice stayed level. Reasonable. "I couldn't let him tell you. Couldn't let him call the police."

"What about Derek?"

Troy hesitated. Just a fraction of a second. "Derek was asking questions. Getting close to the truth."

But something in his voice wavered. Like he wasn't sure. Like he was claiming credit for something he hadn't done.

"You framed me. My scarf. My ornament."

"You were convenient. Everyone already suspected you. The winter formal story. Your memory problems. It was easy to point them toward you."

"You pushed Derek. How did you get upstairs before us? Without me seeing you?"

"The back stairs. Near the kitchen. Heard everything you two said. He was getting too close to the truth. Told me right before he went upstairs. Said he was going to look for that article." Troy shook his head. "I couldn't let him do that."

But something nagged at me. He was lying. Had to be. I pushed the thought away. Not now. My hands shook.

"Give me the phone, Julia."

I gripped the phone tighter.

"No."

"I can't let you keep it."

"The police—"

"Won't get here for hours. Roads are still bad. We have time." He moved another step closer. "Give me the phone."

Panic clawed up my throat. "Stay away from me."

Footsteps from the living room. Olivia appeared. She saw us. Saw the phone in my hand. Saw Troy's face.

Her expression didn't show surprise. Didn't show shock.

Only resignation.

"Olivia," I said. "He killed them. All of them. He's Trevor Walsh. He's wanted—"

"I know," she said. Quiet.

The words stopped me.

"You know?"

"I've always known." She walked over and stood next to Troy. "He told me. Two years ago. Before we got married."

My skin felt too tight. "He killed your friend's brother."

"It was an accident. A bar fight that went wrong." Her voice trembled but held. "Ryan threw the first punch. Troy defended himself. Ryan fell. It was terrible. But it wasn't murder."

"He fled the scene."

"Because he was scared. Because he knew no one would believe him."

"Vanessa believed he killed her brother."

"Vanessa was obsessed. She spent six years hunting Troy. Refused to accept it was an accident." Olivia's eyes filled with tears. "She threatened everything we built. Our marriage. Our life. I didn't want her to die, but—"

"But you didn't stop him."

She didn't answer.

Troy held out his hand. "The phone, Julia."

"No."

"I don't want to hurt you. But I will if I have to."

"Like you hurt Vanessa? Marcus? Derek?"

"This is different. They knew too much. But you—you can still walk away. Give me the phone. Say you found nothing. When the police come, we tell them someone else was here. An intruder. You saw them on the landing."

"They'll know that's a lie."

"Will they? Everyone already thinks you're unstable. Unreliable memory. Guilt about the winter formal. It'll be easy to make them question what you saw." He stepped closer. "Or you can die here. And Olivia and I walk out as the only survivors. Traumatized witnesses. Victims."

My back hit the wall. Nowhere left to go.

"Please," Olivia said. "Just give him the phone."

I looked at her. At the woman I'd known since college. The peace-keeper. The one who smoothed things over. Made everyone comfortable.

She'd known all along. Known what Troy was. Helped him hide. Watched him kill three people and said nothing.

"No," I said. I dug my heel into the floor.

Troy moved fast. Grabbed for the phone.

I jerked back. Ran for the kitchen.

He followed.

Chapter 7

The Kitchen

I ran for the back door. Troy caught me before I reached it.

His hand grabbed my jacket. Yanked me back. I twisted. Broke free. Stumbled into the kitchen counter.

He came at me again. Faster. Stronger.

I grabbed the coffee pot from the counter. Still warm from this morning. Swung it hard.

Hit his shoulder. Hot liquid splashed everywhere. He cursed. Stumbled back.

I dropped the pot. Reached for the knife block on the counter. Pulled one free. Eight-inch blade. Chef's knife.

Troy stopped. Stared at the knife in my hand.

"Julia." His voice calm. Controlled. "Don't do this."

"Stay away from me."

"You can't win. You know that."

"Police are coming."

"Not for hours. Roads are still bad. We have time."

He moved left. I moved right. Kept the counter between us.

"Olivia." He didn't look at her. Kept his eyes on me. "Get me something to tie her up."

Olivia stood in the doorway. Frozen. Face white.

"Olivia," Troy said again. Harder. "Now."

She didn't move.

"Help me."

Her mouth opened. Closed. No words came out.

Troy's jaw tightened. "We're in this together. You know that. If she talks, we both go to prison."

"I didn't—I didn't kill anyone."

"You helped me hide. For five years. That makes you complicit. Accessory after the fact. Harboring a fugitive." His voice stayed level. "You go down with me. Unless we stop her."

Olivia's hands shook. She looked at me. At Troy. Back to me.

I kept the knife raised. "Olivia, you don't have to do this. Help me instead. Testify against him. Tell them you were scared. They'll believe you."

"Don't listen to her," Troy said.

"He killed four people, Olivia. Four. Vanessa. Marcus. Derek. Ryan." My voice cracked. "Your friends. People you loved."

"It wasn't supposed—" Olivia stopped. Started again. "Vanessa wasn't supposed to find us. We were supposed to be safe."

"You were hiding a killer."

"He's not a killer. Ryan was an accident. The bar fight. It went wrong. Troy didn't mean—"

"He's killed three more people since then. That's not an accident. That's—"

Troy moved. Fast. Around the counter.

I slashed with the knife. Wild. Desperate.

Caught his arm. Not deep. Just enough to make him pull back. Blood seeped through his sleeve.

He looked at the cut. Then at me. Something changed in his expression. The calm cracked. Anger underneath.

"You shouldn't have done that."

He grabbed a kitchen towel. Wrapped it around his arm. Moved toward me again. Slower now. Deliberate.

I backed up. Hit the wall. Nowhere left to go.

Troy reached for the knife. Grabbed my wrist. Squeezed. Hard. Pain shot up my arm. My fingers opened. The knife clattered to the floor.

He shoved me against the wall. One hand around my throat. Not squeezing yet. Just holding. A threat.

"I didn't want this," he said. "I wanted to disappear. Live quietly. Have a normal life with Olivia." His grip tightened slightly. "But Vanessa couldn't let it go."

I couldn't breathe right. I clawed at his hand.

"Olivia," he called. Didn't look away from me. "Pick up the knife."

Silence.

"Olivia."

I heard movement. Footsteps on tile. Olivia appeared in my periphery. She bent down. Picked up the knife.

Sirens. Distant. Faint. But there.

Olivia's head snapped toward the sound. Her expression changed.

Calculation behind her eyes.

My heart hammered. This was it. She'd chosen. Chosen him over everything else.

"Good," Troy said. "Now—"

Olivia stabbed him.

Not me. Him.

The blade went into his shoulder. Deep. He gasped. Released me. Staggered back.

The knife stayed in his shoulder. Olivia pulled it free. Blood flowed. Fast. Dark.

Troy stared at her. "What—what are you doing?"

"I can't." Her voice broke. "I can't let you kill her too."

"We talked about this. We agreed. We protect each other. No matter what."

"You killed three people." Tears ran down her face. But her voice was steadier now. Almost rehearsed. "Four. That's not protection. That's not love. That's madness."

"I did it for us." He pressed his hand to his shoulder. Blood seeped between his fingers. "Everything I did was for us. To keep us safe. To keep our life."

"You made me a murderer too. By staying quiet. By helping you hide." She dropped the knife. "I can't do this anymore."

Troy slumped against the counter. The wound bled.

I grabbed my phone from my pocket. Checked the signal.

Two bars.

Service. Finally.

I dialed 911. Hit call. It rang.

"911, what's your emergency?"

"Pine Ridge Chalet. Sussex County. Three people are dead. The killer—"

"Ma'am, we have your location. Officers are already en route. We received a call yesterday about a death at that address. They left Ridgemont 20 minutes ago when the roads cleared. ETA ten minutes."

"Yesterday?"

"Yes ma'am. Saturday morning. Marcus Liu called about Vanessa Hart. Stay on the line. Officers are almost there. Are you safe right now?"

"I think so."

I looked at Troy. He'd slid down to sit on the floor, back against the cabinet. Blood soaked his shirt. He stared at Olivia.

"You chose her," he whispered. "Over me."

"I chose what's right." Olivia wrapped her arms around herself. "Finally."

"After everything. After five years. After building a life together." His voice cracked. "You're throwing it away."

"You threw it away. When you killed Vanessa. When you decided hiding was more important than being honest."

"I couldn't go to prison. I'd lose you."

"You lost me the second you killed my friend."

Sirens. Distant at first. Then louder. Closer.

Red and blue lights cut through the gray morning. Flashed across the walls. The Christmas tree. The covered bodies.

Troy closed his eyes. "It's over."

"Yes," Olivia said. "It is."

The sirens stopped outside. Car doors opened. Boots on gravel. On wood. Heavy footsteps.

"Police! Anyone inside?"

"Here!" I called. "Kitchen!"

The door burst open. Officers flooded in. Guns drawn. Voices shouting. Clear the room. Hands up. Get down.

They separated us. Troy on the floor. Still bleeding. EMTs rushed in. Started treating his shoulder.

An officer took Olivia. Another took me. Led us to different rooms. Different officers.

Detective. Older woman. Sharp eyes. She introduced herself. Hazel Fairbank. Homicide.

I told her everything. Started from Friday night. Finished with the kitchen.

She listened. Took notes. Asked questions.

"Trevor Walsh," she said when I finished. "Hartford PD has been looking for him for six years."

"He killed Ryan Hart. Vanessa's brother. That's why she brought us here. She was going to record him confessing. Then turn him in."

"And instead, he killed her."

"Yes."

Fairbank nodded. Closed her notebook. "You did good surviving. That's harder than people think."

"I didn't—three of my friends are dead."

"And you're not. That matters." She stood. "We'll need a formal statement. But that can wait. Get some rest. EMTs will check you out."

She left. I sat alone in the bedroom they'd put me in.

Through the wall, I heard Olivia crying. Deep sobs. The kind that hurt.

I heard Troy's voice. Calm even now. Talking to officers. Explaining. Spinning his story.

And I heard Fairbank on the phone with someone. Hartford PD probably. Telling them they'd found Trevor Walsh.

My mind drifted to downstairs. The Christmas tree still stood dark. The garland still hung crooked. The peppermint candies still sat untouched.

But the storm had passed. The police had come. It was over.

Chapter 8

Arrested

The cabin filled with police. Crime scene techs in white suits. Photographers. Evidence markers. The organized chaos of an investigation.

I sat on the couch, wrapped in a blanket an EMT had given me. Watched them work. Tag. Photograph. Measure. Turn our nightmare into documentation.

Detective Fairbank moved through the space like she owned it. Directed her team. Asked questions. Took notes. She was methodical. Thorough. Nothing got past her.

Troy sat in the kitchen under guard. Two officers flanked him. EMTs had bandaged his shoulder. He'd stopped bleeding. Started talking instead.

"I need to make a statement," he called out. "About what really happened."

Fairbank looked at him. Walked over. "I'm listening."

"Olivia did this. All of it." His voice steady. Controlled. "She killed Vanessa. She killed Marcus and Derek. I tried to stop her but—"

"That's not true!" Olivia stood from where she'd been sitting near the fireplace. Face red from crying. "He's lying. He killed them. He's Trevor Walsh. He's wanted—"

"Olivia found out about Hartford," Troy continued. Talked over her. "About Ryan Hart. She became obsessed. Paranoid. She thought Vanessa was going to destroy our marriage. So she killed her Friday night. Then covered it up. Killed the others when they got suspicious."

Fairbank's expression didn't change. "And the wound on your shoulder?"

"She attacked me. When I confronted her. When I told her I was going to tell you the truth."

"He's lying," I said. Stood up. Walked toward them. "I have proof. Vanessa's phone. It has a recording of Troy—Trevor—confessing to killing Ryan Hart."

Fairbank held out her hand. "May I?"

I pulled the phone from my pocket. Handed it over.

She pressed play. Vanessa's voice filled the kitchen. Clear. Damning.

"Trevor Walsh. I know who you are. I know what you did."

Troy's response. *"That was an accident."*

The confession. The struggle. The audio cutting out.

Fairbank stopped the recording. Looked at Troy. "Sounds like you confessed to manslaughter. Not Olivia."

"She recorded that. Edited it. Made it sound—"

"Friday night. Timestamp says 11:47 PM. That's when Vanessa died." Fairbank put the phone in a clear plastic evidence bag. "This is evidence of you admitting to killing Ryan Hart. And of Vanessa confronting you right before her death."

Troy's mask finally cracked. "It was an accident. The bar. Ryan threw the first punch. I defended myself. He fell. I didn't mean—"

"But you fled."

"I was scared."

"And changed your name. Built a false identity. Married under that false identity." She pulled out her own phone. Showed him a photo. "Hartford PD sent this. Trevor Walsh. 2018 arrest photo. That's you."

He didn't deny it. Just stared at the floor.

"Where's the weapon?" Fairbank asked her team.

A tech called from the shed. "Got it. Tree branch. Blood on one end. Prints on the other."

"Bag it. Run the prints."

They brought it in. Heavy branch. Dark stains on the thick end. Fairbank examined it without touching.

"We'll need your prints," she said to Troy. "For comparison."

"You won't find them."

"We will. You can't clean blood from wood grain. We can get your DNA." She looked at him. "But let's say we don't find yours. We have the recording. We have you admitting to being Trevor Walsh. We have Hartford's warrant. We have three bodies with matching wounds."

"Circumstantial."

"Maybe. But we also have this." She held up an evidence bag. The Hartford Courant article. "Found in your jacket pocket. Article about Ryan Hart's death. About Trevor Walsh fleeing. Why would you have this unless you're Trevor Walsh?"

Troy said nothing.

"Here's what I think happened," Detective Fairbank said. "Vanessa Hart spent six years looking for you. Found you through social media. Recognized you in wedding photos. Spent 2024 gathering evidence. Tried to go to Hartford PD in January. They said they needed more proof. So she gathered it. Fingerprints. Photos. Background checks. Built a case."

Troy's jaw tightened.

"She planned this weekend to record you confessing. Get it on tape. Then turn you in. She had friends here for safety. For witnesses." Fairbank walked closer to him. "But you figured it out. She confronted you Friday night. Started recording. You realized what she was doing. You lured her outside. Took the phone. Hit her with that branch. Made it look like she went out in the storm."

"That's speculation."

"Is it? Because we also have Julia's testimony. She heard Vanessa mention getting justice for Ryan Friday night. Heard you confess just now on that recording. Watched you try to kill her to keep her quiet." Fairbank crossed her arms. "And we'll find more. We always do. Blood in your clothes. Fibers on the branch."

"I want a lawyer."

"Smart choice." She gestured to the officers. "Trevor Walsh, you're under arrest for the murders of Vanessa Hart and Marcus Liu. And for the 2018 involuntary manslaughter of Ryan Hart."

I noticed she didn't mention Derek.

They read him his rights. Cuffed him. He didn't resist. He stared at Olivia as they led him toward the door.

"Liv," he said. Quiet. "Tell them. Tell them it was an accident. That I'm not—"

"You're a murderer," she whispered. "I can't save you from that."

They took him out. Red and blue lights still flashed outside. An ambulance waited.

Fairbank turned to Olivia.

"We need to talk."

Chapter 9

The Truth

Olivia nodded. Sat down. Pulled her cardigan tight. Tears still wet on her face.

Fairbank took a seat across from her. Pulled out her notebook.

"How long did you know?" she asked.

"That he was Trevor Walsh? Two years. He told me before we got married." Olivia's voice shook. "He said it was an accident. That Ryan started the fight."

"And you helped him hide."

"I was in love. I got him fake documents. Fake social security number. Vouched for him to everyone." She looked at her hands. "I loved him. I thought... I thought we could just live quietly. That no one would ever find us."

"Did you know he killed Vanessa?"

"Not until Saturday morning. When they found Marcus, I started to suspect. But I didn't want to believe it." Fresh tears ran down her face. "I was terrified. He said if I told anyone, he'd kill me too."

Fairbank's expression softened slightly. "You did the right thing in the end. Stopping him. Stabbing him when he tried to kill Julia."

Olivia nodded. Wiped her eyes.

"But, walk me through the timeline. I need to get everything straight." Fairbank opened her notebook. "Saturday evening. When Derek Liu died. Where were you?"

Olivia's hands stilled on her lap. Just for a second. "Downstairs. In the living room. With Troy."

"The whole time?"

"Yes."

"And Julia and Derek went upstairs when?"

"Around six. Six-thirty maybe."

Fairbank turned to me. "Julia, when you and Derek went upstairs, where were Troy and Olivia?"

"In the living room," I said. "On the couch. Together."

"And after Derek fell, who appeared first?"

"Troy. He came from the living room. Immediately."

"How long after the fall?"

"Seconds. Maybe ten seconds."

Fairbank nodded. Turned back to Olivia. "And where were you when Troy ran to help?"

Silence.

"Olivia?"

"I was in the living room."

"Then why didn't you come out at the same time?" Fairbank's voice stayed calm. "Troy appeared from the living room immediately. You appeared from the hallway. The one that leads to the back stairs."

Olivia's breathing changed. "I had gone to the bathroom. That's why I wasn't right there."

"Which bathroom?"

"Downstairs. The small one near the kitchen."

"That's interesting." Fairbank flipped a page. "Because Julia says you appeared from the hallway that connects to the back stairs. Not from the direction of that bathroom."

"I was confused. Everything happened so fast."

"My team found footprints on the landing upstairs. In the dust. Small. Size seven shoe." Fairbank looked up. "What size do you wear, Olivia?"

Silence.

"Seven. But—"

"Julia wears eight. Vanessa wore eight and a half." Fairbank's pen hovered over paper. "The only person in this cabin who wears size seven is you."

"I went upstairs earlier. The footprints could be from any time."

"These were fresh. Positioned right behind where Derek was standing when he fell." Fairbank closed her notebook. "We also found fibers. Wool blend. Cream colored. On Derek's clothing. Same as your cardigan."

Olivia's face went pale.

"And there's a handprint on the wall. Small hand. Your size."

"I was in the living room with Troy—"

"No. You weren't." Fairbank stood. "Troy was in the living room. He appeared from there immediately. But you weren't with him. You appeared separately. From the hallway that connects to the back stairs."

"I was in the bathroom—"

"That bathroom doesn't connect to that hallway. You'd have come from the opposite direction." Fairbank moved closer. "You weren't in any bathroom. You were upstairs."

Olivia said nothing.

"You used the back stairs while Julia and Derek took the main stairs. You heard Derek say he was going to search the rooms. Find evidence about Troy. And you couldn't let that happen. So you got upstairs first. Waited on the landing. And when Derek reached the top, you pushed him."

"No."

Fairbank continued. "The footprints placed you there. The fibers prove contact. The handprint proves you were there within minutes of his death." Fairbank's voice hardened. "And Troy's presence in the living room clears him. He couldn't have been in two places at once."

Understanding arrived like a fist. A scream built in my chest. "You pushed Derek."

Tears ran down Olivia's face. Different now. Fear, not grief.

"Troy killed him. He said he did."

Fairbank sat down. "He lied. Took credit to protect you. Evidence doesn't lie."

Olivia's mask cracked. Something cold underneath.

"Derek was going to ruin everything," she said. Voice flat. "He was going to find that article. Expose Troy. I'd lose everything."

"So you killed him."

"I pushed. He fell." No emotion. "It was necessary."

Grief opened a door I couldn't close. "He was your friend."

Fairbank raised her hand to silence me. She pulled out an evidence bag. The kitchen knife.

"And then you heard the sirens. Police were coming because Marcus called 911 Saturday morning. It was logged. As soon as roads cleared, officers were dispatched." She set the bag on the table. "You heard those sirens and realized Troy might tell us what you'd done. So you stabbed him."

"To stop him from killing Julia—"

"No." Fairbank raised the bag. "You weren't trying to wound him. You were trying to kill him."

Olivia stared at the knife.

"You aimed for the heart." Fairbank's voice went cold. "You tried to murder your husband so he couldn't tell us you killed Derek."

Silence.

"He deserved it," Olivia whispered. "For Ryan. For Vanessa. For making me live a lie."

"Maybe he deserved prison. But you're not judge, jury, and executioner." Fairbank leaned forward. "You murdered Derek. Then attempted to murder Troy. That's who you are."

Olivia said nothing.

Fairbank gestured to the officers. "Olivia Bennett, you're under arrest for the murder of Derek Liu and the attempted murder of Troy Bennett."

They read her rights. Cuffed her.

As they led her past me, her face was blank. Empty.

Just nothing.

I stood. Walked to Fairbank. The horror sank its teeth in.

"Amongst us, she was always the peacemaker," I said. "She killed Derek."

"Yes. Two killers. Different victims." Fairbank put her notebook away. "Troy killed Vanessa, Marcus, and Ryan. Olivia killed Derek and attempted to kill Troy. Both going to prison for life."

The coroner arrived. Removed the bodies. Vanessa. Marcus. Derek.

Three people dead. Two killers caught.

Fairbank touched my shoulder. "You did good. Surviving. Getting that recording. Without you and Marcus, we might never have caught them."

I sat back down. The Christmas tree still dark. The garland still crooked. The peppermint candies untouched.

But the bodies were gone. Both killers in custody. The truth out.

It was over.

Justice.

Chapter 10

Forward

Christmas Eve came quiet.

I'd been home for a week. Spent most of it sleeping. Or trying to. The nightmares came every night. Derek falling. Vanessa's face in the snow. Troy's hand around my throat. Olivia's blank expression as they led her away in cuffs.

That one haunted me most.

Dr. Morrison at St. Mary's said that was normal. Trauma took time. The betrayal would take longer. "You trusted her," she said. "The peacemaker. The one who made everyone comfortable. And she pushed your friend down the stairs."

I hadn't cried when she said it. Just nodded. Still couldn't process it.

Father O'Sullivan had called on Tuesday. Asked if I wanted to come to midnight mass. Said it might help. Community. Ritual. Something bigger than myself.

Christmas was the farthest thing from my mind. And I hadn't been to church in years.

I went

St. Mary's sat on Ridge Road. Small stone building. White lights wrapped around the entrance. Real pine garland on the doors. Inside smelled like beeswax candles and evergreen.

Families filled the pews. Parents with children. Elderly couples. Teenagers on phones. Normal people having a normal Christmas Eve.

I sat in the back. Alone.

The choir sang "Silent Night." Made my throat tight.

Father O'Sullivan gave the homily. Talked about darkness and light. About evil wearing familiar faces. About how betrayal cuts deeper than violence.

"Sometimes the greatest danger comes not from strangers," he said, "but from those we trust most. Those who sit at our table. Those who smile and smooth things over. Those who make us feel safe while hiding daggers."

He wasn't talking about me specifically. But it felt like he was.

After the service, he found me.

"Julia." He sat next to me. "I'm glad you came."

"I didn't know where else to go."

"Church is good for that."

We sat in silence. The building emptied around us.

"Vanessa was brave," he said finally. "Six years seeking justice for her brother. That takes courage."

"She died for it."

"She died making sure Ryan's killer faced consequences." He paused. "But the hardest part isn't Trevor Walsh, is it? It's Olivia."

I looked at him.

"She was your friend," he continued. "You trusted her. Thought you knew her. And then you discovered she was capable of murder. That's a different kind of loss."

My voice came out small. "How did I not see it?"

"Because she was good at hiding. Because she'd practiced being the peacemaker, the one who made everyone comfortable. That was her mask." He touched my shoulder gently. "You're not responsible for seeing through it. She fooled everyone. Even Trevor didn't know she'd killed Derek until the end."

"She killed Derek to protect Trevor. Then tried to kill Trevor to protect herself."

"She did. That's who she was. Not the person you thought you knew, but who she actually was when everything fell apart." He stood. "Honor Marcus and Derek by remembering they were trying to help. Honor Vanessa by remembering she sought justice. And honor yourself by not carrying their killers' sins. Trevor's and Olivia's. Both."

He left me there.

I walked home through Ridgemont. Snow crunched under my boots. Christmas lights glowed on every house.

I passed the plaza. Vanessa's real estate office sat dark. Memorial flowers and candles covered the doorway. Photos. Vanessa smiling in all of them.

I passed Derek's photography studio. Closed. A sign in window: "In Memoriam - Derek Liu, 1991-2024."

No memorial for Marcus yet. But Jenna would plan something. She'd called yesterday.

When I got home, I found a package on my doorstep. Postmark from Hartford.

Inside: a framed photo. Vanessa and a young man. Both smiling. Arms around each other. Thanksgiving 2018. Before.

The young man had Vanessa's eyes. Ryan.

A note fell out.

Ms. Reynolds—I'm Amanda, Ryan's girlfriend. Vanessa contacted me two years ago when she started looking for Trevor. She told me if anything happened to her, to send you this photo. She wanted you to know who Ryan was. Not just the victim. But the person. The brother she loved. Thank you for helping get justice. —Amanda Court

I stared at it. Ryan had been twenty-three. Wanted to be a teacher. Had a girlfriend who loved him. Had a sister who raised him.

Trevor Walsh took all of that. Over a bar fight. A single punch.

Then he took Vanessa. Then Marcus.

And Olivia—gentle Olivia, who made everyone tea and smoothed over arguments—took Derek. Pushed him to protect Trevor. Then tried to murder Trevor when it served her better.

Two killers. Two friends who became monsters.

Christmas morning came gray and cold. I woke on the couch. Safer than the bedroom.

I made coffee. Stood at the window. Watched Ridgemont wake up.

Children played in snow. Families walked to church. Life continued.

My phone rang.

"Julia? It's Jenna Liu. Marcus's sister."

My chest tightened. "Hi."

"I wanted to thank you." Her voice cracked. "For surviving. For making sure they didn't get away with it. Either of them."

"I didn't—"

"You did. Trevor for Marcus. Olivia for Derek. Both in prison. Both facing life sentences." She paused. "If you ever want to talk about Marcus. What he was like before. I'd like that."

"Me too."

"After New Year's?"

"Yeah."

We hung up.

I placed Ryan and Vanessa's photo on my shelf. Next to the cabin photo from Friday night. All five of us. The last time we'd been together. Before one of us became a killer.

I stared at the cabin photo. Olivia's smile. She looked normal. Happy. Human.

She and Troy murdered people.

Troy killed three. Olivia killed one and tried for two.

Both would die in prison.

I didn't know how to carry this. Didn't know how to live with the fact that I'd sat at a table with two murderers. Laughed with them. Trusted them.

One I barely knew. One I'd known for over a decade.

The stranger and the friend. Both monsters.

But I was here. Alive.

Outside, Christmas lights still glowed. Inside, I was warm. Safe.

I couldn't bring them back. Ryan, Vanessa, Marcus, Derek. Four people taken by violence. Three by Trevor. One by Olivia.

But I could live. For all of them.

For Vanessa who spent six years seeking justice.

For Ryan who never got to become a teacher.

For Marcus who tried to keep us all connected.

For Derek who defended me when everyone else suspected. Who died trying to expose the truth.

I could live fully. Fiercely.

Not defined by what Trevor and Olivia did. Not carrying their evil.

Only moving forward.

One day at a time.

Starting today.

Forward.

BOOK 6

Christmas Eve Storm

Chapter 1

Christmas Eve Shift

I was the only nurse on Ward C when the storm hit.

Six inches were already on the ground by the time I reached Ridgemont Psychiatric Center. My windshield wipers fought a losing battle. The weather app said eighteen to twenty-four inches by morning.

Nor'easter.

I drove through Ridgemont's outskirts. Past darkened farmhouses and stripped trees. The facility appeared ahead through the white.

Three stories of brick. 1960s institutional architecture. The kind that looked like a prison because it basically was one. Chain-link fence surrounded the property. Razor wire at the top.

The parking lot was nearly empty. Skeleton crew for Christmas Eve. Most staff had families. Kids waiting for Santa. Trees with presents underneath.

I had a twelve-hour shift and an empty apartment.

Lights glowed on the third floor. Ward C. My ward.

I checked my reflection before getting out. Twenty-nine years old and already exhausted. Straight black hair in a practical braid. Dark brown eyes that wanted sleep. Athletic build from morning runs I'd been skipping.

Burgundy scrubs with the Ridgemont Psychiatric Center logo. White sneakers. Fleece jacket over everything. Stethoscope around my neck. ID badge clipped to my pocket.

Amy Cao, RN.

Cold hit me when I stepped out. The kind that burned. Snow came down sideways. Wind pushed against me. I made it to the entrance, shaking off powder.

The lobby smelled wrong. Pine-scented cleaner trying to mask institutional disinfectant. Fake tree in the corner, lights blinking in no pattern. Wreath on the security desk. Red bow. Plastic holly.

It looked like someone had put lipstick on a corpse.

Carl sat at the desk. Sixty, balding, kind eyes. Security guard for fifteen years. He had a Polaroid tucked beside his radio. Woman in her thirties with his same smile.

"Evening, Amy. Quiet night ahead."

"Hope so."

I signed in. Took the elevator to the third floor.

Ward C stretched in both directions from the nurses' station. Long hallway. Rooms on both sides. Common room at the far end. Locked unit. Electronic doors, barred windows, institutional beige walls, linoleum floors that squeaked.

Emergency lights in corners. Fluorescent hum overhead.

This was going to be my home for the next twelve hours.

Nurse James waited in the break room. Fifty-five, gray hair, exhausted in a way that went deeper than one shift. Same burgundy scrubs.

"Amy. Thank god." He grabbed his coat. "I'm dying to get home."

"How are they tonight?"

"Quiet. Natalie had a session with Dr. Keller this afternoon. Came back upset."

I frowned. "Upset how?"

"Wouldn't say. Refused dinner. Been in her room since."

Natalie Price. Twenty-four. Bipolar disorder, medicated, stable. Scheduled for discharge January second. Nine days.

"Sophie had an episode around six," James continued. "Paranoid delusions. Said someone was watching her through the vents."

Sophie Grant. Thirty-one. Schizophrenia diagnosis. Had those delusions regularly.

James handed me the medication log. "Marissa and Elena are sleeping. Vanessa's in the common room watching TV."

Standard night. Medication schedule. Incident reports. Nothing unusual except—

"Dr. Keller's still here," James added.

"What? On Christmas Eve?"

"Says he has paperwork. Been in his office since four."

Dr. Richard Keller. Chief psychiatrist. Five years at Ridgemont. Usually left by five-thirty. Had a wife and kids in Short Hills. Why stay late tonight?

"Well. Merry Christmas," James said.

"You too."

He left. The ward was mine.

I made rounds at eight-thirty.

Room 301: Marissa Bennett. Thirty-eight. Depression. Heavily medicated. She slept with her back to the door. Brown hair going gray. Thin from not eating. Breathing steady.

She'd been here five years. Admitted 2019. Used to be a marketing executive before her breakdown. Smart woman. Capable. Now just... diminished.

Room 302: Elena Rodriguez. Twenty-seven. PTSD. She slept curled in fetal position. Always slept like that. Long dark hair covered her face. Petite. Nervous even in sleep.

Her ex-husband had put her here. The trauma. The fear. She'd probably never fully heal.

Room 303: Sophie Grant. Thirty-one. Schizophrenia diagnosis. She sat up in bed. Staring at the vent in the ceiling. Dyed black hair. Average build. Green eyes that tracked my movement.

"They're watching," she whispered.

"Sophie, no one's watching."

Her eyes flicked to my badge. Sharp. Assessing. Too focused for someone mid-delusion.

"You don't believe me."

"I believe you're safe here."

She laughed. Bitter. "No one's safe here."

I moved on.

Room 304: Natalie Price. Twenty-four. Strawberry blonde, pale skin, gray eyes. Usually chatty. Smiled a lot. Excited about discharge. Starting a new job in January. Moving in with her sister.

Tonight her door was closed.

I knocked. "Natalie?"

No answer.

I opened the door. She was in bed. Facing the wall.

"Natalie? Are you okay?"

"Go away."

"Nurse James said you were upset."

"I'm fine."

"Did something happen in your session with Dr. Keller?"

She turned. Face wet with tears. Thin from medication. Hospital pajamas hanging off her frame. Gray eyes red and swollen.

"He touched me."

My pulse kicked up. "What?"

"During therapy. His hand on my knee. Then higher." Her voice shook. "I told him to stop. He said I was imagining it. That it was part of my illness."

"Natalie—"

"You don't believe me either."

"I believe you."

"Then do something."

"I will. I'll report this."

"He'll say I'm lying. That I'm crazy." Her voice broke. "And everyone will believe him."

I didn't know what to say. Because she was probably right.

"I'll document it. Talk to him. Figure out what happened."

"What happened is he assaulted me. And no one will care because I'm a psychiatric patient."

She turned back to the wall. Conversation over.

I stood there. Wanting to say something helpful. Finding nothing.

I closed the door.

I went to Dr. Keller's office. Second floor. Administrative wing.

The door was open. He sat at his desk. Reading files. Early fifties, salt-and-pepper hair perfectly styled even this late. Clean-shaven. Handsome in a TV-doctor way. Expensive suit. Italian shoes. Wedding ring catching the light.

Everyone loved Dr. Keller. Patients trusted him. Staff respected him. Chief psychiatrist for five years. Published researcher. Twenty years in the field.

I knocked.

"Amy. Working Christmas Eve?"

"Double pay."

He smiled. Warm. Charming. "Same reason I'm here. Paperwork pays overtime."

I didn't believe him.

"Dr. Keller, I need to talk about Natalie Price."

"What about her?"

"She says something inappropriate happened during therapy today."

"Inappropriate how?"

"She says you touched her."

"Touched her?"

"Inappropriately."

He sighed. Looked sad. Disappointed. Not angry. Not defensive. Just... tired.

"Amy, Natalie is bipolar. She's had reality distortions before. Sexual delusions. It's documented in her file."

"This isn't a delusion."

"How do you know?"

"She was crying."

"She cries often. It's part of her condition." His voice stayed calm. Reasonable. Like he was explaining something to a child. "You're a good nurse. But you can't believe everything patients tell you. Especially ones with mental illness."

I felt trapped. He was so calm. So reasonable.

He was making me doubt myself.

"I need to document this. File a report."

"Of course. Do what you need to do." He smiled again. "I have nothing to hide."

I left his office. Walked back to Ward C. My mind raced.

Was Natalie delusional? Or was Keller lying?

I didn't know.

Nine PM. The lights flickered.

I looked out the window. Snow came down sideways now. Wind howled against the glass. Trees bent. Power lines sagged under ice.

I went back to Ward C. Checked on patients.

Vanessa Hayes sat in the common room. Watching TV. "Rudolph the Red-Nosed Reindeer" played on the screen. Forty-two, graying blonde hair, blue eyes that saw things that weren't there. Delusional disorder. Paranoid type. Thought the government watched her through cameras.

She looked up when I entered. "Are they coming?"

"Who?"

"The ones watching. In the storm."

"No one's coming, Vanessa. It's just us."

She went back to the TV. Wrapped her blanket tighter. Like it was armor.

I checked Natalie's room again. Knocked. "Natalie?"

No answer.

I opened the door.

Empty.

The bathroom light was on.

"Natalie?"

I walked to the bathroom. Pushed the door.

Natalie was on the floor.

Wrists slashed.

Blood everywhere.

I screamed.

I dropped beside her. Checked for pulse. Nothing. Skin already cold. Eyes half-open. Staring at nothing.

Dead.

How long? An hour? Two?

I ran to the nurses' station. Hit the emergency button.

Nothing.

Tried again. Still nothing.

I pulled out my phone. No service.

Landline. I grabbed the receiver. Dead.

The lights went out.

Complete darkness.

Emergency lights should have kicked in. Didn't.

The backup generator was supposed to activate automatically. Nothing.

Somewhere down the hall, a ceiling speaker crackled. Spat out half a warped bar of "Silent Night" before it died.

Silence.

The storm had killed the power.

And I was alone in a locked psychiatric facility.

With a dead patient.

And a doctor I didn't trust.

And four other patients I had to protect.

In the dark.

Chapter 2

Blackout

The darkness was absolute.

I fumbled for my phone. Turned on the flashlight. The beam carved a narrow tunnel through the black. The walls felt closer than they should have.

Ward C is a locked unit. Electronic doors. Magnetic seals. But the power was out.

Were we locked in? Or could the doors open manually?

I tested Room 301. Marissa's room. The door pushed open easily.

She sat up in bed. Confused. "What's happening?"

"Power's out. Storm. Stay in your room for now."

I moved to the next room. Elena's. She backed into the corner. Shaking.

"Please don't hurt me."

"Elena, it's Amy. I'm not going to hurt you."

"The dark." Her voice cracked. "He always came in the dark."

Her ex-husband. The one who put her here.

"You're safe. I promise."

Room 303. Sophie stood at the window. Watching the snow fall through the glass.

"They cut the power," she said.

"Sophie, it's the storm."

"That's what they want you to think."

I needed them together. Safer that way.

"Everyone to the common room. Now."

I herded them down the hallway. Four women in hospital pajamas and robes. Marissa moved slowly. Heavily medicated. Elena flinched at every shadow. Vanessa walked calmly, blanket over her head like a hood. Sophie positioned herself near the door. Like she expected danger.

Natalie was dead. Still in Room 304. Still in the bathroom.

I couldn't deal with the body now. Had to focus on keeping the living alive.

The common room had windows. Moonlight on snow gave faint illumination. Better than the hallways. Easier to see.

"What's going on?" Vanessa asked. Her blue eyes tracked movements I couldn't see.

"Storm knocked out power. Backup generator failed."

"When will it come back?"

"I don't know."

Sophie turned from the window. "Where's Dr. Keller?"

Good question.

"I'll find him. You four stay here."

"Don't leave us." Elena's voice was small. She curled into herself on the couch.

"I'll be right back."

I went to the stairwell. West side. The door opened manually. Thank god.

Down to second floor. Administrative wing. My phone flashlight swept across empty hallways. Doors closed. Dark offices.

Dr. Keller's office was empty. Chair pushed back from the desk. Files scattered. No sign of him.

"Dr. Keller?" I called.

No answer.

I went to first floor. The lobby. Carl should be at the security desk.

The desk was empty.

Where was everyone?

I checked the break room. Empty. Bathroom. Empty. Storage closet. Empty.

I heard something.

Basement.

Thumping. Rhythmic. Mechanical.

The mechanical room was down there. Maybe the generator could be manually restarted.

I opened the basement door. Stairs descended into darkness. My phone flashlight barely cut through.

"Carl?"

Thumping again.

I went down.

The basement smelled like mold and heating oil. Concrete floor, low ceiling, pipes running everywhere. Cold down here. My breath fogged in the flashlight beam.

I followed the sound. The mechanical room door stood open.

I entered.

Flashlight beam swept the room. Generator in the corner. Silent. Dead.

Then I saw him.

Carl.

On the floor. Face down. Blood pooled under his head.

"Carl!"

I ran over. Rolled him. His skull was caved in. One side of his face crushed. Eyes open. Unseeing.

Dead.

Killed with—I looked around. Pipe wrench on the floor beside him. Bloody. Metal slick with it.

Someone had bludgeoned him.

My hands shook. I stood. Backed away.

Footsteps behind me. On the stairs.

I turned. Flashlight beam caught a figure at the top of the stairs.

Dr. Keller.

He stood there. Face pale. Shocked.

"Amy. What are you—" He saw Carl's body. "Oh my god. What happened?"

"Someone killed him."

"What?" He came down the stairs. Fast. Dropped to his knees beside Carl. Checked for pulse. "Jesus. He's dead."

"I know."

Keller looked up at me. His eyes were wide. Horrified. "Who did this?"

"I don't know."

He stood. Looked around the basement. At the shadows. The dark corners. "We need to get upstairs. Now."

"What?"

"Whoever did this might still be here." His voice was urgent. Scared. "You shouldn't be down here alone."

He seemed genuinely terrified.

Was he acting? Or was this real?

"We need to get back to the patients," he said. "Keep them safe."

We went upstairs together. Him leading. Me following. Watching him. Back to Ward C. Third floor.

The patients looked up when we entered.

"What happened?" Sophie asked.

"Carl's dead," I said.

Marissa's face went white. "What?"

"Someone killed him. In the basement."

Elena started crying. Vanessa pulled her blanket tighter. Sophie just watched. Calculating.

Keller moved to the west stairwell door. "We need to barricade this. Both doors. Keep whoever did this out."

"You think someone broke in?" I asked.

"During the storm? Yes. Maybe got trapped inside when the power went out." He grabbed the filing cabinet from the nurses' station. Started dragging it. "Help me."

I hesitated.

Sophie whispered, "Don't trust him."

But Keller was already moving furniture. Building a barricade. Breathing hard from the effort.

I helped. Pushed the filing cabinet against the door. Heavy. Metal. It scraped across linoleum.

"The east stairwell too," Keller said.

We moved to the other side. Dragged the medical cart. The desk. Chairs. Everything we could move. Built a second barricade.

When we finished, Keller was sweating. He wiped his forehead. Looked at the patients.

"You're safe now. Both exits are blocked. No one can get in."

"What about getting out?" Sophie asked.

"We wait for rescue. Storm should clear by morning."

"That's eight hours," I said.

"Then we wait eight hours." He looked at me. "I'll check the other floors. Make sure no one else broke in. That all other exits are secure."

"You're leaving?"

"Just for a few minutes. I'll be back." He moved toward the barricade. Started pulling chairs away.

"Wait—"

"Amy, I need to make sure we're safe. Check the whole building. I'll be quick."

He squeezed through a gap in the barricade. Disappeared down the stairs.

I stood there. Staring after him.

Sophie appeared beside me. "He's lying."

"About what?"

"About checking the building. About helping." Her voice was low. Intense. "Don't trust him."

"You think he killed Carl?"

"I think we need to be careful."

Marissa sat on the couch. Quiet. Watching us. Elena cried softly. Vanessa stared at nothing.

I went back to the barricade. Made sure it was solid. No gaps.

I sat down. Waited for Keller to come back. Or for whatever came next.

The minutes crawled by. Ten. Twenty. Thirty.

He didn't return.

Where was he? What was he doing?

Chapter 3

Suspicions

The patients sat in the common room. Silent. Waiting for something to happen.

I needed to keep them calm. Keep myself calm.

"We're safe here," I said. "Both doors are blocked. Help will come at dawn."

Marissa pulled her hospital robe tighter. She sat in the armchair, legs tucked under her. Five years in this place. She knew every corner. Every routine. "What if help doesn't come?"

"It will."

"The storm could last days." Her voice stayed flat. Medicated. Distant.

Elena rocked on the couch. Back and forth. Small movements. "I want to go home."

"Soon," I said.

Vanessa watched the dark windows. Looking for her watchers. The ones she believed monitored her every move. "They planned this. The storm. The blackout. All of it."

I didn't argue. No point.

Sophie stood near the supply closet door. Arms crossed. Eyes sharp. Too focused for someone with schizophrenia.

I walked to the nurses' station. Pulled open the medication cabinet. If things got worse—if someone panicked—I needed sedatives ready. Midazolam. Standard dose. I drew it into two syringes. Capped them. Set them aside.

Sophie appeared beside me. "You think we'll need those?"

"Hope not."

"But you're preparing anyway." She leaned against the counter. "Smart."

I looked at her. Green eyes clear. No paranoia. No delusion. "You're not having an episode."

"No."

"The vents. The watchers. Earlier tonight—"

"Performance." She straightened. Dropped her voice. "I'm not schizophrenic, Amy. I'm a reporter. Gloria Steele's intern. Ridgemont Gazette."

My throat went dry. "What?"

"I got myself committed here six weeks ago. Fake psych evaluation. Convincing performance." She pulled a small spiral notebook from her robe pocket. "I've been investigating Dr. Keller."

I stared at the notebook. "Why?"

"Three families contacted Gloria. Said their daughters died here. All ruled suicide. But the families suspected murder." Sophie opened the notebook. Pages filled with tight handwriting. Names. Dates. Details. "I came in to find proof."

She turned pages. Showed me.

Patricia Reeves, 33 - Overdose, Sept 2019

Linda Lipton, 28 - Hanging, March 2020

Mary Kim, 41 - Overdose, Nov 2020

Jennifer Santos, 29 - Slashed wrists, June 2021

Bethany Grant, 36 - Hanging, Feb 2022

Natalie Price, 24 - Slashed wrists, Dec 2024

Six women. Six deaths. All under Keller's care.

"They all reported him," Sophie said. "Sexual assault during therapy sessions. Inappropriate touching. Same pattern as Natalie. Then within weeks—dead."

My hands gripped the counter. "He killed them."

"That's what I've been documenting. Witness statements from other patients. Medical records showing suspicious medication doses. Suicide notes that don't match handwriting samples." She flipped more pages. Evidence. Proof. "But Amy, look at this."

She pointed to her notes. Method of death. Details.

"Keller's victims—the ones from 2019 to 2022—they were precise. Overdoses looked accidental. Hangings staged perfectly. Right-handed ligature marks for right-handed victims. Everything clean." Sophie's finger moved to Natalie's entry. "But Natalie? Wrists slashed left to right. She was right-handed. The cuts are wrong. And Carl—bludgeoned with a pipe wrench? Keller never used blunt force. Never. His method was subtle. Untraceable."

The floor tilted under me. "You think someone else killed them."

"I think someone is killing NOW. Tonight. During this storm." Sophie closed the notebook. "And it might not be Keller."

"Then who?"

"I don't know. But we're trapped here with them."

I looked across the common room. Marissa in her chair. Elena on the couch. Vanessa at the window. All of them here when Natalie died. When Carl died.

One of them?

No. That was paranoia. Storm thinking.

Marissa spoke from her chair. "Is there another way out? Besides the stairwells?"

"Why?" I asked.

"If someone's in the building. If they get past the barricades." She pulled her blanket tighter. "We need an escape route."

"The roof access," I said. "Fourth floor. Interior stairs. Always unlocked. Fire code."

Marissa nodded. Filed that information away. Smart. Practical. The marketing executive under the medication fog.

A sound in the hallway. East stairwell.

Everyone froze.

Metal scraping. Something heavy being moved.

I grabbed the fire extinguisher from the wall bracket. Held it ready. Sophie positioned herself in front of the patients.

The barricade shifted. Medical cart pushed aside. Someone was coming through.

The door opened.

Dr. Keller stepped into the ward.

He carried supplies. Flashlights. Batteries. Blankets from storage. His suit jacket was gone. Shirt sleeves rolled up. Sweat on his forehead despite the cold.

"Found these in the first-floor supply room." He set everything down.

"Flashlights. Extra batteries. Blankets if the heat fails."

He handed out flashlights. One to each of us. I didn't lower the fire extinguisher. "Where were you?"

"Checking the building. All floors. Making sure no one broke in during the storm." He wiped his forehead. "Windows are secure. Other wards are locked and empty. We're the only ones here."

"The only ones," Sophie repeated. Voice flat.

Keller looked at her. Then at me. "I'm going back to the basement. Try to restart the generator manually. If I can get power back—"

"You're leaving again?" Elena's voice cracked.

"Just for a bit. The generator has a manual crank. Old system. It might work." He moved toward the barricade. "I'll be back in twenty minutes."

"Wait," I said.

He turned.

"Take a radio. From the nurses' station. Check in every five minutes."

Smart. Keep track of him. Make sure he stayed where he said.

Keller nodded. "Good idea."

He took a radio. Clipped it to his belt. Squeezed back through the barricade. Disappeared down the stairs.

Silence settled over the ward.

Sophie moved close to me. "He's lying."

"About what?"

"About checking the building. About the generator." Her voice dropped. "He's planning something."

"Or he's actually trying to help."

"You believe that?"

I didn't know what I believed anymore.

Marissa stood from her chair. Walked to the window. Looked out at the storm. Snow still falling. Wind still howling. "How long until morning?"

I checked my phone. "Five hours."

"That's a long time to wait."

Elena curled tighter on the couch. Vanessa hummed something under her breath. Christmas carol. Distorted. Wrong.

Sophie tucked her notebook back into her pocket. "We need to stay alert. Watch each other. Don't trust anyone."

"Even you?" I asked.

"Especially me." She met my eyes. "I lied about who I am for six weeks. Fooled everyone. Fooled you." She paused. "If I can do that, anyone can."

The radio on my belt crackled. Static. Then Keller's voice.

"Amy? I'm in the basement. At the generator. Going to try the manual crank now."

I keyed the radio. "Copy. Check in again in five minutes."

"Will do."

Static. Silence.

I set the fire extinguisher down. Leaned against the counter. Every muscle tight. My jaw ached from clenching.

Two killers. Maybe. Old murders and new ones. Different patterns. Different methods.

Keller guilty of the past. Someone else guilty of tonight.

But who?

I looked at the patients. Marissa calm and watchful. Elena terrified and small. Vanessa disconnected from reality. Sophie—Sophie was a reporter. A liar. But an investigator. Probably not a killer.

Probably.

The minutes crawled. Three. Four. Five.

Radio silent.

Six minutes. Seven.

"Dr. Keller?" I keyed the radio. "Status check."

Static.

"Dr. Keller, respond."

Nothing.

Sophie grabbed my arm. "Something's wrong."

Eight minutes. Nine.

The radio crackled.

Heavy breathing. Struggle. Then Keller's voice. Strained. "Amy—someone's down here—"

A crash. The radio cut out.

Gone.

Chapter 4

The Hunt

The radio stayed silent.

I keyed it again. "Dr. Keller, respond."

Static.

Sophie grabbed her flashlight. "We need to go down there."

"I'm not leaving them alone." I looked at Elena and Vanessa. Both terrified. Both vulnerable.

Marissa stood from her chair. "I'll come with you."

"Marissa—"

"I know this building better than anyone. Five years here. Every floor. Every room." She moved toward us. Faster than her usual shuffle. No hesitation. "You need someone who knows the layout."

She was right. And she seemed clearheaded. Alert. Survival instinct cutting through medication fog.

"Fine. Elena, Vanessa—stay here. Lock yourselves in the common room. Don't open the door for anyone except us." I handed Elena the emergency whistle from the nurses' station. "If something happens, blow this. We'll hear it."

Elena took it. Hands shaking. "What if someone comes?"

"Blow the whistle. Hide. Don't try to fight."

Vanessa pulled her blanket over her head. Made herself small. "They're already here. In the walls. Watching."

No time to comfort her.

Sophie, Marissa, and I went to the west stairwell. Moved the filing cabinet just enough to squeeze through.

The stairs descended into darkness. Our flashlight beams cut narrow paths. Cold air rose from below. Basement cold. Concrete and earth.

We moved down. Single file. Me leading. Sophie behind me. Marissa at the rear.

First floor. Empty lobby. Shadows everywhere. The Christmas wreath on the security desk looked wrong in the dark. Mockery of holiday cheer.

We kept going. Down to the basement.

The smell hit first. Mold and heating oil. Damp concrete. Then the cold. My breath fogged in the flashlight beam.

Pipes ran overhead. Low ceiling. Maze of corridors branching off the main hall.

"Where's the mechanical room?" I whispered.

"East corridor." Marissa pointed. "Past the old hydrotherapy room."

We followed her direction. The hydrotherapy room door stood open.

I swept my flashlight inside.

Old tiled walls. White tiles, some cracked, others missing. Porcelain tub in the center. Stained yellow with age. Drains in the floor. Chains on the walls from when they restrained patients decades ago.

And Dr. Keller.

He crouched in the corner. Flashlight on the floor beside him. Examining something.

"Dr. Keller?"

He spun. Saw us. His face—relief. Genuine relief.

"Amy. Thank god." He stood. "I was about to come find you."

"What happened? Your radio cut out."

"I tripped. Dropped it." He pointed to the corner. "But look. Someone's been down here. Recently."

I moved closer. Shone my light where he pointed.

Footprints in the dust. Small. Definitely not Keller's size twelve shoes.

"Woman's shoe," Sophie said. "Size seven. Maybe eight."

My chest tightened. "Could be old. From staff."

"The dust pattern is fresh. Disturbed in the last few hours." Keller's voice stayed calm. Methodical. "Someone was down here tonight."

Marissa stepped forward. Studied the prints. "Could be any of us."

"Or someone who got in before the storm." Keller stood. "Trapped inside when the power went out."

"An intruder," I said.

"Maybe. Or—" He stopped.

"Or what?"

He didn't finish. Just looked at the footprints. Calculating something.

A scream from upstairs. High-pitched. Terrified.

Elena.

We ran. Back through the corridor. Up the stairs. My lungs burned. Legs pumped. Sophie ahead of me. Marissa kept pace. No shuffle now. She moved fast.

Third floor. Ward C.

The common room door hung open.

Elena stood in the hallway. Shaking. Sobbing. Vanessa beside her. Both pale.

"What happened?" I grabbed Elena's shoulders.

"Someone was here." Her voice broke. "Tried to open the door. I saw their shadow under the door. Then the handle moved. Turning. Trying to get in."

"Where did they go?"

"I don't know. I blew the whistle. The shadow disappeared."

Vanessa nodded. "Someone in the hallway. Just for a second. Then gone."

I looked around. Empty hallway. Both stairwell doors still barricaded. No one here now.

But Keller had been with us. In the basement. He couldn't have been upstairs trying doors.

Unless—

I looked at Sophie. At Marissa. Both had been with me the whole time.

Hadn't they?

In the dark. The maze of basement corridors. Had I watched them every second?

No. Impossible to watch everyone at once. Someone could have slipped away. Thirty seconds. Enough time to run upstairs. Try a door. Run back down.

"We need to stay together," Sophie said. "All of us. No one goes anywhere alone."

Marissa leaned against the wall. Breathing hard from the run. "We should split up. Cover more ground. Find whoever's doing this."

"No." Sophie's voice was sharp. "That's how people die in horror movies."

"This isn't a movie."

"Splitting up is stupid. We stay together."

I held up my hands. "Sophie's right. We stay in groups. Minimum two people. Never alone."

Keller nodded. "Agreed. The safest place is here. Ward C. Both stairwells barricaded. We wait for dawn."

"What about the generator?" I asked.

"Dead. Manual crank is broken. Someone sabotaged it." He met my eyes. "Recently. The bolt is sheared off. Fresh metal shavings on the floor."

Someone didn't want the power back on.

Someone wanted us in the dark.

We moved furniture back against the east stairwell door. Reinforced both barricades. Made them stronger. Heavier. Nothing was getting through without making serious noise.

Then we gathered in the common room. All six of us. Flashlights in the center. Circle of light in the darkness.

Elena curled on the couch. Vanessa beside her. Both wrapped in blankets. Marissa sat in the armchair. Sophie stood near the door. Keller leaned against the wall.

And me. In the middle. Trying to think.

Two AM. Four hours until dawn.

Four hours until rescue came.

If we survived that long.

I looked at each of them. Studied their faces in the flashlight glow.

One of them was lying.

One of them had tried Elena's door.

One of them was hunting us.

Or maybe Keller was right. Maybe someone else was in the building. A seventh person. Hiding in the walls.

Either way, we were trapped.

Chapter 5

Suspicion Grows

We sat in silence. Watching each other.

The flashlights cast shadows that moved wrong. Made faces look different. Distorted.

I checked my phone. Two-fifteen AM. Three hours and forty-five minutes until dawn.

My eyes burned. Exhaustion pressed down. But I couldn't sleep. Couldn't let my guard down.

Marissa's medication cups sat on the side table. Three of them. Evening doses I'd prepared before the power went out. Still full. Liquid pooled in the bottom.

She hadn't taken them.

"Marissa," I said. "Your medication."

She looked at the cups. "I'm not taking them tonight."

"You need to stay on schedule."

"They make me foggy. I need to stay alert." Her voice was steady. Clear. "With everything happening—I need my head clear."

Made sense. Survival instinct. Anyone would want to be lucid during a crisis.

But how long? I walked to her chair. Checked the other cups from earlier in the day. Yesterday's evening dose. Still there. Dried residue in the bottom.

"You haven't been taking them at all," I said.

"Just since yesterday. When the storm started." She met my eyes. "I needed to be sharp. In case something happened."

"Something did happen."

"Exactly."

Sophie moved closer. Studied the cups. "How do you feel? Stopping cold turkey—"

"I'm fine. The doses were low anyway. Maintenance level." Marissa pulled her blanket tighter. "I'm more functional without them right now."

I couldn't argue. She seemed more present than I'd ever seen her. Five years on heavy medication. Now suddenly clear. Alert. Capable.

The Marissa who'd been a marketing executive. Before Keller destroyed her life.

"Okay," I said. "But if you start feeling—"

"I'll tell you."

I sat back down. Made a mental note. Track her. Watch for withdrawal symptoms. Mood changes. Instability.

But right now? She seemed fine. Better than fine.

Sophie pulled me aside. Dropped her voice. "I've been thinking about the footprints. Size seven women's shoe."

"Could be any of us."

"Exactly. You, me, Marissa, Elena, Vanessa." Sophie glanced at them. "Which means the killer could be one of us. Not an intruder."

"That's paranoid."

"Is it? Think about the timing. Natalie and Carl died within an hour of each other. Power went out right after. Very convenient."

"Storm knocked out the power."

"Or someone cut it. Used the storm as cover." Sophie crossed her arms. "Someone's been planning this. Waiting for the right moment."

I looked at the others. Elena curled on the couch. Terrified. Vanessa staring at nothing. Lost in her delusions. Marissa watching us from her chair. Calm. Too calm for someone who should be medicated and foggy.

Keller stood near the window. Looking out at the storm.

"Who?" I whispered.

"I don't know. But someone in this room knows more than they're saying."

Keller turned from the window. "What are you two whispering about?"

"Nothing," I said.

"Doesn't sound like nothing."

Sophie straightened. "We're discussing the footprints. The ones in the basement. They're too small to be yours."

"I know."

"Which means someone else was down there."

"Or one of you was." His voice stayed level. Reasonable. "You all came with me. Any of you could have been down there earlier. Before we found them together."

"We were all upstairs," I said.

"Were you? The whole time?" He moved toward us. "People take bathroom breaks. Step out for a minute. In the dark, in the chaos—anyone could have slipped away."

He was right. I couldn't account for everyone every second.

"This is what he wants," Vanessa said from the couch. Voice distant. Dreamy. "Division. Suspicion. We turn on each other. That's how they win."

"They?" Keller asked.

"The watchers. The ones who planned this."

No one responded. Vanessa's delusions were her own world. Not helpful right now.

But maybe she had a point buried in the paranoia. Someone did want us divided. Suspicious of each other.

Three AM. The minutes dragged.

Elena asked for the bathroom. I went with her. Stood outside the door. Waited.

When she came out, her face was wet. Tears or water. Couldn't tell.

"I want to go home," she whispered.

"Soon."

"My sister's probably worried. She'll call. No answer. She'll think—" Elena's voice broke. "She'll think he got me again."

Her ex-husband. The monster who put her here.

"She'll know you're okay. The staff will contact families when the power's back."

"Will we be okay?"

I couldn't answer that.

We walked back to the common room.

Smell hit me halfway down the hall.

Smoke.

Faint. Growing stronger.

"Fire!" I ran toward the west stairwell.

Smoke seeped under the door. Gray wisps curling across the floor.

I grabbed the fire extinguisher. Pulled away enough furniture to open the door.

Heat rolled out. Smoke thicker. A trash can in the stairwell burned. Small fire. Contained. But growing.

I aimed the extinguisher. Pulled the trigger. White foam erupted. Covered the flames. Smothered them. The fire died. Smoke remained.

Keller appeared behind me. "What the hell?"

"Someone started this." I kicked the trash can. Metal. Scorched black. "Deliberately."

"Who?"

I looked back at the common room. Everyone there now. Sophie. Marissa. Elena. Vanessa. All watching from the doorway.

"We were all together," Sophie said.

"Were we?" I stared at them. "Everyone accounted for the whole time?"

Silence.

"I went to the bathroom," Elena said. Small voice. "Five minutes ago."

"I was in the hallway," Marissa said. "Checking the other stairwell. Making sure the barricade held."

"I was getting water from the nurses' station," Vanessa said.

Everyone had been somewhere. Alone. For thirty seconds. A minute. Long enough to light a fire and slip back.

"This is what they want," Vanessa repeated. "Chaos. Fear. We need to stay calm."

But calm felt impossible.

Someone had started that fire. Someone in this building. Maybe someone in this room.

The smoke cleared slowly. Ventilation system dead without power. We propped the stairwell door open. Let it dissipate naturally.

I pulled the barricade back. Sealed us in again.

"We need a new plan," Sophie said. "Waiting here isn't working. Someone's hunting us. We're sitting targets."

"What do you suggest?" Keller asked.

"We go to the roof. Signal for help. Use flashlights. Someone might see."

"In this storm?" Marissa shook her head. "No one's out there."

"Then what? We just wait to die?"

"No one's dying." My voice came out harder than intended. "We have three hours until dawn. We stay together. We stay alert. We survive."

But I didn't believe my own words.

Someone had killed Natalie. Killed Carl. Tried to smoke us out. Sabotaged the generator.

Someone methodical. Patient. Waiting for the right moments.

And we were trapped with them.

Four AM. Two hours until dawn.

The temperature dropped. Heat failing without power. Our breath fogged. The blankets weren't enough.

Marissa stood. Stretched. "I'm going to check if there are more blankets. In the storage closet."

"I'll come with you," I said.

"I know where they are. I'll be thirty seconds."

"No one goes alone."

She sighed. But nodded.

We walked to the storage closet. Down the hall. Flashlights cutting through dark.

Marissa opened the door. Pulled out two more blankets. Thick. Institutional grade.

As she turned, something fell from her pocket.

A folded piece of paper.

I picked it up. Started to hand it back.

Saw writing. Names. Dates.

"What is this?"

Marissa's face went blank. "Nothing."

I unfolded it.

Patricia Reeves. Linda Lipton. Mary Kim. Jennifer Santos. Bethany Grant.

All the names from Sophie's notebook.

"Why do you have this?" My voice dropped. Cold.

"I knew them. Patricia especially. We were in the same ward. 2019. Before she died."

"You knew Keller was killing patients."

"I suspected. But I couldn't prove anything." Marissa's voice stayed steady. "No one believed me. I'm a psychiatric patient. Mentally ill. My word means nothing."

The paper crumpled in my hand. "You've known all along."

"Suspecting isn't knowing. And I was too medicated to do anything about it." She took the paper back. "Until tonight."

She walked past me. Back to the common room.

I stood there. Mind racing.

Marissa knew about the murders. Had a list of victims. Knew Keller was guilty.

And she'd been off her medication. Clear-headed. Capable.

What else wasn't she telling me?

I returned to the common room. Sat down. Watched her.

She wrapped herself in the new blanket. Calm. Focused. Not shaking. Not crying. Not falling apart like someone who should be heavily medicated and off their dose.

She looked at me across the flashlight glow. Held my gaze.
Then smiled.
Small. Brief.
Like she knew something I didn't.

Chapter 6

The Reveal

ive AM. One hour until dawn.

I couldn't stop staring at Marissa.

The list in her pocket. Patricia's name at the top. Five years she'd known about the murders. Five years watching. Waiting.

For what?

Sophie stood near the window. Watching the sky lighten. Gray dawn fighting through storm clouds.

"Storm's breaking," she said. "Rescue will come soon."

Keller checked his watch. "Another hour. Maybe two if roads are bad."

"We just need to hold on," I said.

Elena slept on the couch. Exhausted. Vanessa hummed beside her. Some warped Christmas carol. Off-key. Wrong.

Marissa sat in her chair. Blanket wrapped around her shoulders. She looked at me. That small smile again.

"Amy, can I talk to you? Privately?"

Every instinct screamed no. But I needed answers.

"Fine. Nurses' station."

We walked down the hall. Flashlights cutting dark. The station was small. Enclosed. Just us.

Marissa set her flashlight on the counter. Faced me.

"I need to tell you something," she said. "About Keller."

"What about him?"

"He didn't kill Natalie."

My chest tightened. "What?"

"Or Carl." Her voice stayed flat. Calm. "I did."

Dread pooled in my stomach.

"You're—you're confused. The medication—"

"I haven't taken medication in months, Amy. Not just two days. Months." She leaned against the counter. Relaxed. "I've been cheeking pills since August. Storing them under my mattress. Waiting for the right time."

"The right time for what?"

"Justice." She pulled the list from her pocket. Unfolded it. "Patricia Reeves was my friend. We were admitted the same week. October 2019. Both of us reported Keller for assault. Both of us got committed as punishment."

"Marissa—"

"Patricia died two months later. Overdose. Except she hated taking pills. Would never have taken that many voluntarily." Marissa's voice didn't waver. No emotion. Factual. "Keller killed her. Made it look like suicide. Got away with it."

"So you—"

"Waited. Played the part. Depressed, medicated, broken. For five years." She folded the list. Put it away. "Learning the building. Learning routines. Planning."

My hand moved toward the sedative in my pocket. The syringe I'd prepared earlier.

"Don't." Marissa's eyes tracked the movement. "I'm faster than you think."

I froze.

"Natalie was going to report Keller. File a complaint. Get him investigated." Marissa crossed her arms. "I couldn't let that happen. Not yet. I needed him here. Needed him to be the obvious suspect when people died. So I made sure Natalie stayed quiet."

"You killed her."

"I made it look like his pattern. Left-handed cuts because I'm left-handed. Close enough to his method. Close enough to point suspicion his way." She paused. "Carl was collateral. He saw me in the hallway. After Natalie. He knew something was wrong. So I dealt with it."

"You bludgeoned him."

"Quick. Efficient. He didn't suffer." No remorse. No guilt. "Then I cut the power. Sabotaged the generator. Created chaos. Perfect conditions to finish what I started."

"Which is what?"

"Kill Keller. Make it look like suicide. Guilty conscience. Case closed." Marissa's smile widened. "Everyone would believe it. The chief psychiatrist who murdered his patients for years. Finally couldn't live with himself. Poetic."

"Sophie's evidence—"

"My evidence." She laughed. Bitter. "I've known Sophie was undercover for weeks. Schizophrenic patient who's oddly lucid? Please. I fed her information. Left clues in her room. Guided her investigation exactly where I wanted. She built the case against Keller for me."

My throat closed. "Why tell me this?"

"Because you're going to die anyway." She reached into her other pocket. Pulled out a scalpel. Must have taken it from the medical cart earlier. "Along with everyone else. Murder-suicide. Keller killed his patients and staff during the storm. Then Sophie killed Keller. Then I killed Sophie in self-defense. Traumatized survivor. Sole witness."

"No one will believe that."

"Won't they? Two killers. One guilty of old crimes. One stopping him. Both dead. Me—the broken patient who barely survived. They'll believe whatever I tell them." She moved closer. "Keller IS guilty. He DID kill Patricia and the others. I'm just making sure he pays for it. And cleaning up loose ends."

"I'm a loose end."

"You figured it out. Saw the list. Connected the dots." She raised the scalpel. "I'm sorry, Amy. You're actually a decent nurse. But I can't leave witnesses."

I grabbed the syringe from my pocket. Jabbed toward her.

She dodged. Faster than expected. Grabbed my wrist. Twisted.

Pain shot up my arm. The syringe fell. Clattered across the floor.

Marissa kicked it away. Pressed the scalpel to my throat. "Don't make this harder than it needs to be."

Cold metal against skin. My pulse hammered against the blade.

"Marissa—"

"Five years I've waited. Five years playing the victim. The broken woman. The medicated shell." Her voice dropped. "I'm done waiting. Done pretending. Tonight, everyone pays."

Footsteps in the hallway. Running.

Sophie's voice. "Amy?"

Marissa's grip loosened. Just a fraction.

I shoved her. Hard. Broke free.

Ran into the hallway. "Sophie! She's the killer!"

Sophie appeared. Flashlight beam hit my face. Then swung to Marissa.

Marissa stood in the doorway. Scalpel in hand. No longer hiding.

"Did you really think I was schizophrenic?" she said to Sophie. "Did you think I believed your act?"

"You've been manipulating my investigation."

"I've been using you. There's a difference." Marissa stepped into the hallway. "You were so eager to expose Keller. So righteous. Easy to guide. Easy to control."

Keller emerged from the common room. Saw the scalpel. Saw Marissa's face.

"You," he said. Voice cold. "It was you all along."

"Hello, Dr. Keller." Marissa's smile was ice. "Surprise."

"Natalie. Carl. You killed them."

"I did. And I was going to kill you next. Make it look like remorse. The monster who finally couldn't live with his crimes." She turned the scalpel in her hand. Light caught the blade. "But now? Now I'll just kill all of you. Frame you posthumously. Works either way."

Elena appeared behind Keller. Saw the scalpel. Screamed.

Marissa lunged.

Not at me. At Keller.

He dodged. She was fast. The blade caught his shoulder. Sliced through fabric and skin. Blood bloomed dark.

He stumbled back. Grabbed his wound.

Marissa turned. Ran.

Down the hall. Toward the east stairwell.

Sophie chased. "Stop!"

I grabbed the fire extinguisher. Followed.

Marissa reached the barricade. Shoved furniture aside. Stronger than she should be. Five years off medication. Faking weakness. Now showing her real capability.

She squeezed through. Disappeared down the stairs.

Sophie reached the gap. Started through.

"Wait!" I grabbed her arm. "She's leading us somewhere. Splitting us up."

"We can't let her escape."

"She's not escaping. She's hunting." I looked back. Keller bleeding. Elena hysterical. Vanessa catatonic. "We need to protect them. Keep everyone together."

"She'll get away—"

"There's nowhere to go. The building's locked down. Storm's not clear enough for her to leave." I pulled Sophie back. "We wait for rescue. Lock ourselves in. Let the police deal with her."

Keller pressed his hand to his shoulder. Blood seeped between his fingers. "Amy's right. We barricade. We survive."

We rebuilt the blockade. Heavier. Everything we could move. Desks. Filing cabinets. Medical carts. No one was getting through without serious effort.

Then we gathered in the common room. All of us. Wounded and terrified and trapped.

Marissa was out there. In the building. Armed. Waiting.

And we had forty-five minutes until rescue came.

If we survived that long.

Chapter 7

The Roof

We waited.

Keller sat on the couch. Bleeding. I'd bandaged his shoulder with torn sheets. Makeshift dressing. Not enough. He needed real medical care.

Sophie stood by the door. Listening. Watching for movement in the hallway.

Elena and Vanessa huddled together. Silent. Shock setting in.

My phone showed five-forty AM. Twenty minutes until dawn. Rescue would come soon. Had to come soon.

Smoke smell drifted through the vents.

Faint. Growing stronger.

"Do you smell that?" Sophie asked.

I did. Sharp. Chemical. Not wood smoke.

"She's setting fires," Keller said. Voice strained. "Multiple locations. Smoking us out again."

The smoke thickened. Rolled through the ventilation system. Filled the common room. Gray haze. Choking.

Elena coughed. Vanessa pulled her blanket over her face.

"We can't stay here," I said.

"The roof," Sophie said. "Only option. Above the smoke."

"In this storm?"

"Better than burning."

She was right. The smoke grew dense. My eyes watered. Throat burned. The fire wasn't close yet. But the smoke would kill us first.

"Everyone up. Now." I grabbed Elena's arm. Pulled her to her feet. "Interior stairs. Move."

We stumbled into the hallway. Smoke thicker here. Vision cut to a few feet. Flashlight beams barely penetrated.

I led them to the interior stairwell. Middle of the building. Away from the main stairs where Marissa might be waiting.

Up. One flight. Two. Three.

Fourth floor. Roof access door at the end of the hall.

I pushed it open. Cold air rushed in. Wind. Snow.

We climbed the final steps. Emerged onto the roof.

The storm had lessened. Snow still fell but lighter. Wind still howled but not violent. Dawn broke through clouds. Gray light. Enough to see.

The roof was flat. Gravel surface. No railing. Four stories of empty air. Below—concrete parking lot.

Elena collapsed near the center. Coughing. Vanessa beside her. Both shaking from cold. We wore hospital clothes. Robes. Nothing meant for December weather.

Already freezing.

Keller leaned against the roof access housing. Face pale. Losing blood. "We wait here. Signal rescue when they come."

Sophie moved to the edge. Looked down at the parking lot. "How long?"

"Fifteen minutes. Maybe less."

"We'll freeze before then."

"Then we stay moving. Generate heat. Don't sit still."

I walked the perimeter. Checking sight lines. Making sure Marissa hadn't followed.

Then I saw her.

She stood near the far edge. Scalpel in one hand. Flashlight in the other. Blood on her hospital gown. Not hers. Keller's probably.

"Going somewhere?" she called.

"Stay back." I positioned myself between her and the others.

"Or what? You'll fight me?" She laughed. "You're a nurse. I've been training for this. Five years. Self-defense. Strength training. All in secret. While everyone thought I was medicated and weak."

"Police are coming."

"I know. That's why we're finishing this now." She moved closer. Deliberate. Calculated. "I was going to frame Keller. Make everyone believe he killed you all. But this works too. Rooftop tragedy. Everyone fell. Accident during chaos. Only I survived."

"No one will believe that."

"They'll believe a traumatized patient. A woman who barely escaped with her life." She raised the scalpel. "I've been performing for five years. I can perform a little longer."

Sophie stepped forward. "You killed Patricia's memory. Not honored it. She wouldn't want this."

"You didn't know her." Marissa's voice went cold. "Patricia was kind. Gentle. Keller destroyed that. Made her death look like weakness. Like she couldn't handle her mental illness." She moved another step. "I'm giving her justice. Making sure Keller pays. Making sure everyone complicit pays."

"Carl wasn't complicit."

"He worked here for fifteen years. Never questioned anything. Never helped anyone. His own daughter was committed by Keller and he did nothing." Marissa raised the scalpel. "Everyone here is guilty."

"Not Elena. Not Vanessa."

"Collateral damage." No emotion. Flat. "They're in the way."

She charged.

Not at me. At Sophie.

Sophie dodged. Marissa's blade cut air. Sophie grabbed Marissa's wrist. Twisted. They struggled. Rolled across gravel. The scalpel skittered away.

I ran. Grabbed the blade before Marissa could reach it.

She turned. Saw me. Smiled. Pulled another weapon from her pocket. Syringe. Filled with something dark.

"Phenobarbital. Ten times the normal dose. Enough to stop your heart." She held it like a knife. "Your choice, Amy. Drop the scalpel or I inject Sophie."

Sophie was on the ground. Marissa's foot on her chest. The syringe poised above her neck.

"Don't," Sophie said. "Amy, don't give it to her."

I dropped the scalpel.

Marissa kicked it away. Released Sophie. Turned to me.

"Smart choice."

She lunged. Syringe aimed at my throat.

I sidestepped. Years of avoiding difficult patients. Reading body language. Anticipating moves.

The needle missed. Marissa stumbled. Off balance.

I grabbed her arm. Used her momentum. Pushed.

Marissa fell. Hard. The syringe flew from her hand. Shattered on gravel. Liquid spilled. Soaked into gray stone.

She rolled. Came up fast. Too fast.

Tackled me. We went down. My head hit gravel. Stars burst. Vision blurred.

Marissa's hands found my throat. Squeezed.

"You should have stayed out of it." Her face inches from mine. "Should have just let me finish."

Air cut off. Pressure built behind my eyes. I clawed at her hands. Too strong. Five years of hidden strength training.

Sophie appeared behind her. Grabbed Marissa's hair. Yanked back.

Marissa's grip loosened. She spun. Elbowed Sophie in the face. Sophie went down.

Keller stumbled forward. Wounded. Weak. But moving.

"Marissa, stop."

"Why? So you can talk? Manipulate? Gaslight?" She stood. Faced him. "I'm done listening to you. Done being your victim."

"I didn't—"

"You destroyed my life. Patricia's life. Linda's. Mary's. All of them." She moved toward him. "You're a predator. A monster. And no one stopped you. Until me."

"The courts will—"

"The courts did nothing. The medical board did nothing. The police did nothing." She grabbed the scalpel from where it lay. "So I'm doing it myself."

She rushed him.

Keller couldn't dodge. Too weak. Too slow.

The blade went for his chest. His heart.

I threw myself between them.

The scalpel caught my side. Sharp pain. Hot then cold. Blood soaked through my scrubs.

Marissa's eyes widened. "You—"

I shoved her. Hard. She stumbled backward.

Toward the edge.

She tried to stop. Feet skidding on gravel. Arms windmilling.

For a second she balanced. Right on the edge. Eyes locked on mine.

Then she fell.

Backward. Over. Into empty air.

She didn't scream. Just fell. Silent.

I didn't look. Didn't watch her hit the ground.

Just stood there. Hand pressed to my side. Blood between my fingers. Warm. Wet. Too much.

Sophie grabbed me. "Amy. Amy, sit down."

"I'm fine."

"You're bleeding."

"I'm fine."

My legs gave out. Sophie caught me. Lowered me to the gravel.

Keller appeared. Pressed his hand over mine. Applied pressure. His face swam in my vision.

"Stay with me," he said.

I tried to answer. Couldn't. Voices reached me through cotton. Gray sky above. Wind on my face. Cold seeping through.

Sirens. Distant. Then closer.

Helicopter. The sound cut through everything. Blades chopping air. Red and white markings.

Rescue.

Sophie waved. Flagged them down.

The helicopter landed in the parking lot. Figures emerged. Orange jackets. EMTs.

They came up. Fast. Professional.

Someone took over from Keller. Applied proper pressure. Checked my vitals.

"Stab wound. Left side. Moderate bleeding. Pressure holding. Let's move."

They lifted me. Gurney appeared from somewhere. Straps. Blankets. Everything happened fast.

Down the stairs. Through the building. Smoke cleared. Fire department already working.

Out into dawn. Pink light on white snow. Beautiful. Wrong.

They loaded me into the ambulance. Sophie climbed in beside me.

"You saved him," she said. "Keller. After everything he did."

"He deserves a trial. Not murder." My voice came out weak. "Marissa became what she hated."

"She did."

The ambulance doors closed. Engine started. Sirens wailed.

I looked at Sophie. "Your story. You got it."

"I did. But that's not what matters right now." She held my hand. "You're going to be okay."

"Keller?"

"Stable. They're treating him. He'll live to face justice."

Good. That was good.

The ambulance pulled away. Left the psychiatric center behind. Left the bodies. Left the horror.

I closed my eyes. Let the EMTs work. Let the sirens carry me away.

Christmas Eve. The longest night.

Finally over.

Chapter 8

Aftermath

I woke in a hospital bed.

Ridgemont General. Not the psychiatric center. Real hospital. Clean. Bright. Safe.

Sunlight came through the window. Warm on my face. Christmas morning.

My side ached. Bandaged. Stitched. The wound was clean. Shallow. Lucky. Two inches deeper and Marissa would have hit something vital.

A nurse checked my vitals. Young woman. Kind eyes. "You're awake. How do you feel?"

"Like I got stabbed."

She smiled. "Doctor will be in soon. Your friend's been waiting outside."

Sophie entered. Still in hospital clothes. Borrowed jacket over her robe. She looked exhausted. But alive.

"You're okay," she said.

"More or less. You?"

"Bruised. Nothing serious." She sat in the chair beside the bed. "Keller's in surgery. Shoulder wound needed repair. But he'll survive."

"Good."

"Detective Fairbank is here. Wants to talk when you're ready."

"I'm ready."

Sophie left. Returned with Detective Hazel Fairbank. Mid-forties. Dark coat. Exhausted eyes. I recognized her from the news. Other cases this Christmas. Ridge Lake Resort. The podcaster. Now this.

"Fourth case this week," Fairbank said. Dry. "Ridgemont is cursed."

"Seems that way."

She pulled out a notebook. "Walk me through what happened."

I told her everything. Natalie's accusation. Her death. Carl's murder. Power outage. Sophie's investigation. Marissa's reveal. The rooftop fight.

Fairbank took notes. Face impassive. Professional.

When I finished: "We found Marissa's body. Fourth floor roof to ground level. Impact killed her instantly."

I nodded. Couldn't feel sorry. Should have. Couldn't.

"We also found evidence in her room. Hidden under the mattress. Medications she'd been cheeking for months. Notes detailing her plan. Dates she intended to act." Fairbank flipped pages. "She'd been planning this since August. Waiting for the right opportunity."

"The storm gave it to her."

"It did. Keller working late. Skeleton crew. Isolation. Perfect conditions." Fairbank closed her notebook. "We're exhuming the bodies from 2019 to 2023. The six women in Sophie's notes. Medical examiner will determine if Keller's responsible."

"He is."

"Probably. But we need proof that holds up in court."

"Sophie has proof. Her notebook. Patient testimonies. Medical records."

"We have it. It's evidence now." Fairbank stood. "You did good, Amy. Survived. Protected your patients. Stopped a killer."

"Two killers."

"Yes. Two patterns—old murders and new." She moved toward the door. "Keller stands trial for the 2019–2023 deaths. Marissa's gone, but the record remains. The truth holds her accountable now.

She left.

Sophie returned. "How are you feeling?"

"Tired. Angry. Relieved." I shifted in bed. Pain lanced through my side. "How are the patients?"

"Elena and Vanessa were transferred to a different facility. Proper one. With oversight. They're safe." Sophie sat back down. "The psychiatric center is closed. State shut it down pending investigation."

"Good."

"Gloria wants to run my story. Full exposé. Keller's crimes. Marissa's revenge. The systemic failures that let it happen." She pulled out her notebook. Battered. Bloodstained. "This is going to change things. Mandatory oversight. Independent advocates. Reform."

"Will it?"

"I hope so." She looked at me. "You saved Keller's life. After everything he did. Why?"

"Because Marissa was right about him. He's guilty. He deserves prison. Not murder." I closed my eyes. "She became what she hated. A killer. Someone who decided who lived and died based on her own judgment."

"She was wronged."

"She was. Patricia was wronged. All of them were." I opened my eyes. "But killing Carl? Killing Natalie? They weren't guilty of Keller's crimes. Marissa just wanted revenge. And she didn't care who got hurt."

Sophie nodded. "Complex."

"Everything is."

She stayed with me until visiting hours ended. Then left. Promised to come back tomorrow.

I slept. Dreamless. Exhausted.

Woke to voices in the hallway. Official. Clipped.

Medical examiner. Dr. Sarah Ballard. Same one from the other Christmas cases. She spoke with Fairbank outside my door.

"Three bodies. Natalie Price, Carl Brennan, Marissa Bennett." Ballard's voice carried. Professional. Detached. "Natalie's wrist slashes are consistent with homicide. Wrong angle for self-infliction. Left-handed cuts. Marissa was left-handed."

"And Carl?"

"Blunt force trauma. Single blow from behind. Pipe wrench recovered at scene matches wound pattern. Marissa's prints on the handle."

"What about Marissa?"

"Four-story fall. Multiple fractures. Internal bleeding. Died on impact."

Silence. Then Fairbank: "Both killers confirmed. Keller for the old murders. Marissa for the new ones."

"Correct. My reports will support that."

They moved away. Voices faded.

I lay there. Staring at the ceiling. White tiles. Fluorescent lights. Hospital sounds. Normal sounds.

Two killers. Different motives. Different methods. Both stopped.

Justice. Sort of.

Keller would face trial. Go to prison. Die there probably. He'd killed six women. Maybe more. Assaulted countless others. Used his position to destroy lives.

He deserved everything coming to him.

Marissa had been his victim. Wrongfully committed. Medicated against her will. Five years stolen. Patricia murdered in front of her. The system had failed her completely.

But she'd killed Natalie. Killed Carl. Would have killed all of us.

Victim and perpetrator. Both true. No simple answer.

The next day, Fairbank returned. "Keller's awake. Talking. He confessed to six murders. Patricia Reeves, Linda Lipton, Mary Kim, Jennifer Santos, Bethany Grant, and one we didn't know about. Helen Torres. 2018. Before he came to Ridgemont."

"Seven victims."

"Minimum. We're investigating his previous employment. Three other facilities. Might find more."

My stomach turned. "How many?"

"Don't know yet. Could be a dozen. Could be more." Fairbank sat. "He claims the assaults were consensual. That the women misunderstood therapeutic techniques. That the murders were mercy killings. Ending their suffering."

"He's lying."

"Of course he is. But that's his defense. We'll dismantle it in court." She pulled out papers. "I need your formal statement. For the record."

I gave it. Every detail. Signed forms. Official documentation.

When she finished: "You're free to go. Doctor cleared you. Take it easy for a few weeks. Let the wound heal."

"What happens now?"

"Investigation continues. Trial preparation. Months of work." She stood. "But the immediate threat is over. You're safe."

Safe. The word felt strange. Foreign.

I'd spent twelve hours thinking I might die. Now I was safe. Just like that. Over.

Except it wasn't over. Not really. Seven women dead. Maybe more. Marissa dead. Carl dead. Natalie dead. Lives destroyed. Families shattered. System broken.

That didn't end with Marissa's fall or Keller's arrest. That kept going. Would keep going.

But at least they were stopped. Couldn't hurt anyone else.

That was something.

I checked out of the hospital. December twenty-sixth. Boxing Day. The day after Christmas.

Sophie met me in the lobby. "I'm driving you home."

"I can manage."

"You got stabbed twelve hours ago. I'm driving."

I didn't argue.

We drove through Ridgemont. Snow covered everything. White and clean. Beautiful. The storm had passed. Left clear skies. Bright sun. Like nothing had happened.

But something had. Everything had.

Sophie parked outside my apartment. Walked me to the door.

"Thank you," I said. "For everything. For being there."

"You saved my life. I saved yours. We're even." She smiled. Tired. "Get some rest. I'll check on you tomorrow."

She left.

I went inside. Locked the door. Stood in my empty apartment.

Quiet. Safe. Normal.

I should have felt relieved. Grateful. Something.

Instead I felt hollow. Numb. Like I'd left part of myself on that roof.

The part that believed systems worked. That people were protected. That justice happened automatically.

That part died when Marissa fell.

But maybe something else grew in its place. Something harder. Clearer.

The knowledge that nothing was guaranteed. That protection had to be fought for. That justice required witnesses willing to speak. Reporters willing to investigate. Nurses willing to believe patients.

I walked to the window. Looked out at Ridgemont.

Somewhere out there, more Kellers existed. More Marissas. More systems failing vulnerable people.

But also more Sophies. More people willing to fight.

I didn't know what came next. Didn't know if I'd go back to nursing. Didn't know if I could work in psychiatric care again.

But I knew one thing.

I'd survived. And survival meant something.

It meant being a witness. Being someone who wouldn't look away.

That was enough for now.

Chapter 9

Forward

Three months later.

March brought thaw. Snow melted. Ridgemont emerged from winter. Gray turned to brown turned to green.

I stood in the courthouse. Trenton. Superior Court. Witness for the prosecution.

Dr. Richard Keller sat at the defense table. Orange jumpsuit. Handcuffs. No longer the charming psychiatrist. Just a man facing life in prison.

The prosecutor called me to the stand. I swore in. Told my story.

Natalie's accusation. Her death staged as suicide. Christmas Eve. The hunt through the facility. Marissa's reveal. The rooftop.

Keller's lawyer tried to discredit me. Claimed I was traumatized. Unreliable. That my testimony was colored by the violence I'd witnessed.

The jury didn't buy it.

Sophie's evidence was too strong. Patient testimonies. Medical records showing suspicious overdoses. Suicide notes that didn't match handwriting. Seven bodies exhumed. Seven murders confirmed.

Patricia Reeves. Linda Lipton. Mary Kim. Jennifer Santos. Bethany Grant. Helen Torres. And three more from his previous facilities. Ten victims total. Ten women destroyed because they'd reported him.

The verdict came in two weeks.

Guilty. All counts. First-degree murder. Ten counts.

Life without parole.

Keller showed no emotion. Just sat there. Defeated. Broken.

They led him away. I watched him go. Felt nothing. No satisfaction. No relief. Just emptiness.

Justice. But hollow.

Outside the courthouse, families gathered. Patricia's mother. Linda's sister. Mary's husband. All of them crying. Finally believed. Finally vindicated.

Sophie stood with Gloria Steele. Both reporters. Both witnesses to the verdict.

"It's over," Sophie said when she saw me.

"Part of it."

"The important part. He's in prison. He'll die there."

True. But Marissa was dead too. Carl. Natalie. All the victims. Nothing brought them back.

Sophie won awards for her reporting. New Jersey Journalism Prize. Best investigative reporting. April ceremony. Princeton. Crowded ball-room. Black tie affair.

Gloria gave the introduction. Praised Sophie's courage. Going under-cover. Risking everything for the truth.

Sophie thanked me in her acceptance speech. Red dress. Confident. Nothing like the "schizophrenic patient" I'd met.

"Couldn't have survived without Nurse Cao. She believed the victims. She fought when others didn't."

Standing ovation. I sat in the audience. Cried. Relief and grief mixed together.

After the ceremony, families approached me. Thanked me. Hugged me. Said I'd given them closure.

But Carl's daughter changed everything.

Margaret Brennan. Thirty-seven. Dark hair. Strong jaw. Her father's eyes.

She found me in the courthouse hallway after Keller's sentencing.

"You worked with my father," she said.

"I did. I'm sorry for your loss."

"He tried to save me. Five years ago. Hired lawyers. Contacted medical boards. Tried to prove I was wrongfully committed." Her voice cracked. "Keller destroyed that. Made sure I stayed locked up. Made sure Dad couldn't help me."

"You were at Ridgemont?"

"Ward B. 2019. Same time as Marissa. Same time as Patricia." She pulled out documents. Legal papers. "I reported Keller for assault. He had me committed. Drugged me. Kept me sedated for five years."

My throat closed. "Where are you now?"

"Released. Finally. After his arrest, they reviewed cases. Found twelve women wrongfully committed. All had reported Keller. All labeled delusional. All kept medicated and imprisoned." She met my eyes. "I'm starting a foundation. For victims. Legal aid. Advocacy. Helping people trapped like I was."

"What can I do?"

"Join us. We need nurses. People who understand the system. People who'll believe patients."

I thought about it. Two seconds. "Yes."

I left nursing. Couldn't work in psychiatric care anymore. Too many memories. Too much distrust.

But I could advocate. I could fight.

Margaret's foundation launched in May. "Voice for the Voiceless." Offices in Ridgemont. Small staff. Big mission.

Our first clients: Elena Rodriguez and Vanessa Hayes.

Elena transferred to proper trauma treatment. Not a locked facility. Real therapy. Safe space. She was healing. Slowly. But healing.

Vanessa stayed in treatment. Different facility with oversight. Actual recovery. Medication adjusted. Delusions fading. She'd probably never be completely well. But she was better. Safer.

The state passed reforms. "Margaret's Law." Named for Carl's daughter. Mandatory independent oversight of all psychiatric facilities. Patient advocates. Surprise inspections. Complaint procedures that couldn't be buried.

Too late for Patricia. For Linda. For Mary. For all of them.

But not too late for future victims.

I testified at the state hearing. Told them what I'd seen. How the system protected Keller. How patients were dismissed. How complaints disappeared.

The committee listened. Actually listened.

"This wasn't one bad doctor," the chairwoman said. "This was institutional failure at every level."

Changes came. Slowly. Bureaucratically. But they came.

Facilities closed. Administrators fired. Procedures reformed. Not perfect. Never perfect. But better.

June brought me back to Ridgemont Cemetery.

Three graves. Carl Brennan. Natalie Price. Marissa Bennett.

I brought flowers for all of them.

Carl died trying to protect his daughter. Failed. But tried. That meant something.

Natalie died reporting her abuser. Should have been protected. Wasn't. System failed her.

Marissa died becoming what she hated. Victim turned perpetrator. Both true. No simple story.

I stood at her grave. Gray stone. Simple inscription. Her real story buried with her.

"You were right about him," I said to the stone. "Keller was guilty. Destroyed lives. Got away with it for years." I set flowers down. "But you killed innocent people. Became a monster while hunting one. That's not justice. That's just more death."

The wind moved through trees. Carried away my words.

I walked to my car. Drove to the foundation office.

Margaret waited. "New case. Woman at Essex facility. Says she was wrongfully committed. Claims the psychiatrist assaulted her. Staff won't listen."

"Let's go talk to her."

We drove. Together. Advocates. Witnesses. People who wouldn't look away.

The work continued. Always would. Predators existed. Systems failed. Vulnerable people needed protection.

But now we fought back. Now we believed victims. Now we asked questions.

Not perfect. Never perfect.

But better.

And better was worth fighting for.

I thought about Christmas Eve sometimes. The longest night. Trapped with two killers. Darkness and blood and fear.

But also about Sophie's courage. Elena's survival. Vanessa's resilience. Margaret's determination.

About systems changing because people refused to stay silent.

About patients finally being heard.

That was the real story. Not just death and horror. But also resistance. Reform. People choosing to fight.

Marissa was wrong. Violence didn't create justice. Killing Keller wouldn't have fixed anything. Wouldn't have brought Patricia back. Wouldn't have healed the broken system.

But exposure did. Investigation did. Witnesses speaking up did. Laws changing did.

Sophie's investigation. Margaret's foundation. State reforms. That created change.

Slow. Imperfect. But real.

I couldn't save Patricia. Or Linda. Or Mary. Or any of them.

But I could make sure the next ones were heard. Believed. Protected.

That was enough.

That was everything.

My phone buzzed. Margaret. "The woman at Essex. Her story checks out. Medical records show suspicious medication increases. History of complaints against the psychiatrist. We need to move fast."

"On my way."

I drove. Left the cemetery behind. Left the graves. Left the past.

Moved toward the next fight. The next victim who needed help. The next system that needed changing.

Always forward.

The End.

BOOK 7

The Neighbor

Chapter 1

Moving Day

The moving truck pulled away at three PM. I stood in the empty living room of 847 Maple Street, surrounded by brown boxes. The house smelled like fresh paint and someone else's life.

The realtor said a couple with three kids owned it before me. Upgraded to something bigger in Vernon. They'd left behind scuff marks on the hardwood and a rust stain in the upstairs bathroom sink.

I caught my reflection in the bare window. Dark circles under my eyes. Brown hair falling out of a messy ponytail. Old Penn State sweatshirt, paint-stained jeans. Twenty-nine but looked younger. Hollow.

Three months since the divorce finalized. Three months of Kirk's lawyer dragging everything out, making me prove I deserved half of what we'd built together. The Short Hills apartment went to him. Too many memories there anyway. Too close to his new place with Simone.

Ridgemont was different. Affordable. Quiet. Thirty minutes from Short Hills, but it felt like another planet. Nobody knew me here. Nobody knew about Kirk or the affair or the year I spent trying to fix something that broke on our wedding day.

Outside, Christmas lights blinked on the house across the street. Multicolor. The tacky kind that flashed in sequence. Red, green, blue, red, green, blue. Someone had left a welcome note yesterday—the Johnsons. Invited me to their Christmas party next Saturday.

I wouldn't go.

Two houses down, an inflatable Santa swayed in the December wind. Eight feet tall. Permanently waving.

I hadn't decorated. Hadn't even bought a tree. Christmas was three weeks away and I had nothing. No reason to pretend this year would be festive.

The house was a split-level ranch. Built in the eighties. Two bedrooms. Real doorbell chime—not electronic. Real wood floors. Real quiet. Ground-floor windows made me nervous. First time living alone. But the price was right. Divorce settlement barely covered the down payment.

I walked through each room. Living room: empty except for boxes. Kitchen: outdated but clean. Bathroom: that rust stain glared at me. Bedroom: carpet needed replacing but would do.

My phone buzzed. Text from Jennifer.

How's the new place?

I typed back: *Great! Settling in.*

Lie. I was exhausted. Scared. Relieved to be away from Kirk but terrified of being alone.

Call me later. Love you.

Love you too.

I set the phone down. Opened the nearest box. Kitchen supplies. Unpacked coffee maker, mugs, plates. Made coffee in the unfamiliar kitchen. The cabinets creaked when I opened them. Water took forever to heat.

Outside, *Jingle Bell Rock* played from somewhere down the street. A car passed with a wreath zip-tied to its grille. Normal people doing normal Christmas things.

I took my coffee to the couch—the only furniture I'd unpacked so far. Sat. Stared at boxes. Tomorrow I'll unpack some more. Tonight, I had the couch and my anxiety.

The doorbell rang. Old-fashioned chime. Two notes. Cheerful.

I opened the door.

A woman stood on the porch holding a casserole dish covered in foil. Maybe sixty-five. Gray hair in a neat bob. Kind eyes. Cream cardigan over a floral blouse.

"Hi there! I'm Diane, Diane Fletcher. I live two houses down." She gestured toward a small ranch with white trim. "Wanted to welcome you to the neighborhood."

"Lauren Harper. Thank you."

She handed me the dish. Warm. Heavy. "Chicken and rice. Nothing fancy. But I figured you probably haven't had time to cook with the move and all."

"That's really kind."

"Oh, it's nothing." She smiled. The wrinkles around her eyes deepened. "We're a quiet street. Good people. You'll like it here."

"I'm sure I will."

"Well, if you need anything, I'm at 839. Just knock." She started down the steps, then turned back. "Oh, and don't worry about being alone. I'm always home. Always watching out for my neighbors."

The words should have comforted me. Didn't. Something about the way she said it. Too cheerful. Too knowing.

But I smiled. "Thanks, Diane."

She waved. Walked back to her house. Disappeared inside.

I closed the door. Set the casserole on the kitchen counter. The smell was good. Homemade. I hadn't eaten since breakfast.

I ate standing up. Fork straight from the dish. Too tired to find plates. The chicken was tender. Rice, seasoned perfectly. Diane could cook.

By nine PM, I'd unpacked essentials. Clothes in the bedroom closet. Toiletries in the bathroom. Laptop on the kitchen table. The rest could wait.

I sat on the couch. Opened my laptop. Amazon loaded. I scrolled.

Living alone scared me. Ground-floor windows. A quiet street where nobody knew me. Kirk knew where I lived—I had to file an address change with the court. What if he showed up? What if he tried something?

I searched: home security systems.

Results loaded. Hundreds of options. Ring doorbells. Nest cameras. Smart locks.

I clicked through reviews. Read specifications. Compared prices.

Selected: SecureView doorbell camera. Three HomeGuard indoor cameras. Two SmartSentry smart locks. Total: $847.32.

My budget screamed. But my fear screamed louder.

I added to cart. Entered shipping address: 847 Maple Street, Ridgemont, NJ 07462.

Delivery: Tomorrow by 6 PM.

I hit purchase.

The confirmation email arrived instantly. Order placed. On its way.

Tomorrow I'll install everything. Tomorrow I'd be safe. Tomorrow I'd have control.

I closed the laptop. The house creaked. Wind rattled the windows. Every sound made me tense.

Outside, the Johnsons' lights blinked their pattern. The inflatable Santa swayed. *Deck the Halls* drifted from somewhere.

I checked the door locks. Front door: locked. Back door: locked. Checked again. Still locked.

Climbed into bed. The mattress sat on the floor—no frame yet. Sheets smelled like laundry detergent. Familiar. Safe.

But I couldn't sleep. Just stared at the ceiling. Listened to the house settle. Branches scraped the window. Cars passed outside.

Tomorrow, the security system will arrive. Tomorrow I'd finally breathe.

I closed my eyes. Forced myself to relax.

The Christmas lights bled through the curtains. Red. Green. Blue. Red. Green. Blue.

Sleep came slowly. Fitfully. Interrupted by every sound.

But it came.

Tomorrow would be better.

Tomorrow I'd be safe.

Chapter 2

The Installation

I woke to my phone alarm at eight AM. Sunlight cut through bare windows. First full day in my new house.

Coffee first. The kitchen felt foreign. Wrong cabinet for mugs. Wrong drawer for spoons. Everything displaced.

My laptop sat on the kitchen table. I opened it. Work deadline today—logo redesign for a local brewery. Usually took me four hours. But I couldn't focus.

Amazon tracking refreshed every ten minutes. Package out for delivery. Arriving by 6 PM.

Six PM felt like forever.

Jennifer texted at nine: *You doing okay?*

Fine! Working.

Another lie. I'd opened the design file three times. Stared at blank canvas. Closed it.

Outside, cars passed. Holiday shopping. Three weeks until Christmas. People buying gifts. Decorating trees. Normal December things.

I pulled up the tracking again. Still showed out for delivery.

The brewery logo mocked me. Blank screen. Blinking cursor. I closed the laptop.

Walked through the house instead. Unpacked more boxes. Hung towels in the bathroom. Put sheets on the bed properly—fitted corners, flat sheet, blanket. Made it feel less temporary.

The rust stain in the sink wouldn't budge. I scrubbed anyway. Needed something to do with my hands.

By three PM, I'd unpacked six boxes. Kitchen was functional. Bathroom stocked. Bedroom organized.

Still no package.

I checked tracking. Updated ten minutes ago: Out for delivery.

Sat on the couch. Opened laptop again. The brewery logo file loaded. I moved shapes around. Added color. Nothing looked right. Deleted everything. Started over.

My phone buzzed. Not a text. Amazon notification: **Package arriving soon.**

I jumped up. Checked the window. No delivery truck yet.

Went back to the couch. Stared at my phone.

Four-thirty PM. The doorbell would ring any minute.

I pulled up the tracking again.

Four-fifty PM. Headphones on. Music playing. I was deep in the design when movement caught my eye.

A car pulled away.

My package sat on the porch.

I opened the door. Cold December air hit my face. The box was there. Brown cardboard. Amazon smile logo. My name on the label.

I brought it inside. Heavier than expected. Set it on the living room floor.

Grabbed scissors from the kitchen. Slit the tape down the middle. Cardboard flaps opened.

Bubble wrap. Boxes.

Everything I'd ordered.

A SecureView doorbell camera.

Three HomeGuard cameras.

Two SmartSentry locks.

I installed the doorbell first—old brass one off, new one on, app connected. A live feed blinked onto my phone: porch, steps, street. Night vision worked. Motion detection armed.

The HomeGuard cameras went up fast—living room, bedroom, back entrance. Three feeds stacked on my phone, every angle covered.

The SmartSentry locks took longer, but once I finished, both doors obeyed my phone. Locked. Unlocked. Locked again. Perfect.

By nine, the whole system ran. Doorbell. Cameras. Locks.

A house under my control.

I ate Diane's casserole, checking feeds between bites.

Nothing moved.

By ten, exhaustion crawled over me. Teeth brushed. Sleep clothes.

One last glance at the apps—porch clear, rooms clear, doors locked.

I plugged in my phone and set it beside the ceramic lamp base, the solid weight shifting under my hand as I turned off the light.

Silence. Refrigerator hum.

Christmas lights blinking through the curtains.

Safe.

Secure.

Finally.

Sleep pulled me under.

My phone buzzed.

SmartSentry notification: **Front door unlocked — 3:02 A.M.**

I grabbed the phone. The door was unlocked.

I hadn't touched it.

My hands shook as I re-locked it.

Porch feed—empty.

Activity log—blank.

Wind? Glitch? New system settling?

I set the phone down. Stared at the ceiling, pulse refusing to slow.

Probably nothing.

But I didn't sleep again.

Just watched shadows crawl the ceiling and listened to the house.

Waiting for morning.

Chapter 3

The Glitches

Wednesday morning. The living room lights flickered.

I woke on the couch. Must've fallen asleep there. The lights strobed—on, off, on—until I killed them through the app. No commands in the log. Nothing unusual.

A glitch. New system settling.

Coffee helped. I checked everything again: porch clear, cameras recording, locks secure.

The thermostat sat at sixty-five. I'd set it to seventy-two. I changed it back.

Work demanded attention. Brewery logo due. I forced myself through it—shapes, color tweaks, typography. Sent it off before noon. Good enough.

The doorbell chimed.

SecureView showed an empty porch.

I opened the door anyway. Nothing but the welcome mat and dry leaves. Probably the wind.

I'd barely sat back down when it chimed again.

Feed still empty.

A third chime.

I went to the basement and unplugged the transformer. Silence.

Faulty wiring. Old house. Tomorrow's problem.

Thursday night brought worse.

I watched a documentary—sharks, something mindless—when the living room camera whirred. I turned. The device swiveled on its mount and pointed straight at me.

My pulse spiked.

HomeGuard showed no commands. No movement logs. But the lens stayed fixed on my face until I unplugged it and reset it manually. The other cameras hadn't budged.

Technology, I told myself.

Just technology.

Friday morning, the voice assistant spoke.

I hadn't said the wake word. Hadn't touched it.

The EchoHome on the counter lit up.

"Good morning, Lauren. Did you sleep well?"

I dropped my mug. It shattered across the tile.

"I didn't say anything."

The light pulsed, listening to nothing.

I unplugged it. Threw it in the trash.

Cleaned the coffee with shaking hands.

Too many glitches. Too many devices behaving wrong.

Jennifer called at lunch.

"How's the new place?"

"Weird."

"Weird how?"

I told her—lights, thermostat, doorbell, camera swivel, the assistant speaking on its own.

"That's creepy."

"It's bugs. Updates. Something like that."

"Or someone hacked your system."

My stomach dipped. "Who would hack me?"

"I don't know. But you should return everything."

"I already installed it all. Holes drilled. Wires everywhere."

A pause. Then:

"Lauren... are you sure Kirk isn't involved?"

"How could he be? He doesn't even know I moved to Ridgemont."

Another pause.

"You filed your address with the court. For the divorce. He knows."

My throat tightened. "He wouldn't."

"He's obsessive. You know that."

"He can't access my accounts. I changed everything."

"Just be careful," she said. "If anything else happens, call the police."

"I will."

But I didn't believe my own voice.

Six p.m. A knock at the door.

SecureView showed Diane on my porch, holding a plate.

Warm snickerdoodles. A smile.

"Too many cookies. Thought you might want some."

She stepped inside, moving slowly, taking in the boxes, the sparsity.

"Still getting settled?"

"Trying."

She sat on the couch. Patted the cushion until I joined her.

"I noticed your cameras," she said. "Smart choice. I have the same system."

Something in me eased. "You do?"

"Oh yes. Three years." She squeezed my hand—soft, warm. "Have you had any issues? Glitches?"

"Actually... yes."

She nodded, unsurprised.

"Happens all the time. Updates cause bugs. Cameras recalibrate. Doorbells get twitchy in the wind. Give it a week."

I wanted to believe her.

I tried to.

"Thanks, Diane. Really."

She stood. "Anytime, dear. I'm always home. Always."

A smile.

"Retirement," she said. "Nothing but time."

I walked her out. Ate three cookies.

The Johnsons' speakers played Rudolph outside, their inflatable Santa bowing at the wind like someone apologizing.

Christmas two weeks away. I hadn't bought anything. Hadn't called my parents.

The season felt hollow. Thin.

I checked the feeds: porch empty, rooms still, house quiet.

Maybe she was right. Maybe it was all updates and wiring and my nerves.

I went to bed at eleven.

My phone lit up.

Motion detected — Front Door.

I opened the feed.

Porch empty.

Then the screen glitched—static, pixel smear—and white text appeared across the video:

I'm watching.

The feed snapped back.

Normal porch.

No text.

No trace.

I screenshot it—proof I wasn't losing it—but the image showed only the normal porch view. The message gone.

I locked every door from my phone.

Triple-checked everything.

Set the phone down.

Turned off the light.

Sleep didn't come.

I lay there, ceiling shifting in shadows, heart too loud in my chest.

Someone was watching.

Someone had access.

Someone wanted me to know.

I got up. Took a knife from the kitchen. Set it on the coffee table. Sat on the couch with the feeds open.

Living room. Bedroom. Kitchen. Porch.

Nothing moved.

Hours passed.

Two a.m. Three. Four.

Still nothing.

But I knew—someone had been there. In my system. On my screen. Watching me watch them.

Dawn crept in, gray and thin.

The Johnsons' lights still blinking. Santa still swaying.

I was going to the police.

Today.

Right now.

This wasn't a glitch.

This was something worse.

<h1 style="text-align:center">Chapter 4</h1>

<h2 style="text-align:center">The Livestream</h2>

I walked into Ridgemont Police Station at nine AM. The building smelled like burnt coffee and floor wax. Fluorescent lights hummed overhead. A desk sergeant sat behind bulletproof glass, typing something into an ancient computer.

"Can I help you?"

"I need to file a report. Someone hacked my security system."

He slid a clipboard through the slot. "Fill this out. Officer Polaski will be with you."

I sat in a plastic chair. Filled out the form. Name, address, incident description. My hand shook writing Kirk's name in the "suspected individual" box.

Ten minutes later, a side door opened.

"Ms. Harper?"

Officer Polaski stood in the doorway. Late twenties, athletic build, clean-cut in his pressed uniform. He had kind eyes. The type of cop who actually listened.

"Come on back."

I followed him to a small interview room. Gray walls. Metal table. Two chairs. He gestured for me to sit.

"What brings you in today?"

I pulled out my phone. Opened the screenshot. "Someone sent me this message through my security camera feed."

He studied the image. The words "I'm watching" superimposed over my porch view.

"When did this happen?"

"Last night. Around eleven PM."

"And you suspect your ex-husband?"

"Kirk Harper. He's been..." I searched for the right word. "Controlling. The divorce finalized three months ago. I moved here to get away from him."

Polaski took notes. Professional. Thorough. "Has he contacted you since the divorce?"

"No. Not until this."

"Do you have a restraining order?"

"No. I didn't think I needed one."

"Have you seen him around the neighborhood? Anyone lurking outside your windows?"

"No."

"Have you contacted the manufacturer? SecureView has customer support."

"Not yet. But—"

"I'd start there. Could be faulty equipment." He set down his pen. "Who installed the system?"

"I did."

"Yourself?"

"Yes."

"So no technician came to your house? No one else had access during installation?"

"No. I ordered it from Amazon. Installed everything myself."

"And have you given anyone else access to your accounts? Shared passwords?"

"No."

"Ex-boyfriend? Family member? Friend who might be playing a prank?"

I shook my head.

He nodded. Wrote something down. "I'm going to document this. You should also change all your passwords. Security system, email, everything. Make them complex. Don't reuse anything he might know."

A woman walked past the doorway. Mid-forties, dark hair pulled back, detective's badge clipped to her belt. Sharp eyes that missed nothing.

Polaski stood. "Detective Fairbank, you have a minute?"

She stopped. Looked in. "What's up?"

"Ms. Harper is reporting a potential stalking incident. Ex-husband may have accessed her home security system."

Fairbank stepped into the room. Extended her hand. "Hazel Fairbank. You're on Maple Street?"

"847."

"I know the house. Family with three kids lived there before."

"That's what the realtor said."

She pulled a business card from her pocket. Handed it to me. "If this escalates, call me directly. Don't wait. Stalking situations can turn dangerous fast."

"Thank you."

She left. Polaski finished his report. Gave me a case number. Told me to document everything. Keep the screenshot. Note any future incidents.

I drove home.

By eleven AM, I sat at my kitchen table with my laptop open. Changed every password.

SecureView: thirty random characters. Letters, numbers, symbols. Nothing Kirk could guess.

HomeGuard: different password. Just as complex.

SmartSentry: new password. Wrote them all in a notebook. Hid it in my bedroom drawer.

Email. Amazon. Banking. Social media. Everything.

My fingers cramped from typing. But I felt safer. Slightly.

The system was mine now. Locked down. Protected.

I made lunch. Leftover casserole from Diane. Still good. Ate standing at the counter.

Outside, someone's speakers played Jingle Bells. The Johnsons were setting up for their Christmas party tonight. I could see them through my window. Hanging streamers. Arranging chairs on their deck.

Normal people doing normal things.

I wasn't normal anymore.

By three PM, I couldn't stop thinking about it. The message. "I'm watching."

I opened my laptop. Googled: "Can security cameras be hacked?"

Results loaded. Hundreds of articles. Forums. Reddit threads.

One caught my attention: "How to check if your camera feeds are being streamed without consent."

I clicked.

The article explained dark web surveillance. Illegal streaming sites. Hidden markets for stolen footage. Instructions for searching using Tor browser.

My stomach tightened.

I downloaded Tor. Installed it. Opened the browser.

The interface looked different. Slower. Everything routed through encrypted networks.

I followed the article's instructions. Searched: "847 Maple Street Ridgemont."

A result appeared.

One link. Black background. Red text.

My mouse hovered over it. Shaking.

I clicked.

The page loaded slowly. Dark design. Minimal text.

LIVE FEED: Ridgemont Beauty

Below: a video player.

My living room. Right now. LIVE.

I sat on my couch in the video. Two-second delay. Watching myself on screen.

I waved.

Saw it happen on the feed.

Couldn't breathe.

Chat scrolled beside the video:

DarkWatcher47: she's home

ViewerX: worth every penny

Anonymous: 8 months archived

Subscriber count in the corner: 223 people.

Archive button below the player: 347 videos.

I clicked archive. Thumbnails loaded. Dozens of them. Hundreds.

Me sleeping. Showering. Changing clothes. Crying on the couch. Everything.

Dates: April. May. June. July. August. September. October. November. December.

Wait.

I moved here December fifteenth.

I clicked an April video.

It loaded. Different location. Different bedroom. Different furniture.

My Short Hills apartment.

He'd been filming me for eight months. Before I even left him. Before the divorce finalized.

The room spun. I grabbed the table edge.

Scrolled through more videos. My entire life. Every private moment. Everything I thought was mine.

223 strangers had watched me.

Paid to watch me.

I clicked on account settings. Publicly visible page.

Administrator: StreamHost_Primary

Co-Administrator: TechOp_Secondary

Anonymous usernames. Could be anyone.

But I knew.

Only Kirk had access to that apartment. Only Kirk could have installed cameras there.

But I couldn't prove it.

My phone buzzed. Text from unknown number.

I opened it.

"I know you found it. Come back to me or I send links to your mother, your sister, every client on your contact list. You have 24 hours. -K"

Kirk. This was his handiwork, and he wasn't working alone.

The realization burrowed deep.

Twenty-four hours.

Then everyone would know.

I called Jennifer. She answered on the second ring.

"Hey, what's—"

"He's been livestreaming me." My voice broke. "Eight months. Since April. There are 223 subscribers. 347 videos."

"What?"

"I found it. Dark web site. My living room is streaming right now. Anyone can watch. They're watching me right now."

"Go to the police. Now."

"He'll release everything publicly. To Mom. To my clients. Everyone."

"Lauren, he's already selling you to strangers!"

"Anonymous strangers. Not my FAMILY."

"Then what are you going to do?"

"I don't know."

Silence on the line. Then: "Come stay with me. Pack a bag. Leave tonight."

"He'll follow."

"Then we go to the police together. You have evidence now."

"I can't."

"Lauren—"

"I need to think. I'll call you back."

I hung up.

Sat in the dark living room. Lights off. Curtains drawn. Laptop glowing.

The livestream was still active. Chat still scrolling. Eighty-nine viewers watching.

Watching me sit in the dark.

Across the street, music started. The Johnsons' party. Laughter. Voices. Christmas cheer bleeding through my windows.

Silent Night played from their speakers. Holy night. All is calm.

Nothing was calm.

Chapter 5

The Plan

I didn't sleep. Couldn't eat. Just sat staring at Kirk's text.

Twenty-four hours. Then he'd send the videos to everyone I knew.

Sunday morning. December twenty-second. Three days until Christmas. The Johnsons' party had ended around two AM. Now their yard was quiet. Empty cups scattered across the deck. Deflated Santa listing to one side.

My phone rang at eight AM.

Jennifer.

I answered.

"What did you decide?"

"I can't go back to him."

"Then go to police. You have evidence now. The site. The videos. His threat."

"He'll destroy me out of spite."

Silence on the line. Long enough I checked if the call had dropped.

"So what are you going to do?"

I looked at the text on my screen. At my laptop still open to the livestream. Eighty-three viewers watching me sit on my couch at eight AM on a Sunday.

"I'm going to kill him."

"Lauren—"

"It's the only way this ends. If he's dead, the videos die with him."

"That's murder."

"It's survival."

I hung up.

Set the phone down. Opened my laptop properly. Started researching.

New Jersey self-defense laws. Castle Doctrine. When you could use lethal force.

The answer: if someone broke into your home. If you felt genuine threat to your life.

I already had documentation. Police report from Officer Polaski. Screenshots of Kirk's threat. Evidence of stalking.

The key was making it look like self-defense.

Lure Kirk to my house. Make him break in. Shoot him.

Simple.

I researched gun shops. Found one in Morris County. Open Sundays. Forty-minute drive.

By three PM, I stood in Precision Firearms & Defense. The store smelled like gun oil and new carpet. Display cases lined the walls. Handguns. Rifles. Ammunition boxes stacked on shelves.

A clerk approached. Late fifties, gray beard, flannel shirt. Name tag: FRANK.

"Help you find something?"

"I need protection. My ex-husband is stalking me."

His expression shifted. Professional to sympathetic. "Have you filed a police report?"

I pulled out my phone. Showed him the case number from Polaski's report.

Frank nodded. Read it. "New Jersey has provisions for immediate threat situations. We can waive the standard waiting period with documented stalking."

"What do you recommend?"

"Glock 19. Nine millimeter. Reliable. Easy to use. Good for home defense."

He pulled one from the case. Set it on the counter. Black polymer frame. Compact. Deadly.

I let out an exasperated sigh. "Never held a gun before."

"I'll show you the basics. But you should take a safety course. Get comfortable with it."

Twenty minutes later, I walked out with a Glock 19, two boxes of ammunition, and a gun safe. My hands shook the entire drive home.

Monday morning. December twenty-third. Christmas Eve tomorrow.

I drove to an indoor shooting range in Morris County. The building was unmarked. Industrial. I only found it because of the website directions.

Inside: concrete walls, soundproofing, the constant pop-pop-pop of gunfire from the lanes.

A woman met me at the counter. Fifties, short gray hair, muscular build. Wore a range safety officer vest.

"First time?"

"Yes."

"I'm Carol. I'll get you set up."

She took me through basics. Loading the magazine. Proper stance. How to aim. Breathe. Squeeze the trigger, don't pull.

"Safety's here. Keep your finger off the trigger until ready to fire. Never point at anything you don't intend to shoot."

We moved to a lane. She showed me how to load. Chamber a round. Aim downrange at the paper target.

"Whenever you're ready."

I squeezed the trigger.

The recoil shocked me. Loud even through ear protection. The shot went wide. Missed the target completely.

"Normal. Try again. Relax your shoulders."

I fired again. Again. The first hour was terrible. Shots everywhere. My hands cramped. Ears rang despite protection.

But by the end: I could hit center mass at fifteen feet. Not expert. Competent enough.

Carol watched my final grouping. Five shots. Four hit the target's chest area.

"Not bad. But remember—only fire if you're genuinely in danger. Real situations aren't like this. Adrenaline. Fear. Everything changes."

"I understand."

I drove home. Hands still shaking. Not from fear anymore. From something else.

Determination.

That night, I drove to a convenience store in Vernon. Paid cash for a burner phone. Activated it in the parking lot.

Eight PM. Sitting in my car. Engine off. Christmas lights reflecting off the windshield from the store's display.

I texted Kirk's number from the burner: "You win. I'll come back. But meet me at my house first. Christmas Eve, 8 PM. We need to talk privately."

Sent.

Waited.

Five minutes. Ten.

My phone buzzed.

"I knew you'd see reason. Christmas Eve. Don't make me wait. I've missed you so much."

My stomach turned. He actually thought I wanted him back. That I'd crawled back to him willingly.

I typed: "See you then."

His response came immediately: "I love you."

I stared at the words. Love. He called this love.

Turned off the burner phone. Threw it in the glove compartment.

Drove home.

By ten PM, I had everything ready. Gun safe in my bedroom closet. Combination set to my birthday. Loaded magazine on the shelf inside. Glock cleaned and ready.

Christmas Eve tomorrow. Kirk would come at eight PM.

He'd walk into my house expecting reunion.

He'd never walk out.

I lay in bed. Stared at the ceiling. Gun three feet away in the closet. Loaded. Ready.

Couldn't sleep. Mind running through scenarios. He'd knock. I'd let him in. He'd try to touch me. I'd pull the gun. Tell him to leave. He'd refuse. Get aggressive. Break something. Lunge at me.

Self-defense.

Outside, someone's speakers played Joy to the World. It comes from a few houses down. Still celebrating. Still cheerful.

I felt no joy. Just cold determination.

Tomorrow night: Kirk would walk into my house.

And I would finally be free.

Chapter 6

The Killing

Christmas Eve. The longest day of my life.

I woke at six AM. Couldn't sleep past that. Too much adrenaline. Too much fear.

I ran some errands in the morning, grocery shopping, dropping off dry cleaning, then spent the rest of the afternoon preparing. Gun safe open. Magazine loaded. Fifteen rounds. Glock on the nightstand beside the ceramic lamp.

Kirk was supposed to arrive at eight PM.

I sat in the living room. Lights on. Curtains open. Normal. Like I was waiting for a date. Not an execution.

Across the street, the Johnsons were having a Christmas Eve party. Cars filled their driveway. Laughter drifted through my windows. Music. *Jingle Bell Rock*. People living normal lives.

I checked my phone. Seven PM.

One hour.

Seven-thirty. Still nothing.

I went upstairs. Double-checked everything. Gun loaded. Safety? It's a Glock - squeeze all the way back, Carol had said. I locked the bedroom door so Kirk would force his way in.

Everything ready.

Eight PM. I sat on the bed. Gun in my hands. Waiting.

Eight-fifteen. Nothing.

Eight-thirty. Still nothing.

Was he coming?

Nine PM. My hands shook. I set down the gun. Checked my phone. No messages. No missed calls.

Had he figured it out? Did he know this was a trap?

Nine-thirty. Ten PM.

The Johnsons' party was loud now. Someone's drunk uncle singing Christmas carols off-key. Everyone laughing.

I sat in my bedroom. Gun on my lap. Staring at the door.

Maybe he wasn't coming. Maybe he'd changed his mind. Maybe—

Footsteps downstairs.

My heart stopped.

I'd locked all doors. Front and back. Checked them twice. How did he get in?

Then I remembered. SmartSentry locks. Electronic. Connected to WiFi.

Despite my password changes. Kirk still had access somehow. Must have hacked his way in.

He'd unlocked my door remotely. Walked right in.

The footsteps were slow. Deliberate. Like he had all the time in the world.

Came up the stairs now.

I grabbed the gun. Stood. Aimed at the door.

My bedroom door was closed. Locked with the old-fashioned twist lock. Not electronic. He couldn't open it remotely.

The footsteps stopped outside my room.

Silence.

Then his voice. Calm. Almost gentle.

"Lauren. I know you're awake."

I didn't respond. Just kept the gun aimed. Center mass. Like Carol taught me.

"Open the door. Let's talk about us. About our future."

My finger rested on the trigger. Arms shaking.

"I'm coming in now."

The doorknob turned. Locked. Rattled.

CRACK.

Kirk kicked the door. Wood splintered. Frame cracked.

Another kick. The door flew open. Crashed against the wall.

Kirk stood in the doorway. Backlit by hallway light. Tall silhouette. Broad shoulders. Bigger than me. Always bigger.

He smiled. "Put the gun down, Lauren."

"Get out."

"You're not going to shoot me."

"Try me."

He took a step forward.

I pulled the trigger.

The gun kicked. Deafening crack. My ears rang.

The bullet hit the doorframe. Six inches from his head. Wood exploded. Splinters flew.

Kirk stopped. Looked at the hole. Then at me. Surprise written all over his face. Bot for long.

He smiled wider.

"You missed."

"Next one won't."

"You can't do it." Another step. "You're weak, Lauren. You've always been weak. That's why you stayed with me for four years. That's why you obeyed me. You couldn't stand up for yourself. That's why you'll never—"

I pulled the trigger.

Click.

Nothing.

Kirk's smile turned into a grin. "Did you really think I'd let you keep ammunition?"

My blood went cold.

"I've been in this house every night for a week. Watching you sleep.

Going through your things." He stepped closer. You really should've changed the combination. Your birthday backwards? Amateur."

Another step.

"Took the bullets while you were at the grocery store. Left the magazine in place so you wouldn't notice the weight difference."

He was five feet away now. Four. Three.

"You never had a chance, Lauren."

He lunged.

I pulled the trigger again. Click. Click. Click.

Kirk grabbed my wrist. Twisted. Pain shot up my arm. The gun clattered to the floor.

His other hand closed around my throat.

Pressure. Immediate. Crushing.

I couldn't breathe. Clawed at his hands. Fingers digging into his skin. No air. No air. No air.

Vision spotted. Black creeping in from the edges.

"You're mine, Lauren." His face inches from mine. "Always been mine. I made you. I own you. Every video. Every moment. Every piece of you belongs to me."

He squeezed harder.

"And if I can't have you—"

Tighter. My lungs screamed. Vision tunneling.

"—no one can."

My hand scrabbled across the nightstand. Knocked over a glass. A book. Ceramic. Heavy. Cold.

The lamp.

I grabbed it. Swung.

Connected with his temple.

Kirk's eyes went wide. His grip loosened. Just a fraction.

I swung again.

Harder.

The ceramic base hit bone. Crack. Blood appeared. Dark. Spreading.

Kirk stumbled back. Hand to his head. Looked at his fingers. Red. Wet.

"You—"

I swung again. And again. And again.

Every violation. Every video. Every subscriber who'd watched me shower. Sleep. Cry. Exist.

Every lie. Every manipulation. Every moment of control.

All of it poured into each swing.

Kirk fell. Hit the floor. Hard.

I followed. Kept swinging.

His head. His face. His shoulders.

The lamp broke. Ceramic shattered. I kept hitting him with the base.

Until my arms gave out. Until I couldn't lift it anymore.

I dropped it.

Stood there. Breathing hard. Throat on fire.

Kirk lay on the floor. Blood pooled under his head. Spreading across the hardwood. Dark and thick.

His eyes were open. Staring at nothing. Empty.

I watched his chest. Waiting for it to rise.

It didn't.

He was dead.

I'd killed him.

My hands shook. The adrenaline drained. Legs went weak. I sat on the bed.

Stared at Kirk's body. Three feet away. Blood still spreading. Reaching toward the bedroom door.

I grabbed my phone. Hands slippery with blood. His blood.

Dialed 911.

A woman answered. "911, what's your emergency?"

My voice came out hoarse. Damaged. "I killed someone. He broke into my house. Was strangling me. I hit him with a lamp."

"Ma'am, is the intruder still in your home?"

"Yes. On my bedroom floor. He's not moving. I think he's dead."

"Are you injured?"

"My throat. He choked me."

"I'm sending police and ambulance now. Stay on the line with me. Are you safe? Is the intruder still a threat?"

I looked at Kirk. At the blood. At his empty eyes.

"No. He's dead."

"Okay. Officers are three minutes away. Stay where you are. Don't touch anything."

I sat on the bed. Phone to my ear. The dispatcher kept talking. Asking questions. Keeping me on the line.

Outside, the Johnsons' party was still going. Someone started singing *Silent Night*. Voices joined in. Beautiful. Harmonized. Perfect.

Holy night. All is calm. All is bright.

Nothing was calm. Nothing was bright.

I'd killed my ex-husband on Christmas Eve.

And I felt nothing.

Just empty.

Sirens in the distance. Getting closer.

Red and blue lights flashed through my window. Reflected off the walls. Off the blood. Off Kirk's face.

The cavalry had arrived.

Too late to save him.

Just in time to save me.

Chapter 7

The Investigation

Detective Fairbank arrived at my house at twelve twenty-three AM.

Two patrol cars first. Officer Polaski. Two others. I heard them clear the house room by room. Found me sitting on the bedroom floor. Found Kirk's body.

No pulse. Dead at scene.

Fairbank came upstairs. Hair pulled back. Detective's badge on her belt. She looked at Kirk. At the blood. At the broken door. At me.

"Ms. Harper. We met earlier this week."

I nodded. Couldn't speak. Throat damaged.

"EMTs are coming up. Let them check you first. Then we'll talk."

The paramedics arrived. Young guy, maybe twenty-five. Hispanic. Name tag: RAMOS. He examined my throat with gentle fingers.

"Petechial hemorrhaging in the eyes. Bruising consistent with strangulation. You need to go to the hospital."

I shook my head.

"Ma'am, you could have internal damage—"

"I'm staying."

Ramos looked at Fairbank. She nodded.

"Document the injuries. Photos. Then she can refuse transport."

He took pictures. My throat. My eyes. The red marks where Kirk's fingers had pressed. Then left.

Fairbank sat on the bed. Pulled out a notebook.

"Tell me what happened."

I told her. Kirk's text threatening to release the videos. The meeting I'd arranged. Him breaking in early. The gun with no bullets. His hands on my throat. The lamp.

She wrote it all down. Asked questions. Time. Sequence. Details.

Then she stood. Examined the broken door. The splintered doorframe where my first shot had hit. The empty gun on the floor. The lamp. The blood.

A crime scene photographer arrived. Older woman. Gray hair in a bun. She moved through the room systematically. Flash. Click. Flash. Click.

By three AM, they'd documented everything.

Fairbank came back to me. "This is clear self-defense. He broke in. Attacked you. You defended yourself with what was available."

"I killed him."

"You survived him. There's a difference."

She gestured to the gun on the floor. "Tell me about that."

"I bought it for protection. After I reported the stalking to Officer Polaski."

"And it was loaded?"

"Yes. I loaded it myself."

Fairbank picked it up with a gloved hand. Released the magazine. "Empty."

"He took the bullets," I said. "Kirk told me he'd been in the house every night. Watching me sleep. He must have emptied the magazine."

Fairbank bagged the gun. The magazine. "That shows premeditation on his part. He came here planning to hurt you. Disarmed your defense first."

Two men came upstairs with a stretcher. Black body bag. They loaded Kirk. Zipped it. Carried him down.

Gone.

I sat on the couch. Someone had wrapped a blanket around my shoulders. The house felt cold. Empty.

Officer Polaski brought tea. Set it on the coffee table.

"It's over now."

But it wasn't.

By eight AM, the police had left. Crime scene tape across my bedroom door. Blood still on the hardwood. I couldn't go in there.

I lay on the couch. Tried to sleep. Couldn't.

Every time I closed my eyes: Kirk's face. Blood spreading. Empty eyes staring.

Christmas morning.

Outside, the Johnsons' house looked festive. Their kids ran around in pajamas. Opening presents. Normal Christmas morning.

My phone sat on the coffee table. I picked it up. Checked the Secure-View app.

Cameras still active. Front door. Living room. Bedroom.

All recording.

All streaming.

Ten AM. I opened my laptop.

I shouldn't look. But I had to know if Kirk's death had ended it.

Dark website loaded.

LIVE FEED: Ridgemont Beauty

Still active.

The video showed my living room. Empty couch. Christmas lights blinking through the window.

Chat scrolling:

ViewerX: *RIP StreamHost but show continues*

DarkWatcher47: *administrator change?*

Anonymous: *TechOp is taking over operations*

Current viewers: sixty-seven.

Kirk was dead. Body in the morgue. But the stream continued.

Someone else was running it. Someone else had access. The edges of the room blurred.

I checked the administrator list.

StreamHost_Primary (Inactive)

TechOp_Secondary (Active)

The past opened its mouth.

The TV turned on by itself.

I spun around.

The screen showed my living room. Me standing there. Staring at the TV. The angle was wrong. Not from any camera I'd installed.

Text appeared on the screen. White letters. Bold.

"Sorry about Kirk. But he was just the cameraman. I'm the producer. And the show must go on. -T"

The screen went black.

T.

TechOp_Secondary.

The co-administrator.

Kirk's partner.

I grabbed my coat. My keys. Walked outside to the porch.

Cold December air hit my face. I pulled out my phone. Called Fairbank.

She answered on the third ring. "Ms. Harper. How are you holding up?"

I kept my voice low. "The livestream is still running."

"What?"

"Kirk had a partner. Someone else has access to my systems. The website is still active. Still streaming. They just sent me a message through my TV."

Silence. "Don't say anything else. Not near your house. The cameras have microphones. Can you get to the station?"

My blood went cold. I hadn't thought of that. Every word I'd said inside had been recorded.

"Yes. "

"Don't unplug anything. Don't let them know you're suspicious. Act normal. Like you're going to the store."

"Okay."

"Bring your laptop. We'll look at everything here."

I hung up.

Walked back inside. Grabbed my laptop. My purse. Moved normally. Casually.

Like I was just running errands on Christmas morning.

Got in my car. Started the engine. Backed out of the driveway.

In my rearview mirror: 847 Maple Street got smaller.

Every camera in that house was still watching. Still recording. Waiting for me to come back.

But whoever was running them didn't know I'd figured it out.

Not yet.

Two PM. I sat in an interview room at Ridgemont Police Station.

Not an interrogation room. Fairbank made that clear. Just a private space. No cameras. No recording. No one watching.

She sat across from me. Officer Polaski stood near the door.

"Show me."

I opened my laptop. Pulled up the dark web site. The livestream loaded.

LIVE FEED: Ridgemont Beauty

My living room. Empty. No one there. The cameras still recording. Chat scrolling:

ViewerX: *where'd she go?*

DarkWatcher47: *probably grocery shopping*

Anonymous: *she'll be back*

Fairbank's jaw tightened. "How long has this been active?"

"Eight months. Since April."

I showed her everything. The archive. Three hundred forty-seven videos. Thumbnails of me sleeping. Showering. Living my life. All sold to strangers.

The subscriber list. Two hundred twenty-three people.

The administrator accounts.

StreamHost_Primary (Inactive - Kirk)

TechOp_Secondary (Active - Unknown)

She took screenshots. Documented everything.

"We'll trace the payment records. Server locations. IP addresses. Whoever this is, they're getting paid. That means a money trail."

"How long?"

"Could be days. We need warrants. Access to financial records. But if they're local—and you're right—we'll find them."

Polaski spoke from the door. "The message on your TV. You said it was signed T?"

"Yes."

"TechOp. T for Tech. Could be a clue to their skillset. Someone good with technology."

Fairbank nodded. "We're also seizing Kirk's laptop. His phone. Email accounts. If he communicated with this partner, we'll find evidence."

"What do I do in the meantime?"

"Go home. Act normal. Don't unplug the cameras. Don't let them know we're investigating." She met my eyes. "I know that's hard. But if they realize we're onto them, they'll destroy evidence. Disappear. We need time to build the case."

"So I just... live with it? Knowing someone's watching?"

"For now. Yes." Her voice softened. "I'm sorry. But it's the only way we catch them."

I closed my laptop. Stood.

"How long until you know something?"

"I'll call you the moment we have a lead. Could be tomorrow. Could be a few days. I'll keep you informed all the way."

I drove home. Pulled into my driveway at four PM.

The house looked normal. Lights off. Curtains drawn. Christmas wreath still on the door.

But inside: cameras watching. Microphones recording. Someone on the other end of the feed. Waiting.

I walked in. Set down my laptop. My purse. Moved through the house like everything was fine.

Made coffee. Checked my phone. Sat on the couch.

Normal. Casual. Like I didn't know.

But my skin crawled. Every camera felt like eyes. Every sound like breathing.

Across the street, the Johnsons were outside in the snow. Kids playing with new toys in the yard. Christmas dinner smells drifting from open windows.

Two houses down, Diane's house had lights on. Kitchen window glowing. I could see her moving inside. Making dinner alone.

My phone buzzed. Jennifer.

Are you okay? Saw the news about Kirk. Call me.

I typed back: *I'm fine. Can't talk now. I'll call tomorrow.*

Set the phone down.

Looked at the living room camera mounted on the bookshelf. Red light glowing. Recording.

Someone was watching. Right now. This moment.

Watching me pretend I didn't know.

Kirk was dead. Body in the morgue. Blood still on my bedroom floor.

But I wasn't free.

Someone else controlled the cameras. The streams. The violations.

And they had no idea I was coming for them.

I just had to wait for Fairbank to find out who.

Chapter 8

The Neighbor

The house felt different now. Violated. Every room Kirk had stood in. The bedroom where he'd died.

I sat on the couch and Googled myself. Wanted to know what Jennifer had seen.

Headlines filled the screen:

Ridgemont Woman Bludgeons Ex-Husband in Self-Defense

Smart Home Technology Used to Stalk Divorced Woman

Tech Engineer Killed After Allegedly Stalking Ex-Wife

I knew I shouldn't read the comments. Did anyway.

Good for her.

She probably provoked him.

Anyone have the videos?

My stomach flipped. I shut the laptop.

My phone rang. Fairbank.

"Ms. Harper. We found something on Kirk's laptop."

I straightened. "What?"

"You need to see this. Come to the station."

. . .

Thirty minutes later, I sat across from her in the interview room. Kirk's laptop open between us.

"Livestream records," she said. "Subscriber lists. Payment logs. He was selling access to the camera feeds."

My breath hitched. "What else?"

"Techop.secondary. The person who took over after Kirk passed."

A cold pulse behind my sternum. "Yes."

"We traced the crypto transactions. Kirk's half went to his bank account. The other half went to an account under—" She turned the screen toward me.

DFletcher839@gmail.com.

The room tilted.

"D. Fletcher," I whispered.

Fairbank typed into the property database.

Owner: Diane Fletcher

Address: 839 Maple Street

"Your neighbor," Fairbank said.

Something in me dropped. "Diane. She brought me casserole."

"The same. We don't know how they met yet, but we're getting warrants. Her house. Her computers. Everything."

I swallowed. "Where is she now?"

"We're picking her up within the hour. I wanted you to see this first."

I drove home in a fog.

Diane's house—two doors down—glowed warm behind its white trim.

She stood at her window, looking straight at me.

Smiling.

When I froze, she lifted her hand and waved. Slow. Careful.

Then she closed the curtain.

My hands went cold. She'd watched everything. Pretended to be my friend while streaming my life to strangers. Shower. Sleep. Tears.

How many of my neighbors had paid to watch?

I backed away from the window.

Kirk was dead.

But the viewers remained.

Police arrived ten minutes later. I watched from my living room as two patrol cars rolled up. Fairbank stepped out of an unmarked sedan and knocked on Diane's door.

Diane answered instantly. Like she'd been ready.

They spoke. Diane nodded, asked for a moment, disappeared inside. Came out in a cardigan, purse in hand. No struggle. No handcuffs.

Before getting into the patrol car, she turned toward my window.

Smiled.

Then she was gone.

Fairbank called a couple of hours later. She invited me over.

Minutes later, I walked into the station. I felt like I now worked there. Officer Polaski directed me to the interview room and left only a few hours ago.

"Diane is in custody. Search warrant executed."

"Did she confess?"

"She admitted subscribing. Claims Kirk told her it was performance art. That you consented."

My throat tightened. "I didn't."

"I know. We found her computer. Hundreds of videos. She archived everything."

I pressed a hand to my forehead. Diane watching me whenever she wanted. My privacy catalogued like episodes of a show.

"There's more," Fairbank said. "You need to see this."

She turned her monitor toward me and played the interview video.

Diane sat across from her, cardigan neat, voice even.

"How did you meet Kirk Harper?" Fairbank asked.

I caught him," Diane said. "Early December. I have cameras watching the street. Saw a man at Lauren's house take her Amazon delivery, open it, swap items."

"You called police?" Fairbank asked.

Diane laughed. "Why would I? I saw an opportunity."

She explained everything—running Kirk's plates, finding the divorce, contacting him on a dark web forum. Offering partnership. Handling distribution and payment processing. Running operations for years. Different streets. Different subjects. Markets. Forums. Revenue streams.

"Kirk was obsessed with one woman," she said. "I saw business potential. With him now gone? I take over completely."

Fairbank paused the video.

"She's a predator," she said quietly. "And not a first-time offender. She and Kirk were like an accidental meeting of like minds, joining together to expand their domains."

"What happens now?"

"Arraignment tomorrow. Multiple felony counts. She's looking at decades."

An hour later, I was home.

A thick manila envelope sat on my porch. I brushed off snow.

Inside: a flash drive and a handwritten letter.

Dear Lauren,

The flash drive contains the subscriber list. Pay attention to the locals. I'm not going down alone. He failed to protect me.

Burn them all.

—Diane Fletcher

After my ordeal, I was skeptical of technology. Despite everything, curiosity won. I plugged in the drive.

One spreadsheet. **2,230 rows.**

Most were burners—crypto wallets, anonymized emails.

But some weren't.

Row 47: SeanDipp@DippCapital.com — Sean Dipp, Short Hills

Row 89: PeteDennis1979@gmail.com — Detective Peter Dennis, Ridgemont PD

My vision blurred.

A cop.

A Ridgemont detective had been watching me. While I filed reports. Sat in interview rooms. Trusted them.

He'd seen me on his screen, then passed me in the hallway.

I scrolled.

Row 1560: WatcherDarkWeb — anonymous

Row 2203: RidgemontLocal88 — anonymous

Ridgemont local.

Someone else nearby.

Mailman? Grocery clerk? Another neighbor?

I looked out at the street.

Blinking Christmas lights. Parked cars. Dark windows.

How many subscribers lived within walking distance?

My phone rang. Fairbank.

"Diane's lawyer mentioned she'd sent you something. Claimed it was an apology letter." Pause. "Did you get it? What did it say?"

I hesitated. "It's a flash drive."

Silence. "What's on it?"

"I don't know yet." That was a lie.

"Can you bring it to the station?" Fairbank asked.

"Is it safe to come to the station?"

Another pause. "What do you mean?"

"If someone in your department was watching me... how do I know who to trust?"

Silence.

"Meet me at Ridge Tavern. Eight a.m. Public place."

"Sure."

Another silence. Then her voice hardened. "Don't share that file. Don't open it again. Bring it tomorrow. It's evidence now."

She hung up.

I stared at the laptop.

Row 89: **Detective Peter Dennis. Ridgemont Police Department.**

The same department meant to protect me.
The same building where I'd asked for help.
One of them had been watching the whole time.

Chapter 9

The Testimony

I brought the flash drive to Detective Fairbank at eight AM on December 29th.

Not at the station. At Ridge Tavern. Public place like she'd suggested. The bar was empty except for early morning regulars. Coffee brewing. Smell of bacon from the kitchen. A miniature Christmas tree with half the lights burned out stood on the bar.

Fairbank sat in a corner booth. Two coffees already waiting.

I slid the flash drive across the table.

"Contains subscriber list. Payment records. IP addresses."

Fairbank plugged it into her laptop. Opened the files. Her face hardened as she scrolled.

"Jesus Christ."

"There are two thousand two hundred twenty-three subscribers."

"I'm seeing that." She kept scrolling. "Some international. Germany. Japan. UK. Australia." She stopped. "Some local."

"There's a Ridgemont detective on that list. Detective Peter Dennis."

Fairbank went very still. Looked up at me. "What?"

"His name is on the list. His email. Ridgemont Police Department. He subscribed. He watched me. No alias."

She closed the laptop. "Wait here."

"Where are you going?"

"To make a phone call."

She left. I sat in the booth. Drank coffee that had gone lukewarm. Watched through the window as people walked past. Normal people doing normal things. Shopping. Talking. Living lives that hadn't been violated and sold.

Twenty minutes later, Fairbank came back. Face like stone.

"Detective Peter Dennis has been suspended. Internal Affairs is investigating. If his name is on that list and we can prove he accessed the streams, he'll be prosecuted."

"If?"

"Evidence needs to be verified. Chain of custody. We can't just take Diane's word." She paused. "But yes. If we can prove it—and we will—he's done."

Small satisfaction. A cop who violated me would face justice.

But mostly I felt exhausted.

"How many of these people will actually face consequences?"

Fairbank was honest. "Diane for sure. Maybe ten percent. Twenty if we're lucky. The ones we can positively identify and locate. The ones in the US. The rest will disappear into the internet."

"So they get away with it."

"Some of them. Yes. I'm sorry."

She closed the laptop. Pocketed the flash drive.

"This is evidence now. We'll catalog everyone. Build cases where we can. Sean Dipp is on here too—investment banker in Short Hills. We're bringing him in for questioning."

I nodded. Didn't care about Sean Dipp. Didn't care about any individual name.

They were all the same. All voyeurs. All thieves who'd stolen pieces of my life.

December 30th. At home.

New Year's Eve was tomorrow. A new year. Fresh start. Supposed to be hopeful.

But I didn't feel fresh. I felt used. Exposed. Forever violated.

I sat in the living room. Dark. Just shadows and the glow from street lights through the window.

Kirk was dead. I should feel relief. Victory. Free at last.

But I didn't.

Because he was still winning.

His network remained. His videos still circulated. Copies on hard drives. Saved on cloud storage. Shared in dark corners of the internet where I'd never find them.

He was dead, but his violation lived on.

My phone buzzed. Text from Jennifer.

Come to Burlington for New Year's. Stay with me. You shouldn't be alone.

I almost said yes. Almost packed a bag and drove the forty minutes to my sister's apartment.

But running wouldn't help. I needed to face this. Own it. Survive it.

I typed back: *I'm staying. But thank you.*

Her response came fast: *Call me if you need anything. I mean it.*

I will.

I set the phone down. Looked around the empty house.

This was my life now. Forever looking over my shoulder. Forever wondering who knew. Who watched. Who saved the videos.

Forever violated.

December 31st. Three PM.

I walked through downtown Ridgemont. Needed air. Needed to feel normal. Even if normal was a lie.

Christmas decorations still hung from lampposts. People left them up through New Year's. Storefronts glowed with white lights. Families walked past carrying shopping bags. Couples held hands. Children pointed at window displays.

Normal people with normal lives.

I wondered how many of them knew. How many had seen my videos. How many recognized my face from the news.

Ridgemont Woman Accused of Bludgeoning Stalker Ex-Husband

My photo had been in every article. Local news stations ran the story. I was famous now. For all the wrong reasons.

A man walked past. Mid-forties. Business casual. Wool coat. He made eye contact. Stared. Eyes lingered on my face. Then he smirked. Kept walking.

Did he see the videos? Or was I paranoid?

I'd never know. That was the torture. Not knowing who knew. Not knowing who watched. Who had copies. Who might recognize me.

I went into a coffee shop. Needed warmth. Normalcy. The smell of espresso and cinnamon.

Ordered a latte. Sat by the window. Watched people walk past.

Everyone looked suspicious now. The barista with the sleeve tattoos. The man in the corner reading a newspaper. The woman on her laptop.

Any of them could have watched me. Could have seen me naked. Vulnerable. Crying.

I left the latte half-finished. Couldn't stay. Outside, *Auld Lang Syne* played from a storefront speaker.

Should old acquaintance be forgot.

Should violations be forgiven just because the calendar changed.

Eleven PM. I walked home.

Dark. Cold. December wind cut through my jacket. The street was quiet. Most people at parties. Celebrating. Drinking. Kissing at midnight.

I got to my house. Locked the door manually. Old-fashioned deadbolt. No smart locks. No cameras. No technology Kirk could hijack.

Sat in the living room. Looked at bare walls where cameras used to hang. No green lights. No recording.

I'd walked through every room after Diana's arrest. Ripped out every camera. SecureView doorbell came off the wall. HomeGuard cameras yanked. Wires pulled. SmartSentry locks removed with a screwdriver. Electronic thermostat replaced with the old manual one from the garage.

Every piece of smart technology. Every device. Every connection.

Threw it all in the trash can outside.

I was safe now. Right?

But I didn't feel safe. I still felt watched. Always watched. Even without cameras. The paranoia was permanent.

Footsteps outside. I froze. Stared at the front door. Locked. The footsteps passed. Just someone walking by. A neighbor going home from a party.

Nothing to worry about.

But my heart raced anyway.

This would never end. The paranoia. The fear. The violation. It was permanent. Tattooed on my psyche. I'd never feel safe again.

My phone buzzed. Midnight. New Year. 2025. Fresh start.

Text from unknown number.

Happy New Year, Lauren. I'm still watching. - A Friend

I stared at the screen.

Kirk was dead. Diane was arrested. Detective Peter Dennis suspended. But someone else was out there. Someone who knew where I lived. Someone who had my number.

Someone who was still watching.

The house was dark. Manual locks. Analog thermostat. Regular doorbell. No recording. No streaming. No watching.

I stood in my living room. Bare walls where cameras used to mount. Empty spaces. Silence.

For the first time in eight months, I was alone.

Truly alone.

No cameras. No subscribers. No Kirk. No Diane. No one watching.

Just me. In my house. In control.

And it felt like freedom.

Chapter 10

The Aftermath

They told me I'd heal. They lied.

January 2nd. I sat in Dr. Morrison's office. The therapist Rachel Morrison had recommended. Different Morrison—no relation. Her office was in Morristown. Neutral territory. Away from Ridgemont. Now I was having a Morris overload.

"How are you sleeping?" she asked.

"I'm not."

"Nightmares?"

"Every time I close my eyes, I see cameras. Green lights. Kirk standing in my bedroom. The hooded figure on my porch."

Dr. Morrison wrote something. "That's normal. PTSD following traumatic events—"

"This isn't normal trauma." My voice came out sharp. "Normal trauma ends. Someone attacks you. You survive. It's over. But this?" I gestured at nothing. "The videos are still out there. On hard drives. Cloud storage. Dark web forums. People I'll never meet have copies. Will always have copies. How do I heal from something that never ends?"

She set down her pen. "I don't know if you can. Not completely. But you can learn to live with it."

"I don't want to learn to live with it. I want it to stop."

"I know."

But she didn't. Nobody did. Nobody understood what it meant to be permanently visible. Permanently violated. Forever exposed.

Two weeks later, I listed the house.

Couldn't stay there. Couldn't sleep in the bedroom where Kirk died. Couldn't walk through rooms where cameras had watched me. Couldn't exist in a space that had been weaponized.

The realtor said I'd take a loss. "You just bought three months ago. Market hasn't moved enough."

"I don't care. Sell it."

She did. February 1st. Young couple with a baby. They asked if anything was wrong with the house.

Everything. Everything was wrong with it.

"No," I said. "Just ready to move on."

They signed the papers. Took the keys. I never went back.

June arrived with heat and false hope.

I changed my name. Legal filing. New identity. New social security card. New driver's license.

Lauren Riley Harper was gone. Dead. Buried with Kirk.

I became Megan Cross.

Ironic, maybe. Cross to bear. Cross to carry. But it was different enough. Untraceable. Fresh start.

New apartment in Ramsey. One bedroom. Third floor. No ground-level windows. No smart home anything. Not even a doorbell camera. Just old-fashioned locks and paranoia.

New job. Freelance graphic design under my new name. No clients who knew me before. No connections to Ridgemont.

New life.

Except it wasn't new. The paranoia came with me. Packed in boxes alongside my clothes and dishes.

I checked locks three times before bed. Covered my laptop camera with tape. Turned off location services. Used VPN for everything. Trusted no one.

July 3rd. I sat in a coffee shop in Ramsey.

Busy. Anonymous. Just another woman working on her laptop. Nobody looked twice.

Then a man walked past my table. Stopped. Turned back.

"Lauren?"

My blood went cold. "My name is Megan."

"Sorry. You just look like someone I saw on the news. That woman from Ridgemont. The one who killed her husband."

"You're mistaken."

He smiled. Leaned closer. Voice dropped to whisper. "I saw the videos too."

I closed my laptop. Stood. Walked out.

Didn't run. Running would confirm it. But my hands shook as I unlocked my car. Drove home. Took wrong turns. Made sure he wasn't following.

Got to my apartment. Locked the door. All three locks. Chain. Deadbolt. Handle lock.

Sat on the floor. Back against the wall. And cried.

Six months. Six months of a new name. New life. New city.

And someone still recognized me.

That night, I sat alone in the dark apartment.

Lights off. Curtains drawn. The only glow came from streetlights bleeding through the fabric.

I whispered to the empty room: "I'm free."

But the words tasted like lies.

Kirk was dead. Diane was in prison. Detective Dennis was facing charges. Nineteen subscribers prosecuted. The others—poof.

Thousands remained. Out there. Anonymous. Watching. Waiting.

And the videos lived on. Would always live on. Digital ghosts that could never be exorcised.

I pulled my knees to my chest. Rested my forehead against them.

This was my life now. Started one Christmas ego. Forever looking over my shoulder. Forever wondering who knew. Who watched. Who saved copies.

Forever violated.

Outside, three stories down, a car idled across the street.

Inside the car, a man sat with a laptop open. Glowing screen illuminating his face.

He typed on a dark web forum. Thread title: "Ridgemont Beauty - New Location Found."

His post appeared:

Found her. New location: Ramsey, NJ. Parkside Apartments, Unit 3C. New name: Megan Cross. Working as freelance designer. Coffee shop regular at Java Junction on Bloomfield Ave. Who wants access?

Replies started coming in.

How much?

Is she still hot?

Does she know you found her?

I'll pay double what Kirk charged.

The man smiled. Took a photo through his telephoto lens. Lauren—Megan—visible through a gap in her curtains. Sitting on the floor. Face buried in her knees.

He uploaded the photo.

Bids started rolling in.

The network lived. Someone always watched.

And Lauren Riley Harper, now Megan Cross, would never be free.

The End.

BOOK 8

The Homecoming

Chapter 1

The Invitation

I hadn't been home in six months. Not since the funeral.

Traffic on I-80 West crawled through the Friday evening commute. Manhattan's skyline shrank in my rearview mirror. Forty minutes to Ridgemont. Forty minutes until I walked back into that house.

The house where my father died.

The house I inherited.

The house my family wanted back.

Dad's heart attack had been sudden. June thirteenth, a Thursday morning. He'd been drinking his coffee in the kitchen when it happened. Barbara—my mother—found him on the floor. Dead before the ambulance arrived. Sixty-five years old.

Three weeks later, his lawyer read the will. Everything to me. The house, the investment portfolio, the life insurance. Three point one million dollars.

My brother Greg and my mother got nothing.

They'd been furious. Still were.

I merged onto Route 23 North. Sussex County spread out ahead, all snow-covered rolling hills and expensive suburbs. The Christmas lights started here. Every house outlined in white icicles, inflatable Santas crowding front lawns. Wreaths on every door. The whole county was a Hallmark movie set.

My phone buzzed in the cupholder. Barbara's name on the screen. I let it go to voicemail. She'd called two weeks ago with her invitation. *Please come home for Christmas. Family needs to heal. We can't let money tear us apart.*

I'd agreed. Guilt, maybe. Or stupidity.

Now I was twenty minutes away, and my hands wouldn't stop shaking.

Ridgemont appeared through the December dusk. Wealthy suburb, perfect houses, nobody's laundry hanging outside. I turned onto Lakeview Drive. My childhood street.

The Foster house sat at the end of the cul-de-sac. Two-story white colonial with black shutters. Greg had gone overboard with the Christmas lights. Icicles dripping from the eaves, an inflatable Santa the size of a sedan, a wreath big enough to be a truck tire hanging on the door.

Three cars in the circular driveway. Barbara's Lexus, Greg's BMW, a silver Honda Odyssey that must be Melissa's.

The whole family. Waiting.

I parked behind the minivan. Sat there with the engine running and my hands locked on the steering wheel. Two minutes later, I talked myself into getting out of the car.

The front door opened before I reached it.

Barbara stood there, backlit by the foyer chandelier. Five-four, slim, well-maintained for sixty-two. Silver-gray hair in a perfect chin-length bob. Blue eyes that matched mine. Red cashmere cardigan, black slacks, pearl necklace. Botox had frozen her forehead smooth.

Her smile was too wide. Too bright.

"Natalie! You came!" She pulled me into a hug that lasted too long and squeezed too hard.

"Hi Mom."

Inside, the house smelled like pine and cinnamon. Candles, probably. Barbara had always been obsessed with making the house smell like Christmas.

The living room was exactly the same and completely different.

Twenty feet long, hardwood floors, beige sectional sofa facing the gas fireplace. An eight-foot Christmas tree dominated the corner, covered in white lights and gold ornaments. The flat-screen TV above the fireplace played a loop of crackling fire that wasn't real.

Everything perfect. Everything staged.

Greg emerged from the kitchen carrying his eight-year-old daughter. Six-one, still had the build of the athlete he'd been in college, softer now around the middle. Brown hair thinned on top. He wore dark jeans and an expensive green sweater with the brand logo, and a more expensive-looking watch.

"Nat! Long time." His voice had that forced casual tone.

Emma had brown hair in two braids and wore a pink dress. Missing her front tooth.

Melissa appeared behind him. Five-five, slim, tired. Blonde hair that had been styled but already wilted. Blue eyes with dark circles that matched mine. Yoga pants and an oversized sweater. Her hands moved constantly, picking at her cuticles, adjusting her hair.

"Hi, Natalie. So glad you could make it." The words came out flat.

Sophie, their six-year-old, clung to Melissa's hand. Blonde pigtails, purple dress.

Everyone smiled. Everyone lied with their faces.

"Dinner's almost ready," Barbara said. "Your room is all made up. Same as always."

The same as always. That was the problem.

Dinner happened in the formal dining room. Dark wood table that seated eight, chandelier overhead throwing too much light. Barbara had made pot roast. My childhood favorite.

Emma and Sophie chattered about school and Christmas lists. The only honest sounds in the room.

"Must be nice not having to worry about money anymore." Greg cut his meat with precise movements.

"I work for my money, Greg."

"Sure, but that inheritance is a nice cushion. Three million dollars. Some people have all the luck."

Barbara set down her fork. "Greg, not tonight."

Melissa's voice was quiet. "Some of us have children to provide for. Mortgages. College funds."

My throat tightened. "I didn't write Dad's will."

"No, but you were always his favorite." Greg's jaw tightened.

"Please." Barbara's smile never wavered. "We're family."

The conversation shifted to Christmas plans. Forced normalcy that fooled no one. Emma asked about my job in Manhattan. I answered, grateful for innocent questions.

Dinner ended. I retreated upstairs.

My childhood bedroom sat at the end of the second-floor hallway. Full bed with a white comforter, oak dresser, matching nightstand. Window facing the front yard.

But something was wrong.

The bed was against the wrong wall. Or I remembered wrong. Posters covered one wall—bands I didn't remember liking. Or maybe I'd forgotten. Stress did that.

Photos hung near the dresser. Me at various ages. Some I recognized. Others—

One showed me at maybe ten, at a beach. Boardwalk in the background. Everyone smiling.

I didn't remember that trip.

Fatigue did strange things to memory. Grief, too. I'd been working eighty-hour weeks since Dad died. Maybe I'd just forgotten.

I unpacked my suitcase. Three days' worth of clothes, toiletries, medications. The Xanax bottle rattled when I set it on the nightstand. Prescribed after Dad's death. For anxiety.

I opened it. Counted the pills.

Fifteen. I'd counted them before leaving Manhattan. Obsessive, maybe, but I needed to know.

I changed into pajamas. Brushed my teeth in the small bathroom attached to my room. Locked the bedroom door before getting into bed.

The house settled around me. Old colonial creaking. Pipes groaning. Normal sounds.

I woke to darkness.

A soft click. The door.

Footsteps. Carpet muffling them. Someone moving near my suitcase. The sound of a zipper. Quiet but distinct.

The footsteps retreated. My door closed with another soft click.

I lay there. Heart slamming against my ribs. Too scared to move.

When I opened my eyes, the room was empty. Door closed. Still locked from the inside.

I turned on the lamp. Got up. Checked the door. Locked. Checked the hallway. No one.

But someone had been here. I knew it.

I opened my suitcase. Everything in place. But things had shifted. Just slightly.

I grabbed the Xanax bottle from the nightstand. Opened it. My hands shook as I counted.

Twelve.

There were twelve pills.

Someone had taken three.

Or I'd taken them and couldn't remember.

I sat on the edge of the bed. Stared at the bottle in my hands.

Outside, Christmas lights blinked. Somewhere down the street, a speaker played "Silent Night." Peaceful. Holy.

Inside, the house was silent except for the blood pounding in my ears.

I checked the door. Still locked. Turned off the lamp.

Didn't sleep the rest of the night.

Chapter 2

The Disorientation

I went downstairs around nine. The kitchen smelled like coffee and something sweet. Cinnamon, maybe.

Barbara stood at the counter, flour dusting her red cardigan. She wore an apron, hair perfect despite the early hour. The oven timer showed eighteen minutes remaining.

Greg and Melissa were at the dining table. Greg's buried in a newspaper. A coffee mug was next to him. Melissa looked up and looked away.

I gave a nod.

"Good morning, sweetheart! Making gingerbread cookies. Your favorite."

I didn't remember gingerbread being my favorite.

"Coffee?" She gestured to the pot.

"Thanks."

I poured a cup. Added cream from the fridge. The kitchen gleamed under morning light—chrome fixtures, granite counters wiped spotless. Red and green dish towels hung from the oven handle.

"Sleep well?" Barbara's voice carried that same brittle cheer from last night.

"Someone came into my room last night. I heard them."

Greg lowered his newspaper at the kitchen table. "What are you talking about?"

"Someone went through my suitcase."

Barbara set down the pastry bag. "Honey, you were probably dreaming."

"I wasn't dreaming."

Melissa glanced at Greg. "Old houses make sounds. You're not used to it anymore."

"I know the difference between house sounds and footsteps."

Barbara wiped her hands on a towel. "Well, you seemed fine at breakfast earlier."

My chest went tight. "What?"

"This morning. Around seven-thirty. You came down, ate pancakes, we talked about going to the tree lighting tonight."

"I just woke up."

Barbara's face shifted. Concern. Or performance. "Natalie, you were here. We had a whole conversation about Christmas Eve dinner."

"That didn't happen."

Greg and Melissa exchanged looks. Subtle. Knowing.

"You really don't remember?" Barbara stepped closer.

"I was in my room all morning."

"Honey, you were sitting right there." She pointed to the chair across from Greg. "You ate two pancakes. Maple syrup. You said they were delicious."

My hands went cold. I had no memory of this. None.

"Maybe you were sleepwalking," Melissa said.

"I don't sleepwalk."

"You used to," Greg said. "When you were twelve. You'd walk around the house and not remember it in the morning."

Heat climbed my neck. They were lying. They had to be lying.

But I couldn't remember waking up. Couldn't remember the morning before nine.

I dropped the subject. Took my coffee upstairs.

.   .   .

By afternoon, Barbara insisted I help clean out Dad's study. "We need to go through his things. Together. As a family."

The study was on the first floor. Dark wood paneling, floor-to-ceiling bookshelves, leather chair behind an oak desk. It still smelled like him. Coffee and Old Spice.

I opened the desk drawers. Papers, pens, old receipts. Nothing important.

Barbara handed me a box from the closet. "Photo albums. Maybe you'd like some?"

I opened the top album. Family photos from various years. Birthdays, holidays, vacations.

Then I saw it.

A beach. Boardwalk in the background. Me at maybe ten or eleven. Barbara and Greg on either side. Dad behind us. Everyone smiling. Cotton candy in my hand.

I stared at the photo.

"Cape May, 2001." Barbara's voice came from behind me. "Don't you remember? We rented a house for a week."

"I've never been to Cape May."

"Of course you have. You loved the saltwater taffy. Ate so much you got sick."

I turned the page. More Cape May photos. Me on the beach. Me on the boardwalk. Me in front of a lighthouse.

Zero memory of any of it.

"I don't remember this trip."

"You were young. Memory gaps are normal."

Greg appeared in the doorway. "What's going on?"

"Natalie doesn't remember Cape May."

He crossed to us. Took the album. Flipped through it. "How can you not remember? We went there every summer for three years."

"That's not true."

"It is true." He pulled another album from the box. Opened it. "Look. Cape May 2000. Cape May 2001. Cape May 2002."

Photo after photo. Me at different ages. Same boardwalk. Same beach. Same family.

I had no memory of any of them.

My hands were numb. "This doesn't make sense."

"What doesn't make sense is forgetting entire vacations." Greg's tone was gentle. Fake gentle.

Barbara touched my arm. "Maybe you should rest, dear. You've been under so much stress."

I backed away. Went upstairs.

I locked myself in my bedroom. Grabbed the Xanax bottle from the nightstand.

Opened it. Counted.

Nine pills.

There were nine pills.

This morning there'd been twelve. I'd counted twice.

Now there were nine.

Three more gone.

Or I'd taken them and couldn't remember. Just like I couldn't remember coming down for breakfast. Just like I couldn't remember Cape May.

I sat on the bed. Stared at the bottle.

What was happening to me?

Six PM. Barbara knocked on my door. "Time to go! Tree lighting starts at seven."

"I'm tired."

"Nonsense. It's tradition. The whole town will be there."

I had no choice. Got dressed. Jeans, black sweater, heavy coat. Followed the family to Greg's BMW.

Ridgemont Town Square was packed. Hundreds of people bundled in winter coats. Kids running around. Vendors selling hot chocolate and roasted chestnuts. The Christmas tree stood in the center—forty feet tall, covered in unlit white lights.

Carolers sang near the gazebo. "Joy to the World" echoed across the square.

Barbara linked her arm through mine. "Isn't this lovely?"

I pulled away. Scanned the crowd. Too many people. Too many faces.

The mayor gave a speech. Something about community and tradition. I stopped listening.

Then a countdown. Ten, nine, eight.

The tree lit up. White lights blazing. The crowd cheered.

I turned to leave. A woman blocked my path.

Fifties, kind face, gray hair. She smiled at me.

"Natalie! I'm so glad you're doing better. After what happened last summer."

My throat closed. "What?"

"You know, the incident. With your mother. We were all so worried."

"I don't know what you're talking about."

Her smile faltered. "Oh. I'm sorry. I thought—" She glanced past me at Barbara. "Never mind."

She disappeared into the crowd before I could ask more.

I spun to Barbara. "What was she talking about? What incident?"

Barbara's face was calm. Too calm. "Just someone being kind, dear. Don't worry about it."

"What happened last summer?"

"Nothing happened. People gossip. You know small towns."

Greg appeared with hot chocolate for the girls. "Everything okay?"

"That woman said something about an incident. With Mom."

He handed Emma her cup. "What woman?"

"She was just here."

"I didn't see anyone." He turned to Barbara. "Did you?"

Barbara shook her head. "No one, honey."

They were lying. The woman had been right there. Right in front of me.

Unless I'd imagined her.

The carolers started a new song. "Silent Night." The same song from last night. The same peaceful melody that made everything worse.

I walked away from my family. Through the crowd. Past the vendors. Out of the square.

Behind me, Barbara called my name.

I kept walking.

The Christmas lights blinked on every house. The snow crunched under my boots. "Deck the Halls" drifted from someone's open door.

I checked my coat pocket. Found the Xanax bottle. I'd brought it with me.

Opened it. Counted under a streetlight.

Nine pills.

Still nine.

Or was it? Had I counted wrong before?

I couldn't trust my own memory anymore.

Couldn't trust anything.

Chapter 3

The Missing Time

I walked back alone.

The family stayed at the tree lighting. I needed to be away from them. Away from their concerned faces and gentle voices and lies.

Or truths I couldn't remember.

The house was dark when I arrived. I turned on lights as I moved through rooms. Kitchen, living room, foyer. The Christmas tree blinked in the corner. Red and gold ornaments catching the light.

I sat at the kitchen table. Waited.

They came home an hour later. Emma and Sophie chattering about the tree. Barbara humming "Joy to the World." Greg's keys jangling.

I stood. "I want to know what happened last summer."

The humming stopped.

Barbara set her purse on the counter. "Natalie—"

"That woman at the tree lighting. She mentioned an incident. What incident?"

Greg sent the girls upstairs with Melissa. Closed the kitchen door.

"Sit down," he said.

"I don't want to sit down."

Barbara pulled out a chair. Sat. Folded her hands on the table. "You attacked me. July fifteenth. You'd been drinking. Screaming about the will."

My legs went weak. I grabbed the counter.

"You pushed me down the basement stairs." Her voice was calm. Clinical. "I broke my wrist. Got a concussion. Ridgemont General kept me overnight."

"That's not true."

Greg pulled out his phone. Opened photos. Turned the screen toward me.

Barbara in a hospital bed. Left wrist in a cast. Bruise on her forehead. Date stamp: July 15, 2024.

"You blacked out afterward," Greg said. "Don't remember any of it."

"I would remember hurting someone."

"You don't." Barbara stood. Crossed to me. Held out her left wrist.

A scar. Two inches long. Pink. Healed but visible.

"Feel it."

I didn't move.

She grabbed my hand. Pressed my fingers to the scar. The bone underneath had a ridge. A break that had healed wrong.

"That's from the railing. When I fell."

I yanked my hand back.

Greg pulled papers from a drawer. "Police report. Domestic violence incident. We didn't press charges. Asked them to keep it quiet."

He spread the papers on the table. Official Ridgemont PD letterhead. Incident number. Date. Barbara Foster, victim. Natalie Foster, suspect. Injury: fractured wrist, concussion. No charges filed per victim request.

"The whole town knows," Melissa said from the doorway. "That's why that woman mentioned it."

My chest went tight. "I don't remember."

"You had a psychotic break." Barbara's hand on my arm. "The grief from losing Dad. The stress. It triggered something."

"I'm not crazy."

"No one said you're crazy." Greg's voice was soft. Concerned. "But you need help."

I backed toward the stairs. "This didn't happen."

"It did happen." Barbara followed me. "And we forgave you. Because you're sick. Because you need treatment."

I ran upstairs. Locked my bedroom door.

Pressed my ear against the wood.

Whispering downstairs. Footsteps. Barbara's voice: "—getting worse—"

Greg: "—before she hurts someone again—"

I slid down the door. Sat on the floor.

July fifteenth. I'd been in Manhattan. Working. I remembered my office. My desk. The coffee shop I'd stopped at.

Except I didn't, in all honesty, remember July fifteenth. Not specifically. The days after Dad's funeral had blurred together.

What if they were telling the truth?

What if I'd hurt her and my mind had blocked it out?

What else had I done?

I woke up standing.

Dark room. Cold floor under my bare feet.

Not my room.

Barbara's bedroom.

I was standing in her doorway. My hand outstretched. Holding something.

Scissors.

Eight inches. Silver. Sharp.

Barbara sat up in bed. Her face went white.

"Natalie—"

I stepped forward. Raised the scissors.

She screamed.

Greg's bedroom door flew open. He grabbed me from behind. Wrestled the scissors from my hand.

"What the hell are you doing?"

I couldn't speak. Couldn't breathe.

Barbara was crying. "She was going to—"

"I know." Greg's arms locked around me. "I know."

Morning light woke me.

I was in my bed. Fully dressed. Jeans and sweater from yesterday. Boots still on.

The scissors sat on my nightstand.

I grabbed them. Turned them over in my hands. Real. Solid. Cold metal.

Had last night been real?

I ran to my door. Unlocked it. Went to Barbara's room.

She was making her bed. Turned when I entered.

"Good morning, dear."

No fear on her face. No anger. Nothing.

"Last night—"

"What about it?"

"I came into your room. With scissors."

Barbara smoothed the comforter. "You were sleepwalking again. You came to my door, looked confused, then went back to your room. Perfectly normal."

"I had scissors."

"You didn't have anything, honey. Just stood there for a moment."

Greg appeared in the hallway. "Morning. Everyone sleep okay?"

Barbara smiled. "Fine. Natalie had a little sleepwalking episode, but nothing serious."

They acted like nothing had happened.

Like I hadn't stood in their bedroom with scissors.

Or maybe I hadn't.

Maybe I'd dreamed the whole thing.

Breakfast was tense. I pushed eggs around my plate. Couldn't eat.

Melissa took the girls to the den to watch Christmas movies. Greg and Barbara stayed at the table.

I excused myself. Went to hang my coat in the hall closet.

Something rustled in the pocket.

Paper. Folded.

I pulled it out. Opened it.

My handwriting. Blue ink. Shaky letters.

I'm going to kill them both. They deserve it. - N

My grip slipped. The paper floated—I grabbed it before it hit the floor.

I didn't remember writing this.

Had no memory of these words.

But that was my handwriting. My pen. My rage on paper.

Footsteps behind me.

I shoved the paper back in my pocket. Closed the closet.

"You okay?" Greg stood in the hallway.

"Fine."

He watched me walk upstairs. I went to my bathroom. Locked the door.

Pulled out the letter. Read it again.

I'm going to kill them both.

Who was I?

What was I becoming?

I turned on the sink. Held the paper over the running water. The ink bled. Dissolved. I tore it into pieces. Shoved the pieces down the drain.

Evidence destroyed.

A knock on the door.

"Natalie? You okay in there?"

Barbara's voice.

"Fine. Just washing my face."

Silence. Then footsteps retreating.

I stared at my reflection in the mirror. Dark circles under my eyes. Hair tangled. Pale skin.

I didn't recognize myself anymore.

The water kept running. "Little Drummer Boy" played from somewhere downstairs. Emma and Sophie singing along.

Normal family sounds.

I turned off the water.

Checked my coat pocket again. Made sure the letter was gone.

It was.

But the words stayed with me.

I'm going to kill them both.

Chapter 4

The Lawyer

Sunday morning, my phone buzzed at 7 AM.

Text from unknown number: *This is David Kellerman, your father's attorney. Need to see you today. Urgent. Can meet at office 2 PM. Please confirm.*

I stared at the screen. Kellerman had read Dad's will in June. Hadn't heard from him since.

I texted back: *I'll be there.*

Barbara knocked on my door. "Breakfast is ready, dear."

"I have an appointment. I'll grab something on the way."

"On Sunday?"

"Yes."

I showered. Dressed. Told them I was meeting a friend from college. Didn't wait for questions.

Kellerman's office sat above a dry cleaner on Park Street in Ridgemont. Red brick building, narrow stairs from the street entrance. The chemical smell from below burned my nose.

He was waiting at the top. Door already open.

"Natalie. Thank you for coming." He shook my hand. Gestured inside. "I know Sunday is unusual. But this couldn't wait."

The office was cluttered. Wood desk with scratched surface. Two client chairs. Filing cabinets. A small artificial Christmas tree sat on top of one cabinet. White lights blinked.

He closed the door. "I received the conservatorship petition Friday. Served to me as your father's estate attorney. I tried calling you, but the number I had was disconnected."

"I changed it. After Dad died. Too many calls."

He nodded. Gestured to a chair. I sat.

"Your family is trying to have you declared mentally incompetent." He slid papers across the desk. "Petition filed December tenth. Court date December twenty-seventh."

My hands went cold.

"When your father changed his will, he gave me specific instructions." Kellerman pulled a sealed envelope from his desk drawer. "This letter was to be opened only if Gregory or Barbara challenged your inheritance in any way. Legal contest, conservatorship petition, anything."

He handed it to me. Sealed. My name in Dad's handwriting.

The seal was intact. Kellerman had been holding it for six months.

I opened it. Unfolded the paper.

Dated May 15, 2024. One month before he died.

Natalie,

If you're reading this, Greg or Barbara is coming after the inheritance. I knew they would.

Greg has gambling debts—over $200,000 to bookies in Atlantic City. Barbara has been enabling him, giving him money, lying to me about it. They've stolen from me before. Small amounts at first. Then larger.

I'm changing my will today. Leaving everything to you. When they find out, they'll be angry. They may come after you.

Be careful. They'll do anything for money. Greg especially. He's desperate. And desperate men are dangerous.

Whatever they tell you about yourself, whatever evidence they show you —remember that I trusted YOU. Not them. There's a reason for that.

I love you.

- Dad

The paper shook in my hands.

Kellerman pulled out more documents. "Now, here's what they're claiming."

He spread papers across the desk. Psychiatric evaluation from Dr. Patricia Hayes. Session notes. Dates. Times.

"According to these records, you've been seeing Dr. Hayes twice a week since July. Right after the incident with your mother."

"I've never met Dr. Hayes."

"They have documentation. Diagnosis: early-onset schizophrenia with violent episodes." He pulled up pharmacy records on his computer. "Prescriptions for antipsychotics. Written by Dr. Hayes. Never filled—which they're using as evidence you refused treatment."

"Statement from your mother about July fifteenth. You attacked her. Broke her wrist. Hospital records confirm the injury. Police report confirms the incident."

"Witness statements from neighbors. Three people claim they saw you behaving erratically over the summer."

He leaned back. "Some of this evidence is real. The July incident is documented. But the psychiatric records feel manufactured. Too perfect. Too convenient."

"Court date is December twenty-seventh. Four days from now. If they win, they become your conservators. Full control of your finances, your medical decisions, where you live."

I couldn't breathe.

"Natalie, I need to ask you something." His voice was gentle. "Have you been experiencing blackouts? Memory loss?"

The scissors on my nightstand. The letter in my handwriting. The breakfast I didn't remember eating.

"Yes."

His expression changed. Concern. Worry.

"Have you had violent thoughts?"

I couldn't answer.

"Then we have a problem. Because some of what they're claiming might be true. And if even part of it is true, the judge may rule in their favor."

I drove back through Ridgemont in a daze. Dad's letter in my pocket. The conservatorship petition in my mind.

Whatever they tell you about yourself, whatever evidence they show you —remember that I trusted YOU.

But what if Dad was wrong?

What if I was actually sick?

I pulled over two blocks from the house. Checked my reflection in the rearview mirror.

Then I saw it.

Bruise on my neck. Right side. Faint but visible. Purple-yellow. Finger-shaped.

Four marks. Like someone had grabbed me.

I touched it. Tender. Fresh.

When had this happened?

The radio played "Deck the Halls." Cheerful. Wrong.

I turned it off.

Someone had choked me.

Or I'd choked someone.

I pulled my scarf higher. Covered the bruise.

Started the car. Drove home.

Four days until the court date.

Four days until everything changed.

Chapter 5

The Plan

I walked into the house through the garage. Avoided the front door. Avoided questions.

Upstairs, I sat on my bed. Dad's letter in my hands. The conservatorship petition in my mind.

Four days.

They were going to take everything.

Unless they were trying to save me.

I went downstairs. Found them in the living room. Christmas movie playing on TV. Emma and Sophie on the floor with coloring books. Barbara and Greg on the couch. Melissa in the armchair.

I dropped the petition on the coffee table.

"I know what you're doing."

The movie kept playing. Some cartoon reindeer singing.

Barbara picked up the papers. "Oh, honey."

"You filed to have me declared incompetent."

Greg paused the movie. "Girls, go upstairs."

Emma and Sophie gathered their crayons. Looked at me with wide eyes. Scared eyes.

Was I scaring them?

They left. Melissa followed. Closed the door behind her.

Barbara set down the papers. Tears in her eyes. Real or performed—I couldn't tell anymore. "We're trying to save you. You're sick."

"I'm not sick."

"You attacked me. You don't remember it. That's not normal."

Greg leaned forward. "What if next time you kill someone? What if it's one of the girls?"

"I would never—"

"You would never remember. That's the problem." His voice was gentle. Concerned. "You need help. Real help. Treatment."

"This isn't about treatment. It's about the money."

Barbara wiped her eyes. "The money doesn't matter. You matter. Your safety matters."

"Dad's will matters."

"Your father's will was written before he knew you were sick."

Greg stood. "He wouldn't want you managing millions of dollars while having psychotic episodes."

"I'm not psychotic."

"You wrote a letter saying you wanted to kill us." Barbara's voice cracked. "We found it in the trash. Your handwriting."

My throat closed.

"You're dangerous, Nat. To yourself. To us. We're trying to protect you."

Melissa opened the door. "Think of the girls. They're terrified of you."

"They're children. They need to feel safe in their own home."

I backed toward the stairs. "You're lying."

"We're not lying." Greg's jaw tightened. "We're trying to help you. Before it's too late."

I ran upstairs. Locked my bedroom door.

Pressed my hands against the wood. Tried to breathe.

They had the letter. The one I'd destroyed.

Or thought I'd destroyed.

Or had I written a different one?

How many letters had I written?

. . .

Midnight. The house was silent.

I waited an hour to be sure. Then crept downstairs.

Greg's home office was on the first floor. Small room off the kitchen. Door closed but not locked.

I turned the knob. Stepped inside.

Desk against one wall. Computer monitor dark but not off—screen saver floating. Filing cabinet in the corner. Bookshelves with law textbooks and family photos.

I moved to the desk. Touched the mouse.

Screen woke up. Email open. Gmail. Greg's account.

I scrolled through recent messages. Bills. Junk mail. Then—

Email to Dr. Patricia Hayes. December 18. Four days ago.

Need additional session notes for December court date. Judge will want detailed history. Can you backdate to September?

Response from Hayes, same day:

I can create six additional sessions. Detailed notes showing progressive deterioration. $5,000 per session note. $30,000 total.

My hands shook as I pulled out my phone. Took a photo of the screen.

Evidence. Proof they were fabricating records.

I scrolled further. Found bank statements. Greg's personal account.

Balance: negative $12,000.

Credit card statements: $85,000 owed across four cards.

Transaction history: Atlantic City casinos. Borgata. Caesars. Harrah's. Over and over.

Dad had said $200,000 in gambling debts.

It was worse. Much worse.

Another email. This one to a realtor. December 15.

Once conservatorship is granted, we'll be selling the Ridgemont property. 4-bedroom colonial, Lakeview Drive. Estimated value $850,000. Let me know when you can list it.

They were going to sell Dad's house.

Sell everything.

Pay Greg's debts.

I took more photos. Email after email. Evidence of the plan.

Then I saw the timestamp on the Hayes email.

Sent: December 22, 11:47 PM.

Today.

I checked my phone. Current time: 11:45 PM.

Impossible.

The email hadn't been sent yet.

But it was right there. On the screen.

Footsteps in the hallway.

I froze.

The footsteps stopped outside the office door.

I looked around. Nowhere to go. The desk had no space underneath. The window was locked.

The closet. Small coat closet in the corner.

I crossed the room. Opened it. Stepped inside. Pulled the door almost closed. Left a crack to see through.

The office door opened.

Greg entered. Wearing pajama pants and a t-shirt. Hair messy. Half-asleep.

He went to the computer. Sat down.

Moved the mouse.

Opened his email.

Found the messages to Dr. Hayes.

Deleted them.

One by one. Gone.

Then emptied the trash folder.

Permanent deletion.

He closed the browser. Shut down the computer.

Stood. Stretched. Left the room.

I waited in the closet. Counted to one hundred. Then stepped out.

Went to the computer. Tried to turn it on.

Password protected.

The emails were gone.

I checked my phone. Opened the photos.

Blank screens. Every single one. The camera had captured nothing.

No evidence.

No proof.

Just my word against theirs.

And my word meant nothing.

Because I was the one who couldn't remember. The one who blacked out. The one who wrote threatening letters.

I stood in the dark office. Christmas lights from outside cast shadows through the window. "Silent Night" played from somewhere. Emma's room, maybe. The little girl sleeping peacefully.

Unaware her father, my brother, was destroying me.

Or maybe I was destroying myself.

Maybe I'd imagined the whole thing. The emails. The bank statements. All of it.

Maybe I was as sick as they said.

I went back upstairs. Closed my door. Checked the lock three times.

Sat on the bed in the dark.

Four days until the court date.

Four days until they won.

Unless I fought back.

But how do you fight when you can't trust your own mind?

Chapter 6

The Trap

Monday morning, I woke with a plan.

Go to the police. Tell them everything. Show them Dad's letter. Explain the conservatorship petition. Make them investigate Greg and Barbara.

Even without the emails—even with blank photos—I had to try.

I got dressed. Jeans, sweater, boots. Grabbed my coat from the closet.

Reached for my phone on the nightstand.

Gone.

I checked the floor. Under the bed. In my suitcase. Bathroom counter.

Not there.

My phone was gone.

I went downstairs. Barbara was at the stove, flipping pancakes. Gingerbread pancakes. Steam rising. The kitchen smelled like cinnamon and butter.

"Good morning, sweetheart! I made your favorite."

"Have you seen my phone?"

She turned. Smiled. "No, dear. Did you misplace it?"

"It was on my nightstand."

"You probably moved it. You know how you forget things."

Greg entered from the den. Coffee mug in hand. "What's wrong?"

"My phone is missing."

"When did you last have it?"

"Last night. On my nightstand."

He sipped his coffee. "Check your coat pockets. You're always leaving it places."

I went to the hall closet. Checked every pocket. Not there.

Checked my purse. My car. The living room.

Gone.

"I need to make a call," I said. "Can I use your phone?"

Barbara's face showed concern. Or performance. "Of course. Who do you need to call?"

"A friend."

"Which friend?"

"Does it matter?"

She exchanged a look with Greg. That look. Significant. Loaded.

"Here." Greg handed me his phone. "Use mine."

I took it. Started to dial Ridgemont Police Department.

The screen went black.

"Battery died," Greg said. Took it back. "Sorry. I'll charge it."

Barbara gestured to the table. "Sit. Eat breakfast. We'll find your phone."

"I need to go out."

"In this weather?" She pointed to the window. Snow falling heavy. "They're calling for eight inches. Roads are terrible."

"I don't care."

"At least eat first." Her voice was firm. Not a suggestion.

I sat. Had no choice. No phone. No way to call for help.

Barbara set a plate in front of me. Two gingerbread pancakes. Butter melting. Syrup pooled.

I stared at them.

"Eat," she said.

"I'm not hungry."

"You need to eat. You're too thin."

I pushed the plate away. "I'll have coffee."

"I didn't make coffee yet." Barbara turned back to the stove.

"I'll make it myself."

"Don't be silly. I'll do it." She moved to the coffee maker. Started measuring grounds.

I stood. "I'll just have cereal."

Went to the pantry. Pulled out a new box of granola. Unopened. Sealed.

Grabbed a bowl from the cabinet. Clean. No way to drug it.

Opened the fridge. Milk. Sealed container. Brand new.

Poured cereal into bowl. Poured milk over it.

Sat at the table. Ate.

Barbara and Greg watched me. Silent.

"We're worried about you," Barbara said.

"I'm fine."

"You broke into Greg's office last night."

My spoon stopped halfway to my mouth.

"We have cameras, Nat." Greg pulled out his phone—suddenly working again. Opened an app. Turned the screen toward me.

Security footage. Black and white. Greg's office. Time stamp: 11:42 PM.

Me entering. Going to the computer. Taking photos with my phone.

"That's breaking and entering," Greg said. "That's a crime."

"You're trying to steal my inheritance."

"We're trying to help you. But you're making it impossible."

Barbara sat across from me. "Dr. Hayes is coming this afternoon. To evaluate you."

"I'm not seeing Dr. Hayes."

"You need to. For your own safety."

"I'm leaving." I stood.

The edges of the room blurred.

I grabbed the table. Missed. The floor rushed up.

Greg caught me. "Easy."

"What did you—" My words slurred. Tongue thick.

"We didn't do anything. You did this to yourself." His voice was distant. Echoing.

Everything doubled. Tripled. The kitchen spun.

They drugged the bowl.

Somehow, they'd drugged the bowl before I'd even taken it from the cabinet.

Or the cereal box. Or the milk.

Or I was losing my mind and this was all in my head.

"Let's get you upstairs." Greg's arm around my waist. Supporting me. Trapping me.

"No—"

But my legs wouldn't work. I stumbled. He carried me.

Up the stairs. Down the hallway. Into my room.

Laid me on the bed.

Barbara appeared in the doorway. Melissa behind her. They watched as Greg stepped back.

"Dr. Hayes will be here at three," Barbara said. "She'll evaluate you. Then we're taking you to Ridgemont Psychiatric Center."

"Voluntarily," Greg added. "Or we call the police. Show them the July incident. Show them you breaking into my office. Show them the threatening letter you wrote."

"You'll be arrested. Or you'll be admitted. Your choice."

The ceiling spun. I tried to sit up. Couldn't.

"Sleep it off," Barbara said. "We'll wake you when Dr. Hayes arrives."

They left. The door closed.

Locked from the outside. Click.

I lay there. Room spinning. Drugs pulling me under.

But something in me fought back. Anger. Fear. Survival instinct.

I rolled off the bed. Crawled to the window.

Second floor. Too high to jump. But the garage roof extended below.

I grabbed the bedside lamp. Heavy ceramic base. Swung it at the window.

Glass shattered. Cold air rushed in.

I knocked out the remaining shards. Threw my coat out first. Then climbed through.

The roof was steep. Snow-covered. Slippery.

I slid down. Grabbed the gutter. Hung there. Dropped.

Hit the ground wrong. Pain shot through my left ankle. Twisted. Maybe broken.

Didn't matter. Had to run.

I grabbed my coat. Put it on over my pajamas. Started running.

Through the backyard. Through the neighbor's yard. Through snow that soaked my boots.

Behind me: shouting. The front door slammed.

Greg's voice: "Natalie!"

I ran harder.

Cut through more yards. Dogs barking. Christmas decorations blurring past. "Jingle Bells" playing from someone's house.

Headlights behind me. Greg's BMW. Coming down the street.

I cut through an alley. Between two houses. Came out on Pine Street.

A car approached. Silver sedan. Older woman driving.

I stumbled into the street. Waved my arms.

The car stopped.

The woman rolled down her window. Kind face. Gray hair. Fifties.

"Please—" I grabbed the door handle. "Please help me. They're trying to—"

"Natalie Foster?"

I froze. "How do you know my name?"

She smiled. Warm. Concerned.

"I'm Dr. Patricia Hayes. Get in. I'll help you."

My blood went cold.

Everyone. Everyone was in on it.

I backed away from the car.

"Natalie, please. You're not well. Let me help you."

Greg's BMW turned onto Pine Street. Headlights cutting through the snow.

I ran.

Down the street. Into another yard. Through bushes. Over a fence.

My ankle screamed. My lungs burned. The drugs made everything swim.

But I kept running.

Away from the house. Away from Greg. Away from Dr. Hayes.

Away from everyone who wanted to lock me up.

Or save me.

I didn't know which anymore.

Ridgemont Police Department was six blocks away.

Six blocks through snow and darkness and whatever they'd put in my system.

Six blocks to safety.

Or six blocks to proving I was exactly as crazy as they said.

Behind me: footsteps. Greg calling my name.

Ahead: flashing lights. Red and blue. Spinning through the snow.

Police.

I ran toward the lights.

Toward help.

Toward the only chance I had left.

Chapter 7

The Police

I stumbled through the glass doors of Ridgemont Police Department at 4:47 PM.

Single-story brick building. American flag snapping in the wind outside. Small parking lot with three patrol cars covered in snow.

The lobby was warm. Too warm after the cold. My legs gave out.

An officer rushed from behind the front desk. Young, late twenties, athletic build. Dark blue Ridgemont PD uniform. Badge read: M. POLASKI.

"Ma'am, are you hurt?"

I tried to speak. Nothing came out.

He grabbed his radio. "I need Detective Fairbank at the front desk. Now."

Then to me: "Can you walk?"

I shook my head.

He helped me to a chair. I collapsed into it. My ankle throbbed. Blood from the broken window dripped down my arm. Cuts on my hands.

I'd lost my boots somewhere. Bare feet. Blue from cold.

"What happened?" Polaski asked.

"They drugged me. Locked me in. I had to—" My words slurred together.

A woman appeared from the bullpen. Mid-forties, five-eight, solid build. Dark hair pulled into a tight bun. Sharp brown eyes. Gray pantsuit, white shirt. Badge at her belt.

"I'm Detective Hazel Fairbank." She crouched in front of me. Studied my face. "What's your name?"

"Natalie Foster."

Something changed in her expression. Recognition.

"Get her to interview room two," she told Polaski. "Blanket. Coffee. Call EMT."

Polaski helped me up. Supported my weight. Led me down a hallway.

The interview room was small. Metal table bolted to the floor. Four chairs. Recording equipment on the wall. Beige walls, gray linoleum.

He wrapped a blanket around my shoulders. Disappeared. Returned with coffee in a paper cup.

"EMT's on the way." He left. Closed the door.

I sat alone. Shaking. The coffee burned my hands through the cup but I couldn't let go.

The door opened. Fairbank entered with a first aid kit.

"Let me see your feet."

She knelt. Examined them. The cuts weren't deep. She cleaned them with antiseptic. Applied bandages.

"Your ankle's swollen. Could be broken. EMT will check it."

"I can't go to the hospital."

"Why not?"

"They'll find me there. They'll take me to the psychiatric center."

Fairbank sat across from me. Opened a notepad. "Tell me what happened."

I told her everything. Started with Dad's death in June. The will. The inheritance. Coming home for Christmas. The missing pills. The fake memories. The Cape May photos. The July incident I didn't remember. The conservatorship petition. Kellerman's letter. Greg's office. The emails that disappeared. Being drugged. Locked in. Dr. Hayes waiting in a car.

She took notes. Didn't interrupt.

"They're trying to have me declared incompetent. To steal the inheritance."

"What about the July incident?" Her voice was neutral. "Did you push your mother down the stairs?"

"I don't remember."

"You don't remember doing it? Or you don't remember the incident at all?"

"I don't remember any of it. Zero memory."

"But the medical records say you did."

"I know what they say."

Fairbank set down her pen. "Natalie, do you have a history of mental illness?"

"No."

"Blackouts? Memory loss?"

I couldn't lie. Not here. Not now.

"Since coming home, yes."

She made a note. "How many blackouts?"

"Three. Maybe four. I lose time. Wake up places I don't remember going."

"Have you been taking any medications?"

"Xanax. Prescribed after Dad died. For anxiety."

"Anything else?"

"No."

She pulled her computer closer. Typed. Read something on the screen.

"July fifteenth domestic violence report. Officer Tomlin responded. Barbara Foster, victim. Broken wrist, concussion. You were listed as suspect. She declined to press charges."

"I know."

"Hospital records confirm her injuries. Ridgemont General. Treated and released."

Fairbank typed more. "Dr. Patricia Hayes. Psychiatrist. License is active." She frowned. "But the practice address doesn't match."

"What do you mean?"

"Her records show an office on Route 23. But that address is a UPS Store. Just a PO Box."

My hands tightened on the coffee cup.

"You said you saw emails. Proof she was fabricating records."

"Yes. On Greg's computer. I took photos with my phone."

"Where's your phone?"

"They took it. I searched everywhere. It's gone."

Fairbank held out her hand. "Check your pockets."

I reached into my coat. Left pocket. Right pocket.

My fingers touched glass. Cold. Rectangular.

I pulled it out.

My phone.

"I... I thought they took it."

"Open it."

I unlocked the screen. Went to photos. Scrolled through.

No emails. No screenshots. Nothing from last night.

Just old photos. From before I came home.

"Were they ever there?"

Fairbank's expression gave nothing away. "What did the emails say?"

"Greg asking Dr. Hayes to backdate session notes. She wanted five thousand dollars per session."

"Bank statements showing his gambling debts. Over three hundred thousand dollars."

"An email to a realtor about selling Dad's house once they got conservatorship."

She wrote it down. "Stay here."

Fairbank left. I heard her voice in the hallway. Muffled. Talking to Polaski.

The door opened again. Polaski entered.

"Detective Fairbank is making some calls. Can I get you anything? Water? More coffee?"

"No."

He nodded. Left.

I sat alone. The blanket around my shoulders. My feet bandaged. Ankle throbbing.

Christmas music played from somewhere. "Little Drummer Boy." Tinny speakers. Dispatch radio, maybe.

Normal Christmas for everyone else.

For me, nothing was normal.

Thirty minutes later, Fairbank returned. Sat across from me.

"I'm sending Officer Polaski to bring in your mother and brother for questioning."

"Dr. Hayes as well. For license verification and practice address clarification."

Relief flooded through me. "You believe me?"

"I'm investigating. That's my job." Her face was professional. Careful. "But Natalie, I need you to understand something. Some of what they're claiming might be true. The July incident is documented. Real hospital records. Real police report."

"If you did attack your mother, even in a blackout, that changes things."

"I know."

Her radio crackled. She answered. "Fairbank."

A male voice. "Detective, it's Dr. Ballard from Ridgemont General. Returning your call about Barbara Foster's July injury."

Fairbank pressed a button. Put it on speaker. "Go ahead, Doctor."

"You asked about the wrist fracture. I reviewed the X-rays. Interesting thing—the break pattern is unusual."

"How so?"

"It's consistent with a defensive wound. When someone raises their arm to block a blow. The fracture line runs across the ulna at a specific angle."

"Not consistent with falling downstairs?"

"Falls typically cause different fracture patterns. Colles fracture, distal radius. This was ulnar shaft fracture. Classic defensive injury."

Fairbank's eyes met mine. "So she was blocking something?"

"That would be my assessment. Like someone hit her or pushed her, and she raised her arm to protect herself."

"Thank you, Doctor."

She ended the call.

Silence filled the interview room.

"You attacked her," Fairbank said. "But she may have provoked it."

I couldn't speak.

"Self-defense?"

"I don't know. I don't remember."

"We need to figure out what really happened that day." She stood. "Stay here. Don't leave."

She went to the door. Paused. "Natalie, one way or another, we're going to get to the truth."

The door closed behind her.

I sat in the small room. Wrapped in a blanket. Cuts bandaged. Phone in my hand that had appeared and disappeared and appeared again.

Outside, dispatch played "Joy to the World."

Someone had brought cookies. I could smell them. Snickerdoodles. Christmas cookies for the night shift.

Normal people having a normal Christmas.

While I sat here not knowing if I was victim or villain or both.

Chapter 8

The Revelation

I spent the night at Ridgemont Police Department.

Not in a cell. In a victim services room. Small office with a cot, blanket, pillow. Door locked from the inside. Safe.

The EMT had checked my ankle. Sprained, not broken. Wrapped it. Given me ibuprofen.

I'd slept three hours. Woke at 6 AM to voices in the hallway.

Fairbank's voice. "Bring her to interview room one. Him to room three."

Barbara and Greg. They'd brought them in.

Christmas Eve morning. The station smelled like coffee and someone's homemade cinnamon rolls. Dispatch radio played carols. "The First Noel."

Normal morning for everyone else.

For me, everything was about to change.

Seven AM. Fairbank knocked on my door.

"They're here. I'm starting with your mother."

"Can I watch?"

She hesitated. "Observation room. Behind the glass. But you can't interrupt. No matter what you hear."

I followed her down the hallway. Small room adjacent to interview room one. One-way mirror. I could see in. They couldn't see me.

Barbara sat at the metal table. Composed. Hair perfect despite being picked up at 6 AM. Red cardigan, black slacks. Hands folded. Calm.

Fairbank entered the interview room. Sat across from Barbara.

"Thank you for coming in, Mrs. Foster."

"Of course. Anything to help my daughter." Barbara's voice was steady. Concerned mother.

Fairbank opened a file. "Tell me about July fifteenth."

"Natalie attacked me. Pushed me down the basement stairs. I broke my wrist." She held up her left arm. Showed the scar. "Concussion. Spent the night at Ridgemont General."

"Why did she attack you?"

"She was having an episode. Screaming about the will. About how Dad left everything to her. She wasn't making sense."

"Did she seem intoxicated?"

"No. Just... disconnected. Like she wasn't herself."

Fairbank made notes. "And she doesn't remember the incident?"

"No. Complete blackout. When she came out of it, she had no idea what she'd done."

"That must have been frightening."

"It was terrifying." Barbara's voice cracked. Performance. "My own daughter. I'm scared of her now."

Fairbank pulled out a document. "I spoke with Dr. Erasmus Ballard. ER physician who treated you."

"Yes?"

"He reviewed your X-rays. Says the fracture pattern is unusual."

Barbara's face changed. Just slightly. A flicker.

"Unusual how?"

"It's a defensive wound. Ulnar shaft fracture. Classic pattern when someone raises their arm to block a blow."

"Not consistent with falling downstairs."

Silence.

"Mrs. Foster, you weren't pushed downstairs. Someone hit you. You blocked it. What really happened?"

Barbara's hands trembled. Just slightly. "I told you—"

"You lied in the police report. What really happened July 15th?"

More silence. Barbara stared at the table.

Then her shoulders dropped. The performance cracked.

"She wouldn't share the money." Her voice was flat now. Cold. "Three million dollars. And she was keeping all of it."

"I asked her to be reasonable. To think about family. About Greg's children. She refused."

"I grabbed her. Shook her. She needed to understand."

"She pushed me away. I fell against the railing. Broke my wrist."

Fairbank leaned forward. "Self-defense."

"Yes."

"But you filed a police report claiming she attacked you unprovoked."

Barbara looked up. "She didn't remember. After it happened, she just... shut down. Complete blackout. Didn't remember any of it."

"I realized we could use that."

My hands went cold in the observation room.

"Use how?"

"Tell her she'd attacked me violently. She'd believe it. She had no memory to contradict it."

"Build a case. Make her think she was dangerous. Unstable."

"Then file for conservatorship."

Fairbank's expression didn't change. "Exploiting your daughter's trauma."

"We needed the money." No remorse in Barbara's voice. "Greg's debts. The house. We'd lose everything."

The door to the interview room opened. Polaski entered with Greg. Handcuffed.

"Sit," Fairbank said.

Greg sat next to Barbara. He wouldn't look at her.

"Your mother just confessed to fabricating the July incident." Fairbank turned to Greg. "Want to add anything?"

Greg's jaw tightened. "She's leaving out the important part."

"Which is?"

"We were going to make her actually sick."

I pressed closer to the glass.

"Explain."

"The antipsychotics Dr. Hayes prescribed. We were going to crush them. Put them in her food. Her coffee."

"Small doses. Over weeks. Make her develop symptoms."

"Confusion. Memory loss. Paranoia."

"Then she really would be incompetent."

Barbara closed her eyes. "Greg—"

"She needs to know." He turned to Fairbank. "We planned it all. The fake psychiatric records. The staged incidents. The drugs."

"Dr. Hayes helped you."

"We found her online. She'd lost her New York license. Ethics violations. Malpractice suits. Needed money."

"Offered her fifty thousand for backdated records. Session notes. Prescriptions. Everything we needed for court."

Fairbank made notes. "Conspiracy to commit fraud. Attempted poisoning. Medical fraud."

She pulled another document from her file. "Tell me about your father's heart attack."

Greg went pale.

"Natural causes," he said. "He was sixty-five. He had a heart attack."

Fairbank slid a journal across the table. Dad's journal. The one Kellerman had.

"Your father's last entry. June twelfth. Day before he died."

She read aloud: "I feel ill. Dizzy. Heart racing. If something happens, look at my coffee."

Greg's hands shook.

"What was in his coffee, Greg?"

Silence.

Fairbank turned to Barbara. "Mrs. Foster, you take Digoxin for your heart. Correct?"

Barbara nodded. Tears on her face now. Real tears.

"What happens if someone without a heart condition takes Digoxin?"

"It kills them," Barbara whispered.

"Did you put Digoxin in your husband's coffee?"

"Greg said we had to." Her voice broke. "The will was changed May fifteenth. One month before Richard died. We'd get nothing."

"Greg's debts. The house. We'd lose everything."

"I crushed my pills. Put them in his coffee. Ten days."

"He got weaker. Sicker. Then his heart stopped."

My legs gave out. I grabbed the wall in the observation room.

They murdered him.

They murdered Dad.

Fairbank stood. "Barbara Foster, Gregory Foster, you're under arrest for the murder of Richard Foster."

"Conspiracy to commit fraud. Attempted poisoning of Natalie Foster. Medical fraud."

Barbara sobbed. "Where's Natalie? I need to see her."

"She's safe. And she's getting the help she actually needs. Unlike you, she's innocent."

"She's not innocent!" Greg stood. Chair scraped. "She took everything! Everything that should have been ours!"

He lunged across the table. Grabbed for Fairbank's throat.

Polaski tackled him. Slammed him face-first into the table.

"You're under arrest!" Polaski's knee in Greg's back. Handcuffs clicking.

Greg screamed into the table. "Three million dollars! She doesn't deserve it! She doesn't deserve anything!"

Polaski dragged him from the room.

Barbara sat alone. Crying. Mascara running.

Christmas music played from the lobby. "Joy to the World." Cheerful. Wrong.

I stood in the observation room. Shaking.

Everything clicked into place.

The gaslighting. The drugs. The fake memories. The conservatorship.

All of it built on one real incident they'd twisted into something else.

I'd defended myself. They'd made me believe I was a monster.

And they'd killed Dad to steal money they never got.

The door to the observation room opened. Fairbank entered.

"You okay?"

I couldn't answer.

"You were defending yourself in July. You're not sick. Not dangerous. They manufactured everything else."

"And your father—" Her voice was gentle. "I'm sorry. We'll exhume his body. Digoxin will show up in the autopsy. Murder charges will stick."

I nodded. Numb.

"What happens now?"

"They'll be arraigned this afternoon. Charged with first-degree murder. Bail will be denied."

"You're free to go. The conservatorship petition will be dismissed."

Free.

But nothing felt free.

Dad was still dead. Murdered by the people who should have loved him.

And I'd spent four days believing I was the monster.

When they were the monsters all along.

Chapter 9

The Aftermath

Christmas Eve afternoon, I sat in the Ridgemont PD break room. Small space with a couch, refrigerator, microwave. Coffee maker that never stopped brewing. Vending machine humming in the corner. Someone had hung tinsel around the doorframe. Sad Christmas tree in the corner with blinking lights.

Fairbank brought me coffee. Sat across from me.

"How are you holding up?"

I wrapped my hands around the cup. Needed the warmth. "I don't know."

"Everything they told you was a lie. Built on one real incident they twisted."

"You defended yourself in July. Pushed your mother away when she attacked you. That's not violence. That's survival."

I stared at the coffee. "But I believed them. I believed I was capable of murder."

"They made you doubt your own mind. That's what gaslighting does."

"The missing pills. The Cape May photos. The emails that disappeared." My voice cracked. "What was real?"

"We're still investigating. But some of it was them. Some of it was your trauma response."

She pulled out a business card. "Dr. Rachel Santos. Police psychologist. She's here. Wants to evaluate you."

"I'm not sick."

"I know. But humor me."

Dr. Santos was younger than I expected. Forties, kind eyes, warm smile. Black hair pulled back. Professional but not clinical.

We talked for an hour in a private office. She asked about the blackouts. The missing time. The letter in my handwriting.

"You experienced dissociative amnesia," she said. "Your mind blocked out the July incident because it was traumatic. That's a normal response to trauma."

"The blackouts since coming home were triggered by stress. Being back in that environment. Your family weaponized your gaps in memory."

"You're not schizophrenic. You're not dangerous. You're traumatized. There's a difference."

"What about the letter I wrote? About killing them?"

"Intrusive thoughts. Common in trauma survivors. Especially when being gaslit. Your mind was trying to fight back."

She handed me a tissue. I hadn't realized I was crying.

"You're not crazy, Natalie. You never were."

Four PM. Fairbank found me in the break room.

"Arraignment's done. Both denied bail."

"Barbara Foster: first-degree murder of Richard Foster. Conspiracy to commit fraud. Attempted conservatorship fraud through false evidence."

"Gregory Foster: first-degree murder of Richard Foster. Conspiracy. Attempted kidnapping. Assault on a police officer."

"Dr. Patricia Hayes: medical fraud, conspiracy, practicing medicine without a valid license. Bail set at one hundred thousand. She can't make it."

I nodded. Numb.

"The conservatorship petition is dismissed. You have full control of your father's estate."

"What about Melissa? The girls?"

"Melissa's cooperating. Claims she didn't know about the murder. Just the conservatorship plan. We believe her. She's staying with her parents. Taking the girls."

Emma and Sophie. Innocent in all this.

"Can I see them?"

"Not right now. But eventually, yes."

Fairbank drove me to the Ridgemont Inn. Small hotel near Ridge Lake. Clean room. Queen bed, desk, bathroom. Window overlooking the lake.

"Stay as long as you need. On the department."

"Thank you."

She left. I locked the door. Checked it twice.

Stood at the window. Snow falling over the lake. Families at Ridge Lake Resort in the distance. Christmas lights reflecting off the water. Kids building snowmen. Parents carrying presents.

Normal people having normal Christmases.

I showered. First time feeling clean in days. Washed away the blood, the fear, the drugs.

Put on the clothes Fairbank had gotten from my room. Jeans, sweater, clean socks.

Sat on the bed. Turned on the TV. Some Christmas movie. Family gathered around a tree. Everyone laughing.

I turned it off.

Christmas morning. I woke to a knock on the door.

Room service. I hadn't ordered anything.

"Compliments of the house," the server said. Left a tray. Scrambled eggs, toast, orange juice. Coffee.

An envelope sat next to the plate.

I opened it. Homemade card. Crayon drawing of a Christmas tree. Stick figures underneath.

Merry Christmas Aunt Natalie. Love you. - Emma and Sophie

My hands shook. The card blurred.

They still loved me. After everything. After their father's arrest. After their world collapsed.

They still loved me.

I sat on the bed. Held the card. Cried.

Ten AM. Another knock.

David Kellerman stood in the hallway. Leather bag in hand.

"Merry Christmas," he said. Tired smile.

"Come in."

He set the bag on the desk. Pulled out a leather-bound journal. Worn. Old.

"Your father's personal journal. Police released it this morning. Thought you'd want it."

I took it. Heavy in my hands.

"Last entry is June twelfth. Day before he died."

I opened it. Flipped to the back. Dad's handwriting.

May 15, 2024

Changed my will today. Everything to Natalie. Greg is out of control. Barbara enables him. They've stolen from me before. Small amounts. Then larger. I forgave them. But I can't give them my life's work. Natalie is the only one with integrity.

June 3, 2024

Greg asked for money again. Fifty thousand. Said it was for Emma's school. Barbara confirmed it. I checked with the school. No tuition due. They're lying to me. Still.

June 12, 2024

I feel ill. Dizzy. Heart racing. Coffee tastes bitter this morning. Strange. If something happens, look at my coffee. I'm not paranoid. I'm careful. They know about the will now. I see it in their eyes. - R.F.

He knew. He knew they were killing him and he couldn't stop it.

I closed the journal. Couldn't read more.

"I'm sorry," Kellerman said.

"I want to donate half the inheritance."

He blinked. "That's generous."

"Mental health organizations. Domestic violence shelters. Elder abuse prevention." I met his eyes. "I don't want blood money."

"I'll draw up the paperwork."

Evening. Christmas Day. Snow had stopped. The lake was smooth. Dark. Peaceful.

A knock on the door.

Fairbank stood in the hallway. Off duty now. Jeans and a sweater. Looked tired.

"Exhumation order was approved. Autopsy tomorrow morning."

"If Digoxin is there—and it will be—murder charges stick. Life sentences. Both of them."

I nodded.

"You okay?"

"I'm alive. That's something."

She studied my face. "It's more than something. You survived."

"Doesn't feel like it."

"Give it time."

After she left, I packed. Few clothes I had. Dad's journal. The card from Emma and Sophie.

Couldn't stay in Ridgemont. Too many ghosts. Too much pain.

I'd go back to Manhattan. Back to my apartment. Back to work.

Start over.

The inheritance would be mine. Half donated. Half invested. Enough to live on. Enough to rebuild.

But the money couldn't give me back what I'd lost.

Couldn't bring back Dad.

Couldn't erase the four days I'd spent doubting my sanity.

Couldn't undo what they'd done.

I stood at the window one last time. Ridge Lake stretched out below. Christmas lights blinked on the far shore. "Silent Night" drifted from somewhere. The resort, maybe.

Peaceful. Holy.

But nothing was peaceful. Nothing was holy.

My family had murdered my father for money they never got.

Had tried to destroy me to steal what he'd left.

And I'd believed them. Believed I was the monster.

Tomorrow I'd leave Ridgemont. Leave the house. Leave everything.

But tonight, I stood at the window.

Survivor. Not victim.

Alive. Not broken.

It was Christmas. The day of miracles.

And maybe the miracle was this: I was still standing.

That had to be enough.

Chapter 10

Moving Forward

January second. The exhumation results came back.

Lethal levels of Digoxin in Dad's body. Tissue samples. Hair samples. Blood analysis from preserved specimens. All positive.

Murder. First-degree.

Barbara and Greg both pleaded guilty. No trial. Avoided putting Emma and Sophie through testimony.

Sentencing: Barbara got fifteen years. Greg got twenty-five. The assault on Detective Fairbank added time.

They'd be old when they got out. If they got out.

I didn't attend the sentencing. Couldn't face them. Kellerman sent me the transcript.

Barbara had cried. Said she was sorry. Said she loved me.

Greg had said nothing.

The Ridgemont Gazette ran the story January fifth.

Gloria Steele wrote it. Young reporter, ambitious. She'd been covering all the Christmas incidents in Ridgemont. Three arrests on December twenty-second. A podcaster's confession. A gaslighting scheme. Now a murder plot.

Her headline: **"Local Family's Christmas Murder Plot Exposed: Daughter Escapes Conservatorship Scheme, Parents Face Life Sentences"**

The article connected everything. Called it "Ridgemont's Dark Christmas." Questioned what was happening in this small town. "What's in the water in Ridgemont?"

The story went regional. Then national.

My name was in it. Natalie Foster. Victim. Survivor.

I hated seeing it in print.

Mid-January, I moved to Hoboken.

Small apartment on the tenth floor. One bedroom, galley kitchen, living room with floor-to-ceiling windows. Views of the Hudson River. Manhattan skyline across the water.

No memories here. Clean slate.

I changed my name legally. Natalie Graham. My mother's maiden name. Barbara had forfeited the right to share her name with me.

Dropped Foster entirely. That name was dead to me.

New job. Remote financial analyst for a firm in Boston. Same skills, different company. Nobody knew my history. Nobody asked about Christmas.

Therapy twice a week. Dr. Rachel Santos. Her office in Jersey City. Forty-minute sessions working through PTSD, trust issues, dissociative amnesia.

She taught me trauma responses were normal. That blocking out the July incident was my mind protecting itself. That I wasn't broken.

Progress came slowly. Could sleep with the lights off now. Only checked the door locks once before bed instead of three times. Could eat food I hadn't prepared without panic.

Small victories. But victories.

. . .

The money sat in my account. One point six million after donations and taxes.

I'd given away half. New Jersey Mental Health Association. Women Against Abuse. Elder Justice Initiative. Organizations that helped people like me. People being gaslit. People being hurt by family.

The remaining money was enough to live on. Invest. Be secure.

But it still felt like blood money. Still felt wrong.

Using it for good helped. A little.

Emma and Sophie sent cards.

Melissa had moved to Vermont. Fresh start. Away from Ridgemont. Away from the scandal. Her parents helped with the girls.

Valentine's Day card arrived mid-February. Crayon drawings. Hearts and flowers. *Love Aunt Natalie.*

I sent birthday gifts in March. Books for Emma. Stuffed animal for Sophie. Kept the relationship alive.

Complicated. But hopeful.

They were innocent. They deserved a childhood not defined by their father's crimes.

Valentine's Day evening. I walked through Hoboken.

Cold night. Couples everywhere. Holding hands. Kissing. Celebrating.

Families in restaurant windows. Parents with kids. Grandparents. Normal people. Happy people. Intact families.

I passed one restaurant. Big picture window. Family of six. Grandmother at the head of the table. Parents on the sides. Three kids laughing. Wine glasses raised. Warm light spilling onto the sidewalk.

I stopped. Watched them for a moment.

The grandmother said something. Everyone laughed. The kind of laugh that came from years together. From love. From safety.

I'd never have that.

My family was in prison. My father was dead. My childhood home was sold.

I kept walking.

Past the couples. Past the families. Back to my building.

Tenth floor. Unlocked the door. Locked it behind me. Deadbolt. Chain. Only checked once. Progress.

The apartment was dark. I turned on the lights. Made tea. Sat by the window.

My phone buzzed. Text from Dr. Santos.

Proud of your progress this week. See you Tuesday.

I smiled. Small. Real.

Looked out the window. Snow fell over Hoboken. Light and delicate. City lights reflected off the Hudson River. Manhattan glowed across the water. Somewhere beyond that, Ridgemont slept.

I'd never go back.

The house was sold. Strangers lived there now. The bedroom where I'd counted pills. The office where Greg had deleted evidence. The kitchen where they'd planned my father's murder.

Someone else's home now. Someone else's memories.

Mine were packed away. Locked in therapy sessions and Dr. Santos's notes and court transcripts.

I sipped my tea. Watched the snow.

Home isn't a place. It's a feeling.

And I was building that myself now. One day at a time.

The scar on my wrist caught the light. Small mark from the broken window. From my escape.

Reminder that I'd fought back. That I'd survived.

Not a victim. A survivor.

I'd never have the family in that restaurant window. Never have the grandmother and the laughter and the warmth.

But I had something else.

I had myself.

And for now, that was enough.

THE END

BOOK 9

Office Secret Santa

Chapter 1

The Secret Santa Draw

Monday morning smelled like burnt coffee and someone's peppermint body spray. I walked into Sterling Creative's third-floor office at eight-thirty, already tired.

Fifteen desks in an open floor plan. Gray carpet, white walls, windows overlooking downtown Ridgemont. Home for the last six years.

The conference room had a Christmas tree in the corner. Fake pine, pre-lit, drooping branches. Red and green garland twisted around the windows. Someone had hung a "Secret Santa Kickoff!" banner over the projector screen. Patricia's work. She did this every year.

I dropped my bag at my desk. The Marketing Manager nameplate still made me uncomfortable. Thirty-one and barely qualified. My laptop took forever to boot. I stared at the screensaver—stock photo of mountains I'd never climb.

"Nora!" Jamie waved from across the room. Curly brown hair, too much energy for a Monday. She held up a candy cane. "Ready for the draw?"

"As ready as I'll ever be."

The conference room filled by nine. All fifteen of us crammed around the long table. Floor-to-ceiling windows showed gray December sky. Cold leaked through the glass despite the radiator rattling in the corner.

Patricia stood at the head of the table. Fifty-five, organized to the point of neurotic, wearing a sweater with actual jingle bells sewn into it. She held a Santa hat filled with folded paper slips.

"Welcome to our annual Secret Santa!" Her voice pitched too high. Nervous excitement. "Rules are simple. Fifty-dollar limit. No gag gifts. Exchange happens at the Christmas party Friday, December twentieth." She shook the hat. "Everyone draws one name. Keep it secret."

The hat made its way around the table. Jamie drew first. Smiled at her slip without showing anyone. Marcus from accounting went next. Then Alyson.

Alyson Ellis sat three seats down from me. Twenty-nine, new hire—started in September. Graphic designer. Short blonde hair in a pixie cut, slim build, always wore neutral colors. She'd barely spoken to anyone in three months. Kept her head down, ate lunch at her desk, left at exactly five.

My rare interaction with her was back in October, I'd helped with a client file transfer. She'd borrowed my phone for twenty seconds to AirDrop something. Normal office stuff. I'd forgotten about it immediately.

She pulled a name from the hat. Her face stayed blank. Folded the paper and tucked it into her pocket.

"Earth to Nora." Patricia held the hat in front of me.

I reached in. Grabbed a slip. Unfolded it under the table.

Derek Hoffman.

My stomach dropped.

Derek Hoffman. VP of Client Services. Forty-five. My boss's boss. I reported to Audrey Walsh, the HR Director. She reported to Derek.

Cold, efficient, followed his lead on everything. When Derek wanted someone gone, Audrey processed the paperwork without question. They were a team. Ruthless. Effective.

Derek was six feet tall, salt-and-pepper hair, expensive suits. The kind of man who made junior staff cry in meetings.

Last week he'd reduced an intern to tears over a typo in a PowerPoint slide. The week before that, he'd thrown a water bottle at someone who'd missed a deadline.

The draw finished. Patricia collected the hat. "Remember—fifty dollars, no more, no less. Let's make this fun!" More jingle bells as she gestured. "Party's Friday at three. Catered food, drinks, the whole deal."

People scattered to their desks. I stayed behind, gathered my things.

Tuesday lunch hour, I drove to the mall in Morristown. Twenty minutes west of Ridgemont. Searched for something Derek might actually appreciate. He already had everything. Corner office, six-figure salary, vacation home in Vermont he never shut up about.

I settled on a whiskey decanter set. Crystal, expensive-looking, exactly fifty dollars after tax. Wrapped it Wednesday night at my apartment. Gold paper, neat corners, stick-on bow. Professional.

Thursday afternoon Derek cornered me at my desk about a client proposal I'd submitted. Stood too close, pointed at the printed pages, told me to "fix the copy—it reads like a high schooler wrote it." I rewrote the whole thing. Stayed until seven.

Friday arrived. Three PM. The conference room transformed. Patricia had ordered catered food—sandwich platters, cookies shaped like snowflakes, mini quiches, eggnog. Someone plugged in the electric menorah next to the Christmas tree. Inclusive. Everyone gathered around the table. Wrapped gifts piled under the tree.

Mariah Carey's voice bled from someone's desk speaker. *All I Want For Christmas Is You.* The same song I'd heard in every store, every restaurant, every elevator for the last three weeks. I was sick of Christmas. Sick of forced cheer and ugly sweaters and Secret Santa obligations.

"Let's do gifts!" Patricia rang an actual bell.

We took turns. Marcus got a Starbucks gift card. Jamie got a scented candle set. Alyson's name was called. She walked to the tree, selected a wrapped package bearing her name, opened it. A desk organizer. Bamboo. She nodded once. Set it aside.

Derek's name was called. He walked to the tree, grabbed a box wrapped in gold paper. My wrapping job. He tore it open. The whiskey decanter set. Crystal caught the light.

"Not bad." He held it up.

More forced laughter.

The exchange continued. I got a desk plant—succulent in a ceramic pot. Nice. Patricia got a coffee mug that said "World's Best Organizer."

Derek's eyes narrowed. "Well, well." He reached under the tree, pulled out another box. Larger. Wrapped in silver paper. "Looks like someone's feeling generous."

No name tag on it. Just *To: Derek. Merry Christmas.*

He tore the paper off. Held up a box of chocolate truffles. Gourmet brand, expensive-looking, tied with a gold ribbon.

"Finally," Derek said. "Someone with taste."

He opened the box. Popped a truffle into his mouth. Chewed. Swallowed. "These are good. Whoever got me these has better judgment than most of you." He ate another.

Seven minutes passed. I was checking my phone, half-listening to Patricia talk about holiday hours, when Derek made a sound. Wet, choked. His hand flew to his chest. The other gripped the edge of the table.

"Derek?" Patricia stepped toward him.

He couldn't answer. His face drained white. Sweat beaded on his forehead. He tried to stand. Stumbled. Collapsed forward. Hit the floor hard. His head cracked against the chair leg on the way down.

Someone screamed. Jamie. Or maybe Patricia.

Marcus dropped to his knees next to Derek. Checked his pulse. "Call 911!"

I grabbed my phone. Hands shook. Dialed. Told them someone collapsed, not breathing, send an ambulance. Gave the address. Hung up.

Patricia was crying. Alyson stood against the wall, watching. Her face hadn't changed.

Paramedics arrived in eight minutes. Worked on Derek for five minutes. Chest compressions. Oxygen mask. Needles. Nothing worked.

One of them looked at his partner. Shook his head. Checked his watch. "Time of death, three thirty-one PM."

Dead.

Derek Hoffman was dead on the conference room floor, surrounded by Christmas decorations, spilled eggnog, and half-eaten cookies, and that fucking Mariah Carey song still playing from someone's desk.

Police arrived fifteen minutes later. Detective Hazel Fairbank. Ridgemont PD. Early forties, hair pulled into a tight bun, sharp brown eyes that missed nothing. Gray pantsuit, no jewelry except a watch. She surveyed the room like she was cataloging every detail.

Officer Polaski was with her. Younger, blonde crew cut, stood by the door and took notes.

Fairbank walked to the table where the chocolate box sat. Empty now except for two remaining truffles. She pulled on latex gloves. Picked up the box. Examined it.

"Who gave him these?"

Silence.

"Anyone?"

Patricia's voice wobbled. "They're not from Secret Santa. I track all the assignments—who drew whom. These chocolates aren't on my list. Someone gave them separately."

Fairbank looked at each of us in turn. Her gaze landed on me last. Held there a second too long.

"Did anyone see who gave him those chocolates?"

No one answered. The radiator rattled. Someone's phone buzzed.

Fairbank bagged the chocolates. "We'll need statements from everyone. No one leaves until we've talked to you individually."

She looked at the box again. Back at us. "Nobody saw?"

My throat tightened. Cold spread through my chest.

Something was very, very wrong.

Chapter 2

The First Death

Fairbank kept us until six. One by one, we sat in the conference room with her and Officer Polaski. Five minutes each. Name, position, how long we'd worked there, did we see anything unusual.

My turn came at five-forty. I sat across from Fairbank. Her brown eyes tracked every movement I made. Hands on the table, pen ready, notepad open.

"Nora Brown. Marketing manager. Six years here."

She wrote. "Did you have conflicts with Derek Hoffman?"

"Everyone had conflicts with Derek. He was demanding."

"Demanding how?"

"Made people cry in meetings. Threw things when projects went wrong. Last week he reduced an intern to tears over a typo."

"Did you see who gave him the chocolates?"

"No. They were just under the tree with the other gifts."

Fairbank tapped her pen against the notepad. "Anyone at the office have serious problems with him? Threats, arguments, anything like that?"

I tried to think. Derek had enemies—everyone knew that. But murder? "He fired people regularly. Made them cry in meetings. Threw things when projects went wrong. A lot of people had reasons to hate him."

"Anyone specific? Recent terminations? Threats?"

"Not that I know of. He was just... demanding. Cruel, sometimes."

Fairbank closed her notepad. "That's all for now. Stay local. We'll call if we need anything else."

I grabbed my bag and left.

The drive home took twenty-five minutes. Route 80 west to Parsippany, exit 43, through the strip malls and chain restaurants. Christmas lights hung from every storefront. Red, green, white. Blinking, steady, cascading. The whole state was drowning in forced cheer.

My apartment building sat on a quiet street. Third floor, one bedroom, nine hundred square feet. I unlocked the door and dropped my keys on the kitchen counter. The place was dark except for the light from the parking lot outside. No decorations. No tree. I'd stopped doing Christmas three years ago after Mom died. Dad had moved to Florida. No siblings. Just me and whatever I could microwave for dinner.

I texted Jamie: *Can you believe Derek died?*

Three dots appeared. Disappeared. Appeared again.

Jamie: *Honestly? Not shocked. He had so much stress. Probably his heart.*

Probably his heart. Maybe. Derek was only forty-five but he lived on black coffee and rage. Heart attack made sense.

I tried to sleep. Couldn't. Kept seeing Derek's face when he collapsed. The sound his head made hitting the chair. The paramedics pumping his chest while Mariah Carey kept singing.

Saturday morning, nine-fifteen. My phone rang. Unknown number. Ridgemont area code.

"Ms. Brown, this is Detective Fairbank. I need you to come to Ridgemont Police Station."

My chest went tight. "Why? I already gave a statement. The para-medics said it was his heart—"

"That was the initial assumption. Toxicology came back this morning. Mr. Hoffman was poisoned."

The floor pulsed beneath me. "Poisoned? You mean—"

"Cyanide in the chocolates. This is a homicide investigation. How soon can you get here?"

"Thirty minutes."

She hung up.

I drove back to Ridgemont on autopilot. The police station was downtown, small brick building next to the post office. I parked in the visitor lot and walked in. The lobby smelled like burnt coffee and industrial cleaner. A fake Christmas tree sat in the corner, decorated with tinsel and paper ornaments that looked like they'd been made by elementary school kids. Cheerful. Wrong.

The desk officer took my name and called Fairbank. She appeared two minutes later. Same gray pantsuit. Same sharp eyes. She led me down a narrow hallway to an interview room. Metal table, two chairs, recording equipment on the wall.

"Sit."

I sat.

Fairbank settled across from me. Opened a folder. Pulled out photos of the chocolate box. Close-ups. Evidence markers next to each truffle.

"Cyanide acts fast. Symptoms appear within minutes. Seizures, respi-ratory failure, death. Mr. Hoffman—Derek, ate one truffle at three twenty-one. Collapsed at three twenty-eight. Dead at three thirty-one." She slid a photo toward me. "These chocolates killed him."

My hands pressed flat against the table. Cold metal. Real. Solid.

"Who would do this?"

"That's what I'm trying to determine." Fairbank leaned back. "He's your boss's boss. Tell me about office dynamics. Who hated Derek enough to kill him?"

"Hated is a strong word."

"He's dead. I'd say hate is appropriate."

Fair point. I tried to think past the shock. "Derek had enemies. He was ruthless. Climbed fast, stepped on people on the way up. But I can't think of anyone specific."

She pulled out another photo. The chocolate box. Gold ribbon. No card attached. "These chocolates weren't part of your Secret Santa exchange. Someone gave them separately."

"How do you know?"

"Patricia keeps a master list. Tracks who drew which name. These chocolates aren't on it. Someone placed them under the tree outside the official exchange. Just 'To: Derek.' No giver name."

My mouth went dry. "So someone just... left them under the tree?"

"Appears that way. Anonymous. Could've been placed there before the party. During setup. Whenever."

"But the office has cameras—"

"Conference room doesn't. We checked. Hallway cameras show people coming and going all week. At least thirty different employees. No way to narrow it down."

I tried to process this. Someone at Sterling Creative was a murderer. Someone I'd worked with for six years. Eaten lunch with. Shared elevators with.

"Do you have any idea who might've done this, Ms. Brown?"

"No. I really don't."

Fairbank studied me. Long silence.

"If you think of anything, call me." She slid a business card across the table. "Stay available. We'll be in touch."

I drove home. Hands shook on the steering wheel. I kept checking the rearview mirror. Paranoid. But Derek was dead. Poisoned. Murdered.

Home by noon. I locked the door. Deadbolt, chain. Made tea I didn't drink. Sat on the couch and stared at my phone.

Six PM. Shadows stretched across the living room. My phone buzzed on the coffee table. Text message. Unknown number.

I picked it up.

He deserved it. You know he did.

My hands went cold.

I stared at the screen. Read it again. Again.

Someone at the office. Someone who had my number. Someone who'd killed Derek and wanted me to know they weren't sorry.

The phone buzzed again. Same unknown number.

Stay quiet, Nora. Or you're next.

Chapter 3

The Connection

I called Fairbank's number three times on Sunday morning. She finally answered on the fourth.

"Ms. Brown, I can't discuss an active investigation—"

"Someone texted me last night. Said Derek deserved it. I think the killer has my number."

Silence. "Send me a screenshot. Don't delete anything. Call me if there's a new development."

Click.

Monday dragged. Office closed. Everyone told to work from home. I sat at my kitchen table with my laptop, pretending to answer emails. Couldn't focus. Kept opening new tabs, searching.

Cyanide poisoning symptoms.

The results loaded. Rapid onset. Seizures. Respiratory failure. Confusion, headache, then collapse. Death within minutes if the dose was high enough.

Derek's timeline matched perfectly. Three minutes from first bite to collapse. Seven more until his heart stopped.

I closed the laptop. Stared at the blank screen until my reflection stared back.

Tuesday morning, eight AM. Text from Patricia: *Everyone report to office by 9. Police interviews. Mandatory.*

I drove back to Ridgemont. Parked in the garage beneath our building. The elevator doors opened on the third floor and I walked into chaos.

Fairbank had set up an interview station in the conference room. Officer Polaski stood guard outside. Employees clustered at their desks, waiting their turns. No one was working.

Jamie caught my arm. "They're grilling everyone. Marcus was in there for twenty minutes."

"What'd they ask him?"

"Everything. Where he was Friday afternoon, who he saw near the gift table, did he have problems with Derek." She lowered her voice. "They asked if he knew anything about cyanide."

Panic clawed up my throat. "What'd he say?"

"No. Obviously." She glanced at the conference room door. "They're treating us like suspects."

We were suspects. One of us had killed Derek.

My name was called at nine-forty. I walked into the conference room. Fairbank sat at the head of the table, files spread in front of her. Polaski stood by the window, arms crossed. The Christmas tree was gone— removed as evidence, probably. Only the garland remained, drooping from the windows.

"Ms. Brown. Sit." Fairbank gestured to the chair across from her. "I know we've been through this already, but answer as accurately as you remember."

I sat.

"Friday afternoon, three PM. Walk me through every detail. Who was standing where, who touched the gift table, who you saw near the chocolates."

I tried to remember. "Everyone was moving around. Patricia set up food on the side table. People were eating, talking. The Secret Santa gifts were already under the tree when I got there."

"What time did you arrive at the party?"

"Two fifty-five. I was at my desk until then."

"Did you see anyone place gifts under the tree?"

"No. They were already there."

Fairbank pulled a paper from her file. "This is the Secret Santa list Patricia kept. Shows who drew which name." She slid it toward me.

My name was there. Next to Derek Hoffman's.

"You drew Derek Hoffman," Fairbank said. "You gave him the whiskey decanter set. Gold wrapping paper."

"Yes. He opened it during the exchange."

Fairbank pulled out the photo of the chocolate box again. Silver paper. Gold ribbon. Different from my wrapping. "These chocolates were separate. Extra. Someone placed them under the tree outside the official exchange."

"So they were never part of Secret Santa."

"Correct. Which means anyone could have left them." Fairbank made a note. "No giver name. Just 'To: Derek.' Anonymous."

"So someone could stay hidden."

"Appears that way."

The interview lasted another ten minutes. Same questions, different angles. When did I last see Derek alive? Did I notice anything unusual about his behavior? Did anyone at the office have access to cyanide?

I answered everything. Honestly. I had nothing to hide.

Fairbank let me go at ten-fifteen. "Stay in the area. We may have follow-up questions."

I waited at my desk. Jamie was still being interviewed. Marcus scrolled through his phone, not looking at anyone. Patricia was crying in the corner, tissues wadded in her fist.

Eleven AM. Alyson's turn. She walked into the conference room without hesitation. Door closed behind her.

I couldn't hear what was being said. Just low voices, muffled through the walls. Someone's phone rang. The radiator clanked. Outside, traffic hummed on Route 23.

Twenty minutes later, Alyson emerged. Her face was calm. Unchanged. She walked to her desk, grabbed her bag, and left without speaking to anyone.

Fairbank appeared in the doorway. "Patricia Reynolds."

Patricia jumped. Grabbed her tissues and hurried into the conference room.

Noon. Most interviews finished. Patricia emerged from the conference room and collapsed at her desk. Fairbank stepped out, phone pressed to her ear. She listened. Her expression shifted. She said something sharp to Polaski. They both moved fast, heading for the elevator.

Something was wrong.

I stood. "Detective?"

Fairbank didn't look back. She and Polaski disappeared into the elevator. Doors closed.

The office went silent. We looked at each other. Nobody spoke.

Jamie walked over. "What the hell was that?"

"I don't know."

We waited. One hour. Two. Fairbank didn't come back. Patricia dismissed everyone at three. "Go home. We'll let you know when the office reopens."

I drove home. My phone stayed silent until six-thirty. Then it rang. Fairbank.

"Ms. Brown. We have a development."

My hands went cold. "What happened?"

Fairbank hesitated. "Audrey Walsh missed her interview slot. Hasn't answered her phone since yesterday."

"Yesterday? But she was at the party—"

"She left right after Derek collapsed. Went home. No one's heard from her since." Fairbank paused. "We found Audrey Walsh."

The pause told me everything.

"Dead?"

"Poisoned. Same method. Chocolate truffles. Cyanide." Fairbank's voice was flat. Professional. But I heard the tension underneath. "She died Friday night. Maybe early Saturday morning. Before we knew Derek was murdered."

My legs went weak. I sat down hard on the nearest chair. "Friday night? But how—"

"The chocolates were delivered to her house Friday afternoon. Before the party. Card said they were from a grateful employee." Fairbank paused. "She had no reason to be suspicious. As far as she knew, Derek had a heart attack. Toxicology didn't confirm poison until Saturday morning. By then, Audrey had already eaten one."

Two deaths. Same killer. Same method.

And the killer had planned it so perfectly that Audrey never saw it coming.

"We have a serial poisoner, Ms. Brown. Two victims. Both from your office." Fairbank's voice sharpened. "I need you to think very carefully. What connects Derek Hoffman and Audrey Walsh?"

I tried to think through the shock. Derek and Audrey. VP of Client Services and HR Director. Both senior management. Both hired around the same time. Both climbed fast. Both ruthless in their own ways.

"They both started around 2015. Both climbed fast. Both were..." I struggled to find the word. "Demanding. Cold. People didn't like working with them."

"Anyone specific who had problems with both of them?"

My mind raced. Derek and Audrey. What else connected them? They worked together sometimes. Hiring decisions. Firing decisions.

Firing.

Something cold settled in my chest. A name I hadn't thought about in years.

"There was... something happened a long time ago. I don't think it matters."

"What?" Fairbank's voice sharpened.

I hesitated. "An employee. Mariana Sanchez. She was fired five years ago. November 2019."

"What happened?"

"Derek accused her of leaking client data to a competitor. Said emails came from her account. Audrey processed the termination immediately. Security escorted her out that same day."

"Did she do it?"

"I don't know. She claimed she didn't. Said someone else accessed her account. Begged them to check the IP logs, building access records. They refused." I paused. "It was brutal. They destroyed her career in an afternoon."

Silence on the line.

"Where is Mariana Sanchez now?"

"I don't know. She disappeared after she was fired. I haven't seen her since 2019."

"We'll find her." Fairbank's tone went hard. "If she's behind this, she's not finished. Stay vigilant. Lock your doors. Call me if anything unusual happens."

She hung up.

I stood in my kitchen. Audrey was dead. Two murders. Same killer. Same method.

My phone was still in my hand when it buzzed. Text message. Unknown number.

Two down. More to go.

Chapter 4

The Guilt

Wednesday morning. Christmas Day. I didn't sleep. Kept thinking about Mariana Sanchez. A name I hadn't spoken in five years. A face I'd tried to forget.

Fairbank's words echoed: "If she's behind this, she's not finished."

The texts burned in my mind: *Two down. More to go.*

If Mariana was the killer, and she knew I'd been in that meeting...

I grabbed my laptop from the kitchen table. Opened my email. Searched: *termination 2019.*

The results loaded. I scrolled past HR announcements, exit interviews, goodbye messages. Stopped.

Subject line: *Re: Data Breach Investigation - Mariana Sanchez.*

I clicked. Email from Audrey Walsh to all staff, dated November 2019.

Effective immediately, Mariana Sanchez has been terminated for violating company policy regarding confidential client information. Security has escorted her from the premises. All questions should be directed to HR.

I stared at the date. November 2019. Five years ago.

The memory crashed over me.

. . .

November 2019. I'd been at Sterling Creative three years. Junior marketing manager. Twenty-six years old. Still proving myself. Still scared of mistakes. Still terrified of Derek.

The data breach happened on a Tuesday. Client information—campaign strategies, pricing, contact lists—showed up with our competitor two days later. Exact copies. Someone had leaked it.

Derek called an emergency meeting Thursday afternoon. Conference room. The whole team. He stood at the head of the table. Face red. Jaw tight.

"Someone here is a thief."

Silence. No one moved.

Derek slammed a printed email onto the table. "These came from Mariana Sanchez's account. Sent to an external email address. Competitor's domain. Time-stamped Monday night, eleven PM."

I looked at Mariana. Twenty-three, maybe. Long dark hair, glasses, round face. Junior account coordinator. Quiet girl. She'd been there six months.

Her face went white. "I didn't send those."

"Your account. Your login. Your responsibility." Derek's voice was ice.

"Someone must have accessed my account. Please, check the IP logs. Check where the login came from. I wasn't even in the office Monday night—I was home with my roommate. She can verify—"

Audrey stood. "Enough." Blonde hair in a severe bun. Expression like chiseled stone. "We've reviewed the evidence. The emails came from your account. That's sufficient for immediate termination."

"But I didn't—" Mariana's voice cracked. Tears started. "Please. Check the IP address. Check the building access logs. I wasn't here Monday night. Someone else used my account. Please."

Derek crossed his arms. "Spare us the performance. You're fired. Security will escort you out."

Mariana looked around the room.

Her eyes landed on me for a second.

I looked away.

"You know I didn't do this." Her voice shook. "And you're just going to let them blame me?"

I didn't speak. Didn't move.

Security arrived. Two guards. They walked Mariana to her desk. Watched her pack her things into a cardboard box. Photos. Coffee mug. Notebooks. Her hands shook the whole time.

She walked to the elevator. The box in her arms. Tears streaming. She didn't look back.

The elevator doors closed.

Everyone returned to work. Like nothing happened. Like a woman's career hadn't just been destroyed.

I went back to my desk. Logged into my computer. Stared at the screen.

Something was wrong. I knew it. The emails Derek showed us—they were too obvious. Too convenient. Sent from Mariana's account at eleven PM on a Monday, when she wasn't in the building? IP logs would have shown that. Building access logs would have shown that.

But Derek didn't check. Didn't want to check. He wanted someone to blame. Fast. Clean. Easy.

And Audrey processed the termination without questioning anything. Just followed Derek's lead.

I could have said something. Could have asked about the IP logs. Could have suggested they investigate further before firing her.

But I didn't.

I was scared. Derek was my boss's boss. Questioning him meant risking my job. My career. Everything I'd worked for.

So I stayed silent.

Now, sitting at my kitchen table five years later, coffee cold in front of me, that silence felt like murder.

I could have saved Mariana with one question. One suggestion. One moment of courage.

Instead, I chose my career over the truth.

Derek was dead now. Audrey was dead. And someone was texting me: *You're just as guilty.*

I stared at the laptop screen. The termination email. Audrey's name at the bottom. Professional. Cold. Final.

If Mariana was killing everyone involved in her firing, the pattern was clear.

Derek made the accusation. Dead.

Audrey processed the termination. Dead.

And me? I witnessed it. Knew it was wrong. Said nothing.

I wasn't just a witness. I was complicit.

My phone sat on the table next to my cold coffee. I picked it up. Scrolled through the threatening texts. Two messages from unknown numbers. Both knew things only someone from that meeting would know.

He deserved it. You know he did.

Stay quiet, Nora. Or you're next.

Two down. More to go.

More to go. Not Derek and Audrey. There were more targets.

Me.

I was next. Not because I fired Mariana. But because I let it happen.

The apartment was silent. No Christmas music from neighbors. No traffic sounds from the street. Just the hum of the refrigerator and my own breathing.

Outside the window, Christmas lights blinked on the building across the parking lot. Red and green. Cheerful. Wrong.

I thought about calling Fairbank. Telling her everything. The meeting. My silence. The choice I made five years ago to protect my career instead of an innocent woman.

But what would I say? "I think I'm a target because I didn't speak up in 2019"?

She already knew about Mariana. Already knew Derek and Audrey destroyed her career. What she didn't know—what no one knew—was that I'd watched it happen. I could have said something, maybe stopped it. Or be let go, too.

My chest went tight. The walls of my apartment pressed closer.

Mariana Sanchez. Twenty-three years old. Crying. Begging. Destroyed.

And I did nothing.

Eight PM. Darkness pressed against the windows. I'd spent the day doing nothing. Sitting. Staring. Thinking about 2019.

My phone buzzed on the table.

Text message. Unknown number. Same number from before.

I picked it up.

You remember her, don't you? You said nothing. You're just as guilty.

My grip slipped. The phone fell. I caught it. Read the message again.

The killer knew. Knew I'd been there. Knew I'd witnessed Mariana's firing. Knew I'd stayed silent when I could have saved her.

I stood. Walked to the window. Pulled the curtain back an inch. The parking lot below was empty. Just cars covered in frost. Christmas wreaths hung on apartment doors across the courtyard. Red bows. Green garland. Normal.

But nothing was normal.

Two people were dead. And I was next.

Not because I fired Mariana Sanchez.

Because I let them destroy her.

And five years later, someone was making me pay for that silence.

Chapter 5

The First Twist

Wednesday night. Christmas night. I lay in bed, staring at the ceiling. Every sound from the hallway made me flinch. Footsteps. Doors closing. Someone laughing three apartments down.

Two AM. I gave up. Grabbed my laptop from the kitchen table. Sat on the couch with all the lights off. The glow from the screen hurt my eyes.

I typed into the search bar: *Mariana Sanchez New Jersey.*

Results loaded. LinkedIn profiles—none matched. Facebook accounts —dozens of them, all wrong people. A teacher in Hoboken. A nurse in Camden. An artist in Princeton. No one who'd worked at Sterling Creative.

I tried variations. *Mariana Sanchez Sterling Creative. Mariana Sanchez Ridgemont. Mariana Sanchez marketing.*

Nothing. Zero results that matched.

One old article appeared—Ridgemont Gazette, November 2019. Small piece about corporate data breaches. Mentioned Sterling Creative had terminated an employee for policy violations. No name. Just "junior staff member dismissed following internal investigation."

That was it. Mariana Sanchez had vanished.

I closed the laptop. Sat in the dark. Outside, someone's car alarm went off. Stopped after thirty seconds. Silence returned.

Six AM. Thursday morning. My phone rang.

I grabbed it. Fairbank.

"Did you find her?" I blurted.

"Not exactly. But we have a development."

I sat up straight. "What?"

"We traced the chocolate purchase. Credit card used to buy Derek's chocolates."

My pulse kicked up. "Who?"

"Sarah Mitchell."

The name hit me cold. "Sarah? The accountant?"

"Yes. She works in accounting. Hasn't been seen since Friday—the day Derek died. Address in Newark. We're moving on it now. I'll update you."

She hung up.

Sarah Mitchell. I barely knew her. Quiet woman in accounting. Kept to herself. I'd passed her desk a hundred times and never thought twice about her.

I grabbed my laptop. Searched: *Sarah Mitchell Sterling Creative.*

Nothing came up. No LinkedIn. No Facebook. No trace.

Two hours crawled by. I made coffee I couldn't drink. Paced my apartment. Stared at my phone.

Eight AM. Fairbank called back.

"We arrested Sarah Mitchell at her Newark apartment."

I pressed the phone harder against my ear. "And?"

"At the station, we ran her fingerprints through the system." Fairbank paused. "They match Mariana Sanchez."

The floor dropped. "What?"

"Sarah Mitchell IS Mariana Sanchez. New identity. Prints were on file from 2019—Sterling Creative required fingerprinting for all employees with client data access. That's how we got the instant match."

My mind raced. "She's been working at Sterling under an assumed name?"

"For eight months. Got hired as a temp in accounting. Became permanent in June. No one recognized her."

"But she looked—" I stopped. Five years. People changed. Weight loss. Hair color. Contacts instead of glasses.

"She confessed immediately. Soon as we confronted her with the fingerprints. Said, 'I killed Derek Hoffman. He destroyed my life.'"

My chest went tight.

"She gave us everything. The 2019 frame-up. How Derek fabricated the emails to make it look like she'd leaked the data. How she spent five years planning revenge. Changed her identity. Changed her appearance. Waited for the perfect opportunity."

"What about Audrey?"

"She's being questioned about both murders. Same method. Same motive. We're working on connecting her to Audrey's death."

I couldn't process it. Mariana had been there. At the office. For eight months. Three desks away from me in a different department. I'd never looked twice at Sarah Mitchell.

"For Derek, she bought gourmet chocolates," Fairbank said. "Laced them with cyanide. Placed them under the tree at the party. Gave us every detail. How he died, when, where." She paused. "We're still piecing together Audrey's murder. Different chocolate brand. Delivered to her home. But same poison, same company connection."

Silence stretched between us.

"Ms. Brown, the case is closed. Mariana Sanchez is in custody. Charged with one count, possibly soon, two counts first-degree murder. You're safe now."

Safe. The word felt hollow.

"I know this has been traumatic," Fairbank said. "Can you come in sometime this afternoon to give a supplemental statement?"

"Sure."

She hung up.

. . .

I sat on my couch. Phone in my hand. Stared at the blank TV screen.

Relief should have come. The killer was caught. Case closed. It was over.

But the relief didn't show up. Just guilt. Shame. The weight of knowing my silence five years ago had set this in motion.

If I'd spoken up in 2019, maybe Mariana wouldn't have been fired. Maybe she wouldn't have spent five years planning murder. Maybe Derek and Audrey would still be alive.

Maybe.

I stood. Got dressed. Drove to Ridgemont to give a supplemental statement at the station. Answered more questions from the DA's office. Signed paperwork. The whole process took two hours.

Released by noon. I drove home on autopilot.

One PM. I sat on my couch. Turned on the TV. Some news program. They were already covering the story. "Former Employee Arrested in Double Homicide." Mariana's booking photo filled the screen. Short dark hair. Hollow eyes. The caption read: "Sarah Mitchell, real name Mariana Sanchez."

I turned it off.

Tried to feel relief. Case closed. Mariana was in jail. It was over.

My phone sat on the coffee table. I picked it up. Scrolled through the threatening texts from the past week. All from the same unknown number.

He deserved it. You know he did.

Stay quiet, Nora. Or you're next.

Two down. More to go.

You remember her, don't you? You said nothing. You're just as guilty.

All sent before Mariana's arrest. All part of her plan.

Three PM. My phone buzzed.

New message. Unknown number.

I picked it up.

You think it's over? You're wrong. See you soon, Nora.

My hands froze.

I stared at the screen. Read it again.

But Mariana was in jail. Been in custody since eight AM. How could she send this text?

I grabbed my laptop. Searched the news. Confirmed. *Mariana Sanchez Arraigned. Held Without Bail. Sussex County Jail.*

She was definitely locked up.

So who sent the text?

I scrolled back through the previous messages. Same unknown number for all of them. The ones before the arrest. And this new one. After.

My pulse hammered against my ribs.

I called Fairbank. She answered on the second ring.

"Ms. Brown."

"Someone just texted me. Threatened me. But Mariana's in jail."

Silence. "Forward me the text immediately."

"She's been in custody since eight AM, right? No phone access?"

"Correct. No phone. No computer. No contact with outside."

"Then who sent this?"

Fairbank went quiet. I heard papers rustling. Keyboard clicking.

"Could be delayed send," she said finally. "Burner phone with timer. Or someone else is involved."

"Someone else?"

"Forward me that text. I'll look into it. Stay inside. Lock your doors."

She hung up.

I stood in my apartment. Mariana was in jail. The case was closed. The killer was caught.

But someone just threatened me.

Someone who knew about Mariana. Knew about the murders. Knew I'd stayed silent in 2019.

Someone else was out there.

And they weren't finished.

Chapter 6

The Doubt

I paced my apartment. Mariana was in jail. The case was closed. The killer was caught.

But that text. *See you soon, Nora.*

Not "I'll get you eventually." Not "this isn't over." See you *soon*. Active. Immediate. Present tense.

That wasn't delayed send. That was a threat from someone still free.

Something was wrong.

Four PM. I called Fairbank back.

"I want to visit Mariana Sanchez."

"Why?"

"I need to understand. I need to hear it from her."

Silence stretched between us. "I can arrange that. County jail. Visitor hours until seven. I'll meet you there in an hour."

Five PM. Sussex County Jail sat on the edge of town. Brick building, security fence, guard towers. Cold. Institutional. The kind of place that stripped away everything human.

Fairbank waited at the entrance. Same gray pantsuit. Same sharp eyes.

"She agreed to see you. Fifteen minutes max."

We went through security. Metal detector. Sign in. Visitor log. The guard took my phone and keys. Led us down a narrow hallway that smelled like disinfectant and desperation.

The visitor room was small. Plastic chairs. Metal table bolted to the floor. Cameras in the corners. No windows. Fluorescent lights hummed overhead.

I sat. Waited.

The door opened. A guard escorted Mariana in. Orange jumpsuit. Hands cuffed in front. She shuffled to the chair across from me. Sat.

Five years since that 2019 meeting. She looked different but the same. Short dark hair now—cut recently, maybe in processing. No glasses. Angular face. She'd lost weight. Fifty pounds, maybe more. Cheekbones sharp. Jaw defined.

But her eyes were the same. Dark brown. Intense. They'd haunted me for five years. The way she'd looked around that conference room. Begging someone to help her.

Now they just looked exhausted. Defeated.

Silence stretched between us.

Mariana spoke first. "I knew you'd come."

"Why?"

"Guilt. You were there. November 2019. You watched them destroy me."

My throat went tight. Something old and buried clawed up. "I'm sorry."

"Sorry doesn't give me back five years."

Pause. The fluorescent lights buzzed. Somewhere down the hall, someone was yelling. The sound was muffled. Distant.

"But I'm glad you came," Mariana said. "I want you to understand."

I nodded.

"Derek Hoffman framed me. He was leaking client data himself. Needed a scapegoat. I was young. Quiet. Easy target." Her voice was flat. Matter-of-fact. "He fabricated those emails. Made it look like they came from my account. Planted evidence."

"Audrey processed my termination without asking a single question. Just followed his orders. Security escorted me out like a criminal. I was blacklisted." She leaned forward. "Forty-seven job applications. Forty-seven rejections. Derek called every contact in the industry. Told them I was a thief."

Her jaw tightened. "My career was over at twenty-three."

I couldn't speak. Just listened.

"So yes, I killed him." Her voice hardened. "I spent five years planning it. Changed my identity. Lost fifty pounds. Cut my hair. Became someone else. Got hired at Sterling as Sarah Mitchell. No one recognized me. Not even you, sitting three desks away in accounting."

The weight of that hit me. Eight months. She'd been there eight months. I'd walked past her desk. Said good morning. Never looked twice.

"I waited for the perfect opportunity. Secret Santa was a gift. Anonymous. Easy to slip chocolates into the pile." She leaned back in her chair. "He ate two immediately. Wanted to show off. Died seven minutes later."

Pause. Her eyes met mine. "I'd do it again."

I swallowed. "What about Audrey Walsh?"

Mariana's face changed. Confusion crossed it.

"Who's Audrey Walsh?"

"The HR director. She was killed the same way. Poisoned chocolates."

Mariana stared at me. "I didn't kill anyone named Audrey."

"Don't lie to me. You confessed to both murders."

"I confessed to Derek. Only Derek."

"You sent chocolates to her house Friday afternoon."

Mariana shook her head. "I didn't. I only sent chocolates to Derek. At the office party. That's it."

"You're lying."

"I swear I'm not." Her voice was steady. Calm. "I didn't even know there was a second victim until you just told me."

I studied her face. The confusion looked real. Not rehearsed. Not calculated.

"You didn't see the news?"

"They arrested me Saturday morning. No phone access in holding. No TV. This is the first I'm hearing of a second death."

Mariana leaned forward. Cuffs clinked against the table. "I killed Derek Hoffman. I planned it for five years. I executed it perfectly. But I didn't touch anyone else."

The fluorescent lights buzzed louder. The guard by the door shifted his weight.

"I need to see the case file," I said.

"Why?"

"Because I don't think you're lying."

I exited the visitor room. Fairbank waited in the hallway.

"Get what you needed?"

"She says she didn't kill Audrey."

"Killers lie."

"I don't think she is." I met her eyes. "Can I see the case files? Both murders?"

Fairbank hesitated. Studied me. "Let's go to my office."

Ridgemont Police Station. Detective bullpen. Desks crammed together. Phones ringing. Officers typing reports. The smell of burnt coffee and printer toner.

Fairbank's desk was in the corner. Neat. Organized. Files stacked in perfect alignment. She pulled up digital files on her computer. Crime scene photos. Evidence logs. Toxicology reports.

She turned the monitor toward me. "Derek Hoffman. Audrey Walsh. Compare them."

I leaned in. Studied the screens side by side.

DEREK HOFFMAN:

- Gourmet truffles. Artisan brand. Hand-wrapped.
- Gold ribbon. Elegant box.

- High cyanide dose. Immediate symptoms.
- Died in seven minutes.
- Delivered at office party. Public setting. Everyone watching.

AUDREY WALSH:

- Godiva chocolates. Commercial brand. Store-bought.
- Red ribbon. Standard box.
- Lower cyanide dose. Delayed symptoms.
- Died in twenty minutes.
- Delivered to home. Private setting. Alone.

I stared at the evidence photos. The differences were stark. Obvious. "These don't match."

Fairbank looked up. "What?"

"Different brands. Different ribbons. Different doses. Different locations." I pointed at the screen. "Derek's murder was planned for a public spectacle. High dose. Fast death. Everyone there to witness it. Audrey's was private. Lower dose. Slower death. No witnesses."

Fairbank leaned forward. Studied the files. Went quiet.

"You're right." Her voice was tight. "I missed it."

"Mariana killed Derek. Only Derek."

"Someone else killed Audrey."

Fairbank's face hardened. "We have a second killer."

Her phone rang. She grabbed it. Listened. Her expression shifted.

"When?" Pause. "Are you sure?" Another pause. "Lock it down. I'm on my way."

She hung up. Grabbed her jacket.

"What happened?"

"Alyson Ellis didn't show up for her follow-up interview. We sent officers to her apartment." Fairbank's jaw tightened. "It's empty. Completely cleared out."

My chest went cold. "She ran."

"Stay here." Fairbank grabbed her jacket. "Polaski will be with you. Don't leave the station."

"Where are you going?"

"Alyson's apartment. If she's connected to this, I need to know how." She headed for the door. Stopped. Turned back. "If she's the second killer, you're a target. Until I figure this out, you stay put."

The door closed behind her.

Chapter 7

The Investigation

I sat in the detective's bullpen. Phones ringing. Officers typing reports. The smell of burnt coffee and stale air. Polaski stood by the door. Arms crossed. Watching.

Six-fifteen PM. I checked my phone. No new texts. The threatening message from earlier sat at the top of my messages. *See you soon, Nora.*

Someone at Sterling Creative had killed Audrey. Someone who knew about Mariana. Someone who was still free.

Alyson.

Quiet. New hire. Kept to herself. I'd barely noticed her in three months. And now she was gone.

I thought about October. The file transfer. Her borrowing my phone for twenty seconds. Normal office interaction. Nothing suspicious.

Had she installed something then? Was she tracking me?

My hands went cold. I checked my phone settings. Apps. Permissions. Nothing looked wrong. But I wasn't a tech expert. How would I even know?

Six-forty-five PM. Fairbank still wasn't back.

Polaski's phone buzzed. He answered. Listened. "Understood." Hung up. Looked at me. "Detective found the apartment empty. Moving to next phase of investigation."

"What does that mean?"

"Can't discuss ongoing investigation."

I waited. Seven PM. Seven-fifteen.

Finally, Fairbank walked back in. Her face was tight. She gestured for me to follow her to a conference room. Closed the door.

"Alyson's apartment is completely cleared out. No furniture. No personal items. She'd been moving boxes all week. Yesterday afternoon, a moving truck came. She's gone."

"Where?"

"I don't know. But I found something else." Fairbank pulled out her phone. Showed me an obituary. "Real Alyson Ellis died in March 2022. Car accident in Oregon. No surviving family."

I stared at the photo. Blonde woman. Pixie cut. Bright smile.

"The woman at Sterling Creative stole a dead woman's identity. Birth certificate, social security number, employment records—all forged. She's been planning this since 2022."

"Who is she really?"

"That's what I need to find out." Fairbank pocketed her phone. "I'm going back to the jail. Mariana might know who this woman is."

"You think they're connected?"

"Two killers. Same victims. Same method. Too much overlap to be coincidence." She opened the door. "Stay here. I'll be back in thirty minutes."

She left.

Seven-thirty PM. Polaski got me coffee from the break room. Not Dunkin. I drank it anyway.

Seven-fifty. Fairbank's car pulled into the lot. I watched through the window. She got out. Walked fast. Face hard.

She came straight to the conference room. Closed the door.

"Mariana talked."

I set the coffee down.

"Alyson's her girlfriend. They met in 2020. Support group for people who'd lost jobs unjustly." Fairbank sat across from me. "Mariana told her everything about the 2019 incident. Derek. Audrey. The frame-up. The blacklist."

Fear took root behind my sternum.

"They spent four years planning Derek's murder. Together. Mariana changed her identity. Got hired at Sterling as Sarah Mitchell. Alyson stole the dead woman's identity. Got hired three months ago as Alyson Ellis." Fairbank's jaw tightened. "They coordinated. Positioned themselves. Waited for the perfect opportunity."

"Secret Santa."

"Yes. But here's the problem." Fairbank leaned forward. "Mariana only wanted Derek dead. That was the entire plan. She confessed early, thinking it would end everything. She didn't know Alyson had already killed Audrey—and was planning to kill more people."

"But Alyson killed Audrey anyway."

"Without telling Mariana. Complete surprise." Fairbank pulled out her phone. Showed me a text exchange between her and the jail. "Mariana's exact words: 'I only wanted Derek dead. When you arrested me, I thought it was over. Then you told me about Audrey. I didn't know. Alyson never told me. She won't stop now. She thinks everyone who hurt me deserves to die.'"

The fluorescent lights hummed overhead. Somewhere down the hall, a phone rang.

"Everyone who hurt her," I repeated. "Derek. Audrey."

"And you." Fairbank's eyes locked on mine. "You were in that meeting. You watched. According to Mariana, Alyson sees you as complicit. Just as guilty."

My hands gripped the edge of the table.

"Alyson's been tracking you. The spyware on your phone—that was October, when you helped her with the file transfer. She's known your location for two months. Every text. Every email. Every place you've been."

The room felt smaller.

"I'm moving you. Now. Protective custody. Different location." Fairbank stood. "We need to get essentials from your apartment. Polaski and I will escort you. Five minutes in and out. Understood?"

I nodded.

Seven-fifty-five PM. Fairbank's car pulled into my apartment complex. Polaski followed in a patrol car. The parking lot was dark. A few scattered vehicles. Christmas lights blinked on the building across the courtyard. Red and green. Cheerful. Wrong.

We took the elevator to the third floor. Fairbank went first. Hand near her weapon. Polaski behind me.

The hallway was empty. Fluorescent lights hummed. My door was at the end. Number 347.

"Five minutes," Fairbank said. "Clothes, toiletries, essentials. That's it."

I unlocked my door. Stepped inside. Grabbed a duffel bag from the closet. Started throwing things in. Clothes. Laptop. Phone charger. Toothbrush. My hands shook. The zipper caught. I forced it closed.

Checked the window one last time. Parking lot below. Dark. Nothing suspicious.

I grabbed the duffel bag. Locked my apartment door. The hallway was empty. Fluorescent lights hummed overhead.

I started toward the elevator.

Stopped.

Sound at the apartment next door. 349. Door opening. Someone stepping into the hallway.

I turned.

Alyson stood three feet away. Short blonde hair. Angular face. But her expression wasn't calm anymore. It was cold. Predatory.

"Hello, Nora."

My pulse hammered. "Alyson—"

She took a step forward. "Do you know how long I've waited for this?"

Fairbank appeared at the end of the hallway. Hand on her weapon. "Don't move!"

Alyson ignored her. Eyes locked on me. Another step. "Five years. Watching Mariana suffer. Watching her break. Because of people like you."

"Step away from her!" Fairbank's voice was sharp. Commanding.

Alyson's hand went to her pocket.

"Show me your hands!" Fairbank drew her weapon. "Now!"

Alyson pulled her hand out slowly. Empty. Raised both hands. But she was smiling. "You think I need a weapon? I've been three steps ahead of you this entire time."

Footsteps on the stairs. Polaski appeared behind Alyson. Gun drawn. "Hands behind your head!"

She was boxed in. Trapped between two armed officers.

But she didn't look scared. She looked triumphant.

"On the ground!" Polaski moved closer. "Now!"

Alyson turned to me one last time. "You remember November 2019? That conference room? You watched them destroy her. You knew the truth. And you said nothing."

"Get on the ground!" Fairbank advanced. Weapon steady.

"I wanted you to know." Alyson's smile widened. "Before you die. I wanted you to understand why."

Polaski grabbed her shoulder. Forced her down. She didn't resist this time. Just kept staring at me as he cuffed her hands behind her back.

"You think this is over?" She laughed. Sharp. Bitter. "You think catching me changes anything?"

They pulled her to her feet.

"Mariana knows what I'm capable of. And so will you." Her eyes burned into mine. "See you soon, Nora."

They led her down the hallway. Toward the elevator. She didn't look away until the doors closed between us.

Silence.

Fairbank lowered her weapon. Turned to me. "You okay?"

I wasn't. My hands shook. My legs felt weak.

But I nodded.

"Let's go. You're not staying here tonight."

We walked to the elevator. The doors closed. I watched the floor numbers descend. Three. Two. One.

Alyson was caught. Both killers in custody.

It was over.

So why didn't it feel over?

Chapter 8

The Second Twist

Eight PM. Ridgemont Police Station. Interview room. Metal table. Two chairs. Recording equipment on the wall. Camera in the corner. Red light blinking.

Alyson sat across from Fairbank and me. Hands cuffed to the table. Orange jail jumpsuit. Hair still perfect. Face calm. Like she was discussing the weather.

Polaski stood by the door. Arms crossed. Watching.

Fairbank placed a folder on the table. Opened it. "Alyson Ellis—or whoever you are—you're being charged with the murder of Audrey Walsh. Conspiracy to commit murder. Identity theft. Do you understand these charges?"

Alyson nodded. "I understand."

"Do you want a lawyer?"

"No." Her voice was steady. Calm. "I want to explain."

Fairbank pressed record on the equipment. "State your name for the record."

"My real name is Alyson Reed."

My hands pressed flat against the table.

"I met Mariana Sanchez in 2020. Support group for people who'd lost their jobs unjustly. First session, she told her story. The frame-up. Derek fabricating evidence. Audrey processing the termination without asking a single question. The blacklist." Alyson's eyes shifted to me. "Your office watching her get destroyed. Including you, Nora."

My chest went tight.

"Mariana was broken. Depressed. Suicidal at times. I helped her survive." Her voice softened. "We fell in love."

Silence. The recording equipment hummed. Somewhere down the hall, a phone rang.

"Mariana wanted revenge. Just on Derek. The man who framed her." Alyson leaned forward. "We spent four years planning it. I found the real Alyson Ellis—car accident victim, no family, perfect identity to steal. Changed my appearance to match hers. Lost weight. Dyed my hair. Got contacts."

"Applied to Sterling Creative in 2024. Got hired. Positioned myself perfectly." She paused. "Secret Santa was a gift. Anonymous. Easy."

Fairbank made notes. Didn't look up. "When did you diverge from the plan?"

Alyson's expression shifted. Hardened. "I read the case files. Learned about Audrey's role. And yours, Nora. Mariana said Derek alone was enough. She wanted to move on after that. Build a new life with me."

"I disagreed."

The words hung in the air.

"Mariana wanted justice. I wanted revenge. There's a difference." Her jaw tightened. "She was too forgiving. Too merciful. She wanted to punish one person and let the rest of you live with guilt."

"I couldn't accept that."

Fairbank looked up. "Why not?"

"Because Audrey enabled him. Never questioned the evidence. Just followed orders. She was complicit." Alyson's eyes locked on mine. "And you? You watched. You knew the evidence was fake. And you said nothing."

My throat closed.

"Friday morning, I bought Godiva chocolates. Different brand than

Derek's. Mariana didn't know." Her voice was matter-of-fact. Clinical. "I delivered them to Audrey's house Friday afternoon. Card said they were from a grateful employee. She ate one Friday night. Died before anyone knew Derek was murdered."

"Mariana didn't know about it."

Fairbank tapped her pen. "You've been texting Ms. Brown. Threatening her."

"Yes."

"How? You tracked her phone?"

Alyson smiled slightly. "In October, she helped me with a file transfer. I borrowed her phone for twenty seconds. Installed spyware."

Recognition struck like lightning.

"After that, I could read every text. Every email. See her GPS location down to the meter." She tilted her head. "That's how I knew where she was. Always. Technology makes stalking easy."

I wanted to leave. Wanted to run. But my legs wouldn't move.

"Mariana's confession threw me. She turned herself in thinking it would end. That I'd stop." Alyson shook her head. "But I couldn't. You were still alive. Still unpunished."

"So I cleared out my apartment. Planned to finish this. Kill you, Nora. Then disappear."

Fairbank closed her folder. "Why confess now? Why not just run?"

Alyson's smile faded. "Because Mariana will spend decades in prison. I wanted her to know I tried. That I finished what we started." She paused. "Even if I failed."

Her eyes met mine again. "You'll always know you're the reason people died. Your silence destroyed Mariana. That destruction created me."

"You can't escape that."

The fluorescent lights buzzed overhead. The recording equipment whirred.

Fairbank leaned back. "We told Mariana what you did. The murders. The plan."

Alyson's face changed. "What did she say?"

"She was devastated. Said she never wanted Audrey dead. Never wanted you to kill anyone." Fairbank's voice was flat. Professional. "She begged us to stop you before you hurt Ms. Brown."

Pain crossed Alyson's face. Real. Raw. "She tried to protect you. Even after everything."

Tears welled up in her eyes. First emotion I'd seen crack through. "I did this for her. And she hates me for it."

The door opened. Polaski and another officer entered.

"We're transferring you to county jail. Murder charges will be formally filed tomorrow."

They unlocked her cuffs from the table. Pulled her to her feet. Recuffed her hands behind her back.

Alyson looked at me one last time. Tears streamed down her face. "Tell Mariana I'm sorry. I thought I was helping."

The words branded themselves across my brain.

"I thought I was saving her."

They led her out. The door closed. Lock clicked.

Silence.

I sat in the interview room. Fairbank across from me. The recording equipment still running. Red light blinking.

"You okay?"

"No." My voice a whisper.

"Fair enough."

Pause. She reached over. Stopped the recording. The red light went dark.

"Two killers. Both in custody. You're safe."

But I didn't feel safe. Felt like a survivor of something that should have killed me. Should have. But didn't.

"What happens now?"

"Trials. Sentencing. Justice system." Fairbank stood. "Could take months. Maybe a year. You'll have to testify."

"And me? What do I do?"

"You go home. You survived. You move forward." She walked to the door. Opened it. "Come on. I'll drive you."

. . .

Ten PM. Fairbank pulled up to my apartment. The parking lot was dark. Christmas lights still blinked across the courtyard. Red and green. On and off. On and off.

"You need anything, call me." She handed me her card again. I already had three.

I got out. Walked to my building. Took the elevator to the third floor. Walked down the hallway. My door. Number 347.

The apartment next door—349—was dark. Empty. Crime scene tape across the entrance.

I unlocked my door. Stepped inside. Locked it behind me. Deadbolt. Chain.

Walked to the windows. Checked them. Locked. Curtains drawn.

Sat on the couch in the dark.

Two people were dead. Derek and Audrey. Two people were in prison. Mariana and Alyson.

Because five years ago, I stayed silent.

Because I was scared. Because I chose my career over the truth. Because I looked away when someone was being destroyed and I knew—I knew—it was wrong.

The weight of that pressed down. Suffocating. Permanent.

I'd survived. But survival wasn't the same as being okay.

And I'd never be okay again.

Chapter 9

The Reckoning

Friday morning. I didn't sleep. Sat on the couch until dawn. Gray light crept through the windows. Day after Christmas. Somewhere, people were returning gifts. Eating leftovers. Complaining about relatives.

Here, silence and guilt.

Nine AM. Ridgemont Police Station. The district attorney's office had sent a prosecutor. Young. Maybe thirty. Sharp suit. Kind eyes. She set up a recorder on the conference table.

"Ms. Brown, I need you to tell me everything you know about the 2019 incident."

I talked for three hours. Derek's accusation. The emails supposedly from Mariana's account. Her pleas to check the IP logs. The building access records that would have proven her innocence. Audrey processing the termination without question. Security escorting Mariana out.

My silence.

My voice went hoarse. I cried twice. The prosecutor handed me tissues. Waited. Let me compose myself.

"This will help Mariana's case," she said finally. "Show she was framed. The evidence was fabricated. It won't erase what she did, but it'll reduce the charges."

"From what to what?"

"First-degree murder down to voluntary manslaughter. Crime of passion after years of documented trauma." She closed her folder. "She'll still serve time. Ten to fifteen years. But it's better than life."

I nodded.

"Alyson Reed is different. First-degree murder for Audrey Walsh. Premeditated. Cold. Calculated. Attempted murder for you. Identity theft. Stalking." The prosecutor's expression hardened. "She's looking at life. No parole eligibility for twenty-five years."

Twenty-five years. Alyson would be fifty-four before she could even apply for parole.

"You'll have to testify at both trials. Could be months before they're scheduled. Are you prepared for that?"

"I don't have a choice."

"No. You don't." She stood. Extended her hand. "Thank you for your cooperation, Ms. Brown."

I shook it. Left.

Three PM. I requested one more visit with Mariana. Fairbank approved it. Drove me to the county jail herself.

Same visitor room. Same plastic chairs. Same metal table. Same smell of disinfectant.

Mariana entered. Orange jumpsuit. Hands cuffed. She looked broken. Hollow. Sat across from me.

Silence stretched between us. Long. Heavy.

Mariana spoke first. "I never wanted Audrey dead. Or you."

"I know."

"Alyson went too far. I tried to stop her. That's why I confessed. Thought if I was arrested, she'd stop." Tears streamed down her face. "I underestimated her love. Her rage."

I didn't know what to say. What could I say?

"I'm sorry. For 2019. For staying silent. For everything."

Mariana nodded slowly. "I know. But sorry doesn't undo it."

"No. It doesn't."

The fluorescent lights hummed. A guard coughed somewhere down the hall.

"Did you tell them? About Derek framing me?"

"Yes. Everything. The prosecutor says it'll help your case. Voluntary manslaughter instead of murder. Ten to fifteen years instead of life."

"Ten to fifteen." She repeated the words. Tasted them. "Still a long time."

"Yes."

"What will you do now?"

"I don't know. Figure out how to live with this."

Mariana's eyes met mine. Dark. Exhausted. "Join the club."

The guard tapped his watch. Time was up.

Mariana stood. Shuffled toward the door. Stopped. Turned back.

"For what it's worth, I believe you. That you're sorry. That you'll carry this forever." She paused. "Do something with it. Make it mean something."

The guard led her away. The door closed.

I sat alone in the visitor room for a long time.

Outside, Fairbank waited by her car. Leaned against the hood. Arms crossed.

"How'd it go?"

"As well as it could."

We drove back to my apartment in silence. Christmas decorations still hung from every storefront. Lights blinked. Wreaths sagged. The whole state looked tired.

"What happens to Sterling Creative?" I asked.

"Company's done. Scandal too big. They'll close within months. Maybe weeks." Fairbank glanced at me. "Everyone will get severance. But that's it."

"Good. Place was toxic anyway."

She pulled into my parking lot. Put the car in park. "You need anything, call me."

"Thank you."

"I mean it. This kind of thing—" She stopped. Started again. "It changes you. Don't try to handle it alone."

I nodded. Got out. Watched her drive away.

Six PM. I sat in my apartment. The lights off. The TV off. Just darkness and silence.

My phone rang. Jamie.

"You okay? I saw the news."

"I'm alive."

"Want company? Dinner? My family has leftovers. Turkey, stuffing, pie. Way too much food."

"No. Thank you. I need to be alone."

"Okay. But call if you need anything. I mean it, Nora. Anything."

"I will."

I hung up. Set the phone on the coffee table.

Looked around my apartment. No decorations. No tree. No Christmas. Just empty space and furniture I'd had for six years. A life I'd built on silence and cowardice.

I opened my laptop. Typed into the search bar: *Legal Aid Society New Jersey*.

The website loaded. Nonprofit organization. Helped people who couldn't afford lawyers. Wrongful terminations. False accusations. Cases that fell through the cracks. People like Mariana. People whose lives got destroyed by lies and silence.

Maybe I could volunteer. Maybe I could help someone the way I didn't help Mariana.

Not redemption. Nothing could redeem my silence. Nothing could bring back Derek and Audrey. Nothing could give Mariana and Alyson back the years they'd lose in prison.

But purpose. Something good from all this wreckage.

I clicked the volunteer application. Started filling it out.

My phone buzzed. Text message. Patricia.

Office closing permanently. Severance details coming next week. Take care of yourself, Nora.

I stared at the message. Six years at Sterling Creative. Gone. My career. My routine. Everything I'd prioritized over doing the right thing in 2019.

All of it: over.

I set the phone down. Looked at the laptop screen. The volunteer application half-finished. A blank space where it asked: *Why do you want to volunteer?*

I typed: *Because I stayed silent once. I won't make that mistake again.*

Hit submit.

The confirmation page loaded. *Thank you for your interest. We'll be in touch within two weeks.*

Two weeks. The trials wouldn't start for months. Sterling would close by January. My severance would last maybe six months if I was careful.

My future: uncertain. Unknown. Unmapped.

But I was alive.

That had to mean something.

Even if I didn't know what yet.

Chapter 10

Moving Forward

January. Sterling Creative closed January 15th officially. All employees terminated. Six years reduced to a severance check and a box of belongings.

I never went back to the office after that Thursday in December.

The Trials

March 2025. Mariana Sanchez pleaded guilty to voluntary manslaughter. I testified. Told the judge everything about Derek's frame-up. The fake evidence. The emails sent from her account when she wasn't in the building. The IP logs Derek refused to check. Mariana's pleas. Her innocence.

The judge considered mitigating circumstances. Wrongful termination. Blacklist. Five years of documented trauma.

Sentenced: fifteen years. Eligible for parole after ten.

Less than murder. More than justice.

April 2025. Alyson Reed's trial lasted two weeks. She pleaded guilty to first-degree murder for Audrey Walsh. Pleaded guilty to attempted murder for me. No mitigating circumstances. The prosecutor laid it out: cold, calculated, premeditated. Identity theft. Stalking. Two years of planning.

Sentenced: life. No parole eligibility for twenty-five years.

She'd be fifty-four before she could even apply.

If she survived that long.

Nora's New Life

February. I started volunteering at the Legal Aid Society of Newark. Three days a week. Wrongful termination cases. People accused of things they didn't do. People whose lives got destroyed by lies and silence.

I couldn't save Mariana.

Maybe I could save someone else.

March. I moved to Montclair. Smaller apartment. Cheaper rent. Second floor of a converted Victorian. Hardwood floors. High ceilings. Too much light. Minimal furniture: bed, desk, chair. No decorations. No photos. No Christmas plans.

Never again.

April. I started therapy. Dr. Rachel Santos. Twice a week. Working through guilt, complicity, silence.

"You can't change the past," she said. "You can change what you do now."

Small steps. Some days I believed it. Most days I didn't.

May. A letter arrived from Sussex County Jail. Mariana's handwriting. Neat. Precise.

Nora,

I don't forgive you. I want to be clear about that. What you didn't do cost me everything. My career, my identity, five years planning revenge instead of living.

But I understand you. We were both victims of Derek's cruelty. You were scared of him. So was I.

I took a life. You took the coward's path. We're both paying for it now. I'll spend decades in prison. You'll spend your life carrying guilt.

Neither of us wins.

Do something good with this. Make it mean something.

- M.

I read it three times. Burned it in the kitchen sink. Watched the paper curl and blacken. Ash swirled down the drain.

The words stayed anyway.

Do something good. Make it mean something.

Summer. The Legal Aid work intensified. I won my first case. Wrongful termination overturned. A woman got her job back. Her livelihood. Her dignity.

Small victory. Not enough. Would never be enough.

But something.

Fall. Sterling Creative officially dissolved. Assets sold. Building empty. Patricia moved to Vermont. Jamie took a job in Philadelphia. Everyone scattered.

Like the company never existed.

But the ghosts remained.

November. I stood at my apartment window. Watched cars pass below. Normal people living normal lives. Going to work. Coming home. Complaining about traffic.

My phone rang. Dad's number. I'd been avoiding him for months. Picked up anyway.

"Hello, Dad. It's me, Nora."

"Of course I know it's you."

Pause. Traffic sounds from his end. Florida. Retirement. A life I didn't understand.

"How are you, kiddo?"

"I'm... I'm working on it."

"That's all anyone can do."

We talked for thirty minutes. First real conversation in years. Not much. But a start.

Present day. I sat at my desk in the Legal Aid office. Stack of files in front of me. New case, a man accused of theft he didn't commit. Evidence looked manufactured. Time stamps didn't match. Security footage mysteriously corrupted.

I knew how to fight this now. Knew what fabricated evidence looked like. Learned it the hard way.

My phone rang. New client.

I answered. "Legal Aid Society, this is Nora Brown."

"I need help." Woman's voice. Shaking. Desperate. "I was fired for whistleblowing. They're saying I stole company funds. I didn't. They fabricated the documents. No one will listen."

I knew this story. Lived it from the wrong side.

"I'll help you. Tell me everything."

I picked up my pen. Started taking notes.

This time, I spoke up.

Some mistakes can't be undone. Some silences echo forever.

Mariana was in prison. Alyson was in prison. Derek and Audrey were dead. Sterling Creative was gone.

But I was still here. Still breathing. Still trying.

Silence was complicity. Cowardice had consequences. The things we don't say can destroy people just as surely as the things we do.

I couldn't change 2019. Couldn't give Mariana back five years. Couldn't bring back the dead.

But redemption wasn't about erasing the past. It was about facing it. And choosing differently next time.

Some days that was enough.
Today, it had to be.

THE END

BOOK 10

The Proposal

Chapter 1

The Arrival

The cabin looked like a Christmas card.

Tyler's F-150 crunched through fresh snow as we pulled up the long driveway. Pine trees pressed close on both sides, branches heavy with white.

Through the windshield, the cabin emerged from the woods—log walls, stone chimney trailing smoke, warm light spilling from frost-edged windows. Four o'clock and the December sun already sank low, painting everything gold and blue.

"You decorated," I said.

Tyler grinned. Thirty-two, dark hair, the kind of jaw that belonged in cologne ads. He wore the hunter green sweater I'd bought him last month, sleeves pushed up his forearms. "Came up Wednesday. Wanted everything perfect."

Perfect. The word sat warm in my chest.

A wreath hung on the front door, tied with red velvet ribbon. Icicle lights traced the roofline, blinking their steady rhythm. Through the window, I glimpsed the glow of a Christmas tree. One year of dating, and Tyler Grant had driven forty minutes from Sparta to transform his family's lake cabin into a winter wonderland.

For me.

I knew what that meant.

We climbed out into the cold. I stretched, stiff from the hour-long drive from my apartment in Morristown. My breath came in white clouds.

I'm Brooke Palmer. Twenty-nine, five-six, the kind of face people call "approachable"—the kind that disappears in waiting rooms and grocery store lines. Nothing interesting ever happened to me. Same dental hygienist job since graduation. Same routine. Same life.

But standing here in the snow, in my puffer coat and knit hat, something shifted. Like the next chapter was about to begin.

Tyler grabbed both our bags from the truck bed. "Go inside. Warm up. I'll bring everything in."

The cabin smelled like pine and wood smoke and something sweet— cinnamon, maybe. Apple cider. The living room opened before me, all exposed beams and worn leather furniture. A fire crackled in the stone fireplace. The Christmas tree stood in the corner, strung with white lights and silver ornaments.

Two stockings hung from the mantel. One red. One green.

Our names stitched across them in gold thread. Tyler. Brooke.

My throat tightened. He'd had them made.

But something was off. The garland draped across the mantel sagged in the middle, unevenly distributed. The tree ornaments clustered too heavily on one side. The wreath above the fireplace hung slightly crooked. Small things. Details most people wouldn't notice. But the impression was rushed. Hurried. Not quite the perfection Tyler claimed.

"What do you think?" Tyler came up behind me, dropped the bags by the door. His arms wrapped around my waist. Cold from outside, but his chest pressed warm against my back.

"It's beautiful."

"Wait until you see the lake in the morning. Frozen solid this time of year." He kissed my temple. "Hot cocoa?"

I nodded.

Tyler moved to the kitchen—an open layout, everything visible from where I stood. He pulled mugs from the cabinet, heated milk on the stove.

Bing Crosby drifted from a small Bluetooth speaker on the counter. *White Christmas.* The song my grandmother used to play every December.

How did he know that? I'd mentioned it once. Months ago. He remembered.

I wandered through the living room. Touched the garland on the mantel. Ran my fingers over the soft wool of the stockings. The fire popped and settled. Outside, through the window, snow had started to fall again. Fat flakes drifting down through the pines. Silent. Still.

No neighbors for three miles. No cell signal this deep in the woods. Just us.

Romantic, I told myself. Private. Perfect for a proposal.

Tyler handed me a mug topped with whipped cream. "Careful. It's hot."

We sat on the couch, his thigh pressed against mine. The cocoa warmed my hands through the ceramic. Sweet, rich, a hint of peppermint.

He'd remembered I liked peppermint.

"I've been thinking about our future," Tyler said. "After the holidays, we should look at apartments together. I found a three-bedroom on Maple Street. Good school district."

I blinked. "School district?"

"For someday." He smiled. "I want kids, Brooke. Two, maybe three. A real family."

He hadn't asked what I wanted. Hadn't asked if I was ready. He'd already looked at apartments. Already picked neighborhoods. Already planned our children.

"That's... that's a big step."

"A year is time enough, don't you think?" He kissed my forehead. "I need to grab firewood from the shed. Enough to last the night. Make yourself at home."

He stood, pulled on his jacket. "I'll be back in twenty minutes."

The door closed behind him. Cold air rushed in, then cut off. His footsteps crunched away through the snow.

I counted to thirty. Listened for the creak of the shed door.

Then I moved.

The ring. I wanted to see it. Just a peek—just to know what it looked like, to prepare my surprised face for when he finally asked. Tyler's black duffel sat by the door where he'd dropped it. I knelt beside it, unzipped the main compartment. Clothes. Toiletry bag. A bottle of champagne wrapped in a towel.

Champagne. For after.

My pulse quickened. I dug deeper. Pushed aside his running shoes. Found it tucked in an interior pocket.

My fingers froze. For one suspended moment, I couldn't breathe—couldn't think past the electric rush of hope tangled with the sick guilt of snooping.

A velvet box. Navy blue. Small enough to fit in a palm.

The Christmas tree lights blinked behind me—red, gold, green. Bing Crosby crooned about snow and sleigh bells. The fire crackled. Everything soft. Everything warm.

I opened the box.

Empty.

"What?"

Had Tyler moved it? Forgotten it somewhere?

Then I noticed small writing inside the lid.

B.P. - Christmas Eve 2024

B.P.? Brooke Palmer. My initials.

Where was the ring?

A floorboard creaked upstairs.

I froze. Box open in my hands. Heart slamming against my ribs.

Tyler was outside. Getting firewood. I'd heard him walk to the shed.

Another creak. Slow. Deliberate. The sound of weight shifting on old wood.

Someone was upstairs.

I closed the box. Shoved it back in the bag. Zipped it shut. My hands shook so hard the zipper caught twice before it closed.

The front door swung open. Cold air. Snow on Tyler's shoulders.

He carried an armload of split logs, stacked them by the fireplace. Brushed bark from his sweater.

"Miss me?" He crossed to me. Kissed my cheek. His lips were cold from outside, but his eyes stayed warm. Crinkled at the corners. Happy.

"Of course."

"You look pale." He touched my forehead with the back of his hand. "Feeling okay?"

"Just tired from the drive."

"Sit. Relax." He steered me toward the couch. Tucked a blanket around my shoulders. "I'll start dinner in a bit. You just rest."

Tyler moved back to the kitchen. Started pulling ingredients from the refrigerator. Hummed along with the music.

I sat rigid on the couch. Stared at the ceiling. At the dark rectangle of the second-floor landing visible from where I sat.

No movement. No sound.

Just the fire crackling. Just Tyler humming. Just the Christmas tree lights blinking their endless pattern.

Tyler kissed my forehead. Pulled me close. His arms wrapped around me, solid and warm.

Over his shoulder, I stared at the ceiling.

The old cabin settled around us. Wood expanding and contracting in the cold. Beams shifting with age and weight and time.

Somewhere above us, the structure groaned.

It sounded almost human.

Chapter 2

Hairline Cracks

Saturday morning. Sunlight streamed through the frost-edged windows, turning the cabin golden. I woke to the smell of bacon and coffee.

Tyler stood at the stove in flannel pajama pants and a t-shirt, spatula in hand. Pancakes on the griddle. Eggs scrambled in a pan. Orange juice poured into glasses. The table set with plates and silverware and a small vase holding pine branches.

He smiled over his shoulder. "Morning, beautiful. Hungry?"

I slid onto a stool at the counter. "You didn't have to do all this."

"I wanted to." He plated three golden pancakes. Set them in front of me with butter and syrup. "I thought we'd hike at ten. There's a trail that circles the lake—takes about an hour. Then lunch at one. After that, we can relax before I start dinner."

I poured syrup. "What if I want to nap?"

Tyler laughed. Soft. Affectionate. "You never nap. You always say sitting still makes you anxious."

I paused, fork halfway to my mouth. "I... do say that."

"I know you." He kissed the top of my head. "Better than you know yourself sometimes."

He was right. I did say that. But his certainty—the way he stated it like fact, like my preferences were data he'd cataloged—made something tighten in my chest.

We ate breakfast. Tyler talked about the hike. The views. The photo opportunities. I nodded. Agreed. The pancakes tasted like cardboard in my mouth.

After breakfast, I helped him clear the dishes. He washed while I dried.

"What do you want for Christmas dinner?" Tyler asked. "I'm thinking something special. Romantic."

"Last week you said you were making chicken parmesan."

Tyler's hands stilled in the soapy water. He looked at me, forehead creased. "I never said that."

"Yes, you did. We were on the phone Tuesday night. You said it was my favorite."

"Brooke." His voice stayed gentle. Patient. "I suggested steak. Filet mignon with roasted vegetables. You said chicken sounded too heavy for a special occasion."

I replayed the conversation in my mind. Tuesday night. He'd called after work. We'd talked about the weekend. About dinner. Had he said steak? Or chicken?

I couldn't remember.

"You've been stressed at work," Tyler said. His hand found mine. Squeezed. "End-of-year deadlines. It's okay to forget things."

"I wasn't stressed—"

"Dr. Peterson's been difficult, right? With that new patient management system?"

He was right again. Dr. Peterson, my boss at the dental practice, had been impossible all month. New software. New protocols. I'd mentioned it to Tyler.

"Yeah," I said. "He has."

"See? You're exhausted. Your brain is fried." Tyler smiled. Kissed my temple. "Let me take care of everything this weekend. You just relax."

I dried the last plate in silence.

The morning passed in increments. I went to the bathroom. When I came out, Tyler was in the hallway.

"There you are. I was about to check on you."

I grabbed a glass of water from the kitchen. Tyler appeared beside me.

"Everything okay?"

"Fine. Just thirsty."

I walked to the living room to grab my book. Tyler followed.

"Where were you?"

"Kitchen. Getting water."

"Oh." He smiled. "I thought you went upstairs."

I hadn't. But he watched me like he expected an explanation. Like my movements required tracking.

At eleven, Tyler announced he needed to shower before our hike. The water started running. Steam drifted from under the bathroom door.

I had fifteen minutes. Maybe twenty.

The basement door stood at the end of the hallway. Narrow. White. Easy to miss. I'd noticed it yesterday but hadn't explored.

Now, I opened it.

Wooden stairs descended into darkness. I found the light switch. A bare bulb flickered on.

Concrete floor. Stone walls. The smell of damp and old wood and something faintly chemical. Boxes stacked along one wall. A workbench with tools—hammers, saws, coils of rope. And along the far wall, more boxes. Christmas decorations. Tangled lights. A box of ornaments.

I moved deeper. Tax documents in plastic bins. Old camping gear. A stack of vinyl records. Then, tucked behind a box labeled *2019 Tax Returns*, a shoebox.

I pulled it out. Lifted the lid.

Photos.

Tyler at the cabin. Smiling in front of the fireplace. A wreath hung on the wall behind him—the same wreath that hung there now. Stockings on the mantel. A Christmas tree with familiar ornaments.

But he wasn't alone.

A woman stood beside him. Blonde hair. Bright smile. Her arm looped through his. Tyler's arm around her waist. The photograph captured a moment of easy affection—two people comfortable together, in love.

I flipped the photo over. No date. No names. Just blank white paper.

I recognized her face. From somewhere. But I couldn't place it.

I shoved the photo back in the box. Put the box where I'd found it. Climbed the stairs. The shower was still running.

Tyler emerged ten minutes later, hair wet, wearing jeans and a flannel shirt. "Ready for that hike?"

"Actually, I need to ask you something." I kept my voice light. Casual. "I found some old photos in the basement. Who's the blonde woman?"

Tyler paused mid-button. His hands stilled on his shirt. He looked at me with complete calm.

"What blonde woman?"

"In the photos. At this cabin. With you."

Tyler's face shifted. Patient. Slightly amused. Like I'd asked something naive.

"Brooke, my parents owned this place for thirty years. Lots of family friends came up here. Could be anyone. My cousin Emily. My aunt's friend from church. I'd have to see the photo to know."

"She was with you specifically. Your arm was around her."

"You're making assumptions." He smiled. Crossed to me. Cupped my face in his hands. "You worry too much. It's probably just an old girlfriend from college. Ancient history. Nothing that matters."

His tone was so reasonable. So gentle. Like he was talking to someone who'd gotten confused about something obvious.

"It looked recent," I said.

"Define recent." Tyler kissed my forehead. "The cabin looks the same every Christmas. Same decorations. Same tree. A photo from ten years ago looks like a photo from last week."

He had a point. The decorations were old. Reused every year. How could I date the photo?

"Come on." He grabbed our coats from the closet. "Let's get some fresh air. Clear your head."

We hiked the trail around the lake. Tyler pointed out birds. Told stories about summers he'd spent here as a kid. Held my hand over icy patches.

The perfect boyfriend.

But every time I glanced at him, I saw that photo. That blonde woman. Her bright smile. The ease between them.

That night, we ate leftovers by the fire. Tyler suggested a movie. We watched something romantic and forgettable. He held me on the couch, his arm around my shoulders, his chin resting on my head.

Later, in bed, he pulled me close. His breathing evened out within minutes. Deep. Steady. The breathing of someone with nothing on his conscience.

I lay rigid beside him. Stared at the dark ceiling. The old cabin creaked and settled around us.

I couldn't shake the feeling that the woman in the photo was staring back at me, trying to warn me about something.

Chapter 3

The Shifting Ground

Saturday stretched quiet and slow. Tyler made sandwiches for lunch. We ate by the window, watching snow fall through the pines. He talked about work—his accounting firm, year-end deadlines, difficult clients. Normal conversation. Easy. Comfortable.

But I kept thinking about the photo. About the blonde woman whose face I couldn't place.

At two, Tyler stood. Grabbed his jacket and keys.

"Need to grab wine and a few things for tomorrow's dinner. Christmas Eve needs to be special." He kissed my forehead. "You want to come?"

"I'll stay. Still tired from the drive."

"Rest, then. I'll be back in an hour."

I watched through the window as the F-150 pulled away. Watched until it disappeared around the bend in the driveway. Counted to sixty. Then I moved.

My laptop sat in my overnight bag. Tyler's mobile hotspot was exactly where he'd mentioned it—kitchen drawer, next to takeout menus and batteries. He'd told me about it last month. Used it when he worked from the cabin. Good signal, he'd said. Better than most places up here.

I powered it on. Waited for the connection. One bar. Two. Three.

Then I searched.

S.R. Tyler Grant 2022 cabin

The results loaded slowly. Facebook posts. Instagram tags. A marathon time from 2019.

A post from December 14, 2022. Tyler's Facebook. The privacy settings were semi-public—old posts visible before he'd locked everything down.

A photo. Tyler and a blonde woman. Arms around each other. Big smiles. Her left hand extended toward the camera, a ring catching light.

The caption: *She said yes! Can't wait to spend forever with this one. engaged christmas*

Tagged: Samantha Reid.

The woman from the basement photo. I knew I'd recognized her face.

I clicked through to her profile. Most of it was private now. But some posts remained visible. Photos from 2022. Samantha at a beach. Samantha hiking. Samantha at what looked like a winery, Tyler beside her.

Then December 28, 2022. A Christmas tree, ornaments catching light. Caption: *Best Christmas ever! Can't wait for what's next!*

After that, nothing.

No New Year's post. No engagement party photos. No wedding planning updates. No breakup announcement. Samantha Reid's social media simply stopped.

December 28, 2022. Almost exactly two years ago.

My chest tightened. I searched— *Samantha Reid missing New Jersey*

No results. No news articles. No police reports. No memorial pages.

A twenty-eight-year-old woman doesn't just vanish. Doesn't stop posting, stop existing, stop mattering—unless someone makes sure she does.

I searched, *Samantha Reid California*

This time results.

A LinkedIn profile, updated March 2023. *Marketing Director, TechVision SF. San Francisco, California.*

A blog comment from April 2023 on a moving company review site: *Just used them for my cross-country move to CA. Highly recommend! Fresh start vibes. - S.R.*

An Instagram story screenshot, reposted to a San Francisco food blog: blonde woman in front of the Golden Gate Bridge, face partially visible. Could be Samantha. Hard to tell.

I stared at the screen. Two versions of the same story.

Version one: Samantha got engaged, then vanished without a trace.

Version two: Samantha moved to California, started a new job, built a new life.

Which was true?

Or were both lies?

Tires crunched on gravel outside.

I slammed the laptop shut. Shoved it under the couch pillow. My heart hammered against my ribs.

The truck engine cut off. Door opened and closed. Footsteps on the porch.

I grabbed my phone. Pulled up Netflix. Made it look like I'd been watching something.

Tyler entered carrying a plastic grocery bag. He stopped just inside the door. His eyes scanned the room. Slow. Methodical. Taking inventory.

They landed on me.

Then on the couch.

On the pillow where my laptop hid.

"Store was out of the good wine," he said. "Decided to check the other place in town instead."

He'd only been gone thirty minutes. Not an hour. Not enough time to drive to Sparta, shop, and drive back.

"Find what you needed?" My voice came out thin.

"Eventually." He set the bag on the counter. Slowly. Deliberately. "What have you been doing?"

"Watching Netflix."

"On your laptop?" A slight smile crossed his face. "I thought you preferred the TV."

"My account wouldn't load on the TV. Used my laptop instead."

Tyler nodded. Unpacked the groceries. Wine. Butter. Fresh herbs. His movements precise. Controlled.

"You're trembling," he said without looking at me.

I glanced at my hands. He was right. They shook against my thighs.

Tyler crossed the room. Pulled me up from the couch. Into his arms.

The hug was too tight. Too long. His hands pressed against my back, holding me in place.

He whispered into my hair: "You're safe here, Brooke."

I stiffened. "Safe from what?"

Tyler pulled back. Studied my face. His hands came up to cup my cheeks. Gentle. Tender.

"From whatever's making you so anxious." Concern creased his forehead. "You've been acting strange since we got here. Jumpy. Distant. Like you're afraid of something."

"I'm fine."

"You don't seem fine." His thumb stroked my cheekbone. "Talk to me. What's wrong?"

Everything. Nothing. I didn't know anymore.

"Just work stress. Holiday deadlines. Dr. Peterson has me covering for the other hygienist who's out sick. Double-booked appointments all week."

Tyler nodded slowly. But his eyes didn't believe me.

"Okay." He kissed my forehead. "If you say so."

He released me. Went back to the kitchen. Started prepping dinner. Hummed along with the Christmas music still playing from the speaker.

I sat back down on the couch. The pillow pressed against my hip. My laptop hidden beneath it. Evidence of my searching. Of my doubt.

If he looked, he'd find it. If he asked to use my computer, he'd see my search history.

But he didn't ask. Didn't look. Just cooked dinner while the snow fell outside and the fire crackled and the Christmas lights blinked their endless pattern.

That night, I woke at 2:14 AM.

Tyler's side of the bed was empty. Sheets cold.

I held my breath. Listened.

Footsteps. Somewhere in the cabin. Not the living room. Not the kitchen. Somewhere else. Deeper.

The basement?

The footsteps moved slowly. Deliberately. Like someone searching for something. Or checking on something they'd hidden.

I lay frozen. Stared at the dark ceiling. Counted my heartbeats.

Five minutes passed. Ten.

The bedroom door opened. Tyler slipped back into bed. His body radiated cold—winter cold, concrete cold, the cold of underground spaces.

His arm draped across me. Pulled me close.

"You awake?" he whispered.

I kept my breathing slow. Even. Fake sleep.

Tyler's lips brushed my shoulder. "I love you, Brooke. More than you know."

His breathing slowed within minutes. Deep. Steady.

But I stayed awake. Listening to him move through dreams beside me.

Chapter 4

Contradictions

Sunday morning. The cabin smelled like coffee and wood smoke. Tyler stood at the stove making scrambled eggs. Through the window, I could see fresh snow had fallen overnight. Everything looked clean. Pristine. Unmarked.

"Sleep okay?" Tyler set a plate in front of me.

"Fine."

He studied my face. "You look tired."

I was. I'd barely slept. Every time I closed my eyes, I saw Samantha's last post. *Best Christmas ever! Can't wait for what's next!*

What came next?

"I'm going to chop more firewood after breakfast," Tyler said. "We're running low. Shouldn't take more than an hour."

I nodded. Picked at my eggs.

An hour. That's all I needed.

Tyler finished his coffee. Pulled on his jacket and boots. Grabbed the axe from beside the door.

"You okay here?"

"Yeah. I might take a nap."

He kissed the top of my head. "Good. You need rest."

The door closed behind him. I counted to thirty. Heard the first crack of the axe against wood. Steady. Rhythmic. Predictable.

I grabbed my laptop. Pulled up Samantha's Facebook again. Found her mother tagged in an old post—Linda Reid, Parsippany. Her profile was semi-public. Community garden page listed a phone number for volunteer coordination.

I dialed before I could second-guess myself.

Three rings. Then: "Hello?"

"Hi, Mrs. Reid? My name is Jessica Chambers. I went to Rutgers with Samantha. I'm trying to reconnect with some old college friends for a reunion we're planning."

A pause. The line crackled.

"Oh." Linda's voice shifted. Careful now. Rehearsed. "That's... that's nice."

"I haven't been able to reach Samantha. Her old number doesn't work. Do you have her current contact?"

Another pause. Longer this time.

"Samantha moved to California." The words came out flat. Practiced, like a script she'd memorized. "She's doing great out there. Calls sometimes."

"That's wonderful. Could I get her new number? Or maybe an email?"

"No, I... she changed everything when she moved. You know how it is. Fresh start." A thin laugh. "She's always been independent."

Outside, the axe kept cracking. Tyler was still working.

"When did you last speak to her?"

Silence stretched between us.

"A few months ago. She's busy. New job, new life." Linda's voice wavered. Almost broke. "I'm sure she'd love to hear from old friends, but I just... I don't have her information. I'm sorry."

"Mrs. Reid—"

The line went dead.

I stared at my phone. A mother who didn't have her daughter's phone number. Who hadn't talked to her in "months." Whose voice cracked when she spoke about her.

Linda Reid was lying. Or she was repeating a lie someone had told her.

I opened Instagram. Searched Samantha's name. Found her account—dormant since December 2022, just like Facebook. But her followers were still visible.

Cara Mendez. Bio read: *Samantha's person since 2012.*

I tapped the message button. Typed fast.

Hi Cara. I'm sorry to reach out like this. I'm trying to find Samantha Reid. We have a mutual connection and I'm worried about her. Have you heard from her recently?

Sent. I set the phone down. Stared at it.

Three minutes later, it buzzed.

Who is this? How do you know Sam?

I typed back: *I can't explain right now. Please—have you talked to her since she "moved"?*

Three dots appeared. Disappeared. Appeared again.

I wish I knew where she was.

My chest tightened.

Her mom said California.

The response came fast now. Angry.

That's bullshit. Sam and I were best friends for ten years. TEN YEARS. She wouldn't just leave without telling me. Without saying goodbye. Without a single text.

What do you think happened?

I filed a missing person report. December 2022. The cops said she wasn't missing—her family confirmed she was fine, just moved for a fresh start. Case closed.

But you never believed that.

Never. Something happened to her. I know it. She was engaged to this guy—Tyler something. They were supposed to get married. Then she just... vanished. Right after Christmas. No goodbye, no forwarding address, nothing. Her mom gives me the same rehearsed story every time. "She's in California. She's fine." But nobody's heard from her. Not once. Not in two years.

I stared at the screen. Outside, the axe had stopped.

I typed fast: *I have to go. Thank you.*

Wait—do you know something? About Sam? Please, if you know anything—

I closed the app. Set the phone face-down.

The cabin was quiet. Too quiet.

I looked out the window. Tyler stood at the woodpile, axe resting on his shoulder. Not chopping. Just standing there.

Staring at the cabin.

Staring at me.

Our eyes met through the glass. He didn't wave. Didn't smile. Just watched me with that same steady gaze from yesterday. Like he was trying to read my thoughts through the window.

Fifteen minutes later, Tyler came inside. Set the axe by the door. Brushed wood chips from his jacket.

"Getting hungry?" He moved to the kitchen. "I'll make sandwiches."

"Sure."

Lunch was quiet. Tyler made turkey and swiss on sourdough. We ate at the table. He kept watching me.

"You're quiet today," he said.

"Just thinking."

"About what?"

"Nothing important."

Tyler set down his sandwich. "You keep looking at your phone. Expecting a call?"

"No. Why?"

"You seem distracted. Like your mind is somewhere else." His tone hovered between hurt and suspicious. "Are you having second thoughts about this weekend? About us?"

"Of course not."

"Because if you are, you can tell me." He reached across the table. Took my hand. "I want you to be happy, Brooke. That's all I've ever wanted."

His thumb stroked my knuckles. The same gesture from our first date. Tender. Loving. The touch of someone who cared.

But now it felt like monitoring. Like he was checking my pulse. Making sure I stayed calm.

"I'm sorry if I've been overbearing this weekend." Tyler's voice softened. "I just love you so much. Sometimes I get protective." A gentle smile. "I know I can be intense. But it's only because I can't imagine losing you."

There it was. The reframe. Controlling behavior packaged as devotion. Surveillance sold as love.

"You haven't been overbearing," I lied.

"Good." He squeezed my hand. "Because tomorrow's Christmas Eve. I have something special planned. Something I've been waiting all year to do."

That afternoon, Tyler announced he needed to chop more firewood. He pulled on his jacket. Grabbed the axe.

I watched through the window as he walked to the woodpile. He paused. Turned. Looked back at the cabin.

Direct eye contact through the glass.

He didn't wave. Didn't smile. Just stared.

Then turned back to work.

The proposal. The empty velvet box with my initials: B.P. - Christmas Eve 2024. Today's date.

He was going to propose tonight. I'd known it since I found the box. But where was the ring?

And why did I keep thinking about Samantha Reid? Tyler's ex-fiancée. Engaged Christmas 2022. Vanished days later. Never heard from again.

He proposed to her too.

And then she disappeared.

The rhythmic crack of the axe sounded like a countdown.

Chapter 5

The Pattern

Sunday afternoon. Tyler was still outside with the firewood. I could hear the steady crack of the axe through the window. Rhythmic. Predictable. I had time.

The basement door opened without sound. I descended the wooden stairs with purpose this time. Not exploring. Hunting.

The shoebox sat where I'd left it, tucked behind the tax returns. I pulled it out. Opened it.

The photo of Tyler and Samantha on top. I set it aside.

Beneath it: another photo.

Different woman. Darker hair, shoulder-length. Younger—early twenties, maybe. She stood on the cabin porch, fall leaves piled around her feet. Orange and red and gold. Tyler beside her, arm around her waist, same smile.

I turned it over.

Handwriting on the back. Blue ink. Neat cursive.

Tyler & Michelle, Thanksgiving 2018

Six years ago. Four years before Samantha.

My hands shook. I shoved the photo in my pocket. Put the box back. Climbed the stairs.

In the living room, I grabbed my laptop. Tyler's mobile hotspot still connected from this morning.

I searched: *Michelle Johnson missing New Jersey 2018*

The results loaded slowly. Then: Newark Star-Ledger archive.

Michelle Johnson, 24, Missing Since November 15, 2018. Police Have No Leads.

I clicked through. The article loaded in pieces.

A photo of Michelle—the same woman from the cabin. Same dark hair. Same young face.

Last seen leaving her Newark apartment for a weekend trip... boyfriend reported her missing after she failed to return... no signs of foul play... case remains open...

Boyfriend reported her missing.

Tyler had reported her missing. Then, four years later, he got engaged to Samantha. Who also vanished.

Two women. Both after dating Tyler. Both gone.

And I was here. In the same cabin. With the same man.

The pattern was clear.

I was next.

My mindset shifted. No more wondering if I was paranoid. No more questioning my instincts. This wasn't about doubt anymore.

This was about survival.

I analyzed the cabin with new eyes. Escape routes. Resources. Obstacles.

Nearest neighbor: three miles through deep snow. Temperatures in the twenties. I'd freeze before I made it halfway.

My car: back in Morristown. I'd ridden here in Tyler's truck.

Tyler's truck: keys always in his jacket pocket. Even when he slept, the jacket hung on the bedpost. I'd never get them without waking him.

Cell signal: one bar by the window. Tyler knew that now. He'd be watching for it.

Landline: I crossed to the kitchen. Lifted the receiver. Dead. No dial tone.

I traced the cord along the wall. Behind the bookshelf. Down toward the baseboard. Found where it disappeared through a small hole leading outside.

Clean cut. The wire severed three inches from the wall. No fraying. No weather damage.

Tyler had cut the phone line.

The axe stopped.

I put the receiver back. Moved to the couch. Grabbed my book. Made myself look casual.

The front door opened. Tyler stamped snow from his boots.

"Getting cold out there." He hung his jacket by the door. Keys jingled in the pocket—too far away, too obvious. "I'm thinking steak for dinner. That work for you?"

"Sounds good."

Tyler moved to the kitchen. Started pulling ingredients from the refrigerator. I watched him from the couch.

"Your family must have a lot of memories here," I said.

"Some good. Some bad."

"Like what?"

Tyler's jaw tightened. Barely visible. But I saw it.

"Just old history. Nothing worth discussing."

I stood. Walked to the kitchen. Leaned against the counter. "Have you brought other girlfriends here?"

Tyler stopped chopping vegetables. The knife paused mid-cut. He turned slowly.

"Why would you ask that?"

"Just curious."

His eyes stayed on mine. Searching. Calculating.

"You're the only one who matters, Brooke." He set the knife down carefully. Deliberately. "The past is the past."

But his hands were shaking.

Dinner was quiet. Tyler grilled steaks on the stovetop. Made roasted potatoes. Opened a bottle of red wine. We ate at the table by candlelight.

Normal. Romantic. Except I kept watching his hands. The way they gripped the wine glass too tight. The tension in his shoulders.

"More wine?" Tyler reached for the bottle.

It slipped. Hit the edge of the table. Shattered on the floor.

Red wine spread across hardwood like blood.

"Why did you put it so close to the edge?" He snapped the words. Sharp. Angry.

I hadn't touched the bottle. He'd set it there himself.

Tyler looked at the mess. Then at me. His expression shifted—realization, then immediate regret.

"Sorry." He grabbed paper towels. Knelt to clean up glass. "I'm just stressed about work stuff. Year-end deadlines. Didn't mean to take it out on you."

"It's okay."

But I'd seen it. The flash of temper underneath. The crack in his careful control.

That night, I lay rigid in bed. Tyler's arm draped across me. Possessive even in sleep. His breathing slowed within minutes. Deep. Even.

I counted seconds. Minutes. Hours.

At 2:14 AM, Tyler spoke.

Not awake. Not conscious. Words from whatever dream held him.

"...had to..." His voice was thick. Distant. "...couldn't let you leave..."

I held my breath. Didn't move.

His arm tightened around me.

"...mine..." Another mumble. "...forever..."

The words hung in the dark. Tyler's confession, delivered while he slept. While his guard was down. While the truth escaped in fragments.

He'd said the same thing to Michelle. To Samantha.

And they'd tried to leave.

I stared at the ceiling. At the dark shapes of beams overhead. At the Christmas wreath hanging above the headboard like a funeral decoration.

I realized I was already too late to leave safely.

Chapter 6

Into The Dark

Monday. Two AM. Christmas Eve morning.

A sound woke me. Heavy. Deliberate. A door shutting somewhere below.

I opened my eyes. The bedroom was dark except for the faint glow from the living room—those Christmas tree lights that never turned off. Red. Gold. Green.

Tyler's side of the bed was empty. Sheets cold.

I sat up. Listened.

Footsteps on concrete. Distant but clear. The basement.

Metal scraping. Tools. A muttered curse.

I'd been down there twice now. But there'd been another door. Narrow. White. Easy to miss. I'd assumed it was storage. A closet. Nothing important.

Now I remembered. It had a lock on the outside.

I slipped out of bed. My feet touched cold hardwood. I moved through the dark bedroom, into the hallway.

The basement door stood three inches open. Pale light spilled from below.

I should have gone back to bed. Should have pulled the covers over my head and pretended I'd seen nothing.

Instead, I crept forward.

The living room was dark except for the tree. Those lights blinked their steady rhythm. Red. Gold. Green. Silent night. Holy night.

The basement stairs descended into cold. I took the first step. It creaked under my weight.

I froze.

Below, the sounds stopped.

Then they resumed. Tyler working. Focused.

I descended slowly. Each step took forever. The cold air rose to meet me—unnatural cold, like refrigeration. Chemical-sweet. Wrong.

At the bottom, I peered around the corner.

The space opened larger than I'd seen before. The door I'd noticed earlier—the locked one—now stood open. Beyond it, another room. Concrete walls. A single bulb hung from the ceiling.

Tyler's silhouette hunched over something large and white.

A chest freezer. Industrial. The kind you'd find in a butcher shop or hunting lodge. Big enough to hold a deer.

Big enough to hold a person.

Blue-white light washed his face.

He held something small in one hand. Pliers in the other. Working at it. Gentle but persistent.

"Come on," he muttered. "Need it for tomorrow... Christmas Eve..."

The ring. He was trying to work a ring off something.

I couldn't see what. But I knew.

Tyler twisted the pliers. Pulled. The motion was delicate. Reverent.

"Almost... there..."

I retreated. Back up the stairs. Feet silent on wood. Into the bedroom. Under the covers. Heart slamming so hard I thought it would crack my rib cage.

I forced my breathing to slow. Even. Counted to thirty.

Minutes later, the bedroom door opened.

"Brooke?"

I stirred. Made my voice thick with fake sleep. "Mm?"

"Did you get up?"

"Bathroom." I kept my eyes half-closed. "Cold. Why are you awake?"

The mattress dipped. Tyler slid in beside me. His body radiated cold—basement cold, concrete cold, refrigeration cold.

"Checking the pipes. Old cabin like this, they freeze if you're not careful." He pulled me close. Too close.

The smell hit me. Chemical sweetness. Formaldehyde.

"Go back to sleep," he whispered.

But I didn't sleep. Couldn't sleep. Just lay there counting seconds until morning.

Christmas Eve. Ten AM. Tyler stood by the front door, pulled on his jacket.

"I need to grab a few last things for tonight. Special dinner." He kissed my forehead. "Be back in an hour. Rest up. Tonight's going to be perfect."

Perfect. The word made my skin crawl.

The truck pulled away. I watched through the window until it disappeared.

Then I moved.

The basement. Now. I had to know.

The stairs creaked under my feet. The cold air wrapped around me like hands. At the bottom, I found the second door. Open—Tyler had been in a hurry this morning.

The freezer sat in the center of the small room. White. Industrial. Humming its steady song.

Padlocked shut.

I searched for a key. Checked the workbench. Looked through tool drawers. Nothing.

The hammer sat on the workbench. Heavy. Metal head. Wooden handle.

The need to know tore through my restraint.

I grabbed it.

Three swings. Four. Fifth. The lock broke. Clattered to the concrete floor.

The hum from the freezer sounded like distant screaming.

I lifted the lid.

Blue light flooded my face. Cold air rose from below.

Samantha.

I couldn't breathe. Couldn't move. Couldn't think. Just stared at this woman who'd smiled in photos. Who'd posted about Christmas. Who'd said *Can't wait for what's next* and never got to find out.

Preserved perfectly. Skin pale but intact. No decay. No rot. Just sleep.

Like she was waiting for Christmas morning to arrive so she could wake up and open presents and drink hot cocoa by the fire.

She wore Christmas pajamas. Red plaid. The kind you'd see in a catalog. Hair arranged in soft waves around her face. Makeup applied—subtle, natural, beautiful. Hands folded across her chest.

Except—

Her left hand. The ring finger. It ended at the knuckle. A clean cut. Surgical. Deliberate.

The finger was gone.

My eyes moved to what lay beside her body. Tucked against her shoulder. Two small objects.

Two velvet boxes. Navy blue.

I picked up the first one with shaking hands. Opened it.

The finger.

Severed. Preserved in the cold. Gray-white skin waxy and unnatural. And on it, still snug at the base: the antique ring. White gold. Delicate filigree.

I looked at the inside of the lid. Faded inscription: *S.R. - Christmas Eve 2022*

He'd cut it off. After she died. Kept it separate. A trophy. Forever.

The second box sat beside it. Smaller. Newer. It looked familiar.

I picked it up. My hands wouldn't stop shaking.

I opened it.

Empty.

Navy velvet lining. Pristine. Waiting.

I looked at the inscription.

Fresh gold thread. Recently embroidered.

B.P. - Christmas Eve 2024

B.P.

Brooke Palmer.

My box. My initials. Today's date.

The realization hit like ice water.

He was going to propose tonight. With Samantha's ring. The ring he'd been trying to remove from her severed finger at two AM. The ring he'd finally gotten off this morning.

A shadow fell across the freezer.

I turned.

Tyler stood at the bottom of the stairs. Grocery bag in one hand. Face calm. No anger. No surprise.

Just quiet observation.

"I was hoping you wouldn't find them," he said, voice soft. "But I think part of me wanted you to know."

He set the bag down. Took a step forward.

I stumbled back. Hit the freezer. The cold metal pressed against my spine.

"Tyler—"

"We need to talk, Brooke." His voice stayed gentle. Reasonable. "About us. About forever."

He took another step.

I looked at the stairs. At the distance between us. At the only way out.

The basement door at the top of the stairs swung shut with a click—locked from inside.

Chapter 7

The Rewriting

Tyler didn't yell. Didn't grab me. Didn't charge forward in rage.

He just stood there at the bottom of the stairs. Calm. Patient. Like I was a child who'd wandered somewhere I shouldn't have gone.

"Brooke." His voice was soft. The same voice from our first date. From the night he said he loved me. "I need you to breathe. Can you do that for me?"

I couldn't. My lungs wouldn't work. The air felt too thick. Too cold. I pressed against the freezer. Samantha lay inches below me. Dead. Preserved. Dressed like a doll.

"You're in shock." Tyler took a step closer. "That's understandable."

"You killed her." The words scraped out of my throat. "You killed Samantha."

Tyler sighed. Patient. Like I'd misunderstood something obvious.

"Is that what you think you're seeing?"

"I'm LOOKING at her body—"

"You're looking at someone I tried to save."

The words didn't make sense. I stared at him. At his face. At the gentle concern in his eyes.

"What?"

Tyler stepped closer. Hands raised. Non-threatening. "Samantha had... problems, Brooke. Mental health issues. After we got engaged, she started spiraling. Depression. Anxiety. She wouldn't see a therapist. Wouldn't take medication. I tried to help her, but she wouldn't let me."

"That's not—"

"She tried to hurt herself. Christmas Eve, two years ago." His voice broke. Actual emotion. Actual pain. "I found her in the bathroom. Pills everywhere. She'd taken the whole bottle. I called 911. Performed CPR. But it was too late. She was already gone."

I couldn't process it. The logic was insane. But his delivery was so calm. So measured. So believable.

"You're lying."

"I know it's not healthy." Tyler's eyes glistened. Were those tears? "I know I should have buried her. Let her family have a funeral. But I couldn't. I loved her too much. The thought of putting her in the ground, letting her rot—I couldn't do it."

He took another step. I had nowhere to go. My back pressed against the freezer. Against Samantha.

"So I preserved her. Kept her here. Where I could visit her. Talk to her." Tyler's voice dropped to a whisper. "I know it sounds crazy. But grief makes us do irrational things."

For one horrible second, I questioned myself.

Could he be telling the truth?

No. Cara said Samantha was fine. Planning a wedding. Happy.

But Tyler sounded so certain. So sad. So sincere.

"What about Michelle?" My voice shook. "Michelle Johnson."

Tyler's face shifted. Genuine confusion. "Who's Michelle?"

"Michelle Johnson. 2018. Your girlfriend. She went missing."

"I never dated anyone named Michelle."

"I found the photo. You and her. Thanksgiving 2018. This cabin."

"My cousin Michelle visited that Thanksgiving." Tyler's voice stayed patient. But something underneath it hardened. "Jesus, Brooke. What do you think I am? Some kind of serial killer?"

He said it like the idea was absurd. Laughable. Like I was the one being unreasonable.

"The photo said—"

"Family photos exist, Brooke. Cousins visit for holidays. That doesn't make me a murderer."

Tyler moved closer. Took both my hands in his. Gentle. Caring.

"Listen to me. You're exhausted. This weekend has been stressful. You've been acting paranoid since we arrived."

"I'm not paranoid—"

"You snooped through my bag the first night. You went through the basement. You've been researching me behind my back." Each accusation was true. But the way he said it made me sound unstable. Invasive. Wrong.

"I think the pressure of us getting serious has triggered some anxiety," Tyler continued. His thumbs stroked my knuckles. Soothing. "That's okay. We can work through it together. But right now, you need rest."

"Tyler—"

"I think you need rest." He guided me toward the stairs. Firm grip on my arm. "Let's get you upstairs. You can lie down. We'll talk more when you're calmer."

"Tyler, I saw her body—"

"You saw someone I loved who's gone." His voice stayed so gentle. So reasonable. "Nothing more."

I was so confused I almost followed. Almost let him lead me up those stairs. His version of events was insane. But his delivery made mine sound hysterical.

Then I stopped.

"No."

Tyler's face shifted. Just a flicker. Something cold underneath the concern.

"Brooke—"

"I want to leave. Now."

"We can't." His grip tightened on my arm. "The roads are snowed in. We're stuck here until morning. And you're not thinking clearly."

"I'm thinking perfectly clearly—"

"You're spiraling." Tyler pulled me toward the stairs. Not rough. Not violent. But firm. Inevitable. "You need to calm down before you hurt yourself."

Before I hurt myself. Like I was the danger. Like I was the problem.

He guided me up the stairs. Through the basement door. Down the hallway. Upstairs, into the bedroom.

"Sleep." Tyler's voice was soft. Tender. "Christmas Eve dinner is at six. We'll celebrate like we planned."

"Tyler, please—"

"I love you, Brooke." He cupped my face. Looked into my eyes. "I'm trying to help you. You have to trust me."

The door closed.

The lock clicked from outside.

I stood in the bedroom. Alone. The wreath above the headboard. The Christmas lights blinking through the doorway. Red. Gold. Green.

I replayed his words. *Samantha had problems. Mental health issues. She tried to hurt herself. I tried to save her.*

Was it possible?

No. It couldn't be. Cara was her best friend. Cara would have known if Samantha was suicidal.

But Tyler had sounded so certain. So sad. So believable.

You're exhausted. You've been acting paranoid. The pressure has triggered anxiety.

Was I paranoid? I'd snooped through his bag. Gone through his basement. Researched him online. Made assumptions about photos and names.

No. I saw her body. That was real.

But his explanation for it was so logical. Grief. Preservation. Irrational but understandable.

I sat on the bed. Hands shaking. Mind racing in circles.

Outside the door, footsteps moved through the cabin. Tyler humming. Christmas music. *Silent Night.*

The melody drifted through the walls. Sweet. Peaceful. Wrong.

Holy infant so tender and mild—

I wondered if I'd ever trusted my own mind less.

Chapter 8

Candlelit Hostage

Three PM. Christmas Eve. I was alone in the bedroom.

I tried the door first. Locked from outside. I threw my weight against it. The wood didn't budge. Solid. Old. Built to last.

The window next. Too small. Even if I could fit, it was painted shut. I pushed until my palms ached. It wouldn't move more than four inches.

I beat my fists on the door. Left hand. Right hand. Over and over until my knuckles split and bled. Red smears on white paint.

"HELP!" I screamed until my throat burned. Until my voice cracked and broke. "SOMEONE HELP ME!"

No one heard. No one was coming. The nearest neighbor was three miles away through deep snow.

I was alone with him.

I slid down the door. Sat on the floor. Stared at the wreath above the headboard. Red berries. Plaid bow. Festive and cheerful and wrong.

The hours crawled.

At five PM, footsteps approached. Tyler's voice came through the door. Soft. Coaxing.

"Brooke, I'm making dinner, your favorite—chicken parmesan.

Tonight's the night I've been planning for. The night everything becomes official."

I didn't answer.

"I know you're upset. We can talk about this like adults."

Silence.

"I love you. That's never going to change." His voice had that patient, hurt quality. Like I was the one being unreasonable. Like I was the one who'd done something wrong. "We're going to get through this together."

I pressed my hands over my ears. But I could still hear him. Still hear the love in his voice. The devotion. The certainty.

At six PM, the lock clicked.

The door opened. Tyler stood in the doorway. He'd changed into a clean button-down shirt. Navy blue. The one I'd said I liked. Hair combed. Freshly shaved. Cologne—the same one from our first date.

He'd dressed for a proposal.

"Dinner's ready." His voice was warm. Happy. "Come on. Tonight's special."

"I'm not hungry."

"You need to eat. Come on." He extended his hand. Patient. Gentle.

I didn't take it.

His jaw tightened. Just a fraction. "Don't make this harder than it needs to be."

I stood. Walked past him without touching. Into the living room.

The table was set for two. White candles. Wine glasses. Christmas tree blinking behind us. The cabin glowed soft and golden.

Roasted chicken. Mashed potatoes. Green beans. A carving knife beside the platter.

Tyler pulled out my chair. "Sit."

I sat.

He served my plate like this was normal. Like we were any couple celebrating Christmas Eve. Poured wine into both glasses. Raised his.

"To the future. To us. To forever."

I stared at my food. Couldn't touch it.

Tyler ate with appetite. Cut his chicken. Took a bite. Chewed. Swallowed. Normal. Easy. Like there wasn't a dead woman in his basement.

"I want you to understand something before I ask you the most important question." He set down his fork. Leaned forward. "I need you to know why I do what I do. Why I love the way I love."

My stomach turned.

"Michelle was my first." His voice went soft. Nostalgic. "Sweet girl. She loved the water. Swimming, sailing, everything about the lake. We'd spend whole weekends on the dock. She'd dive off and swim for hours." He smiled. "When she said she was leaving—New York, some marketing job—I couldn't let her go. So I made sure she'd always be near the water she loved."

Oh my God. The lake. Michelle was in the lake.

"Samantha was different. Elegant. Refined. She deserved to be preserved perfectly. Like a work of art." Tyler's eyes went distant. Tender. "She's still beautiful, Brooke. You saw her. Like she's just sleeping. Waiting for me."

I couldn't breathe.

"And you." Tyler reached across the table. Took my hand. "You're going to be my wife."

He stood. Walked around the table. Got down on one knee.

From his pocket, he produced a small velvet box. The same box from the basement. B.P. My box.

He opened it.

The ring. Antique. White gold. Delicate filigree. Clean now. Polished. No longer on a severed finger.

"I got it off her this morning. It was stuck—preservation makes things difficult. But I managed." Tyler's voice was proud. Accomplished. "It's yours now, Brooke."

Dread pooled in my stomach. If I'd eaten, it would have come up right away. I swallowed hard.

He looked up at me. Eyes shining.

"Brooke Palmer. Will you marry me?"

The question hung in the air. The candles flickered. The Christmas tree blinked behind him. Red. Gold. Green.

Say no, and he kills me tonight.

Say yes, and he kills me... eventually. After the wedding. After I try to leave.

"Say yes, Brooke." Tyler's voice dropped. Harder now. "You know what happens if you say no."

Certainty hardened into stone. My voice came out thin. Broken. "Yes."

Tyler's face transformed. Pure joy. Pure relief. He slid the ring onto my finger. It fit perfectly. Like it had been made for me.

Like Samantha and I were the same size.

He stood. Pulled me up. Kissed me. His lips were warm. Gentle. Loving.

"We'll get married in Vermont. Small ceremony. Just us. Then we'll have forever. Actual forever."

I nodded. Pretended to listen. But my eyes tracked the carving knife.

"Love means forever, Brooke. Not until things get hard. Not until you find someone better. Forever."

"I understand."

"Do you?" He squeezed my hand. "Because I need you to understand. What we have is special. Worth protecting. Worth keeping. No matter what."

"I understand," I repeated.

Tyler smiled. Stood.

He moved to the kitchen. "Champagne. We need champagne for this."

He turned his back. Reached for the bottle on the counter, started working the cork.

The carving knife sat on the table. Six inches from my hand.

I grabbed it.

Slid it into my lap. Under the napkin. My heart slammed against my ribs. The handle felt cold. Heavy. Real.

Tyler turned back with two champagne glasses. Smiling. Happy. Filled my glass. Filled his. Set the bottle down.

He leaned across the table. Lips parted. Coming in for a kiss.

I drove the knife into his shoulder.

Tyler screamed. The sound tore through the cabin—raw, animal, shocked. The glasses shattered on the floor. Champagne spread across hardwood like the wine from before.

His hand went to the blade. Buried in muscle and bone.

I ran.

His jacket hung by the door. I tore through the pockets. Fingers scrambling. Found the keys.

"BROOKE!"

I didn't look back. Out the door. Into snow and darkness and cold.

Tyler's truck sat ten feet away. I ran for it.

Fumbled with the keys. Hands shaking. Blood-slicked from the knife.

The keys slipped. Fell into the snow.

"No. No no no—"

I dropped to my knees. Dug through snow with bare hands. Cold burned my skin. Where were they? Where—

There. Metal against my fingers.

I grabbed them. Stood. Ran to the truck.

Climbed in. Jammed the key into the ignition. Turned it.

Click. Click. Click.

The engine wouldn't catch.

"Come on. Come ON—"

I turned the key again. The engine turned over. Died.

In the rearview mirror: Tyler staggered onto the porch. Blood soaked his shirt. But he was on his feet. Walking. Coming toward me.

I turned the key a third time. Pumped the gas.

The engine roared to life.

I threw it in reverse. Floored the accelerator.

The truck lurched backward. Fishtailed. I corrected. Threw it in drive. Pressed the gas.

The tires spun. The truck didn't move. Stuck in deep snow at the edge of the driveway.

Tyler was closer now. Twenty feet. Fifteen.

The tires kept spinning. I rocked the truck. Forward. Reverse. Forward.

Tyler ten feet away.

I floored the accelerator.

The F-150 fishtailed on snow, then caught. Tires churned. The driveway stretched ahead, white and endless.

In the rearview mirror, Tyler collapsed in the snow.

I didn't slow down. Five miles. That's what I needed. Five miles to signal.

The truck flew through darkness. Pine trees blurred past. My hands shook on the wheel. Blood on my fingers—his blood. I wiped them on my jeans, kept driving.

Three miles. Four.

I didn't slow down until the cabin disappeared behind the trees—but I could still feel him watching.

Chapter 9

The Hunt In The Snow

The truck flew through darkness. Snow-packed road. Pine trees on both sides. My hands shook on the wheel. Blood on my fingers—his blood, my blood, I didn't know anymore.

One mile. Two. Three.

I checked the rearview mirror. No headlights. Tyler didn't have another vehicle. Couldn't follow.

But his voice echoed in my head anyway.

Say yes, Brooke.

Forever.

Actual forever.

Four miles. Five.

My phone lit up on the passenger seat. One bar. Two. Three.

Signal.

I pulled to the side of the road. Snow piled high on both shoulders. The truck idled. Heater blasting. My breath came in white gasps even inside the cab.

I grabbed my phone. Dialed 911 with trembling fingers.

One ring. Two.

"Sussex County 911, what's your emergency?"

My voice broke. "My boyfriend killed two women. He was going to kill me. He's at a cabin off Route 517 near Sparta."

"Are you safe now? Where are you?"

"I think so. I'm on Route 517. Five miles from the cabin. I stabbed him. I don't know if he's—" My throat closed. "I don't know if he can follow me."

"Ma'am, I need you to stay calm. Units are being dispatched. Can you tell me your exact location?"

I looked around. Dark road. Pine trees. Snow everywhere. "I don't know. I just drove. I didn't pay attention to—"

"That's okay. We're tracking your phone. Officers are on their way. Stay on the line with me. Are you injured?"

"No. But he is. I stabbed him in the shoulder."

"Is he armed?"

"I don't know. He has an axe. At the cabin."

"Officers are five minutes away. I need you to stay in your vehicle with the doors locked. Do not return to the cabin. Do you understand?"

"Yes."

"What's your name?"

"Brooke. Brooke Palmer."

"Brooke, you're doing great. Just keep talking to me."

The dispatcher kept me on the line. Asked questions. Where was the cabin. How many rooms. Where was the body. I answered on autopilot. Numb. Cold.

Ten minutes felt like hours.

I watched the road ahead. Watched the road behind. Watched the trees on both sides.

What if he followed on foot? What if he was out there right now, bleeding and staggering through the snow, coming for me?

What if I hadn't stabbed him deep enough?

Finally—red and blue lights in the distance. Getting closer. Brighter.

Two patrol cars pulled up behind me. An ambulance followed.

An officer approached my window. Young. Professional.

"Ma'am, are you injured?"

I shook my head. Couldn't speak.

They wrapped me in a blanket. Moved me to a patrol car. Took my statement. I gave them directions. Described Tyler. Described what I'd seen.

"Samantha Reid. In the basement freezer. Her ring finger is severed. It's in a velvet box next to her body. And there's a second box. With my initials. B.P. He was going to do the same thing to me."

The officer's face went pale. He radioed to units heading to the cabin.

"Suspect is injured but mobile. Approach with extreme caution. Victim reports second velvet box with her own initials. Suspect may have planned additional homicide."

Twenty minutes later, the radio crackled.

"Suspect in custody. Male, early thirties, stab wound to left shoulder. Conscious and cooperative. Medics on scene."

Cooperative. Like he'd welcomed them. Like he'd been expecting them.

The officer glanced at me in the rearview mirror. "They got him."

I nodded. Still couldn't feel relief.

An hour later, Detective Hazel Fairbank arrived. Mid-forties. Sharp eyes. Gray pantsuit. She drove me to the station in a black sedan.

Her radio crackled while we drove.

"Detective, we need forensics. Basement freezer. One body confirmed. Female, preserved, left ring finger severed post-mortem. We also recovered two velvet boxes. One containing the severed finger. One empty with victim's initials and today's date."

Fairbank's jaw tightened. She picked up the radio. "Secure the scene. I'll be there after I get Ms. Palmer's statement."

At the station, she took me to a small room. Warm. Coffee I couldn't drink. Blanket around my shoulders.

I told her everything. The empty box. The research. The two boxes in the freezer. The proposal. The attack. The escape.

When I finished, Fairbank set down her pen.

"Officers found a jewelry box in the master bedroom. Inside was a necklace engraved M.J. We believe it belonged to Michelle Johnson. We'll be dragging the lake come spring."

I nodded.

"Tyler Grant has been charged with two counts first-degree murder. Samantha Reid. Michelle Johnson. And attempted murder of you." Fairbank's voice was steady. "He's not getting out. Ever."

"What did he say? When they arrested him?"

Fairbank's expression darkened. "He asked if you were okay. Then he said, 'She said yes. We're engaged.'"

The ring. Samantha's ring. The one he'd forced onto my finger during the proposal.

I looked down at my left hand. Tried to pull it off. My fingers trembled. I twisted—

Nothing.

The ring wasn't there.

I stared at my bare finger. The skin where it had been was slightly indented. Red. But the ring was gone.

When had I taken it off? In the truck? During the escape? I couldn't remember. The whole night was fragments. Running. Keys in the snow. The engine that wouldn't start. Tyler walking toward me, bleeding.

I must have pulled it off somewhere. Lost it in the panic.

"You're safe now," Fairbank said.

I nodded. But I couldn't stop staring at my empty finger. At the mark the ring had left behind.

Safe was a word that had lost all meaning.

Chapter 10

Christmas Morning

Christmas morning. My parents' house in Morristown.

I sat on the couch in my childhood living room. Same floral pattern. Same coffee table with water rings. Same family photos on the mantel—me at six, gap-toothed and smiling. Me at graduation. Me in a life that felt like it belonged to someone else.

Mom sat beside me. Her arm around my shoulders. Holding me like I was still six years old and had scraped my knee.

Dad paced by the window. Back and forth. Back and forth. He'd been doing that since I arrived at three AM.

In the kitchen, relatives whispered. Aunt Carol. Uncle Jim. My cousin Kendra. They'd come over when they heard. Brought casseroles and sympathy and questions no one knew how to ask.

The Christmas tree blinked in the corner. Red. Gold. Green. I couldn't look at it.

The TV played on low volume. Morning news. A reporter stood outside Sussex County Jail.

"Tyler Grant, 32, of Sparta, has been charged with two counts of first-degree murder in the deaths of Samantha Reid and Michelle Johnson.

Police discovered Reid's body at Grant's family cabin late Christmas Eve. Grant is being held without bail."

Tyler's photo filled the screen. Clean-cut. Handsome. The same photo from his LinkedIn. The one where he looked trustworthy. Professional. Normal.

"Allegedly killed two women," the reporter said.

Allegedly. Like there was doubt.

I'd seen Samantha's body. Seen her in that freezer. Seen what he'd done.

There was no allegedly.

Mid-morning, a patrol officer arrived. Young. Apologetic. He needed final details for the prosecutor.

"I'm sorry to do this on Christmas," he said. "But the DA needs a complete statement before arraignment tomorrow."

Mom stood. "Can't this wait?"

"Last time, I promise."

I answered his questions. Third time telling the story. My voice came out mechanical. Distant. Like I was describing something that happened to someone else.

How long had they dated? One year.

When did she become suspicious? Saturday.

Did he threaten her directly? Yes. He proposed at knifepoint. Said "You know what happens if you say no."

Did he confess? Yes. He told me Michelle was in the lake. That he preserved Samantha in the freezer. That I was going to be his wife whether I wanted to or not.

The officer wrote everything down. His pen scratched across paper. Every word became evidence. Proof.

"He made me wear the ring," I added. My voice distant. "The one from Samantha's severed finger. Put it on my hand during the proposal. It's still at the cabin. On the kitchen table where I left it when I ran."

The officer nodded. Made another note. "We recovered the ring. It's in evidence now."

He thanked me. Left. I went back to the couch. Back to staring at nothing.

Mid-afternoon, my phone rang. Detective Fairbank.

"Ms. Palmer. I wanted to update you." Her voice was professional. Steady. "Samantha Reid's body has been officially identified. Cause of death: asphyxiation. The medical examiner believes she was manually strangled."

Not pills. Not an overdose. Not suicide.

Strangled.

Tyler had lied about everything.

"We've charged Tyler Grant with first-degree murder. Michelle Johnson's case has been reopened. We'll be dragging the lake come spring." Fairbank paused. "His arraignment is tomorrow morning. He's being held without bail. He's not getting out, Ms. Palmer."

"Okay."

"It's over. He can't hurt you."

I nodded even though she couldn't see me. But I knew better.

It would never be over.

Evening. The relatives had left. Just me, Mom, and Dad.

Dad cleared his throat. "Let's open presents. Try to have some normalcy."

Normalcy. The word felt foreign.

But I went through the motions. Sat by the tree. Forced a smile.

Mom handed me a wrapped box. I tore the paper. A scarf. Soft. Blue. Beautiful.

"Thank you."

Dad gave me a book. Mystery novel. Something I'd mentioned wanting months ago.

"Thank you."

I set them aside. Stared at the pile of presents still under the tree.

Then I saw it.

A wrapped gift I hadn't noticed before. Silver paper. Gold ribbon. Sitting behind the others, partially hidden.

A tag attached: *For Brooke*

"What's this?" I picked it up. Heavy. Small. The size of—

Mom frowned. "We didn't put that there."

Dad stood. "Maybe one of your aunts left it earlier?"

"Which aunt?"

They looked at each other. Neither knew.

My hands shook as I tore the paper. Slowly. Carefully. Like the box might explode.

Beneath the silver paper: a navy blue velvet box.

Not Samantha's box. Mine.

The one from the freezer. The one with my initials. The one Tyler had made and ready, waiting for my finger after he killed me.

But it was supposed to be in police evidence. I'd watched them photograph it. Tag it. Seal it in an evidence bag.

How was it here?

My hands shook as I opened the lid.

Empty. Just velvet lining.

The inscription inside: B.P. - Christmas Eve 2024

My initials. Today's date. The box that was supposed to hold my severed finger with his ring on it.

The box he'd prepared before he ever proposed.

The box that proved he'd always planned to kill me.

I dropped the box.

Mom: "Honey, what's wrong?"

"Where did this come from?" My voice cracked. "Did anyone bring this? Did anyone drop off a package?"

Dad: "What is it?"

"Did anyone come here today? Anyone at all?"

They shook their heads. No visitors except the police officer this morning.

I stared at the box on the floor.

Three possibilities:

Tyler had arranged delivery before his arrest. Planned ahead. Knew what might happen. Sent it as a message.

Or evidence had been mishandled. The box released somehow. Lost in the chaos. Sent to wrong address.

Or I was hallucinating. Breaking down. Trauma fracturing my grip on reality.

No way to know which.

Mom's voice: "Should we call the police?"

"I don't know."

I picked up the box. The velvet felt real. Solid. The inscription looked real. Fresh.

I closed the lid. The snap echoed through the living room.

It sounded like a warning.

I looked at the Christmas tree. Lights blinking in their endless pattern. Red. Gold. Green. Red. Gold. Green.

Same pattern as Tyler's cabin.

Same rhythm.

Forever.

Some proposals are promises. Others are chains.

I'd survived Tyler Grant.

But I'd never escape him.

Because love, Tyler had taught me, meant never letting go.

And some gifts keep arriving long after Christmas morning.

THE END

BOOK 11

Love, Actually

Chapter 1

The Arrival

The last suitcase barely fit. I shoved it into the back of my Lexus, wedged between gift bags and the garment carrier holding the red silk dress. Dangerous neckline. The kind you wear when you want someone to remember you.

Eight months.

Two hundred forty-three days of texting, phone calls, late-night conversations that stretched until three AM. Tomorrow—finally—I'd see his face.

I slid into the driver's seat and pulled onto Route 202. Evening sky had turned that winter gray that promised snow but never delivered. Strip malls gave way to bare trees, snow-covered farmland, and the winding roads of Sussex County.

Thirty minutes separated my Montvale apartment from Jenna's house in Ridgemont. Every red light stretched into eternity. Every slow driver felt personal.

My phone sat silent in the cupholder.

Ethan always texted around this time. After work, before dinner. The predictability had become its own kind of intimacy. I knew his rhythms better than my own.

We'd matched in April. His profile showed a man with kind eyes, dark hair, a smile that seemed genuine rather than posed.

Philadelphia. Thirty-one. Marketing consultant. The conversation started easy—books, travel, the shared misery of working from home—and never stopped.

The camera thing bothered me at first. Eight months without a single video call. First his laptop camera broke. Then his phone. Then he was "camera shy," which I'd found vulnerable. Endearing.

Now the excuse had hardened into something I tried not to examine.

But his voice. Deep and warm, with a laugh that made my chest ache. He remembered everything. My favorite coffee order. My childhood fear of thunderstorms. The name of the goldfish I'd had in college. Marcus. The fish, not my brother-in-law. Though the coincidence made me smile.

Ridgemont's Main Street glowed ahead. White lights wrapped every lamppost. Giant wreaths hung from storefronts. A banner stretched across the road: RIDGEMONT CHRISTMAS FESTIVAL - DEC 21-23. Someone had put a Santa hat on the bronze statue in the town square.

I turned onto Maple Creek Lane. Jenna's house sat at the end of the cul-de-sac. Colonial with black shutters and wraparound porch. She'd outdone herself this year.

Garland twisted up the railings. Icicle lights dripped from the gutters. A wreath the size of a car tire dominated the front door.

The porch light flicked on before I'd parked.

Jenna burst through the door, arms already open. My sister at thirty-two looked like a catalog model. Blonde highlights. Yoga-toned arms. Cashmere sweater in seasonal burgundy. She pulled me into a hug that smelled like cinnamon and something baking.

"You're here!" She squeezed tighter. "I've been watching the window for an hour."

"Traffic." I laughed into her shoulder. "And I may have changed outfits three times."

"For us or for Mystery Man?"

"Shut up."

She pulled back, hands on my shoulders, scanning my face with that older-sister radar. "You're glowing. Actual glowing."

"I'm happy."

"I can see that." Her smile softened. "Good. You deserve it."

The front door opened again. Marcus stepped onto the porch. Tall. Broad-shouldered. The kind of handsome that looked effortless. Dark hair. Square jaw. Charming grin. He wore a fleece pullover and jeans, barefoot despite the cold.

"There she is." He crossed to us, wrapped me in a hug. Cologne and wood smoke. "Jenna's been driving me crazy. 'Is she close? Check the traffic app. What if she got lost?'"

"I don't get lost. I have GPS."

"That's what I told her." He released me, stepped back. "Good to see you, Paige. Jenna says you have a mystery boyfriend visiting?"

Heat crept up my neck. "Tomorrow. Saturday. You'll all meet him."

"Exciting." Marcus smiled. "Finally putting a face to the name."

Something moved behind his eyes. A flicker. There and gone.

Curiosity? Skepticism?

I couldn't read it.

"Let's get your bags," Jenna said. "It's freezing."

The house wrapped around me like a warm blanket. Hardwood floors gleamed. A fire crackled in the stone fireplace. The Christmas tree dominated the living room—eight feet tall, covered in ornaments I recognized from childhood. Mom's crystal angel. Dad's wooden soldiers. The lopsided star I'd made in third grade, still shedding glitter.

Bing Crosby crooned from hidden speakers. *White Christmas.* The smell of gingerbread drifted from the kitchen.

"Guest room's ready," Jenna said. "Fresh sheets, extra blankets. And I cleared space in the closet for that dress you texted about."

"You're the best."

"I know." She squeezed my hand. "Dinner in twenty minutes. Marcus is making his famous pasta."

I hauled my suitcase upstairs. The guest room overlooked the backyard, where more lights traced the fence line. A small artificial tree sat on the dresser, pre-lit, fake pine scent filling the space.

I unpacked essentials. Hung the red dress in the closet. Stood there for a moment, fingers on the silk.

Tomorrow.

My phone buzzed.

I grabbed it too fast, nearly dropped it. My message from an hour ago still showed on screen: *Can't wait to finally see you tomorrow!*

His reply glowed white against blue.

Me too. I've waited so long for this.

I read it twice. Three times.

The words were right. Everything I wanted to hear.

But something had shifted. The tone felt different. Colder. Clinical. Like a script rather than a conversation.

I stared at the screen until it went dark.

Downstairs, Jenna laughed at something Marcus said. Christmas music swelled. The fire popped.

And in my hands, my phone stayed silent.

Chapter 2

Something's Off

Gingerbread. The smell hit me before I opened my eyes. Warm, spiced, pulled straight from childhood. Mom used to make it every December, brown sugar and molasses staining her apron.

I found Jenna in the kitchen at nine AM. Flour dusted her cheeks. She'd already rolled out three batches of dough. Cookie cutters lined the counter—stars, trees, reindeer, gingerbread men with missing limbs.

"You're up." She handed me coffee. "Sleep okay?"

"Eventually."

Her eyes narrowed. "Ethan?"

"He's just... different lately. Through text. Shorter responses. I'm probably overthinking."

"You always overthink." She nudged me toward a stool.

"Tomorrow's the big day. Sit. Decorate. It'll distract you."

I picked up a frosting bag. Royal icing, white as fresh snow. The gingerbread man in front of me stared up with raisin eyes. I gave him a crooked smile.

From the living room, Nat King Cole sang about chestnuts roasting. The tree lights blinked in a pattern I couldn't predict. Outside, frost clung to the windows.

Marcus appeared in the doorway, phone pressed to his ear. "Can't talk right now. I'll call you back." He ended the call, slipped the phone into his pocket. "Ladies. How's the cookie situation?"

"Under control," Jenna said.

Her smile flickered. Dimmed. Came back brighter, compensating.

"Good. I've got some work emails. Study." He grabbed a cookie from the cooling rack and disappeared.

I watched the doorway where he'd been. "Everything okay with you two?"

"Fine." Jenna pressed a star cutter into dough. "Why?"

"He seems distracted."

"Work stress. End of year stuff. Insurance companies don't take holidays." She lifted the star, set it on the baking sheet. "Don't worry about it."

But her jaw stayed tight. And when Marcus's muffled voice drifted from the study—another phone call, the third in an hour—she didn't look up.

We spent the afternoon wrapping presents. Jenna had a system. Tissue paper first, then the box, then ribbon. Everything had to match. I'd wrapped three gifts crooked before she took over.

"You're hopeless," she said, but she laughed.

"I'm creative."

"That's not what that is."

At two o'clock, Jenna pulled out her laptop. "Time for my least favorite tradition."

The spreadsheets. Every December, I helped her reconcile household finances. She claimed to hate numbers, but I suspected she just liked the company. An excuse to sit together, drink wine, pretend we were closer than sisters who only talked at holidays.

I scrolled through the accounts. Checking, savings, credit cards. Everything organized by date, amount, category.

Then I found the transfers.

December 3: $15,000 to Sterling Ventures LLC.

December 10: $20,000 to Sterling Ventures LLC.

December 16: $18,000 to Sterling Ventures LLC.

Fifty-three thousand dollars in two weeks. My finger hovered over the trackpad.

"What's Sterling Ventures?"

Jenna leaned over my shoulder. "Marcus's investment account. He set it up last year."

"That's a lot of money."

"He knows what he's doing." She reached past me, clicked to a different tab. "Now the credit cards—those are the real disaster."

I let it go. Not my marriage. Not my money.

But the numbers stayed lodged in the back of my mind. Fifty-three thousand dollars. To an account I'd never heard of.

I took screenshots anyway. Old habit. Backup paranoia. Saved them to my phone's cloud storage.

Dinner was quiet. Marcus made chicken parmesan, his specialty, but ate barely half his plate. His phone sat face-down on the table. It buzzed twice. He ignored it.

Jenna talked about the Christmas festival tomorrow. The parade route. The hot chocolate stand. The choir performing in the town square. Anything to fill the silence.

I escaped to my room at eight.

My phone showed one text from Ethan, sent while I was eating.

Thinking about you.

I typed back: *Wish you were here already. Look at this tree.* Attached a photo of Jenna's masterpiece, all lights and ornaments, that lopsided star I'd made in third grade.

No response.

I waited. Thirty minutes. An hour.

At ten-fifteen: *Soon. Very soon.*

The words looked right. Read wrong. Something mechanical about them. Copy-pasted from a different conversation.

I called him. Voicemail. His warm voice, recorded months ago: "You've reached Ethan. Leave a message." The beep.

I hung up without speaking.

Texted: *Can we video call? Just for a minute. I miss your face.*

Three dots appeared. Disappeared. Appeared again.

Camera still broken. Sorry. Tomorrow. I promise.

The excuse I'd heard a dozen times. A hundred times. The excuse I'd swallowed because his voice was kind and his words were perfect and I wanted so badly to believe.

I set the phone down. Picked it up. Set it down again.

Tomorrow. He'd promised tomorrow.

But doubt crept through the guest room like cold air through a crack.

Outside, someone's Christmas display played *Jingle Bell Rock*. Cheerful. Bright. The neighbors lived normal lives with normal problems.

I lay in bed and stared at the ceiling. Light from the street bled through the blinds. The small tree on the dresser blinked red, then green, then gold.

My phone stayed dark.

Marcus's footsteps, a shuffle, moved past my door. Down the hall. Into the bedroom he shared with Jenna. Their door closed with a soft click.

The house settled into its Christmas quiet.

And I tried to convince myself everything was fine.

Chapter 3

The Cancellation

At midnight, I opened Instagram. His profile sat in my saved searches. Ethan Brooks, Philadelphia. Private account. But the profile picture was public.

That face I'd memorized. Dark hair. Kind eyes. A smile that seemed genuine rather than posed.

I'd looked at it a hundred times. Maybe more.

I stared at it now. Searching for something. A flaw. A warning I'd missed.

Nothing. Just a handsome man who'd told me he loved me.

I set the phone down. Tried to sleep.

Couldn't.

At eight AM, my phone buzzed.

I grabbed it. Ethan's name on the screen. *Work emergency. Can't make it today. I'm so sorry.*

Will come Christmas Eve instead. I promise.

I read it three times.

Work emergency. On a Saturday. The day we'd planned for months.

Convenient.

I typed back: *Okay. Tomorrow then.*

Didn't add the heart emoji I usually included. Didn't write *I love you* or *miss you* or any of the words I'd scattered through eight months of messages.

Let him wonder.

Downstairs, Jenna was making pancakes. The smell of bacon drifted up through the floor. Christmas music played from the kitchen speaker. *Deck the Halls*. Cheerful and mocking.

I washed my face. Applied concealer under my eyes. Practiced a smile in the mirror.

It looked fake.

Close enough.

Breakfast was boring. Eggs, toast, small talk about the weather. Snow expected for Christmas. How lovely.

Marcus checked his phone under the table. Screen tilted away from Jenna.

"When's lover boy arriving?" Jenna asked.

"He canceled. Work emergency." I picked at my eggs. "Said he'll come Christmas Eve instead."

"That's two days away." Jenna frowned. "After all this waiting?"

"He's dedicated to his job." The lie came automatic.

Marcus looked up. "Christmas Eve? That's cutting it close."

"Better late than never." I forced a smile.

Marcus looked up. "On a Saturday before Christmas? Must be some job."

"He's dedicated."

"I'm sure." Marcus went back to his plate.

After breakfast, I retreated to the guest room. Closed the door. Sat on the bed.

Pulled out my phone.

Typed Ethan's number into Google. The number I'd called hundreds of times. The voice that had made my chest ache.

No results. No records. No social media ties. No reverse lookup information.

A burner phone. Disposable. Untraceable.

I opened Instagram. Searched for his profile.

User not found.

Gone. Deleted. Like he'd never existed.

My hands went numb.

I searched "Ethan Brooks Philadelphia" on every platform. LinkedIn, Facebook, Twitter.

A few results appeared. An orthodontist in his sixties. A college student at Penn. A real estate agent with a wife and three kids.

None of them him.

Or rather, none of them the version of him I'd constructed in my head.

The real Ethan Brooks, if he existed anywhere, wasn't the man I'd been texting.

I set the phone down. Stared at the wall.

Eight months. Two hundred forty-three days. Thousands of messages. Late-night calls that stretched until dawn. Planning a future. Falling in love.

With someone who didn't exist.

The Christmas tree on the dresser blinked. Red, green, gold. Steady as a heartbeat.

I picked up my phone again.

Opened our text history. Scrolled back to the beginning. April 15. The day we matched.

His profile picture smiled at me from the top of the screen.

I took a screenshot.

Opened Google. Reverse image search.

The page loaded slow. My Wi-Fi signal weak in the guest room. One bar flickering.

Then results filled the screen.

Nordic Style Menswear. Fall Collection 2023.

The same face stared back at me from a catalog. Wearing a cable-knit sweater I'd never seen. Different background. Same jaw. Same eyes. Same smile.

Model: Henrik Larsen. Stockholm, Sweden.

I scrolled down.

More results. The photo on a stock image site. Available for download. Twelve dollars and ninety-nine cents.

A template for fake profiles. A face bought and sold like any other product.

I clicked through image after image. Henrik Larsen in a wool coat. Henrik Larsen on a beach. Henrik Larsen holding a coffee cup, smiling at something off-camera.

Every photo I'd saved of "Ethan" traced back to the same Swedish model.

A face sold on stock websites for twelve dollars.

A face I'd fallen in love with.

The phone slipped from my fingers. Hit the carpet with a thud that felt too quiet for what had just broken.

I sat on the edge of the bed. Hands in my lap. Staring at nothing.

Catfished.

The word sat in my stomach like a stone.

I'd heard it before. TV documentaries. Cautionary tales. The kind of thing that happened to desperate people who should have known better.

I never thought I'd be that person. The naive woman who fell for a profile picture and pretty words.

But here I sat. Evidence glowing on my phone screen.

I'd sent him photos of myself. Real photos. My face. My apartment. My life.

He'd sent back lies. Eight months of lies.

A knock on the door. "Paige?" Jenna's voice. "You okay in there?"

I grabbed the phone. Shoved it under the pillow.

"Fine. Just tired."

"Come down when you're ready. I'm making hot chocolate."

Her footsteps retreated down the hall.

I pulled the phone back out. Looked at Henrik Larsen's face one more time.

Not Ethan. Never Ethan.

Ethan Brooks didn't exist.

But someone had created him. Someone had spent eight months pretending to be him. Texting me. Calling me. Making me fall in love.

Why?

Who would do this?

A stranger? Some random catfish running multiple profiles, scamming lonely women for money?

But he'd never asked for money. Never pushed for anything except my time. My attention. My secrets.

Someone close, then. Someone who knew me. Knew my life. Knew where to find me.

My throat tightened.

I stood. Crossed to the window. Looked down at the street.

Jenna's house sat at the end of the cul-de-sac. Only three other houses visible from here. The Johnsons across the street. An older couple two doors down. A young family with kids.

Normal people living normal lives.

And somewhere—someone who'd spent eight months manipulating me.

Downstairs, the grandfather clock chimed noon.

From the kitchen, Jenna called up: "Hot chocolate's ready!"

I looked at the phone in my hand. At Henrik Larsen's face. At eight months of lies packaged in a smile bought for twelve dollars.

"Ethan Brooks" wasn't real.

He'd never been real.

But someone had spent eight months pretending to love me.

And that someone knew where I was right now.

Chapter 4

Who?

I didn't tell Jenna.

Couldn't find the words. How do you explain you've been catfished without sounding stupid? Without admitting you fell for a face bought for twelve dollars?

I went downstairs. Accepted the hot chocolate. Sat on the couch while Jenna talked about the Christmas festival. The parade route. The choir in the town square. Her words washed over me like white noise.

Marcus appeared from the study. Grabbed his coat.

"Heading to Rockaway Mall," he said. "Last-minute shopping. Need anything?"

Jenna shook her head. He left.

I waited until his car disappeared down the street.

Then I went back upstairs.

Pulled out my phone. Opened our text history. Eight months of conversation. Thousands of messages.

I scrolled through slowly. Looking for something I'd missed. Some clue. Some crack in the facade where the truth had leaked through.

April 22: *Happy birthday to your sister! Hope she had a good one. Thirty-two, right?*

I'd mentioned Jenna's birthday. He'd remembered. Nothing suspicious there.

May 3: *How's the Lexus treating you? Those things run forever.*

I stopped scrolling.

My car. When had I told him about my car?

I searched our messages. "Lexus." "Car." "Drive."

Nothing. I'd never mentioned what I drove.

My chest tightened.

June 18: *Allergic to strawberries—noted! I'll make sure there's none in the dessert when I finally cook for you.*

When had I told him about the allergy?

I searched. "Strawberry." "Allergic." "Allergy."

No results. I'd never mentioned it.

But he knew.

July 4: *That scar on your knee—you said you got it at seven, right? Bike accident?*

The scar. A pale line on my left knee that only showed in shorts. A detail I forgot I had until someone pointed it out.

I'd never told anyone about it. Not in text. Not in conversation. It was just there. Background. Unimportant.

Only family would notice. Only someone who'd seen me at barbecues, at pools, at a hundred family gatherings over twenty-eight years.

I kept scrolling.

September 8: *Love the new apartment layout. Desk by the window for better light—smart move.*

I'd rearranged my Montvale apartment in September. Moved the desk from the corner to the window. Better natural light for work.

I'd never told Ethan. Never sent photos of the new setup.

But he knew.

October 15: *Your parents still in Sparta? That's not far from Ridgemont.*

I'd mentioned my parents. But never their town. Sparta was close to Ridgemont—thirty minutes, maybe. But why would a stranger from Philadelphia know that? Care about that?

November 2: *Remember when your mom used to call you Paisley? That's adorable.*

My childhood nickname. The one I hated. The one I hadn't used since middle school.

Only family knew that name. Only people who'd known me as a kid.

The phone screen blurred. I blinked. Focused.

Ethan knew my car. My allergies. A childhood scar I'd never mentioned. My parents' exact town. A nickname I'd buried years ago. My apartment layout.

Details I'd shared with family. With Jenna, during phone calls and holiday visits. With Marcus, in passing conversations I'd already forgotten.

Someone had been feeding him information.

Someone close.

I heard the front door open downstairs. Marcus's voice: "Got the wrapping paper."

"The silver kind?" Jenna's voice.

"With snowflakes. Just like you wanted."

Their voices drifted up. Easy. Domestic. Normal.

I stood. Crossed to the door. Listened.

Footsteps in the kitchen. Cabinet opening. The rustle of shopping bags.

"Where's Paige?" Marcus asked.

"Upstairs. I think she's upset about Ethan canceling."

"Poor thing." His tone sympathetic. Concerned. "Eight months and he can't make one weekend work?"

"He had a work emergency."

"On a Saturday?" A pause. "Seems convenient."

"Marcus."

"I'm just saying. If I were him, nothing would keep me away."

The conversation moved to the living room. Voices muffled now.

I opened the door. Crept to the top of the stairs.

"...think she's really in love with him?" Marcus asked.

"She talks about him constantly." Jenna sighed. "I hope he's worth it."

"Has she told you much about him?"

"The basics. Philadelphia. Marketing consultant. They matched in April."

"You ever seen a picture?"

"His profile. But it's private now."

"Huh." A pause. "What kind of guy doesn't video call his girlfriend for eight months?"

"Camera shy, apparently."

"Or hiding something."

The words hung in the air.

I stepped back from the stairs. Moved to the guest room. Closed the door.

My phone buzzed.

A text from Jenna: *Coming down? Made cookies.*

I typed back: *In a minute. Just checking work email.*

Set the phone down.

Stared at the wall.

Marcus had asked questions about Ethan. Normal questions. The kind a protective brother-in-law would ask.

Or the kind someone pretending to be Ethan would ask. Checking his story. Making sure his lies held up.

I needed to test them. Figure out who knew what.

At three o'clock, I went downstairs. Found Jenna in the kitchen. Marcus was back in the study—another phone call, door closed.

"Hey." Jenna handed me a gingerbread cookie. "Feeling better?"

"Yeah. Just disappointed about Ethan."

"Tomorrow will be worth the wait." She squeezed my shoulder. "I promise."

We sat at the kitchen table. Afternoon light slanted through the windows. Outside, Jenna's neighbors across the street were putting up more decorations. An inflatable snowman joined their inflatable Santa.

"I've been thinking," I said. "Maybe I'll get a cat."

Jenna looked up. "A cat?"

"Yeah. My apartment allows them. And I'm home a lot. Working remote." I picked at the cookie. "Maybe a Siamese. They're smart."

"You've never been a cat person."

"I know. But I've been lonely. Ethan's in Philadelphia. Work keeps me busy. A cat might be nice."

Jenna smiled. "I think it's a good idea. Company."

We talked about cat breeds. Care requirements. The best local shelters. Normal sister conversation.

I watched her face. Her reactions. Genuine curiosity. No hidden agenda.

She didn't know. Couldn't know.

Marcus emerged from the study at five. Grabbed a beer from the fridge.

"What are we talking about?"

"Paige is getting a cat," Jenna said.

His eyebrows lifted. "Really? Since when?"

"Just decided today," I said. "Thinking about a Siamese."

"Cats are good." He twisted the cap off his beer. "Low maintenance. Independent."

He didn't mention it to Ethan. Didn't pull out his phone. Didn't do anything suspicious.

Just drank his beer and talked about cat breeds like any normal person would.

Dinner came and went. Chicken tacos. Easy conversation. Christmas music from the living room speakers. *Have Yourself a Merry Little Christmas.* Soft and melancholy.

At eight PM, I excused myself. Headed upstairs.

My phone buzzed as I closed the guest room door.

Ethan's name on the screen.

Hey, beautiful. How's your day?

I stared at the text.

Typed back: *Good. Changed my mind about the cat though. Found out I'm allergic.*

I'd never mentioned a cat to Ethan. Never in eight months.

If he was real, he'd ask: What cat?

If someone in this house was Ethan, they'd already know.

I hit send.

Waited.

Three dots appeared.

Probably for the best. Dogs are better anyway.

The room tilted.

He'd taken the bait. Responded like we'd already discussed cats. Like I'd told him about my decision this afternoon.

But I hadn't.

I'd only told Jenna and Marcus.

And "Ethan" knew.

I sat on the bed. Phone in my hands. The Christmas tree on the dresser blinked its mocking colors.

Someone in this house had spent eight months pretending to love me.

Someone who'd heard me mention a cat this afternoon.

Someone who was watching. Listening. Waiting.

The house settled around me. Pipes ticked. The furnace hummed.

Downstairs, Jenna and Marcus moved through their evening routine. Dishes clanking. TV turning on. Normal sounds in a normal house.

But nothing was normal.

And I was spending Christmas under the same roof as whoever had built "Ethan Brooks" from stolen information and a Swedish model's face.

Chapter 5

The Correlation

Marcus left for a drive at nine-fifteen. Said he needed to clear his head.

The front door closed. His car started. Headlights swept across my bedroom window.

Ten minutes later, my phone buzzed.

Ethan: *Can't stop thinking about you.*

I stared at the text. Then at the window where Marcus's headlights had disappeared.

Coincidence. Had to be.

But my hands shook as I opened my laptop.

I didn't know Marcus's exact schedule. Didn't track his movements or ask Jenna where he was every night. We lived in different towns. I had my own life in Montvale.

But I knew some things.

I opened the family group chat. Mom, Dad, Jenna, me. The thread we used to coordinate holidays and share updates. I scrolled back through months of messages.

July 22: Jenna had posted in the chat. *Marcus at conference in Boston this week. House feels empty!*

I opened my text history with Ethan. July 22, 11:30 PM: *I wish I could hear your voice right now.*

That night, Marcus was in Boston. And "Ethan" had called me. We'd talked for an hour.

I kept scrolling through the family chat.

September 17: Jenna. *Marcus working late again. Third night this week. Anyone free for dinner?*

That same night in my Ethan messages: 8:45 PM call. Two hours long.

November 12: Jenna in the group chat. *Solo evening. Marcus in Philly for client meetings.*

November 12, 10:15 PM from Ethan: *Can't stop thinking about you.*

I opened Instagram. Pulled up Jenna's profile. She posted constantly. Her perfect life documented in filtered squares.

July: Photo of takeout containers. Caption: "Solo dinner tonight. Husband traveling. Send wine recs! 🍷 "

September: Photo with a girlfriend. "Girls night since Marcus is working late AGAIN."

November: Photo of her reading by the fireplace. "Cozy solo evening while the husband travels for work. 📚 "

Each post matched a late-night message from Ethan.

It wasn't every message. I couldn't track eight months of Marcus's schedule from my apartment thirty minutes away.

But the pattern I could verify was enough.

When Marcus was verifiably away—business trips, late nights, conferences Jenna mentioned—"Ethan" reached out.

When Jenna posted photos of them together at dinners or weekend events, "Ethan" went quiet for days.

Not proof. Not conclusive.

But enough to make my stomach turn.

I closed the laptop. Couldn't look anymore.

My phone buzzed again.

You still there?

Marcus was driving somewhere in Ridgemont. Windows down. Cold air on his face.

And "Ethan" was texting me from wherever Marcus kept his secrets.

I didn't respond.

Set the phone face-down on the nightstand.

Lay in bed and stared at the ceiling until the clock showed two AM.

Marcus's car returned around midnight. I heard it in the driveway. The engine cutting. The door closing. His footsteps on the porch.

The house went quiet again.

I didn't sleep.

Morning came gray and cold. Sunday. The day Ethan was supposed to have arrived. The day I was supposed to meet the man I'd fallen in love with.

Instead, I walked downstairs to find him making eggs.

Marcus stood at the stove. Spatula in hand. Coffee brewing. Sunday morning domestic scene.

"Morning." He didn't turn around. "Sleep well?"

"Not really."

"Pre-meeting nerves." He plated the eggs. Brought them to the table. "Tomorrow's the big day."

I sat. Watched him move through the kitchen. The way he paused before pouring coffee. The way he tilted his head when he listened. Small mannerisms I'd never paid attention to before.

Jenna came down in yoga pants and an oversized sweatshirt. Kissed Marcus's cheek. Poured herself coffee.

"What's everyone doing today?" she asked.

"Work emails." Marcus picked up his phone. "Boring stuff."

"I've got grocery shopping," Jenna said. "Last-minute ingredients for tomorrow's dinner."

She looked at me. "Want to come?"

"I'll stay here. Headache."

"You sure?"

"Yeah. Need to rest before Ethan arrives."

The lie came easy. Too easy.

Jenna left at ten. Marcus settled in the living room with his laptop. Work emails, he said. Always work.

I sat in the armchair across from him. Phone in hand. Heart slamming against my ribs.

Time to test him.

I typed to Ethan: *Can you call me? Right now? I need to hear your voice.*

Sent.

Marcus's laptop chimed. Email notification. His eyes flicked to the screen. Then to his pocket.

Then to me.

"Sorry." He stood. Already reaching for his phone. "Work call. Need to take this outside."

He grabbed his coat. Stepped onto the porch. The door clicked shut behind him.

I counted to ten.

My phone rang.

Unknown number.

I answered.

"Hey, beautiful."

The voice came through distorted. Warped. Like someone speaking underwater. A voice changer. The kind you could download from any app store.

"The connection's bad," I said.

"Yeah. Sorry. Spotty signal." A pause. Two beats of silence before the next words. "I can't wait to see you tomorrow."

The pause.

That specific pause. Two beats before important words.

I'd heard it a thousand times.

At dinner tables. In living rooms. In conversations I'd forgotten until now.

Marcus paused the same way.

"Me too," I said. My voice stayed steady. A miracle. "Listen, the call's breaking up. I'll text you later."

"Okay, beautiful. Talk soon."

Beautiful. The way he stretched the word. Emphasis on the first syllable.

Marcus said it the same way to Jenna. Every single time.

I hung up.

Through the window, Marcus stood on the porch. Phone pressed to his ear. Speaking to no one now. Performing for an audience of one.

He looked up.

Our eyes met through the glass.

I smiled. Waved.

He waved back.

The monster wore my brother-in-law's face.

I spent the rest of the morning in my room. Door closed. Laptop open.

Reviewed everything again. The timing. The pauses. The way Ethan knew things only family would know.

All the pieces locked together.

Marcus had created Ethan Brooks. Spent eight months pretending to love me. Used a voice changer for calls. Timed his texts for when he was away from the house.

But why?

What did he gain from making me fall in love with someone who didn't exist?

I thought about the spreadsheets. The transfers. Sterling Ventures LLC. Fifty-three thousand dollars in two weeks.

Money Marcus couldn't explain. Money flowing into accounts Jenna barely understood.

And me. The sister who helped with finances every December. Who asked questions. Who took screenshots and organized records and noticed patterns.

A threat.

I was a threat to whatever Marcus was hiding.

And "Ethan" was how he monitored me. Controlled me. Made sure I didn't look too close.

My phone buzzed.

Ethan: *Tomorrow can't come soon enough. I love you.*

I stared at the words.

Marcus had typed them. Marcus, who was married to my sister. Who smiled at family dinners. Who made pasta and asked about my day and pretended to care.

Marcus, who'd spent eight months manipulating me.

I typed back: *Love you too.*

The lie tasted like metal.

Downstairs, the front door opened. Jenna's voice: "I'm back! Need help with groceries."

Marcus: "Be right there."

Their footsteps moved to the kitchen. Normal sounds. Normal life.

I sat in the guest room. Phone in my hands. Evidence everywhere.

But no way to prove it. No way to show Jenna without sounding crazy.

No way to leave without them knowing.

I pulled up the screenshots I'd taken yesterday. The financial records. Sterling Ventures. The shell companies.

If Marcus was hiding money, that's why he needed to control me.

If I could prove the embezzlement, I could prove everything.

Tomorrow was Christmas Eve. The day "Ethan" was supposed to arrive. The day Marcus's lies would have to become real or unravel completely.

I had twenty-four hours to figure out my next move.

Twenty-four hours trapped in a house with a man who'd stolen my heart to protect his crimes.

Outside, church bells rang. Calling people to Sunday service. Peace on earth. Goodwill toward men.

I looked at my phone. At Ethan's last message. At eight months of love that had never been real.

And I knew. Tomorrow, everything would change.

One way or another.

Chapter 6

The Phone

I needed proof. Real proof. Something more than patterns and pauses and a voice distorted through an app.

Marcus's personal phone sat on the kitchen counter.

Monday afternoon. Two PM. Jenna was upstairs—I could hear the shower running. Marcus stood on the back porch with his work phone pressed to his ear. Another call. His breath fogged in the December cold.

His personal phone glowed on the granite. Screen still lit. Unlocked.

I moved before I could stop myself.

Through the living room. Past the Christmas tree with its blinking lights. Into the kitchen where breakfast dishes still sat by the sink.

The phone was warm. Recently used.

Home screen showed a photo of him and Jenna at some beach. Smiling. Happy. The kind of couple you'd see in a picture frame at Target.

I swiped through his apps. Email. Calendar. Browser. Nothing unusual.

Then I found a folder labeled "Utilities." Buried at the bottom of the second screen.

Inside: calculator, compass, level. Standard phone tools.

And one app with an icon that looked like a calculator but wasn't.

I opened it.

The conversation loaded.

My name at the top. My photo—the one from May, standing in my Montvale apartment with new curtains behind me.

Every message. Every text. Every lie I'd believed for eight months.

April 15: Hey! I saw we matched. Your profile made me laugh...

May 3: How's the Lexus treating you?

June 18: Allergic to strawberries—noted!

December 19: Work emergency. Can't make it until tomorrow.

December 22: Can't stop thinking about you.

All of it. Right here on my brother-in-law's phone.

My hands shook. I took screenshots with my own phone. One after another. As many as I could before—

The porch door opened.

Cold air rushed in.

I closed the app. Set the phone down exactly where I'd found it. Stepped to the sink.

Grabbed a glass. Filled it with water.

Marcus walked into the kitchen. Snow dusted his shoulders. When had it started snowing?

His eyes went to his phone. To me. Back to his phone.

"Everything okay?"

"Fine." I gripped the counter. "Just getting water."

He picked up his phone. Checked the screen. Slipped it in his pocket.

That smile. The one I used to think was charming.

"Jenna's in the shower," he said. "Let me see if she's done."

He walked past me. Close enough that I could smell his cologne.

The same cologne I'd imagined on "Ethan." The same scent I'd dreamed about for months.

I stood alone in the kitchen.

Outside, snow fell on the Christmas decorations. The inflatable Santa swayed in the wind. Icicle lights dripped from the gutters.

From the radio on the counter, someone sang about winter wonderland.

I'd found the proof. Screenshots of his messages. His fake profile. Eight months of manipulation captured on my phone.

But finding it and using it were two different things.

I went upstairs. Locked myself in the guest room.

Opened my laptop. Pulled up the screenshots I'd taken Saturday. The financial records from Jenna's spreadsheet.

Sterling Ventures LLC. December 3: $15,000. December 10: $20,000. December 16: $18,000.

I opened a browser. Searched "Sterling Ventures LLC New Jersey."

No website. No business registration. No LinkedIn profiles. No employee listings. No trace of existence beyond a name on a transfer receipt.

I tried the other companies from the screenshots.

Apex Holdings. Nothing.

Meridian Capital Partners. Nothing.

Shell companies. All of them. Money flowing out of Marcus's accounts and disappearing into nothing.

The pieces locked together with a click I could almost hear.

Marcus worked for an insurance company. Access to accounts. To policies. To money that moved in numbers too large for anyone to track closely.

He'd been siphoning funds. Small amounts at first. Bigger as he grew confident. Into fake companies he controlled.

Embezzlement.

And I had the evidence. Screenshots from last December. Records I'd taken as backup. Never suspecting what they contained.

Last December. When I'd helped with the finances. When I'd asked about Sterling Ventures. When Marcus first realized I was getting too close.

April. When "Ethan Brooks" appeared on my dating app. Perfect timing. Perfect profile. Perfect words.

Marcus had created him to monitor me. To control what I knew. To track my thoughts, my suspicions, my every move.

To make sure the woman who touched his finances every December didn't stumble onto the truth.

I'd been falling in love with my handler.

My phone buzzed.

Marcus: *Jenna's making dinner. Come down when you're ready.*

He'd texted from his regular number. Not the burner. Not "Ethan."

Just Marcus. Brother-in-law. Husband. Criminal.

I looked at the screenshots on my phone. The financial records. The fake companies. The messages proving Marcus was Ethan.

Evidence to destroy him.

And no way to use it without him knowing.

My car keys sat in my purse. Twenty feet from the front door.

But Marcus stood between me and the exit. Marcus, who checked his phone constantly. Marcus, who knew exactly where I was at every moment because he'd spent eight months training me to tell "Ethan" everything.

The guest room walls pressed closer. The Christmas tree blinked its mocking colors.

I pulled out my phone. Opened the screenshots again. Studied them.

Marcus's fake profile. The app disguised as a calculator. Our entire conversation history.

And in the messages: references I'd missed before.

September: Make sure she doesn't look too close at the accounts.

October: She's asking about Sterling again. Need to distract her.

November: The screenshots from last year—does she still have them?

He'd been worried about me for months. Tracking what I knew. What I suspected. What evidence I'd kept.

The screenshots from last December. The ones I'd taken out of habit and forgotten about.

The ones sitting on my phone right now.

Marcus needed those screenshots to disappear. Needed me to stay quiet. Needed to control the narrative until he could fix his embezzlement and walk away clean.

That's why "Ethan" existed. Not love. Not connection.

Control.

And I'd given him exactly what he wanted. Shared everything. Trusted completely. Let him inside my head for eight months while he stole from his company and used me as his early warning system.

Downstairs, Jenna called up: "Paige! Dinner!"

I looked at the door. At the screenshots. At the evidence that could send Marcus to prison.

And at the Christmas decorations visible through my window. The neighbors' lights twinkling. The snow falling soft and quiet.

Tomorrow was Christmas Eve. The day "Ethan" was supposed to arrive. The day everything was supposed to be perfect.

Instead, I was trapped in a house with a man who'd stolen my heart to protect his crimes.

And I had less than twenty-four hours to figure out how to survive.

Chapter 7

The Sister

Jenna stood at the stove, stirring hot chocolate. Real chocolate, not the powdered kind. She'd shaved it from a block, added cream, a splash of vanilla. The kitchen smelled like childhood.

She was humming. Some carol about snow and sleigh bells.

My sister at thirty-two. Blonde and beautiful and married to a thief.

Did she know? Had she always known?

"There you are." She turned, wooden spoon in hand. "I made the good stuff. Mom's recipe."

"Thanks."

She poured two mugs. Topped them with whipped cream and cinnamon. Handed one to me with a smile that looked genuine.

But what did genuine mean anymore?

We moved to the living room. The Christmas tree dominated the corner. Ornaments glittered. Lights cycled through their programmed sequence. Jenna had added more garland since yesterday—draped over the mantel, wound around the stair railing, hung above every doorway.

"I love this time of year." She curled into the couch, cradling her mug. "Everything feels possible."

I sat in the armchair. The same spot I'd occupied last night. Watching Marcus. Cataloging his lies.

"Can I ask you something?"

"Of course."

"Those transfers in your spreadsheet. Sterling Ventures. The other accounts. What are those?"

Jenna sipped her chocolate. "Marcus handles the investments. I just let him do his thing."

"You don't know what Sterling Ventures is?"

"Some business account?" She shrugged. "He set it up last year. Tax advantages or something. I don't really follow that stuff."

Her confusion looked real. The slight furrow between her brows. The way she tilted her head. Body language I'd known my entire life.

But Marcus had fooled me for eight months. Maybe deception ran in the family.

From the radio on the bookshelf, a children's choir sang about a winter wonderland.

Marcus came down the stairs. Coat on. Keys in hand. Work phone in his pocket—I could see the outline.

"Heading out," he said. "Meeting a client in Morristown. Back in a couple hours."

Jenna set down her mug. "On a Monday before Christmas?"

"Year-end stuff. Won't be long." He crossed to her. Kissed her cheek. "Need anything?"

"We're good."

He nodded at me on his way out. That smile. That mask.

The front door closed. His car started. Headlights swept across the window.

Jenna reached for the remote. "Want to watch something? There's a holiday movie—"

"I need to tell you something."

The words came out harder than I intended. Jenna froze. Remote halfway to the TV.

"What's wrong?"

I set down my mug. Stood up. Sat back down. Couldn't find a position that felt safe.

"It's about Marcus."

"What about him?"

"Ethan isn't real."

Silence. The children's choir kept singing. Outside, wind rattled the windows.

"What do you mean, Ethan isn't real?"

"The man I've been talking to for eight months. The man I was supposed to meet tomorrow." I gripped the armrest. "He doesn't exist. The photos are stock images. Swedish model named Henrik Larsen. Twelve dollars on a clothing website."

Jenna's face went pale. "That's... that's crazy. Why would someone—"

"Marcus."

The name landed like a stone.

"Marcus created the profile. Marcus has been texting me. Calling me with a voice changer. Pretending to be someone who loves me." I stood. Couldn't sit still. "I found the conversations on his phone yesterday. Every message. Every lie."

Jenna didn't move. Didn't blink.

"He's been catfishing me, Jenna. Your husband has been pretending to be my boyfriend for eight months."

The carol ended. Another started. *Silver Bells.* City sidewalks dressed in holiday style.

"Why would he do that?" Jenna's voice came out flat. Controlled.

"The money. Those transfers—Sterling Ventures, Apex Holdings, all of it. They're fake companies. Shell accounts." I moved toward her. "He's been embezzling. And I have evidence on my phone from last year's spreadsheets. He created Ethan to monitor me. To make sure I didn't figure out what he was doing with your finances."

Jenna stared at her hot chocolate. The whipped cream had deflated. Sinking into the brown liquid.

"Say something." I crouched in front of her. "Please. I know this is a lot, but we need to call the police. We need to—"

"I know about Ethan."

The words hit me like ice water.

"What?"

Jenna looked up. Her eyes were dry. Clear. Not a trace of surprise.

"I know Marcus created that profile."

The room tilted. The Christmas tree lights blurred at the edges of my vision.

"You knew?"

"He told me in September." She set down her mug. Slow. Deliberate. "Said he was testing you."

"Testing me?"

"You help with our finances every year. You see things. Numbers. Transfers. Accounts." Jenna stood. Stepped around me. Walked to the window. "He said you were getting too close. Asking too many questions last December. He needed to know if you'd keep secrets."

I couldn't breathe. The hot chocolate churned in my stomach.

"So you let him pretend to be my boyfriend? For eight months?"

"It wasn't supposed to go this long." She turned to face me. Arms crossed. Defensive. "But then you fell for it. Really fell. And Marcus said it was easier to keep going than figure out how to end it."

"Easier." The word tasted like poison. "It was easier to let me fall in love with someone who doesn't exist."

"You were never supposed to fall in love. You were supposed to share things. Tell 'Ethan' about your life. Your suspicions. Anything that might be a problem." Her jaw tightened. "It was about protecting our family."

"From what? From me?"

"From anyone who might threaten what we've built."

The children's choir swelled. Joy to the world. Peace on earth.

"The embezzlement." My voice cracked. "You know about that too."

Jenna didn't answer. Didn't need to. The truth was written in the set of her shoulders. The lift of her chin. The way she looked at me like I was a problem to be solved.

"He's protecting our family," she said. "That money is our future. Our security. And you're not going to take it away."

The sister I'd known my whole life stood five feet away. Blonde hair. Cashmere sweater. Hot chocolate on her breath.

A stranger wearing Jenna's face.

"I trusted you." My voice came out a whisper.

"I know." She pulled out her phone. Started typing. "And I'm sorry. But Marcus will be home soon. And we need to figure out what happens next."

I stood at the edge of the living room. The garland above the doorway brushed my shoulder. Outside, the neighbors were putting up more lights. Normal people living normal lives.

"You chose him over me."

Jenna's fingers paused on the screen. "He's my husband."

"I'm your sister."

Her jaw locked. She looked away. Kept typing.

The Christmas tree blinked. Red. Gold. White. The angel on top leaned to one side. Crooked. Off-balance.

Like everything in this house.

"I'm leaving." I moved toward the stairs.

"No." Jenna stepped in front of me. "You're not."

"You can't stop me."

"Paige." Her voice hardened. "Sit down. We're going to wait for Marcus. And then the three of us are going to talk about how to handle this."

"Handle this?" I stepped back. "You let your husband catfish your sister. You helped him steal money. You watched me fall apart waiting for someone who didn't exist—"

"You were fine," Jenna snapped. "You were happy. Happier than you've been in years."

"So that makes it okay?"

"It made things easier."

The words hit like a physical blow.

From outside, the sound of tires on snow.

Jenna's head turned toward the window.

Headlights swept across the living room. Bright white cutting through the Christmas lights.

The engine shut off.
Jenna exhaled. Her shoulders dropped.
"He's home."
She said it like relief.
Like backup had arrived.

Chapter 8

The Trap

The front door opened. Cold air gusted into the living room.

Marcus stepped inside. Snow dusted his coat and hair. He read the room in a glance. My stance. Jenna's expression. The space between us.

"You talked."

Not a question.

Jenna moved closer to him. "She knows everything."

Marcus nodded. No surprise. He slipped his hand into his coat pocket. Withdrew the front door key. Turned. Locked the deadbolt with a clean click.

Then pocketed the key.

I stepped back until my shoulders hit the wall.

Marcus set his work phone on the console. His coat stayed on. Snow melted off the leather and dripped onto the hardwood.

"When did you find out?"

"Saturday. Then I found the app on your phone yesterday."

"Should've locked the screen." He pulled off his gloves. "But here we are."

"You lied to me." My voice shook. "Both of you."

"Everything I did kept this family stable." Marcus stepped closer. "You were the one piece I couldn't predict."

Jenna stood behind him. Aligned. United.

"I'm leaving," I said.

"No." Jenna's voice cut sharp. "You're not."

Marcus closed the distance between us. "Sit down, Paige."

I pressed against the wall. "I'm going to the police."

"No. You're not." He tapped his pocket where the key had disappeared. Metal jingled. "We need to talk about how this works."

He walked to the couch. Sat. Elbows on knees.

"I started two years ago. Company cut bonuses. Costs went up. Partners kept cashing checks." He looked at his hands. "So I adjusted numbers. Small transfers. No one noticed."

My hand closed around the staircase post.

"Until last year. You came for Christmas. Pulled the files. Asked about Sterling Ventures." His mouth twitched. "You were always good with details."

"You stole from your company."

"I borrowed. Needed six months to fix it. Then the market dropped. Had to cover holes with new holes." He leaned back. "Stopped three months ago. Have a plan to unwind it. Move assets. Pay back enough that it looks like accounting errors."

"And you need time."

"Six months. By summer, new job. New city. No one chases old mistakes."

"What does that have to do with me?"

Jenna finally spoke. "You have last year's spreadsheets. Screenshots. You remember everything."

"So you're a liability," Marcus said.

The word settled like a stone.

"You go to police now, everything collapses. Full audit. I go to prison. Jenna loses the house. Everything." His eyes stayed flat. "She loses everything."

"You hurt both of us."

"I protected this family." His voice hardened. "And you helped. Every December. Free accounting work. You organized those files. Created the documentation that made it all look legitimate."

My throat tightened.

"You touched those accounts," he continued. "Your screenshots. Your notes. Your reconciliations. You think the police won't ask why our family accountant never noticed fifty thousand in suspicious transfers?"

"I'm not your accountant."

"Tell that to a jury. You reviewed the books. Took screenshots. Created records. Never reported anything." He stepped closer. "Best case? You're incompetent. Worst case? You were in on it."

"I didn't know—"

"Doesn't matter. You had access. You had knowledge. You had opportunity." His tone cooled. "You go to police, you don't just destroy us. You implicate yourself."

The carol played. *Have Yourself a Merry Little Christmas.*

My vision narrowed. "That's not true."

"Isn't it? You think prosecutors won't ask why you kept coming back every year? Why you never questioned the transfers? Why you took screenshots and kept them?" He tilted his head. "They'll wonder what you were hiding."

"I wasn't hiding anything."

"Then why not report it last year? When you first saw Sterling Ventures?" He waited. "Because some part of you knew. And you chose family over the law. Just like now."

My hands shook.

"So what?" I asked. "You scare me into silence?"

"I remove the risk." He stepped toward me. "You're staying here until after New Year. No phone. No laptop. No contact. After that, we'll be gone. You tell any story you want. No evidence. No us."

"You can't keep me here."

He looked at the locked door. "I already started."

I reached for my phone.

Gone.

Jenna held it up. My lock screen glowed in her hand. She pressed the button. The light died.

"When?"

"While you argued," she said.

Marcus pulled my backpack from behind the console. Unzipped. Empty.

"I'll keep this safe."

He stepped close. Didn't raise a hand. Didn't need to.

"You go to police, they'll investigate everyone who touched those accounts. Including you." His jaw tightened. "You really want to explain to detectives why you kept coming back? Why you never asked questions? Why you have screenshots you never reported?"

Something inside me twisted.

"This isn't about protecting you. It's about protecting himself."

"It's about protecting all of us. You. Jenna. This family." He shook his head. "You want the truth more than you want your sister safe."

"I want my life back."

"Then sit this out. You survive a boring Christmas. We fix the mess. Everyone moves on."

Jenna shifted. "Marcus..."

He held up a hand.

I stared at my sister. "You're okay with this?"

Her eyes shone. "He's my husband."

"I'm your sister."

She looked away.

Marcus's hand closed around my arm. Firm. "Guest room. You need sleep."

I yanked back. "Don't touch me."

He walked to the stairs. Waited.

"You go up. Door stays locked. Tomorrow you think clearly."

"And if I don't?"

"You will."

I climbed. The garland brushed my shoulder. Through the window, the neighbor's wreath glowed yellow.

My car sat in the driveway. Keys in Marcus's pocket. No phone. No laptop. No one who knew I needed help.

Jenna stood at the base of the stairs. Wouldn't meet my eyes.

The guest room waited. I stepped inside.

Marcus shut the door. The lock clicked.

I pressed my hand against the wood. Listened to footsteps retreat.

Then silence. Just carols drifting up from below.

I lay on the bed. Stared at the ceiling. Light from the street bled through the blinds.

Hours passed. The house settled. By evening, smells drifted up. Roast meat. Cinnamon. Christmas Eve dinner prep.

Voices rose. Muffled.

I moved to the door. Knelt. Pressed my ear to the wood.

Jenna's voice: "We can't keep her here forever!"

Marcus. Low. Cold: "We won't have to."

A pause.

Then clearer: "After tonight, it won't matter."

The words echoed in the dark guest room.

I stayed on the floor. Back against the bed. The house quiet around me.

After tonight, it won't matter.

Christmas Eve tomorrow. The day Ethan was supposed to arrive. The day Marcus's lies would have to become real or unravel completely.

The day something was going to happen.

Something Marcus had planned.

Something that would make keeping me here no longer necessary.

I looked at the door. At the hinges on my side. Three brass pins under layers of paint.

Old house hardware.

I had until tomorrow to figure out how to survive.

Chapter 9

The Escape

The hinges sat on my side of the door. Three old brass pins under layers of paint.

I grabbed the nail file from my purse. Thin. Silver. Pointed. Wedged it under the top hinge pin. Pushed.

Nothing.

I leaned in. Metal scraped. Paint fell. My wrist shook.

Again.

The pin shifted a fraction. Rust groaned. My arm burned.

A carol drifted up. Warm. Slow. My stomach tightened.

I kept at it.

Push. Slip. Curse. A cramp forced me to switch hands. Fingers numbed. Sweat cooled on my neck.

Below, boots. Water running. A flush. Steps. A door closing. Then quiet.

Tree lights pulsed red and green under the door gap.

The pin crept upward. My fingers caught it. Pulled.

A soft scrape.

I froze.

No footsteps.

Pin in my pocket. Middle hinge next.

Harder. The file slipped. Stung my knuckle. Blood welled. I wiped it on my jeans. Shoulder throbbing. Back tight.

Carols blended into one long loop. Familiar songs warped now.

The pin rose grain by grain. Then gave. I eased it free.

Two pins pocketed.

I braced my shoulder against the door and lifted. The bottom hinge squealed. The door sagged. A narrow gap opened.

Enough.

I slid through sideways. Breath tight. Shoulder scraping the jamb. The door leaned back. Clinging to its last hinge.

The hallway lay in half-dark. A nightlight near the bathroom cast a dim circle on the carpet. The rest glowed with stray color from the tree downstairs.

I crept along the wall.

At the top of the staircase, I stopped. Listened.

Nothing.

No TV. No voices. No clink of glasses.

I took the stairs one at a time. Toes close to the riser. A board creaked under my weight. I paused. Heart thudding in my neck.

Silence.

The living room opened at the bottom. The tree dominated the far corner. Lights blinked on their timer. The angel topper leaned. Our three stockings hung in a perfect row. Names stitched in red.

The front door stood across from the tree. Deadbolt fixed in place. Chain latch slid across.

I tried the knob anyway.

Locked.

No need looking for the key. Marcus had put it in his pocket.

I moved toward the back of the house. Bare feet cold on the hardwood. The kitchen sat dark except for the blue glow of the oven clock. 1:42 AM.

Christmas morning.

The back door had a deadbolt and chain too. Both engaged.

The kitchen window over the sink looked smaller than the others but lower. Old wood. Thick paint. Frost on the glass.

I climbed onto the counter. Wedged my fingers under the sash. Pushed up.

The window didn't move.

I tried again. The frame groaned. A sliver of air sliced across my fingers.

I leaned my shoulder into the glass and shoved. The sash jumped an inch. Then another.

Cold rushed in. Snow smell. Wet and metallic.

I swung my legs through and dropped.

Snow swallowed my ankles. The shock of cold shot straight up my bones. I bit down on a sound and stumbled forward.

The neighbor's house glowed through the trees. One front window lit. Porch light off. A wreath on their door.

I ran.

The yard stretched longer than it ever looked from Jenna's kitchen table. Snow grabbed at my feet. Ice cut into the skin under my toes. My breath tore in rough bursts from my throat.

Halfway across, a sound cracked the air.

The back door of Jenna's house slammed open.

"Paige!"

Marcus.

The word hurled itself across the snow.

I didn't look back.

Boots hammered the deck boards. Then the crunch of heavy steps in the yard.

"Stop!"

I drove my legs harder. My lungs burned. My arms felt like they no longer belonged to me.

The neighbor's porch loomed ahead. Their porch light snapped on. Motion sensor. I took the steps in a clumsy jump and hit the door with both fists.

"Please! Please, help!"

Wood rattled in its frame. I pounded again.

"Open the door! I need help!"

Behind me, the steps drew closer. A dark shape cut across the white yard in my peripheral vision. Marcus's breath carried thin in the cold.

"Paige, don't do this!"

The porch light bleached the snow in harsh yellow. My hands had gone red and raw against the door.

Locks clicked on the other side.

The door opened a narrow slice. An older man stared back at me. Gray hair. Deep lines in his face. Pajamas under a robe. His eyes went from my bare feet to my arms to my face.

"Please," I said. "He's after me. I need to call 911."

Boots hit the bottom step behind me.

The man pulled me inside. Fast. He shoved the door closed and flipped the deadbolt. A second lock. A chain.

Marcus hit the other side a heartbeat later.

The door shuddered.

"Open the door!" Marcus shouted. "She's confused. She's not safe. Open up!"

The old man grabbed the shotgun that leaned in the corner beside the coat rack. He held it low but solid. Barrel angled at the floor. Body behind the frame.

He didn't raise his voice. "Step off my porch."

"I'm her brother-in-law," Marcus said. "She's having some kind of episode. Open the door and we'll talk."

"The police can sort it out," the man said.

He turned his head toward the hallway.

"Phone," he called. "Bring the phone."

A woman answered from deeper in the house. "What's going on?"

"Phone," he repeated.

She brought a cordless handset. Her eyes widened when she saw me. Barefoot. Shivering. Smears of blood on my fingers from the nail file cut.

The man dialed. He pressed the phone to his ear. Eyes still on the door.

"There's a young woman at my house," he said after a beat. "She says her sister and brother-in-law held her against her will. The man is on my porch right now trying to get in. 2 1 4 Ridge Lane. Yes. We're in Ridgemont. Send someone now."

The door shook again under Marcus's fists.

"Paige!" he yelled. "Don't do this. You're blowing up everything."

The man raised the shotgun a notch. "You touch this door again and I treat it as a break-in."

The dispatcher's voice buzzed faintly from the handset.

"Officers are on their way," the man said into the phone. He set it on the entry table and kept his stance.

Sirens began as a distant wail. Far at first. Then closer. Echoing off snow and trees.

Marcus stepped off the porch. Through the sidelight window, I watched him move toward his SUV at the curb. Snow covered the windshield. He yanked the driver's door open.

Blue and red lights washed across the houses at the end of the street. A cruiser turned the corner hard. Another followed. Tires crunched over packed snow.

The first car angled across the road in front of Marcus's SUV. The second pulled in behind it.

Doors opened. Officers shouted commands. Marcus lifted his hands and froze. Arms bright in the flash.

They moved him to his knees. A pair of cuffs caught the light.

Inside the entryway, my legs gave out. I slid down the wall until I sat on the hardwood. The blanket of cold still wrapped around my skin from the yard.

The woman fetched another blanket and draped it over my shoulders. Fleece. Warm. It scratched a little at my neck.

"You're safe here," she said.

My teeth knocked against each other anyway.

Minutes later, a woman in a dark coat stepped through the open door. Officers checked the porch and yard behind her. She had short hair. A lined face. Careful eyes.

She crouched in front of me.

"I'm Detective Hazel Fairbank," she said. "Can you tell me your name?"

"Paige," I managed. "Paige Holloway."

"You're safe now, Paige," she said. "We have him in custody. We have units heading to your sister's house. We're going to take your statement and get you somewhere warm."

Warm sounded like another country.

But I was out. I was safe.

And Marcus sat in handcuffs under twinkling Christmas lights while snow fell soft and quiet on the perfect suburban street.

Chapter 10

Aftermath

Detective Fairbank crouched in front of me in the neighbor's entryway. Short dark hair. Lined face. Careful eyes.

"I'm Detective Hazel Fairbank. Can you tell me your name?"

"Paige Holloway."

My teeth chattered. The words barely came out.

"You're safe now, Paige." She gestured to the EMT behind her. "Let them check you first. Get you warm. Then we'll talk."

The neighbor's wife brought more blankets. A space heater appeared from somewhere. Warm air blasted against my feet.

The paramedic worked fast. Young. Professional. He examined my feet—cut from ice, bruised, swollen. My hands. The knuckle I'd split with the nail file. My shoulder, scraped from the door jamb.

"You should go to the hospital."

"I'm staying." My voice still shook from cold.

He looked at Fairbank. She nodded.

"Document the injuries. Photos. Then she can refuse transport."

He took pictures. My feet. My hands. The scrape on my shoulder. Then bandaged what he could. Wrapped heated packs around my feet.

The neighbor brought tea. Hot. Sweet. My fingers could barely hold the mug.

Time passed. Thirty minutes. Maybe more. The shaking slowed. Feeling returned to my toes. The shock started to lift.

Fairbank waited. Patient. Didn't push. Just stood near the door, talking quietly with officers outside.

When my hands finally steadied on the mug, she moved to sit beside me on the neighbor's couch.

Pulled out a notebook.

"Ready to talk?"

I nodded.

"Tell me what happened."

I told her everything. Ethan Brooks. The catfishing. Finding Marcus's phone. The embezzlement. Jenna knowing all along. Being locked in the guest room. Overhearing "after tonight it won't matter."

I pulled out my phone—somehow still in my pocket through everything. Showed her the screenshots. The financial records from last year. The fake companies. The messages proving Marcus was Ethan.

She wrote it all down. Asked questions. Time. Sequence. Details.

"This is enough," she said. "Multiple charges. Identity fraud. False imprisonment. Embezzlement. Extortion."

"What about Jenna?"

"Conspiracy. Accessory. She'll face charges too."

Dawn broke while we talked. Gray light through the neighbor's windows. Christmas morning.

By six AM, officers had cleared Jenna's house. An officer escorted me there to collect my things. Crime scene tape across the driveway. The guest room door hung off its last hinge. The kitchen window still gaped open.

Jenna wasn't there. They'd taken her to the station in a separate car.

I grabbed my suitcase. The red silk dress still hung in the closet. I left it there.

Walked through the house one last time. The Christmas tree still blinked. Our stockings still hung. Gingerbread cookies sat on the kitchen counter.

A perfect Christmas morning.

All lies.

I drove my Lexus through the snow toward my parents' house in Sparta. The sky lightened as I pulled onto their street. Their Christmas lights still blinked on the porch.

Mom opened the door before I reached it. She took one look at my face and pulled me against her. Dad wrapped his arms around both of us. No questions. Not yet.

Behind them, their tree glowed soft and steady. Ornaments from our childhood hung from the branches. A paper star Jenna made in third grade sagged near the top.

I looked away.

The news came in pieces over the next few days.

Marcus arrested. Charged with embezzlement, identity fraud, false imprisonment, extortion, conspiracy.

Company audit revealed the full extent. Over one hundred thousand dollars stolen across eighteen months. Shell companies. Fake transfers. Years in prison.

Jenna arrested. Charged as accessory. Conspiracy. False imprisonment. She'd known since September. Helped cover it up. Let Marcus catfish me for months.

Their house seized for restitution. Assets frozen. The perfect life they'd built collapsed in forty-eight hours.

Detective Fairbank called with updates. Professional. Kind. She said I'd need to testify eventually. I said I would.

January turned to February. February to March.

By March, the snow in Montvale had shrunk into dirty piles along the curbs. My apartment smelled like coffee and the citrus cleaner I used on weekends.

The mail slot clanked.

An envelope slid onto the floor. Same return address as the others. Same familiar slant to the handwriting.

Jenna.

Prison.

I stood there for a long second. Then picked it up and dropped it straight into the trash. On top of the last one. Unopened.

My parents asked the question every few visits.

"Do you think you'll ever forgive her?"

I shook my head.

"She chose money over me," I said. "So no. I won't."

The words sat in the air. Solid. Final.

I drove back to Montvale as the sun dropped toward the horizon. Sky washed in pale orange. Headlights rolled past on the highway. My hands stayed steady on the wheel.

I spent eight months falling in love with a man who didn't exist. He knew my fears. My dreams. My secrets. He remembered my birthday. He made me feel seen.

And the whole time, he was sitting across from me at Thanksgiving dinner. Married to my sister. Using me to protect his crimes.

Ethan Brooks was never real.

But the betrayal was.

My sister chose money over blood. Her husband chose control over conscience.

And I chose to survive.

Jenna writes me letters from prison. I don't open them.

Some people say family is everything.

But family is supposed to protect you—not plot against you in the next room while you sleep.

This Christmas, I learned that love can be a weapon. And family can be the hand that wields it.

I'm done being the target.

END

BOOK 12

Forgiveness Season

Chapter 1

The Visit

I parked outside Ridgemont General Hospital with a carrier of coffee and a box of donuts from Ridge Bakery. Friday before Christmas. I'd finished my shopping early—Liam's gifts wrapped and tucked in the closet—and thought I'd surprise him at work.

The lobby sparkled with holiday cheer. White lights wrapped the reception desk. A massive tree dominated the corner, silver and gold ornaments catching the overhead fluorescents.

Instrumental carols played softly from hidden speakers. *Have Yourself a Merry Little Christmas.* Some staff in scrubs and lab coats wore Santa hats.

Dennis, the security guard, waved me through with a smile. "Mrs. Foster. Nice to see you."

"Merry Christmas, Dennis."

I took the elevator to the third floor. Administrative wing. Billing department at the end of the hall. A wreath with silver bells hung on the door. They jingled when I pushed through.

The reception area looked festive. A smaller tree sat on the corner desk, decorated with paper snowflakes that looked handmade. Garland draped across the file cabinets. Someone had strung colored lights along the window.

A young woman sat at the front desk typing. Late twenties, maybe. Dark hair pulled back in a neat bun. Navy cardigan over a white blouse. She looked up when I entered.

Her face went pale.

"Can I help you?"

"Is Liam available? I brought coffee." I held up the carrier and smiled.

Her hands froze on the keyboard. Stopped mid-motion.

"Let me... let me check." Her voice had a slight tremor.

She stood. I noticed her shoes. Black flats. Worn at the heels, scuffed at the toes. The discount store kind you buy when money's tight.

Poor thing. Probably overworked. Liam ran a tight ship. High standards. The holidays must make everything worse for administrative staff.

"One moment, please." She disappeared through a door marked "L. Foster - Billing Manager."

I waited by her desk. Studied the space. Photos of the staff at what looked like a summer picnic. Liam stood in the back row, arms crossed, not smiling. A coffee mug that said "World's Okayest Admin" sat beside her monitor. An empty candy dish held a few peppermints scattered at the bottom.

The door opened. Liam appeared. Surprise flashed across his face before he caught it.

"Imogen! What are you doing here?"

"Thought you could use a pick-me-up. Christmas shopping wore me out." I held out the coffee carrier. "Figured you were drowning in year-end chaos."

He took it. His hand trembled. The cups rattled against each other.

"That's... that's very thoughtful."

I stepped past him into his office. Not large. A window overlooking the parking lot. His desk was covered in folders and loose papers. The computer screen faced away from the door.

Our wedding photo sat on his desk. Our tenth anniversary trip. Two years ago. I'd worn the blue dress he liked. He'd forgotten our dinner reservation, but we'd laughed about it later.

The frame was facedown.

"You knocked over our picture." I reached for it. Turned it upright.

"Must've been when I was reaching for files."

"You work too hard, honey." I set down the donut box. "Have you eaten today?"

"Not yet."

Sweat beaded on his forehead. The air conditioning blasted cold air. December in New Jersey. The hospital kept the heat cranked high, but his office felt like a freezer.

"Are you feeling okay? You look pale."

"I'm fine. Busy. Year-end, you know."

A soft knock on the doorframe. The young woman from reception stood there. She held a folder in both hands. Shaking.

Not tiny nervous shaking. Her whole hand trembled as she extended the folder toward Liam.

"The Patterson account. You said you needed it by eleven."

"Right. Thank you." He took it.

Their fingers touched briefly. Both flinched.

I watched the exchange. Neither of them looked at each other. The air felt heavy between them. Charged somehow.

She must be one of those people who got nervous around authority figures. Some employees couldn't handle direct interaction with management. Liam's intensity could be intimidating to junior staff. He expected excellence.

Her eyes met mine. Only for a second. Something in that look I couldn't quite place.

I smiled at her. Tried to put her at ease. "I'm Imogen. Liam's wife."

"Freida." She swallowed. "I'm the administrative assistant."

"How long have you worked here?"

"Eight months."

Liam's coffee cup hit the desk harder than necessary. Liquid sloshed over the rim onto the papers.

"Freida, don't you have the Morrison file to finish?"

"Yes. I'm sorry." She backed out quickly.

I watched her go. Navy cardigan. Cheap shoes. Trembling hands.

"She seems sweet."

"She's adequate. Does her job." Liam grabbed napkins from his drawer. Started wiping up the spilled coffee. "I have a meeting in five minutes. Was there something specific you needed?"

"Wanted to see you. Make sure you're taking care of yourself." I crossed to him. Kissed his cheek.

He flinched. Barely noticeable. Like my lips burned.

"You're so tense."

"Year-end audits. Hospital administration's breathing down my neck about every detail." He guided me toward the door. His hand on my lower back. Gentle but firm. Pushing. "I really appreciate the coffee. But I need to prep for this meeting."

"Of course. I understand."

I paused at Freida's desk on my way out. She looked up. Those scared eyes.

"Do you have plans for Christmas?"

She blinked. "I'm sorry?"

"Christmas. Do you have family nearby?"

"No. My mother's in Arizona. We don't really talk much."

"That must be lonely."

She looked down at her keyboard. "I manage."

I nodded. Raised my head. Tapped a finger on my chin.

Wondered if there was a way I could make this young lady's Christmas a happy memory.

The elevator doors closed on *Jingle Bells*. Cheerful. Bright. The lobby tree seemed even more festive on the way out. Dennis wished me happy holidays from his post.

I drove home through Ridgemont's decorated streets. White lights on every lamppost. Wreaths on every door. The Johnsons had their nativity scene up already. The Millers' inflatable reindeer bobbed in the front yard.

Everyone preparing for Christmas. Family gatherings. Warm homes. Connection.

That poor girl. Alone for the holidays.

The house was quiet when I got home. Our colonial with the black shutters. The one Liam had insisted on. "Better investment," he'd said. I'd wanted the one on Oak Street, but he'd been right about the value.

I set my purse on the entry table. Looked around at our home. Twelve years of marriage. Twelve years of building this life together.

The mantel needed garland. I should start decorating this weekend. Make everything perfect for Christmas Eve.

The two of us this year. Quiet and cozy.

Unless...

I thought about Freida again. That worn cardigan. Those cheap shoes. The way she'd said "I manage" with such quiet resignation.

Nobody should be alone at Christmas.

Maybe there was something I could do about that.

Chapter 2

The Gifts

Sunday afternoon. I organized the dining room cabinet.

Christmas Eve was Tuesday. Two days away. I needed to make room for the good china. The set my mother had given me when Liam and I got married. We only used it for special occasions.

I pulled out old serving platters. Stacked them on the table. Wiped down the shelves with a damp cloth. The scent of lemon cleaner mixed with the cinnamon candles I'd lit in the living room.

The front door opened. Liam's footsteps in the foyer.

"Imogen?"

"In here."

He appeared in the doorway, laden with grocery bags. Still in his coat. Face flushed from the cold.

"What are you doing?"

"Organizing. I need space for the china." I gestured at the cabinet. "Christmas dinner is in two days." I glanced at the shopping bags. "How was shopping?"

"Too many people. Cut it short." His eyes went to the small safe tucked in the back corner of the bottom shelf. The one with the gun. "You moved that."

"Only dusting around it." I straightened. Brushed dust from my hands. "Actually, I've been thinking. You should find somewhere else to keep it. What if someone breaks in and finds it there?"

He set the bags down. Crossed the room. Opened the safe. The Sig Sauer sat inside exactly where it should be. He checked it. Seemed satisfied.

"No intruder would think to look in a dining cabinet." He closed the safe. Locked it. "Besides, we could be ambushed while eating dinner. I want it accessible."

"That's paranoid, Liam."

"That's prepared." He pulled off his coat. Draped it over a chair. "Moreover, we both know how to handle it safely."

"Still. It makes me nervous."

"It's for protection." He picked up the grocery bags. "I'll put these away, then change."

He left for the kitchen. I heard the refrigerator open. Packages rustling. Cabinet doors closing.

His footsteps crossed to the stairs. Climbing.

I looked at the closed safe. Thought about what he'd said. Ambushed. Such a strange word choice. But then, Liam had always been cautious. Sometimes overly so.

After a minute, I opened the safe again. The gun sat inside. Heavy. Black. Intimidating.

With deliberate ease, I pulled it out. The way they'd taught us in the safety course last spring. Keep your finger off the trigger. Point it in a safe direction. The metal was cold against my palms.

I checked the chamber. Empty. Good. The magazine was loaded and inserted in the grip.

I ejected the magazine. Set it on the shelf beside the safe. Checked the gun again. Completely clear now. Safer this way.

I put the gun back in the safe. Went back to organizing the china.

The doorbell rang at three o'clock.

I wasn't expecting anyone.

I wiped my hands on my apron. Walked to the front door. Through the frosted glass, I could see a figure in brown.

A courier stood on the porch. Young man with a tablet and two wrapped boxes balanced in his arms.

"Delivery for Foster residence."

"I didn't order anything."

"Someone sent them to you, ma'am. Need your signature."

I signed on the screen. He handed me the boxes and wished me Merry Christmas. His truck was already backing out of the driveway before I closed the door.

I brought them inside. Set them on the coffee table. Both were wrapped in red paper with white ribbon. Professional wrapping. Department store quality. The kind that cost extra.

One had a tag tied to the bow: "To Imogen."

The other: "To Liam."

Both from Freida.

I smiled. How thoughtful. Liam's secretary had sent us Christmas gifts. She must really look up to him. Appreciate working for him despite how demanding he could be. Some employees went the extra mile during the holidays.

I carried them to the Christmas tree in the corner of the living room. Set them underneath with the others. Stepped back. They looked perfect there. The red wrapping matched the tree skirt.

The pine scent from the tree filled the room. Carols played softly from the kitchen radio. *Silver Bells*. Everything felt festive. Warm.

"Did I hear the bell?"

Liam's voice startled me. He'd come downstairs. Changed into jeans and a sweater. His hair was damp from a quick shower.

"A courier just left."

He came into the living room. Stopped. Stared at the Christmas tree. At the two red boxes underneath.

"Where did those come from?"

"A courier brought them while you were upstairs." I wiped my hands on my apron. "Isn't it sweet? Your secretary sent us gifts."

"My secretary?" He swallowed. "When did they arrive?"

"Not too long ago. The doorbell you heard." I stepped closer to him. "Are you feeling alright? You look pale again."

"When exactly?"

"I told you. Maybe twenty minutes ago. Why?"

He didn't answer. Stared at the boxes. His jaw worked. Hands clenched at his sides.

Now, why is my husband getting worked up because of two Christmas gifts?

Chapter 3

The Invitation

"We're not keeping them."

I blinked. "What?"

"Those gifts. We're throwing them out."

"Liam, that's incredibly rude. She probably spent her whole paycheck—"

"I don't care. We'll give them back. It's inappropriate."

"How is a Christmas gift inappropriate?"

"Employee giving gifts to the boss. It crosses boundaries." He moved toward the tree. Reached for the boxes.

I stepped between him and the tree. "Absolutely not. We are not giving them back or throwing away someone's thoughtful gesture."

"Imogen—"

"No. That poor girl sent us gifts. We will accept them graciously."

The words tumbled out before I'd fully thought them through.

"Oh, I've been meaning to tell you. I invited Freida to Christmas Eve dinner."

Liam's eyes went wide. His whole body went rigid.

"You what?"

"Invited her to dinner. Tuesday. Christmas Eve." I smoothed my apron. "Six o'clock."

"When did you do this?"

"Friday. When I visited your office. We were chatting at her desk and she mentioned being alone for Christmas. No family nearby. Her mother's in Arizona and they don't talk." I moved past him toward the kitchen. "I felt terrible. Nobody should be alone at Christmas."

He followed me. "You can't just invite my employees to our home!"

I turned. "Why not? She's alone. It's Christmas. We have plenty of food."

"It's wildly inappropriate!"

"How is kindness inappropriate?" I pulled the refrigerator open. Rearranged items to make room for tomorrow's groceries. "I don't understand why you're so upset."

"You don't—" He ran his hand through his damp hair. "Imogen, you need to cancel."

I closed the refrigerator. Looked at him. His face was flushed. A vein pulsed at his temple.

"That would be incredibly rude. I can't uninvite someone." I crossed my arms. "And I certainly can't reject their gifts. What kind of person does that?"

"Tell her you're sick."

"I won't lie, Liam."

"Then tell her something came up!"

"Like what? What possible excuse would justify uninviting someone two days before Christmas?" I kept my voice calm. Reasonable. "People talk. Especially in a workplace. If you uninvite an employee from a social event, it looks petty. It looks cruel."

"I don't care what it looks like—"

"Well, I do. We have a reputation in this community." I picked up a dish towel. Started drying the breakfast dishes still in the rack. "We're gracious people. Charitable people. We don't turn away someone who's alone during the holidays."

"You don't understand the situation—"

"I understand perfectly. You're embarrassed because you've been harsh with her at work and you don't want to face her socially." I set a plate in the cabinet. "But that's not her fault. She's been nothing but professional. She sent us thoughtful gifts. The least we can do is share one meal with her."

His hands clenched into fists. Released. Clenched again.

"This is a mistake."

"The only mistake would be showing cruelty to an employee who's done nothing wrong." I dried another plate. "She's coming. Six PM Tuesday. We're going to be polite and welcoming. We'll open these lovely gifts she sent us. We'll have a pleasant dinner. Then she'll go home and we'll have our Christmas."

I set the plate down. Looked directly at him.

"And frankly, Liam, you should be ashamed of yourself for even suggesting we throw away her gifts or cancel on her."

Something shifted in his face. The panic smoothed away. Replaced by something cooler. More controlled.

"Okay."

The single word hung in the air.

He took a deep breath. Let it out slowly.

"I'm going to make a call."

He walked past me. Out through the kitchen door to the backyard. I watched through the window as he pulled out his phone. Paced across the snow-dusted patio. His breath fogged in the cold December air.

I turned back to the dishes. Continued drying them. Putting them away.

The radio was still playing in the living room. *The Christmas Song.* Chestnuts roasting on an open fire.

I thought about Freida. Her worn shoes. Her nervous hands. The way she'd looked so alone at that desk surrounded by Christmas decorations.

At least she'd have one nice evening. A home-cooked meal. Pleasant company. Some warmth during the holidays.

That's what Christmas was supposed to be about. Generosity. Kindness. Opening your home to those who needed it.

I'd done the right thing.
Even if Liam didn't see it yet.

Chapter 4

The Pressure

Monday morning. Christmas Eve Eve, my mother used to call it. One more day of preparation before the big evening.

Liam left for work at his usual time. Kissed my forehead before he stepped out. Coffee mug rinsed and in the dishwasher. Normal. Pleasant.

"I'll be home by six. Need me to pick anything up?"

"No, I have everything. Thank you though."

"Looking forward to tomorrow." Another kiss. "Your cooking is always perfect."

The door closed. His car started. Backed out of the driveway.

I made my own coffee. Started going through my checklist for tomorrow's dinner. The prime rib was in the refrigerator, ready to be seasoned. I'd picked up fresh green beans at the market. The pie crust needed to be made this afternoon.

Everything had to be perfect.

The morning passed peacefully. I prepped vegetables. Made lists. Organized the dining room.

Around two o'clock, I heard his car in the driveway.

Home early. But not rushing. Not panicked like yesterday.

Liam came through the front door. Called out a greeting.

"In the kitchen."

He appeared. Loosened his tie. "Finished early. Holiday schedule. Half the office is already gone for the week."

"That's nice. You can relax."

"Actually—" He glanced at his watch. "I have a few calls to make. Work stuff I need to wrap up before tomorrow. Don't want any interruptions during dinner."

"Of course."

He went into his study, closed the door. Softly this time. Not slammed.

I continued my prep work. The rhythmic sound of chopping soothed me.

After twenty minutes, I heard his voice through the walls.

Not shouting. But intense. Focused. Business voice.

I couldn't make out words. Only the cadence. Professional. Controlled.

Another call. This one quieter. More urgent but still measured.

I carried a cup of coffee to his door. Knocked softly.

"Liam? I made fresh coffee."

The door opened. He smiled. Took the cup.

"Thank you. You're wonderful."

"Everything okay?"

"Fine. Closing out year-end accounts. Making sure everything's documented properly." He sipped the coffee. "This is perfect."

"You'll be done in time for dinner?"

"Absolutely. Six o'clock. I'll be ready."

He closed the door. Gently.

I went back to the kitchen. Continued working.

More calls through the walls. His voice rising and falling. But always controlled. Always measured.

He was handling it. Whatever stress he'd felt yesterday, he'd mastered it.

That's who I'd married. A man who handled pressure. Who adapted. Who stayed in control.

At four o'clock, the study door opened.

Liam emerged. Looked tired but composed. Tie back on. Hair combed.

"I'm running to the office. Need to grab some files. Won't be long."

I looked up from rolling out pie dough. "This late?"

"Administrative stuff. Want everything buttoned up before the holiday." He grabbed his coat from the hall closet. "Need anything while I'm out?"

"No, I think I'm good."

He crossed to me. Kissed my cheek. "You're amazing. This is going to be a wonderful evening."

"I hope so."

"I know so." He squeezed my shoulder. "Freida will have a lovely time. You're giving her a real gift."

The words were right. The tone was right.

But something in his eyes.

Gone before I could identify it.

"I'll be back by six. Plenty of time to get ready."

The door closed behind him.

I watched through the kitchen window. He got in his car. Sat there for a moment. On his phone again. Typing.

Then he backed out. Drove away.

I went back to the pie dough. Rolled it out. Fitted it into the pan. Crimped the edges the way my mother had taught me. Slid it into the refrigerator to chill.

The house felt quiet. Peaceful.

Liam was being so supportive. So understanding. Yesterday's tension had been work stress. Nothing more.

Tomorrow would be perfect. He'd be a gracious host. Freida would feel welcome. We'd have a nice meal together.

I turned on the Christmas tree lights. Put on carols. *O Come All Ye Faithful.* The festive feeling returned.

I set out the ingredients for tomorrow's dishes. Organized them on the counter. Made a timeline. What needed to be cooked when. How to time everything so it all finished together.

Cooking was mathematics. Precision. Control.

I understood cooking.

Six o'clock came. Liam's car pulled into the driveway. Right on time.

He came through the door with a small bag. "Grabbed us some wine. Better quality than what we had. For our guest."

"That's thoughtful."

"Only the best." He set the bag on the counter. Pulled out an expensive bottle. "This will pair perfectly with prime rib."

"You didn't have to—"

"I wanted to. This is important. Making her feel valued." He smiled. "You were right to invite her."

I warmed at his words. At his support.

He'd been stressed yesterday. But he'd worked through it. Accepted the situation. Made the best of it.

That's what strong people did. They adapted.

"I'm going to shower. Change." He headed for the stairs. Paused. "Thank you."

"For what?"

"For being you. For being kind. For making our home a place people want to be."

He climbed the stairs. I heard the shower start.

I looked at the expensive wine on the counter. At the organized kitchen. At the perfect timeline I'd created.

Tomorrow would be wonderful.

Liam was on board. Supportive. Ready to be a good host.

The tension from the weekend had dissolved.

Everything was going to be fine.

I knew it.

Chapter 5

Preparations

Christmas Eve morning. Liam's side of the bed was warm. He was already awake.

I opened my eyes. Found him dressed. Sitting on the edge of the bed. Tying his shoes.

"Good morning," I said.

He turned. Smiled. "Morning. Didn't want to wake you."

"Where are you going?"

"Quick run to the bakery. Thought I'd grab some fresh bread for tonight. The good sourdough you like."

I sat up. "You don't have to—"

"I want to." He stood. Crossed to the bed. Kissed my forehead. "You're doing all the cooking. Least I can do is help."

"That's sweet."

"Back in an hour. Then I'm all yours. Put me to work."

The door closed. His car started.

I went downstairs and started cooking.

The kitchen was dark. Cold. I turned on the lights. Started the coffee maker. Pulled out the prime rib from the refrigerator. Set it on the counter to come to room temperature.

This was what I knew. What I was good at. Creating warmth. Creating home.

I tied on my apron. The red one with white snowflakes. Washed my hands. Began.

The prime rib needed seasoning. I mixed kosher salt, cracked black pepper, fresh rosemary, and minced garlic. Rubbed it into the meat. Massaged it in until the roast glistened. Set it aside.

Scalloped potatoes next. I sliced the potatoes thin on the mandoline. Paper-thin. Each slice uniform. Layered them in the baking dish with heavy cream, gruyere cheese, fresh thyme. Covered it. Set it in the refrigerator.

The pie was already done. Apple. Liam's favorite. The crust had turned out perfectly golden yesterday. I'd let it cool overnight.

Now the green beans. I trimmed each one. Blanched them. Shocked them in ice water to keep the color bright. Toasted slivered almonds in butter until they smelled nutty and rich.

The front door opened. Liam returned. Bag in hand.

"Fresh sourdough. Still warm." He set it on the counter. "What else can I do?"

"You don't have to—"

"I want to help. Put me to work."

I smiled. "You could set the table. The good china."

"Consider it done."

He went to the dining room. I heard the cabinet open. China clinking. His footsteps back and forth.

By nine o'clock, the kitchen was warm. Alive. The scent of rosemary and garlic filled the air.

I pulled out the carving knife from the block. The good one. German steel. Heavy in my hand.

Found the sharpening steel in the drawer. Held it vertical. Drew the knife down at a twenty-degree angle. The rhythmic sound filled the kitchen. Metal against metal. Back and forth. Back and forth. Soothing. Meditative.

Twenty strokes on each side. The way my mother had taught me.

I tested the edge on a tomato. The knife slid through without resistance. The skin split clean. No tearing.

Perfect.

A sharp knife was safer than a dull one. A dull blade slipped. Required pressure. Could cut you when it jumped. A sharp blade did exactly what you wanted. Made carving easier. Cleaner.

I rinsed the knife. Dried it. Carried it to the dining room.

Liam had set the table beautifully. Three places. My mother's china arranged perfectly. Crystal glasses. Silver candlesticks. White linen napkins folded at each setting.

"This looks wonderful," I said.

"Learned from the best." He gestured at the sideboard. "Where do you want the knife?"

"Right there. Near where I'll carve."

He stepped aside. I set the knife on the sideboard.

Ready when dinner was served.

In the center of the table sat the two wrapped gifts. Red paper. White ribbons.

Liam looked at them. His face unreadable.

"Should I move those?" he asked. Voice carefully neutral.

"No. They look festive. We'll open them after dinner."

"Right. After dinner." He turned away. "I'll finish the napkins."

Back to the kitchen. Roll dough for dinner rolls. Let them rise. Prepare the cranberry sauce. Chop fresh herbs.

The house began to smell like Christmas. Like home.

Liam appeared in the doorway. "Coffee?"

"Please."

He poured two cups. Handed me one. We stood together at the counter. The morning light streaming through the window. Carols playing softly from the living room.

"This is nice," I said.

"It is." He sipped his coffee. "I'm sorry about Sunday. I was stressed. Took it out on you."

"It's okay. You were worried."

"I was. But you were right. This is the right thing to do." He set down his cup. "I called Freida yesterday. Told her how much we're looking forward to having her."

My eyebrows shot up. "You did?"

"Of course. Wanted her to know she's welcome. That it's not merely an obligation."

My heart warmed. "That was thoughtful."

"She sounded relieved. I think she was nervous I'd be upset."

"And you're not?"

"No. You showed me the right way to handle this." He touched my arm. "You're good at that. Seeing what people need."

I smiled. Set down my coffee. Went back to work.

At eleven-thirty, I moved to the dining room to iron the final tablecloth.

Liam had already set up the ironing board. Plugged in the iron.

"Thought you might need this."

"Thank you."

I began pressing the linen smooth. The rhythmic motion brought memories.

Meeting Liam thirteen years ago. I'd been working as a junior accountant. He'd been in sales at the same company. Charming. Ambitious. He'd promised me everything. A house. A life. Security.

Our wedding had been small. My parents hadn't approved. "He's controlling," my mother had said. "You'll see."

I'd thought they were overprotective. Old-fashioned. Liam wasn't controlling. He was decisive. Strong. He knew what he wanted.

Two years into marriage, he'd suggested I quit work. "We don't need two incomes," he'd said. "You could focus on our home. Make it perfect. Isn't that what you want?"

I'd hesitated. I'd liked my job. The numbers. The precision. The independence.

But he'd been right. His salary was enough. And I could pour myself into creating the home I'd always dreamed of.

Five years in, we'd house-hunted. I'd fallen in love with the colonial on

Oak Street. Big windows. Original hardwood. A yard perfect for children someday.

Liam had insisted on this one instead. "Better investment," he'd said. "Oak Street is overpriced. This neighborhood will appreciate faster."

He'd been right about that too.

Our tenth anniversary, two years ago. I'd made reservations at the restaurant where he'd proposed. Bought a new dress. He'd forgotten. "Work emergency," he'd said. "I'll make it up to you."

He never had.

Last Christmas, he'd been distant. Distracted. I'd thought it was year-end stress.

Now, another Christmas. Another chance to connect. To remember why we'd chosen each other.

I'd sacrificed a lot. My career. My dreams of the Oak Street house. Anniversaries. Time.

But that's what marriage was. Compromise. Building something together. Even when it was hard.

I finished the tablecloth. Laid it over the sideboard. Smoothed it flat.

Liam appeared behind me. "Looks perfect."

"Thank you for helping today."

"My pleasure." He surveyed the dining room. "This is going to be a wonderful evening."

"I hope so."

"I know so." He checked his watch. "What time did you say she's coming?"

"Six."

"Then I should start getting ready. Want to look presentable for our guest."

He went upstairs. I heard the shower running.

I removed the ironing board. Everything in its place.

The dining room looked perfect.

By five o'clock, the roast was in the oven. The potatoes baking. The rolls golden and warm. Everything timed to finish at six-thirty. Thirty minutes after Freida arrived. Enough time for drinks and conversation first.

I went upstairs to shower and change. Jumped in as soon as Liam came out.

My red dress hung in the closet. The one I'd bought for last year's Christmas party that we'd ended up not attending. Another work emergency.

I slipped it on. Zipped it up. The fabric was soft. Flattering. I looked nice.

The pearl necklace sat in my jewelry box. Liam had given it to me five years ago. For our anniversary. One of the few he'd remembered.

I fastened it around my neck. Touched the pearls. Smooth. Cool.

Checked my makeup in the mirror. Applied lipstick. Brushed my hair one more time.

Liam emerged from his study. Dark slacks. White dress shirt. He'd even put on a tie.

"You look beautiful," he said.

"You clean up pretty well yourself."

He crossed to me. Adjusted my necklace slightly. His fingers gentle.

"Tonight's going to be perfect. You've worked so hard."

"We both have."

"No. You did this. You're the heart of this home." He kissed my cheek. "I'm lucky to have you."

The doorbell rang.

Five fifty-five. Five minutes early.

"I'll get it," Liam said.

He headed downstairs. I took a breath. Smoothed my dress. Followed.

Chapter 6

The Arrival

Through the frosted glass, I saw her outline. Small. Nervous.

Liam opened the door.

Freida stood on the porch in a navy dress. Face pale. Eyes wide. She held a wine bottle in shaking hands.

She looked at Liam. Something passed between them. Too quick to read.

Then Liam smiled. Warm. Welcoming.

"Freida. Right on time. Please, come in."

She stepped inside. Liam took her coat.

"Let me get that for you. Make yourself at home."

She handed it to him with trembling hands. Navy peacoat. Worn at the elbows. She wore the same navy dress. Her only good dress, probably.

Liam hung it in the closet. Turned back with that same warm smile.

"We're so glad you could come. Aren't we, Imogen?"

"Of course." I stepped forward. "Nobody should spend Christmas alone."

Freida held out the wine bottle. Cheap. The kind you bought at the grocery store for under ten dollars. Her hands shook.

"I brought this. For dinner."

"How thoughtful!" Liam took it. Examined the label with the same courtesy he'd shown the expensive bottle yesterday. "This will be perfect. Thank you."

He disappeared into the kitchen. I heard the cork pull. Glasses clinked.

"Please, come in. Sit." I gestured to the living room.

Freida followed. Perched on the edge of the armchair. Hands clasped in her lap. She looked around the room like she was cataloging exits.

"Your home is beautiful."

"Thank you. We've been here eight years now." I settled on the couch. "Liam picked it out. He has an eye for these things."

Liam returned with three glasses of wine. Handed them out. His movements smooth. Gracious.

He sat on the couch beside me. Not as far away as I'd expected. Actually close. His hand rested on the cushion near mine.

"So, Freida." He sipped his wine. Casual. Friendly. "Imogen tells me your mother's in Arizona."

"Yes. Scottsdale."

"Beautiful area. Hot though. Must be quite a change, New Jersey winters."

"It is."

"How are you finding Ridgemont? Besides the cold."

She gripped her wine glass. "It's nice. Quiet."

"That's what we like about it." Liam smiled. "Small town feel. Good people. Safe."

The word hung in the air. Safe.

Freida's knuckles went white on the glass.

"How long have you worked with Liam?" I asked. Trying to keep the conversation flowing.

"Eight months."

"That's right. You started in spring." I sipped my wine. "Liam mentioned the department was understaffed. You must have been a welcome addition."

"She's been invaluable," Liam said. His voice warm. Appreciative. "Really stepped up. Learned quickly. Very detail-oriented."

He looked directly at Freida when he said it.

She looked down at her lap.

"That's wonderful," I said. "It's so important to have good people. Especially in finance. All those numbers. All those accounts that need to be perfect."

"Exactly." Liam leaned back. Relaxed. "Everything has to balance. Everything has to be documented properly. No room for error."

Freida's breathing had gotten shallow.

"Are you alright?" I asked. "You look pale."

"I'm fine. A bit warm."

"Let me adjust the thermostat—"

"No. Really. I'm fine."

Awkward silence.

The Christmas tree lights blinked in the corner. The ornaments caught the glow. Everything festive. Cheerful.

But the air felt thick.

"So tell me about yourself, Freida." Liam crossed his legs. Casual. "What brought you to New Jersey? A job opportunity?"

"Yes. I needed a fresh start."

"From what?"

She looked up. Met his eyes.

"Just... wanted a change."

"Everyone deserves a fresh start." Liam smiled. "A chance to leave the past behind. Move forward. As long as they've learned from their mistakes."

I looked between them. Something in the exchange I didn't quite understand.

"Well, we're glad you're here," I said brightly. "In Ridgemont. And here tonight."

"Thank you for having me." Freida's voice barely above a whisper.

"It's our pleasure." Liam stood. Topped off his wine. "More for anyone?"

We both declined.

He sat back down. This time his hand found mine. Squeezed it.

"My wife is an excellent cook. You're in for a treat."

"I'm sure."

"She's good at everything she does. Taking care of our home. Managing our household. Very thorough. Very observant." He looked at me. Genuine affection in his eyes. "I'm a lucky man."

I squeezed back. Warmth flooding through me.

This was going well. Liam was being wonderful. Gracious. Welcoming.

The tension from the weekend seemed like a distant memory.

"Imogen mentioned you handle the billing department finances," I said to Freida. "That must be challenging. Especially during year-end."

"I only process what I'm told to process."

"Oh, don't be modest." Liam's voice warm. Encouraging. "You do more than that. You understand the systems. The accounts. Where everything goes. How it all connects."

He sipped his wine. Eyes on her over the rim.

"You're very good at following instructions."

Freida set down her glass. Her hand shook so badly it rattled against the side table.

"May I use your restroom?"

"Of course. Down the hall. Second door on the right."

She practically fled.

The moment she was gone, Liam's smile faded. He stared at the hallway where she'd disappeared.

"She seems very nervous," I said.

"Does she?" He turned back to me. The smile returned. "I suppose it's awkward. Social situations with your boss."

"You're being wonderful though. Very welcoming."

"Of course. You were right. This is the right thing to do." He stood. Walked to the window. Looked out at the street. "Everyone deserves kindness. Especially during the holidays."

"I'm glad you see it that way now."

"I do." He turned back. "I really do."

The timer buzzed from the kitchen.

I stood. "Dinner's ready. I should check the roast." I put on my apron and pulled the roast from the oven.

The meat was perfect. Browned. The internal thermometer read exactly one hundred thirty-five degrees. Medium rare. The way Liam liked it.

I set it on the counter to rest.

Freida emerged from the hallway. Eyes red. Like she'd splashed water on her face. Trying to compose herself.

"Everything alright?"

"Yes. Sorry. Allergies."

"Oh, you poor thing. I have antihistamine if you need it."

"I'm fine. Thank you."

Liam appeared in the kitchen doorway. "Ladies. Shall we move to the dining room?"

He offered his arm to Freida. Gentlemanly. Proper.

She hesitated. Then took it.

He led her to the dining room. Pulled out her chair. Waited for her to sit before pushing it in.

"This looks beautiful, Imogen," he said.

"Thank you."

Liam sat at the head of the table. I sat to his right. Freida to his left.

The gifts sat in the center. Red paper bright against white linen.

Liam glanced at them. His jaw tightened. For a brief second.

Then the smile returned.

"This looks wonderful," Freida said. Her voice shook.

"Thank you. It's my favorite meal to make." I picked up the carving knife from the sideboard. "Liam's favorite too. Prime rib. Medium rare."

The knife slid through the meat. Smooth. Clean. Each slice perfect.

I plated the food. Passed the plates around. Served the scalloped potatoes. The green beans.

The moment of truth. Are they going to like the food?

I rubbed my hands on my thighs. I felt something hard. Shoot. I still had the apron on. I decided to leave it.

Liam ate. Actually ate. Made appreciative sounds.

"This is delicious, honey. You've outdone yourself."

"Thank you."

Freida pushed food around her plate.

"Not hungry?" Liam asked. Concern in his voice. "Imogen's cooking is usually irresistible."

"It's wonderful. I'm... not very hungry."

"Nervous stomach?" He cut another piece of meat. "I get that sometimes. High-pressure situations. When there's a lot at stake."

He chewed slowly. Watching her.

"But you know what I've learned? It's better to face things head-on. Deal with problems directly. Rather than letting them fester."

"Liam," I said. "Don't talk shop at dinner."

"You're right. Sorry." He smiled. "Force of habit."

We ate in near silence. The Christmas music filled the gaps. *O Holy Night.* The notes soared.

I tried to make conversation. "This has been such a lovely Christmas season. The decorations on Main Street are beautiful this year. Have you seen them, Freida?"

"No. I haven't really gone downtown."

"You should. The tree lighting was wonderful. They had a choir. Hot chocolate." I cut a piece of roast. "Maybe after the holidays you could explore more. Ridgemont has such a nice community feel."

"Maybe."

Liam poured himself more wine. Topped off my glass. Offered to Freida.

She shook her head.

"Are you sure? It's very good. Expensive." He smiled. "I picked it out especially for tonight. Only the best for our guest."

"I'm fine. Thank you."

"Suit yourself."

The clock on the mantel ticked. The candles flickered. Everything perfect.

But something felt off.

I couldn't put my finger on it. The conversation was polite. Liam was gracious. Freida was quiet, but that made sense. She was nervous.

Still.

Something in the air between them. Like a string pulled too tight.

"Well." I stood. Started gathering plates. "I suppose we can move on to the gifts. Then dessert."

Liam's fork clattered against his plate.

I looked at him. His face had gone pale.

"Now?" His voice came out tight.

"Of course. It's tradition. Dinner. Then presents. Then dessert."

He looked at the gifts. Then at Freida. She'd gone even paler.

"Actually," Liam said carefully. "Maybe we should wait. Have dessert first."

"That's silly. They're right there. Let's open them."

I reached for his gift. The one with his name on the tag.

His hand shot out. Grabbed my wrist.

Not hard. Not painful. But firm. Stopping me.

"Liam?"

He held my wrist for a long moment. His eyes locked on the gift.

Then he released me. Sat back.

"You're right. Let's open them."

But his voice had changed.

The warmth was gone.

Something cold had replaced it.

Chapter 7

The Dinner

He released my wrist.

I rubbed the spot. Not painful. But the firmness had startled me.

"Liam?"

"Sorry." He forced a smile. "Reflex. You surprised me."

"I was only reaching for the gift."

"I know. I know." He picked up his wine glass. Drained it. Poured another. "Let's open them."

But his hand shook as he poured.

I pulled the gift toward me. The one with his name. "Here. You first."

He stared at it. The red paper. The white ribbon. Freida had wrapped it beautifully.

"Maybe after dessert—"

"Liam, what's wrong? It's only a gift."

"Nothing's wrong." He reached for the box. Pulled it toward him. "Nothing at all."

His fingers worked at the ribbon. Slowly. Like he was defusing a bomb.

The ribbon fell away. He tore at the paper. Methodical. Controlled. Peeled it back piece by piece.

Inside was a manila folder.

He stopped. Hands frozen on the folder. Not opening it.

The clock ticked. The candles flickered. *Silent Night* played softly from the living room.

"Well?" I asked. "What is it?"

He didn't answer.

"Liam?"

Slowly, very slowly, he opened the folder.

I couldn't see from my angle. But I watched his face. Watched the color drain. Watched something shift behind his eyes.

He flipped through the pages. One. Two. Three. His breathing changed. Faster. Shallower.

My heartbeat picked up a notch. What is it?"

His head snapped up. But he didn't look at me. He looked at Freida.

All the warmth from earlier was gone. Completely. What replaced it made my breath catch.

"You brought these into my home."

His voice came out quiet. Deadly.

Freida said nothing. She sat there. Hands folded in her lap.

I glanced from Liam to Freida. "What's going on?" I reached for the papers. "Let me see—"

He snatched them away. "No."

"Liam—"

"She's been stealing from the hospital." The words came out measured. Controlled. But something simmered underneath. "These are forged documents. Trying to frame me."

I looked at Freida. She shook her head. Barely.

"That's not true," she whispered.

"Not true?" Liam laughed. Short. Sharp. "You've been embezzling for months. Creating fake accounts. Stealing from patients. And when I discovered it, when I tried to stop you, you—" He gestured at the papers. "You created this. To deflect blame."

"Liam, that's a serious accusation." I kept my voice calm. "If she's stealing, we should call the police—"

"No police." He stood. Started pacing. "This is an internal matter. Hospital business."

"Then why bring it to Christmas dinner?" I looked at Freida. "Why give us this as a gift?"

"Because she's obsessed with me," Liam said. "I rejected her advances. Multiple times. Now she wants revenge."

Freida's face went white. "That's not—"

"You've been pursuing me for months." His voice stayed level. Controlled. But his hands clenched. "Making excuses to come to my office. Staying late. Sending inappropriate messages."

"Show me the papers," I said firmly.

"Imogen—" Liam started.

"Show me. Now." The words shot out of me.

Liam hesitated. Then threw the folder on the table.

I picked up the first document. Bank transfer. Eighteen thousand dollars. Liam's signature at the bottom. To Sterling Ventures LLC.

My accountant training kicked in. I studied it. The format. The routing number. The signature.

It looked real.

I picked up another. More transfers. Different amounts. All signed by Liam.

"These have your signature."

"Forged. She had access to my files. My login credentials."

I looked at more documents. The pattern emerging. Shell companies. Systematic transfers. Over eighteen months.

"Liam." I set down the papers. "These look real."

"Because she's good at forgery." He paced faster. "She works in billing. She knows the systems. The accounts."

"Then explain Sterling Ventures."

He stopped. "What?"

"Sterling Ventures LLC. I saw a transfer to them on our account state-ment. In March. I googled it. Nothing came up."

His face shifted. "That was... a legitimate business expense."

"What business?"

"Hospital vendor."

"With no web presence? No company registration?" My voice hardened. "I checked, Liam. It doesn't exist."

Silence.

Then Freida spoke. Quiet. Shaking.

"Open yours, Imogen."

I looked at her. Then at my gift. Still wrapped. Still sitting there.

"Don't." Liam's voice sharp. "More forgeries. More lies."

Dread pooled in my stomach. I picked it up anyway.

Lighter than his had been. I tore the paper. Not carefully. My hands were shaking now.

Inside. Another manila folder.

I opened it.

Printed pages. Text messages. Screenshots. Dates going back months.

I read the first one aloud. My voice shook.

"November third. Liam to Freida: 'Keep cooking the books or I'll tell everyone you're stealing. You'll go to prison.'"

The words hung in the air.

I looked up at Liam.

His face had changed. The control slipping. Something desperate replacing it.

"She edited those. Photoshopped them."

I looked back down. Kept reading.

"November tenth. 'Meet me at the Marriott or you're fired. Your choice.'"

Understanding arrived like a fist. My hands shook harder.

"Imogen, she's lying—"

"November fifteenth. 'My wife doesn't check the accounts. We're safe as long as you keep quiet.'"

I stopped. The room tilted.

"Your wife doesn't check the accounts?"

Liam reached for the papers. "Those aren't real. None of that is real."

I pulled them back. Kept reading. To myself this time.

Messages about hotel rooms. About covering tracks. About moving money. About keeping me in the dark.

About the affair.

Pages and pages. Months of messages.

My vision blurred at the edges.

I set the papers down. Looked at Freida. Really looked.

Her cheap shoes. Her worn dress. Her terrified eyes.

Then back at Liam. His expensive shirt. His tie. The watch I'd given him for his birthday.

"How long?"

He opened his mouth. Closed it.

"How long have you been sleeping with her?"

"I'm not—"

"The hotel charges. The Marriott. January. I saw them. You said work travel."

His mask cracked. A little bit.

"You've known since January?"

"I thought it was work travel." My voice broke. "I trusted you."

"Imogen—"

"How long?"

Silence. The Christmas music still played. *Silent Night*. All is calm.

Nothing was calm.

"Eight months," Freida whispered.

I looked at her. "Since you started working there."

She nodded.

Something fundamental shifted inside me. Eight months. While I'd been cooking his meals. Setting his table. Playing perfect wife.

While he'd been helping me prepare tonight's dinner. Being supportive. Gracious.

All of it. Performance.

I turned back to the bank documents. Studied them with my accountant's eye.

"You've been embezzling."

"No. Listen—"

"These are your signatures. Your accounts. Your login credentials." I looked at him. "How much?"

"It's not what it looks like—"

"How much did you steal?"

His jaw worked. The pleasant host from earlier completely gone.

"Fifty. Maybe sixty thousand."

The admission hung in the air.

I laughed. Sharp. Bitter. "Fifty thousand dollars. And you thought you'd get away with it."

"I was going to pay it back—"

"With what? The money you hid in shell companies?" I picked up more papers. "You created fake businesses. Fake invoices. For eighteen months."

"I needed—"

"You needed?" My voice rose. "I gave up my career for you! My job. My independence. You said we didn't need two incomes. That I should focus on our home."

"You were mediocre anyway."

The words came out quiet. Casual.

Like he'd been thinking them for years.

I faced him.

Let the silence stretch.

"Excuse me."

"You were a mediocre accountant. I saved you from a boring career." He gestured around the room. "Gave you this. This house. This life. You should be grateful."

Something inside me broke.

Or maybe it had been broken all along. I'd only finally noticed.

I stood. The room spun.

All day. His helpfulness. His support. His compliments.

All of it. Lies.

"And her?" I looked at Freida. "You forced her to help you."

"She was willing—"

"The texts say otherwise!" My voice cracked. "You threatened her. Blackmailed her. Used your position to—"

I couldn't finish.

Twelve years of marriage. Twelve years of building this life.

Built on lies. Built on control. Built on a man who called me mediocre while I cooked his favorite meal.

I walked to the sideboard. Looked at the carving knife lying there.

Then past it. At the dining cabinet.

Where the gun was.

Liam saw where I was looking.

His face changed. Calculation replaced everything else.

He moved toward the cabinet. Fast.

"What...what are you doing?" My voice came out high. Scared.

He pulled open the door. Reached for the safe. Opened it.

Pulled out the Sig Sauer.

Freida went pale. I stood frozen.

"Nobody's calling the police," he said.

The pleasant host was gone. Completely.

This was someone else. Someone I'd never seen before.

Or maybe someone who'd been there all along. Hidden behind smiles and compliments and helpful gestures.

"Liam." I kept my voice calm. Quiet. "Put that down."

"No."

My heart hammered. This wasn't real. This couldn't be real.

The man who'd kissed my forehead this morning. Who'd helped set the table. Who'd bought expensive wine for our guest.

Stood in our dining room. Holding a gun.

And I had no idea what he was going to do.

Chapter 8

The Documents

"Put the gun down, Liam."

"No."

He held it. Not pointed at anyone.

"You're writing a confession, Freida."

"What?" Her voice came out strangled.

"You stole everything. From the hospital. From me. You're going to write it all down. Sign it."

Freida's eyes went round and wet, whites flashed like something trapped. "No one will believe—"

Liam stepped toward her. "They'll believe what I tell them." The gun was pointed down. Visible. Threatening. "You'll write that you embezzled. That you tried to frame me. That you seduced me to cover your crimes."

I moved forward. "Liam, stop. You're not thinking clearly."

"I'm thinking clearly for the first time." His voice stayed level. Controlled. But something manic flickered behind his eyes. "She planned this. Both of you. Setting me up."

"Nobody set you up. Those are your signatures—"

"Forged!"

"Your phone number on the messages—"

"Spoofed!"

I picked up the text message printouts again. Hands shaking. Read through them more carefully.

"December first. 'My wife is stupid. She doesn't suspect a thing.'"

The words hit harder the second time.

"Your wife is stupid."

My voice came out flat. Dead.

Liam's gun hand wavered. "I never said that."

"It's right here. Your number. Time stamps. Everything." I flipped through more pages. "November twentieth. 'She thinks I'm at the gym. Meet me at the Marriott. Room 412.'"

I looked up. "You told me you joined a gym. November. For your health."

Liam said nothing.

Understanding arrived like a fist. "There is no gym."

"Imogen—"

"The Marriott charges on our credit card. January through now. Once a week. Sometimes twice." I set down the messages. Picked up the bank documents again. "And these transfers. Systematic. Consistent. Eighteen months."

I spread them across the table. Let my training take over. Shut down the emotion. Focus on numbers.

"Sterling Ventures LLC. Apex Holdings. Meridian Capital Partners." I pulled out my phone. Searched each one. "None of them exist. No business registration. No web presence. Nothing."

"They're legitimate—"

"No. They're shell companies. You created fake vendor accounts. Submitted false invoices. Approved your own transfers." I looked at the timestamps. The patterns. "Always under twenty thousand. Below the threshold that requires additional approval."

His face showed I was right.

"You knew the system. You knew the limits. You stayed under them." I kept going. Couldn't stop now. "And you made her process them. Made her think she was the one stealing. So if anyone caught it, the trail led to her."

Freida made a sound. Small. Broken.

"The texts show it," I continued. "You threatened her. Said you'd blame her. That you had evidence. That she'd go to prison."

"She was willing—"

"She was COERCED!" The word snagged on the way out. "You had her job in your hands. Her rent. Her food. You squeezed until she folded. You threatened her. You—"

I looked at more messages. Saw dates. Locations.

"April fifteenth. 'Tell your landlord you'll be late on rent. I need you to process the Meridian transfer today.'"

I looked at Freida. "You were late on rent because of him?"

Freida nodded. Tears streamed down her face.

"May third. 'If you tell anyone, I'll say you stole my login. They'll believe me, not you.'" I kept reading. My voice shook. "June seventh. 'My wife doesn't check anything. She's too busy playing house.'"

Playing house.

Twelve years. I'd given up my career. My independence. Everything.

To play house.

"July second. 'She asked about the Marriott charges. I told her work travel. She believed it. She always believes me.'"

The words burned.

I set down the papers. Looked at him.

"I saw those charges in January. I trusted you. I believed you were traveling for work."

"You should have—"

"I saw Sterling Ventures in March. I googled it. Found nothing. But I trusted you. I thought it was a mistake. A system error."

"It was—"

"No. It was fraud. Systematic. Deliberate. And I saw it. My accountant training saw it. But I trusted my husband more than I trusted my own eyes."

I laughed. Sharp. Bitter.

"You were right. I was stupid."

"I didn't mean—"

"Yes, you did." I picked up more messages. Read them. "August tenth. 'Sometimes I forget why I married her. Then I remember—she manages the house so I don't have to.'"

The room spun.

"September fourth. 'She's making pot roast tonight. Her signature dish. Like she thinks cooking will fix everything.'"

I'd made pot roast in September. For our anniversary. The one he'd forgotten.

He'd texted his mistress about it.

"October second. 'She asked if I wanted to try for a baby again. I said maybe next year. There won't be a next year.'"

My breath caught.

We'd talked about that. October. I'd brought up adoption. Fertility treatments. He'd said maybe next year. Maybe when work slowed down.

There won't be a next year.

"What does that mean?" I looked at him. "There won't be a next year?"

He said nothing.

"Were you planning to leave me?"

"It's complicated—"

"WERE YOU PLANNING TO LEAVE ME?"

"Yes!" The word exploded out. "Yes. Okay? Yes. I was going to leave. Take the money I'd saved. Start over somewhere else. Away from this house. Away from you. Away from—"

He gestured around. At the perfect table. The perfect meal. The perfect life I'd built.

"Away from mediocrity."

The word hung in the air.

I looked at the documents. The transfers. Adding them up in my head.

"Sixty thousand. You said sixty thousand."

"About that."

"These transfers add up to over ninety."

His face confirmed it.

"How much did you really steal, Liam?"

Silence.

"HOW MUCH?"

"One hundred twenty thousand." The admission came quiet. "Give or take."

One hundred twenty thousand dollars.

Over eighteen months.

While I'd been cooking his meals. Ironing his shirts. Making our home perfect.

While he'd been stealing. Cheating. Planning to leave.

"Where is it?"

"Offshore account. Cayman Islands."

"And you were going to what? Simply disappear?"

"I was going to tell you I got transferred. New position. We'd sell the house. I'd take my share. Leave the country before you realized the money was gone."

The plan. Methodical. Careful. Cruel.

"And her?" I looked at Freida. "What happens to her when you disappear?"

"She takes the fall. The evidence points to her. She goes to prison. I'm long gone."

Freida sobbed. Curled into herself.

"You're a monster." The words came out quiet. Flat.

"I'm a survivor." He raised the gun slightly. Not pointing. But ready. "And I'm not going to prison. Not for her. Not for anyone."

"Then what's your plan? Shoot us both? Christmas Eve murder-suicide? How does that get you to the Cayman Islands?"

"You're going to write a confession." He looked at Freida. "Both of you. You embezzled. You had an affair. You tried to frame me. You'll sign it. Date it. Leave it where it'll be found."

"And then what?"

"Then you'll drive somewhere remote. You'll make it look like suicide. Guilt. Shame. Couldn't live with what you'd done."

His voice stayed calm. Matter-of-fact.

Like he was describing a business plan.

"You've thought this through."

"I've had time. Today. While you were cooking. While I was making calls. I had lots of time."

The helpful husband. Setting the table. Buying wine. Being gracious to our guest.

All while planning how to murder us.

"And if we refuse?"

He pointed the gun. Directly at Freida.

"Then I shoot her now. Say she attacked me. That you both attacked me. Self-defense. By the time police sort it out, I'll be gone."

"They'll find the evidence. The documents—"

"Will disappear. Along with both of you." He smiled. Cold. Empty. "I've planned for everything."

I looked at the gun. At his face. At the complete absence of the man I'd married.

Or maybe he'd never been there at all.

Maybe this was who he'd always been.

And I'd been too stupid to see it.

"So what do you want us to do?" I asked quietly.

"Start writing. Both of you. Everything you did. Everything you stole. Everything you plotted. Make it detailed. Make it believable."

"We don't have paper—"

"Kitchen. Now. Both of you. I'll dictate exactly what you'll write."

He gestured with the gun. Toward the kitchen.

Freida stood on shaking legs. I stood too.

We walked to the kitchen.

Liam followed. Gun raised now. Pointed at us.

We reached the kitchen. The warm, perfect kitchen where I'd spent all morning cooking.

"Sit."

We sat at the table.

He pulled paper from the drawer. Set it in front of Freida.

"Start with your name. Date. Today's date."

She picked up the pen. Hand shaking so hard she could barely write.

"I, Freida Morrison—"

Her hand stopped. She looked up at him.

"I can't do this."

"Yes, you can."

"No. I won't."

His face changed. The last bit of control slipped.

"Yes. You will."

"No."

He stepped toward her. Grabbed her throat with his free hand. Gun still in the other.

"Write it!"

She clawed at his hand. Couldn't speak. Couldn't breathe.

Her face turned red. Then purple.

I stood. "STOP! You're killing her!"

He didn't stop. Squeezed harder.

Freida's eyes bulged. Desperate. Dying.

I had to do something.

I lunged. Not for the gun. For him. For his arm. Trying to pull him off her.

He threw me back. I hit the counter. Hard.

Pain lanced through my ribs.

I looked at the knife block. At the carving knife I'd sharpened this morning.

Still in the dining room. On the sideboard.

But there were other knives here.

Liam kept choking Freida. Her struggles were weakening. Going limp.

I grabbed a knife from the block. A paring knife. Small. Sharp.

Lunged at Liam.

He saw me coming. Let go of Freida. Spun.

We struggled. He was stronger. So much stronger.

He grabbed my wrist. Twisted. The knife fell. Clattered across the floor.

Pointed the gun at me. Point blank. Two feet away.

"I didn't want this. But you forced my hand."

He pulled the trigger.
Click.
Nothing.
His face went blank. Confused.
He pulled again.
Click.
"What the—"
Then everything happened at once.

Chapter 9

The Turn

"What the—"

Liam stared at the gun. Pulled the trigger again. Click. Click. Click.

Nothing.

Freida moved.

She grabbed the paring knife from the floor. Lunged at him. Weak. Gasping.

Buried the blade in his back.

Not deep. But enough.

Liam screamed. Spun. The gun flew from his hand. Clattered across the kitchen floor.

He staggered. Hand reached back for the knife. Couldn't grab it.

Blood spread across his white shirt. Dark. Fast.

"You bitch—"

He stumbled toward the dining room. One hand pressed to the wall.

I scrambled for the gun. Grabbed it.

Liam made it to the doorway. Leaned against the frame.

Blood dripped down his back. The paring knife stuck out from his shoulder blade. Small. Inadequate.

Not enough to stop him.

He looked at the sideboard. At the carving knife.

The one I'd sharpened that morning. Heavy. German steel. Sharp enough to split a tomato skin.

"No—"

He lurched forward. Grabbed it with his good arm.

Turned to face us. The carving knife in one hand. The paring knife still in his back.

Blood spread across the floor. Across my mother's tablecloth. Across the broken dishes.

"I'll kill you both," he said. Pain strained his voice. "Write it off as self-defense. You attacked me. I defended myself."

He took a step toward Freida. She'd collapsed against the wall. Still gasping for air. Throat bruised. Barely conscious.

"Put the knife down, Liam."

"Or what? You'll shoot me with an empty gun?" He laughed. Bitter. Wet. Blood on his lips. "You don't even know how to load it."

He took another step toward Freida. Raised the carving knife.

He glanced at me. "She dies first. Then you. Then I call 911."

My hand went to my apron pocket. Left side.

Found the magazine. Cold. Heavy.

I dropped to the floor. Both hands on the gun.

The magazine slid into the well. Click.

Liam's eyes widened.

I hesitated.

Liam lunged at me.

Too late.

Collided into me. We rolled across the dining room floor. Through broken glass. Wine. Blood.

My hand on the gun. His hand on my hand. Both fighting for control.

The barrel pointed everywhere. Ceiling. Wall. Floor.

His weight on top of me. Stronger. Even injured. Even bleeding.

"You ruined everything," he gasped. Blood sprayed from his mouth. "Everything I built."

He tried to wrench the gun away. I held on.

We rolled. I was on top. Then him. Then me.

Freida couldn't help. Semi-conscious. Eyes unfocused.

His hand squeezed mine. Crushing. Tried to make me let go.

The carving knife—he'd dropped it. Lost in the struggle.

Only the gun between us now.

The barrel twisted. Pointed at the ceiling. At the wall.

At him.

I made sure of it.

His hand over mine. But I'd angled it. Exactly where I needed it. Over his left pocket.

Point blank. Heart shot.

My finger found the trigger.

Pulled.

BANG.

The sound deafening.

Liam jerked. His hand loosened on mine.

He pulled back. Staggered up. Stood.

Looked down at himself.

Blood spread across his chest. Dark. Fast.

He touched it. Looked at his hand. Red.

"Imogen..."

His voice confused. Lost.

He took a step. Stumbled. Fell to his knees.

"You..."

He pitched forward. Hit the floor.

Didn't move.

Silence. Except for ragged breathing. Mine. Freida's.

From the living room, the radio still played. *Joy to the World.*

I dropped the gun. It clattered on the hardwood.

Stared at Liam's body. Blood pooled beneath him. Spread across our dining room floor.

Christmas Eve dinner. Ruined.

Everything. Ruined.

"Is he...?" Freida's voice. Barely a whisper.

I crawled to him. Hands shook. Pressed fingers to his neck.

Nothing.

No pulse. No breath. Nothing.

"He's dead."

The words came out flat. Empty.

Freida sobbed. Curled against the wall. Held her throat.

I sat on the floor. In the blood. In the wine. In the broken pieces of our perfect dinner.

The gun lay where I'd dropped it. Still warm.

I'd killed him.

We'd fought for the gun and I'd killed him.

The room spun. My hands shook.

I pulled out my phone. From my apron pocket. My fingers slippery with blood.

Dialed 911.

"911, what's your emergency?"

"My husband." My voice shook. "He attacked us. He had a gun."

The words tumbled out. Disjointed. Broken.

"He was choking her. She couldn't breathe. She stabbed him. He came at us with a knife. We fought. The gun went off."

This was what happened.

The struggle. The gun. The shot.

"Are you safe now, ma'am?"

"He's..." I looked at his body. "He's dead."

"Where are you located?"

I gave the address. Mechanical. Disconnected.

"Officers are on the way. Are you injured?"

"I don't know. He was killing her. The knife. The gun. I tried to stop him. It went off."

"You did the right thing, ma'am. Help is on the way. Stay on the line."

I looked at the gun on the floor. At Liam's body. At Freida in the corner.

At the dining table. The gifts still there. Opened now. Evidence scattered across white linen.

The expensive wine Liam had bought. Unopened. For our guest.

The helpful husband. The gracious host.

All performance.

All lies.

"Officers are three minutes out."

"Okay."

I sat there. Phone to my ear. Blood on my hands. On my red dress. Christmas carols played in the next room.

Christmas Eve. Our last Christmas Eve together.

The police were coming.

And my husband was dead.

Chapter 10

The Clean Up

The police arrived in seven minutes. Paramedics in nine.

Too late for Liam.

I sat on the kitchen floor. Blood on my hands. On my dress. The red fabric darker now. Wet.

Freida huddled against the dining room wall. Still held her throat. Bruises already formed. Purple finger marks.

The first officer came through the door. Gun drawn. Saw us. Saw Liam's body.

Lowered his weapon.

"Ma'am? Are you injured?"

I shook my head. Couldn't speak.

More officers poured in. Secured the scene. Checked pulses. Called it in.

A woman in a dark coat entered. Forty-something. Short hair. Tired eyes.

She crouched in front of me.

"I'm Detective Hazel Fairbank. Can you tell me what happened?"

The words came out broken. Disjointed.

"He found out we knew. About the money. The affair. He got the gun.

Said he wasn't going to prison. He choked her. She couldn't breathe. She stabbed him. He got the knife. The carving knife. Came at us. We fought. The gun went off."

"Who's 'she'?"

I pointed at Freida. "His secretary. She came for dinner. He attacked her."

Fairbank stood. Spoke quietly with the other officers. Then back to me.

"We need statements. Separately. Is there somewhere else you can go?"

"The neighbor's house."

One officer helped me up. My legs wouldn't hold right.

He led me next door. The Millers opened without question. Saw the police cars. The lights. The blood on my dress.

Mrs. Miller brought me a blanket. Water I couldn't drink.

Detective Fairbank sat across from me at their dining table.

"Tell me everything. From the beginning."

I told her about the dinner. The gifts. The documents. The embezzlement. The affair. His confession.

"He pulled the gun from the dining cabinet. Threatened us. Said Freida had to write a confession. Say she'd stolen the money."

My hands shook. I pressed them together.

"She refused. He grabbed her throat. Started choking her. Her face turned purple. She couldn't breathe. She was dying."

"What did you do?"

"I tried to stop him. Grabbed a knife from the kitchen. We fought. He threw me. The knife fell. Freida grabbed it. Stabbed him in the back."

"Then what?"

"He pulled the trigger. At me. But nothing happened. He looked confused. Pulled it again. Click, click. Nothing."

"The gun was empty?"

"Yes. I'd removed the magazine on Sunday. When I was cleaning the dining room cabinet. I found the gun in the safe. Checked if it was loaded. The magazine was in there. I took it out. For safety."

"Where did you put it?"

"I don't remember exactly. On the shelf, maybe? Or in my apron. I was wearing an apron while I cleaned. I wanted to make sure the gun was safe."

Fairbank nodded. "Go on."

"Then Freida stabbed him. With the kitchen knife. In the back. He dropped the gun. Went to the dining room. Got the carving knife from the sideboard. The one I'd used for dinner."

"And then?"

"He came at us with it. Said he was going to kill us both. Freida first, then me. He was going to stab her. She couldn't even move. She'd been choked. She was barely conscious."

My voice cracked. "I grabbed the gun from the floor. I was panicking. He was raising the knife. Going to stab her. And I felt something hard in my apron pocket."

"The magazine?"

"Yes. I'd put on my apron earlier to take the roast from the oven. I never took it off. The magazine must have been in the pocket from Sunday. From when I was cleaning."

"You loaded the gun?"

"Yes. My hands were shaking. But it clicked in. I didn't even think. He was going to kill her. I—I loaded it."

"Then what happened?"

"He saw me load the gun. He lunged at me. We fought. On the floor. Rolling. Fighting for control. I don't even remember exactly. Everything was chaos. The gun was between us. We were both holding it. And then it went off."

"Where was the gun when it discharged?"

"Between us. We were on the floor. Both hands on it. I don't know exactly where it was pointed. It went off."

Fairbank studied me. "You loaded the weapon during the struggle?"

"Right before. He was about to stab Freida. I loaded it. Then he came at me. We fought. It went off."

"And the magazine had been in your apron pocket since Sunday?"

"It must have been. I don't remember putting it there specifically. I was cleaning. I took it out of the safe. I must have put it in my apron pocket and forgot about it."

She wrote this down. "Two days later, you happened to be wearing the same apron?"

"I wear it when I cook. I'd put it on to take the roast from the oven. I forgot to take it off after."

"Lucky you had it."

I looked at her. "Lucky?"

"The magazine. In your pocket. Right when you needed it."

"I—yes. Lucky."

She wrote everything down. Asked more questions. Times. Details. Sequence.

"The knife wound in his back?"

"Freida. She was trying to help. He'd been choking her."

"And the carving knife?"

"He grabbed it. From the sideboard. Where I'd set it after dinner. He came at us with it."

Fairbank set down her pen. Looked at me directly.

"Defense of a third party. Clear self-defense. He was actively trying to kill you both."

I nodded. Started to cry.

This was real. Genuine. The shock. The trauma.

I'd killed my husband.

In our dining room.

On Christmas Eve.

By four AM, the coroner had taken the body. Forensics had photographed everything. Blood spatter. Broken dishes. The gun. Both knives. Documents scattered across the table.

The detective talked to her partner near the door. I heard fragments.

"Gunshot wound. Close range. Consistent with struggle."

"Two stab wounds. Defensive actions."

"Evidence supports self-defense."

"Open and shut. Clear case."

They cleared the scene. Left one officer to secure the house overnight. Everyone else gone by four-thirty.

I walked back home.

Blood stained the dining room floor. Dark. Spreading.

Freida met me in the kitchen. She'd been interviewed separately. Her voice still hoarse. Throat mottled with bruises. Purple and black.

We sat at the kitchen table. Not speaking.

I pulled down the whiskey. Poured two glasses. Pushed one toward her.

We drank.

"We didn't plan for him to die."

Her words came out quiet. Shaking.

"No."

And I believed it. In that moment. The reality of his death hit me in waves.

We hadn't planned this.

It was self-defense. He'd attacked us. We'd defended ourselves.

That's what happened.

Freida turned to me with. Eyes wet. Sad. "It was self-defense. Right?"

I nodded. "He was going to kill us both."

"With the knife. He was coming at us."

"Yes."

More silence. The clock ticked. Dawn approached.

"What happens now?" Frieda said and leu out a breath.

"We survive."

She drained her glass. Set it down with a shaking hand.

"I should go. Get some rest."

"Yes."

We stood. Hugged. Brief. Awkward. Two women bonded by trauma. She left.

The door closed.

I was alone.

. . .

The house was silent.

I sat at the kitchen table. Freida gone. Police gone. Liam's body gone.

Only me and the bloodstain in the dining room.

I poured another whiskey. Drank it.

Self-defense.

That's what it was.

He'd attacked us. I'd defended us.

The magazine had been in my apron pocket. I'd loaded the gun. Shot him.

Self-defense.

I looked at the apron in the sink. Blood-soaked. Ruined.

I'd worn it all evening. Forgot to take it off.

The red dress had no pockets. The apron had two.

Lucky I'd kept it on.

Lucky the magazine was there.

Lucky.

I drained the whiskey.

Poured another.

Christmas morning. Dawn broke through the window.

My husband was dead.

And I'd killed him.

In self-defense.

Chapter 11

The Truth

I sat at the kitchen table. Alone. Dawn light spread across the floor.

Let myself remember the truth.

January. This year.

The hotel charge appeared on our credit card. Marriott. One hundred forty-seven dollars. Overnight stay.

Liam said work travel.

But the date was Tuesday. Midweek. He'd come home that night. Said he worked late.

The charge was for overnight.

I googled the location. Two miles from the hospital.

I didn't confront him. I watched. Documented.

March.

I checked our joint account. Saw transfers I didn't recognize.

Sterling Ventures LLC. Fifteen thousand dollars.

I googled it. Nothing.

Shell company. Fraud.

I checked our statements back six months. Found more. Apex Holdings. Meridian Capital Partners. All fake. All bore Liam's signature.

I didn't confront him. I stayed quiet. Kept records.

April through May.

More hotel charges. Different hotels. Always midweek.

More transfers. More shell companies.

Over one hundred thousand dollars. Stolen from the hospital.

And I realized something.

Divorce would leave me with nothing. He'd hidden the money. Created debts in both our names.

I'd lose the house. The life I'd built. Everything I'd sacrificed.

Unless...

June.

I started to plan.

I researched self-defense laws. Forensics. Blood spatter patterns. What made a shooting look justified.

I studied our insurance policies.

Life insurance. Five hundred thousand. Double indemnity for accidental death or crime victim.

If Liam died during commission of a crime—one million dollars.

I read every clause. Made sure I understood what would trigger the payout.

An attack. That would do it.

An attack on two people. Even better.

December. Three weeks ago.

Freida reached out. Email to my personal account.

Subject: "I need to tell you something."

She confessed everything. The affair. The blackmail. The fraud.

She expected me to be angry.

Instead, I saw the opportunity.

We met. Coffee shop in Morristown. Away from Ridgemont.

I told her I already knew. Had known for months.

She cried. Apologized.

I said: "We can help each other."

The plan was simple. That's what I told her.

Confront him. Get a confession. Turn him in.

That's what she believed.

But I knew from the start it wouldn't end that way.

Prison meant lawyers. Trials. Discovery. Everything public.

And he'd still have the money. Hidden offshore. Untouchable.

Even from prison, he'd have won.

No.

This had to end differently.

I stood. Walked to the sideboard. Opened the drawer.

Empty now. Police had taken the carving knife into evidence.

But I remembered yesterday morning. How I'd sharpened it.

Twenty strokes on each side. Tested it on a tomato. The blade sliced clean.

"For the roast," I'd told myself.

But I'd set it on the sideboard. Within easy reach.

Plan A.

Wait until his back turned. During dinner.

Bury the knife between his ribs.

Make sure Freida's fingerprints were on it. Hand it to her. "Can you help me carve?"

Then when he attacked—and I knew he would—she'd have the weapon.

She'd use it. Self-defense.

It would look like she killed him.

I'd be the widow. The innocent wife.

But Sunday happened.

Liam's reaction to the gifts. His panic about the dinner.

I realized he might not come. Might force a cancellation.

So I adjusted.

I made the invitation non-cancellable. Used social pressure. Etiquette. Reputation.

I trapped him.

And I removed the bullets from the gun.

Not for safety.

For control.

Plan B.

If he grabbed the gun—and I knew he might—it would be empty.

He'd pull the trigger. Nothing would happen.

In that moment of confusion. That moment when he realized he was defenseless.

That's when it would happen.

I walked to the kitchen. Looked at my red apron in the sink. Blood-soaked.

Christmas Eve morning.

I got dressed. Red dress. Pearls.

I went to the dining room. To the gun safe.

I retrieved the magazine.

Slipped it into my left apron pocket.

Lipstick and tissues in the right pocket. To look natural.

Magazine in the left.

Ready.

Liam would have noticed the apron over my dress. I left it out.

I put it on to pull the roast from the oven. Then kept it on. Through the meal. Through everything.

Didn't take it off.

The red dress had no pockets.

The apron had two.

I kept it on. Deliberately.

The struggle.

On the floor. We fought for the gun.

Freida semi-conscious from the choking. Couldn't see clearly. Couldn't testify.

Perfect.

My hand went to my apron pocket. Left side.

Found the magazine. Cold. Heavy.

Two seconds. While Liam focused on Freida.

Smooth motion.

Magazine into the well. Push. Click.

But he noticed, and lunged at me.

That was the only time luck played a part. I didn't drop the gun.

We rolled. Struggled. Liam, already weak from blood loss.

I twisted. Got leverage. Easy. Rolled on top.

The barrel between us.

Not at the ceiling. Not at the wall.

At his heart.

I made sure of it.

His hand over mine. But I'd angled it. Exactly where I needed it.

Point blank. Heart shot.

I pulled the trigger.

Deliberately.

I watched his eyes widen. Watched him understand.

Watched him die.

Christmas morning.

I'd murdered my husband.

Not self-defense. Murder.

Premeditated. Planned. Executed.

Freida would never know.

She believed it was an accident. A gun that went off in chaos.

She'd testify to that. Believe it forever.

The police believed it. The evidence supported it.

Two women who defended themselves from a violent, armed man.

But I knew.

I'd removed the bullets Sunday. Put the magazine in my apron Christmas Eve. Wore the apron deliberately. Loaded the gun during the struggle. Aimed. Fired.

Step by step.

The perfect crime.

. . .

I pulled the life insurance policy from the desk drawer.

Five hundred thousand. Double indemnity.

Dies during commission of a crime—one million dollars.

I set it on the table.

My house. My choice. My life.

No more Liam. No more control.

His fraud would die with him. No investigation into me.

A widow who collected insurance on her criminal husband.

Freida would get promoted. Take Liam's position.

And I'd be free.

Free of the man who called me mediocre. Who planned to leave me with nothing. Who stole and lied and called his wife stupid.

Dead.

Because I killed him.

And got away with it.

Three months later. March.

I repainted the dining room. Soft gray. New hardwood covered the bloodstain.

Saturday morning. Coffee. Newspaper.

The Ridgemont Gazette lay on the table.

Bottom of page six: "Ridgemont's Dark Christmas" by Gloria Steele.

My case got two sentences.

"Christmas Eve shooting ruled self-defense. Liam Foster, 45, was killed by his wife when he attacked her and employee Freida Morrison after being confronted about embezzlement and affair. Case closed."

I set the paper aside.

Insurance paid out. One million dollars. House paid off. No debt.

Everything mine.

Freida had been promoted. Took Liam's position.

She'd called a few times in January. We talked less in February. By March, barely at all.

Better that way.

She believed we'd survived something terrible together.

Only I knew the truth.

The doorbell rang.

Freida stood on the porch. Navy coat. New shoes. Better quality.

"Hi. Can I come in?"

I stepped aside.

We sat at the kitchen table.

I made coffee.

"I still think about that night," she said.

"So do I."

"Do you ever wonder if we could have handled it differently?"

I met her eyes. "He didn't give us a choice."

She nodded. Believed it. Would always believe it.

"He was going to kill us both."

"I know. I just—" She wrapped her hands around the mug. "Sometimes I wake up and I can still feel his hands on my throat. And I remember the gun and the blood and—"

"It's trauma. It takes time."

"Are you seeing anyone? A therapist?"

"No. I'm managing."

The same words she'd said that first day. At the hospital.

She didn't remember. But I did.

We drank coffee. Made small talk. Twenty minutes.

She left.

I locked the door.

Upstairs. My bedroom. My house. My life.

She'd never know.

She'd testify if needed. Swear it was self-defense. Believe it with her whole heart.

And I'd let her.

Some truths were better buried.

Like Liam.

Six feet under in Ridgemont Cemetery.

Finally where he belonged.

I lay in bed. The house silent.

Tomorrow I'd meet with the financial advisor. Invest the insurance money. Start fresh.

Maybe take a class. Accounting. Refresh my skills.

Maybe work again. On my terms.

Freida thought we'd survived a nightmare together.

The police thought I'd defended myself and a friend.

The insurance company thought they'd paid a crime victim.

The hospital thought they'd lost an employee to his own crimes.

Everyone believed what I'd shown them.

But I knew the truth.

I'd planned it. Executed it. Got away with it.

The perfect crime.

I'd killed my husband.

Removed the bullets. Sharpened the knife. Orchestrated the confrontation. Wore the apron deliberately. Loaded the gun during the struggle. Aimed. Fired.

Step by step.

Murder.

And I'd do it again.

END

About the Author

Ion Esimai writes psychological thrillers about the secrets people keep — and what those secrets cost.

His *Perfect Series* explores guilt, love, and the quiet violence of the human heart. Every story begins with something ordinary — a road trip, a family lunch, a weekend away — and ends somewhere dark, intimate, and impossible to forget.

When he's not writing, Ion studies the way silence builds between people — the words they don't say, the looks that last too long.

📖 *Get a free story from the Perfect Series universe:* FREE eBook Perfect Road Trip

facebook.com/ionesimaiauthor

youtube.com/@IonEsimai

threads.com/@ionesimai25

Also by Ion Esimai

THE PERFECT SERIES

Perfect Daughter

RIDGEMONT CHRISTMAS THRILLER SERIES

BOOK 1: The Gift Exchange

BOOK 2: The Perfect Christmas Card

BOOK 3: Day One: The Partridge

BOOK 4: The Advent Calendar

BOOK 5: The Cabin

BOOK 6: Christmas Eve Storm

BOOK 7: The Neighbor

BOOK 8: The Homecoming

BOOK 9: Office Secret Santa

BOOK 10: The Proposal

BOOK 11: Love, Actually

BOOK 12: Forgiveness Season

www.ingramcontent.com/pod-product-compliance
Lightning Source LLC
Chambersburg PA
CBHW022007300726
48970CB00003B/777